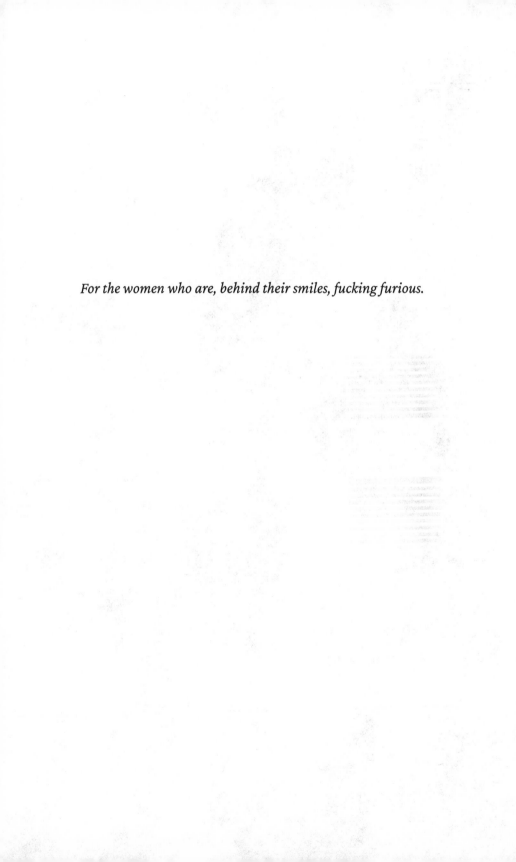

For the women who are, behind their smiles, fucking furious.

Pearlwort to save you from the faeries.
Pearlwort to guard your heart.

— ALBIONIC FOLKLORE

The moon was a sliver in the sky, a few days from disappearing altogether—a few nights from the Wild Hunt riding.

It gave me enough light to see by as my sabrecat, Vespera, picked through the undergrowth in silence. I rolled my hips with her gait, keeping my thighs loose: I didn't need speed from her, yet. Her ears flicked and her black coat gleamed, a stark contrast to how dull my red hair had grown this past year.

Beyond the trees and their shadows, the road was grey in the moonlight. And empty. I scowled and touched the butt of my pistol, like that would bring the prey I hunted.

If we wanted something more than cabbage and courgette on our plates next week, it needed to. We were down to the last of the flour, and I hadn't tasted meat in weeks. If I were a decent hunter, I'd come out in the day with bow and arrow.

But that was a big *if*.

I was a great shot, but an abysmal hunter. The butler,

Horwich, had been passable, bringing rabbits to the table on the regular, but a slip on the ice last winter had ended his hunting career.

So instead, I rode at night seeking a different kind of quarry, one that frequented balls... Like the one this evening.

Once upon a time, the Viscountess Lady Katherine Ferrers had been invited to *everything,* but not anymore. She'd stopped accepting invitations so many years ago, drawing rooms were no longer abuzz with speculation. It had been a long while since anyone had called me lady anything. It was just Kat now.

Still, I got to hear about these things. And although I couldn't attend parties—wearing the same tatty gown every time would win me nothing but sneers—I could make use of them. And this way was much more practical.

I cocked my head. Was that a sound? With a gloved hand to her shoulder, I stilled Vespera and held my breath, listening.

At first, I was sure I must've imagined it. Wishful thinking.

But a distant pounding thrummed through the air, felt more than heard, and beneath me Vespera coiled like a spring.

After all these years, the adrenaline still kicked through me, making my skin tingle and my heart hammer. This was the only time I broke the rules, even my own.

They were simple. Some places and actions were safe. Home. Tending our vegetables. Grooming Vespera. And other places and actions weren't safe: almost everywhere and everything else. I didn't go there or do those. Except for when I rode at night.

Because it was less dangerous than the alternative, which was losing my home.

Besides, I was clever about it. I crept through the night,

and I knew all the best routes for escape. I hid behind a hood *and* mask. And I'd have wagered my sabrecat was faster than any other in Albion.

There were a lot of reasons I'd never been caught.

Thank the gods. After all, the sentence for highway robbery was death, especially for the infamous Wicked Lady, as the papers called her—called *me*.

Thirty seconds after the initial thrum of paws on the road, came the squeak and rumble of a carriage in movement.

Partygoers heading home. Drunk and tired. And with any luck, their coachman had entertained himself with a hip flask —that would make my job easier.

Squeezing my thighs, I eased Vespera to the very edge of the forest. We'd wait here until the last possible moment when I'd block their way, pistols drawn—

A shriek pierced the night. The air in my lungs stilled. Even Vespera, so well-trained for any situation or surprise, lifted her head.

It almost sounded like a person. *Almost.*

But I knew that sound. A fox.

I peered out along the road. My quarry was a coach pulled by four sabrecats—that meant money. Lots of money. They could afford to pay my toll.

Again, the screech raked through the forest's darkness.

Shit.

If the coachman thought it was a woman screaming, he'd turn back. And then there would be no toll.

This would all have been for nothing.

Yes, there would be other nights, but tonight? It was my best bet—the lords and ladies travelling from the ball would be dripping in jewels. Although I wouldn't get their full value from my fence, I'd get enough.

With a near empty larder, I'd settle for enough.

Another shriek.

The carriage slowed.

"Shit," I muttered, making Vespera shift her weight.

I needed to chase off that fox.

WE CHARGED THROUGH THE FOREST, far enough from the carriage that they wouldn't hear the slight rustle Vespera couldn't help making at this speed. Even if they did, they'd put it down to the damn fox screaming like a woman being disembowelled.

Leaves and branches whipped past, forcing me to duck close to Vespera's back as I peered ahead. She wound between thick oaks and leapt over fallen trunks, breaths steaming in the chill of night.

Then we were in a moonlit clearing, a gap in the canopy big enough to see that sliver of ghostly white slashing through the night sky. And ahead, a flash of red, as bright as autumn.

The fox that was trying to fuck up my entire evening.

Except it looked like the poor thing was having a worse night than me, because glinting in the dim light was the thin line of a snare's wire. One end fastened to a tree, the other was buried in the thick fur of the creature's neck.

It didn't snarl or shrink away from me.

Brown eyes wide but calm, it watched as though wondering what I'd do. Which was a stupid thing to imagine, because animals didn't think like that, but...

It watched. And it waited.

Even in this silvery light, its thick fur was the richest red I've ever seen, deeper than my auburn hair. Its tail was a magnificent sweep of the same red tipped with white, and my fingers clenched around the reins, aching to test how soft it felt, how thick.

When they weren't taking chickens from our now empty coops, I'd always liked foxes. Clever and quiet, not obviously dangerous like a wolf or sabrecat. They snuck in, took what they needed, and vanished into the night.

This one was the most beautiful creature I'd ever seen.

And beautiful wasn't useful, but...

Blood specked the white of its throat. It was in pain.

Despite myself, despite my quarry back on the road, it tugged on my heart.

Besides, if I left it here in the snare, it would only scare away the coach. This was a matter of practicality.

"This is just so I can do my job," I told it with a nod before dismounting.

My leather gloves should give me some protection if it tried to bite, but I'd do my best to grab it by the scruff of its neck like a sabrecat cub.

Hands held wide, head bowed, I approached. "It's all right." I kept my voice soft and low. "I'm going to help you." *Quickly, so I can get back to that carriage and its fat purses.*

Even as I closed in, an arm's length away now, the fox didn't strain away at the end of the snare. It didn't react at all, just sat and waited.

Everyone knew a wild animal, even a semi-tamed one, would lash out when cornered and injured. Not this fox. In fact, its calm had grown eerie now, making the back of my neck prickle.

My feet stilled, telling me to turn and run.

Just some irrational fear. Listening to it would cost me the night's hunt.

I forced myself to take another step. "That's it." I wasn't sure if that was for the fox or my own skittish self. I'd been doing this—haunting the roads at night—for more years than I cared to remember. I couldn't afford fear. I certainly couldn't afford to give in to it.

"That's it. Nice and quiet." My heart pounded, louder than the sabrecats on the road, as I lunged in, grabbing it by the scruff.

But it didn't dart away or snap at my hands.

And my bones ached with the wrongness.

"Unsafe. *Unsafe*," they whispered.

It was too late, because I had a handful of its fur. It looked up at me with eyes full of pain and far too much under-standing for a fox.

My throat closed as I slipped a finger under the wire looped around its neck and drew my dagger.

You could kill it. That would keep it quiet.

It would. And it would quiet the feeling of wrongness slithering under my skin.

But...

Other than making me uncomfortable, this fox had done nothing wrong. Chances were that feeling was my mind playing tricks on me—the pressure of tonight's hunt making me foolish enough to entertain the idea a fox trapped in a snare was something more than just that.

"Pull yourself together, Kat." I yanked my blade through the wire.

Despite everything I told myself, I took a long step back.

As the snare dropped to the ground, the creature turned its

neck side-to-side, something eerily human about the gesture. Then it stood. It was much larger than any fox I'd heard of.

I swallowed and didn't sheath my dagger. "There," I said, voice firmer than I felt, "you're free."

It regarded me with those large brown eyes for a long while before bowing its head. Its tail was the last thing I saw as it disappeared into the forest in silence.

Goosebumps picking their way across my skin, I hurried back to Vespera and mounted.

When we returned to the road, the carriage was gone. Only its tracks remained, leading away into the distance.

I slumped in the saddle. "Shit."

T he next day I woke feeling like crap. That probably had something to do with the home brewed elder-berry wine I'd used to drown my sorrows at the night's failure.

Sickness lurking at the back of my tongue, I dug in the vegetable beds, sowing seeds, coating my hands in mud like no "lady" should. Across the path, old roses watched, their thorns pricking me with my failures even from this distance.

Last night, I'd lurked on the forest's fringes, holding out for another carriage taking partygoers home. When dawn's pallor touched the sky, I had to accept I'd missed my chance.

Damn fox. I drove my trowel into the soil, sending up a spray of crumbly dirt.

In the sunlight, it felt utterly stupid that I'd even enter-tained the idea of the creature being anything more than an animal trapped in a snare. Fae weren't so stupid to get them-selves caught. And save for the retinue that had presented itself to the queen recently, they hadn't been seen in Albion since before I was born.

It was just a fox. And I'd let the waning moon and promise of the Wild Hunt whip my mind into a foolish frenzy that saw strangeness and danger where there were none.

"Idiot," I muttered as I dropped seeds into the loosened soil.

Cursing that fox and myself, I worked past noon sowing, weeding, thinning out seedlings, and hunting slugs and snails. Since we'd been forced to slaughter the ducks last winter, it was my job to find the slimy bastards beneath stones and behind plant pots and squash them.

If the choice was between a slug and my vegetables, I chose my vegetables every time.

Just like I should've chosen my prey last night instead of that fox.

With a sigh, I finally went inside the third time the cook, Morag, called me from the kitchen door.

My head was about ready to explode and the heat kicked out by the oven didn't help. I slid into a rickety chair with a groan, depositing the radishes and salad leaves I'd harvested between my slug-murdering.

"Suppose you haven't eaten yet."

I didn't need to look up to know Morag was giving me That Look. The one where her lips were flat and her brow low—all disapproval and hard love. I'd learned to read people long ago. It was a useful skill—a survival skill with a family like mine.

"Felt too sick first thing," I muttered, shoving hair from my face where it had fallen loose while I worked.

"And I wonder why that is." I could *hear* the arched eyebrow in her tone. "Get this down you." She plonked a chipped mug on the table, the fresh scent of peppermint rising in its steam.

The smell didn't turn my stomach; I chanced a sip. It beat away the sick taste on the back of my tongue, so I kept drinking while she waved her rolling pin at me, eyes glinting.

"Look at the state of your hair. When was the last time you brushed it?"

I couldn't even summon the energy to wince. Although I hadn't looked in a mirror in... Gods, how long had it been?

"My hair doesn't matter."

"You need to look after yourself." She shook her head, tutting. "Out all night." Her look was meaningful, and I knew she knew what I did when I disappeared on Vespera, even if I never told her outright. "Then drinking that rubbish past dawn."

"I will." I tilted the cup as I shrugged. "Just as soon as the cabbage is harvested, the beds all weeded, the courgettes planted out, the hen house repaired, the gate re-hung, that hole in the back fence patched up... And I'm sure there's something else I'm forgetting. *Then* there'll be time to look after myself."

That Look made a return, but the lines between her brows were deeper and the shadows cast on her eyes darker. "And what if it's too late?"

Too late? I snorted. "I'll survive."

With a huff, Morag turned and stomped to the oven. Steam billowed out, carrying a sweet scent that had my mouth watering at once, all queasiness forgotten.

I frowned at her, even as I smacked my lips. "You didn't."

"I did." The little cake tins clashed against the tray as it thudded into the cork mat on the table.

The floral notes of honey in the air pulled a soft sound

from my throat, but I clenched my hands. "We're supposed to be selling the honey, not eating it." My stomach growled, though, and my fatal weakness for sweet treats had me leaning over the table, inhaling as deeply as I could. Good gods, they smelled amazing. It had been so many months since I'd eaten anything so tasty, I could've wept with longing.

"Aye, well, I only used a tablespoon. The rest is in jars for selling." Her mouth softened as she looked at me, hands on her hips. "Treating yourself isn't a sin, you know."

Maybe it was that softness, maybe it was my weakness for the scent of fresh honey cakes, but part of me cracked as I looked back at her. I had to hold my breath and wait for the stinging in my eyes to fade.

Because I was tired.

So. Fucking. Tired.

Maybe that had made me prickly, not to mention ungrateful. So I sat up and nodded at Morag as she tipped one of the cakes from its tin onto a cooling rack. "Thank you."

At last she smiled, the hard glint gone from her eyes. "That's my girl."

When I reached for a cake, she swatted my hand. "Let them cool down first!"

I scoffed, rising and darting for the cooling rack before she could swat me off again. The sponge was hot and moist, perhaps too hot, but... "No time for that. Work to do."

As I backed away, she folded her arms and shook her head, That Look firmly back in place.

Standing in the doorway, I took a bite of the honey cake and sighed. Morag had lived and worked here since she was a girl. It was the only home she knew. Lucky for me, because she was good enough to work in any stately home she wanted. Yet she remained here in this crumbling manor where I could barely afford to keep up her wages. Selfish as it may be, I was intensely grateful as the cake's sweetness bloomed across my tongue.

Floral honey and the rich caramel flavour of brown sugar consumed me.

I sank into it. Lost myself in it. Just for a moment. Just that one spark of pleasure that eased my shoulders for a handful of seconds. Glorious and brief and, most importantly, *mine.*

I opened my mouth to take a second bite when a pounding came from the front doors.

Morag tensed, head canted in a question, eyebrows twitching together in something that was part-confusion and part-concern.

"Looks like you get your way and I have to let it cool down." I grinned and deposited the rest of my precious cake on the cooling rack as I left the room.

Who the hells came to Markyate Cell? The once great estate had hosted balls and parties before I'd lived here. But it was a long time since we'd been able to afford to feed anyone outside the household. Recently, it had been challenging enough to feed the three of us.

I was untying my apron when the hammering knock sounded again, echoing through the empty halls. Not only a visitor, an impatient one.

Oh no. A chill crept over me. Not that prick's secretary again.

Some called my husband Lord Robin Fanshawe, but I preferred other, more inventive names. I hadn't seen the man in years, which suited me very well. I only heard from him when he needed money, which took the form of an invoice sent directly to the house from a landlord or tailor. Or, when I was *really* unlucky, when his secretary came to help himself to the contents of the safe on behalf of his master.

Such a loyal dog.

Jaw ratcheting tighter and tighter, I opened the large front door. "Mr Smythe, you're going to have to tell—"

The words withered on my tongue.

Because it wasn't the gangly secretary at the door.

3

A man stood on the top step, his charcoal suit smart but not *too* smart. Some sort of professional—the kind who worked in an office. An attorney, perhaps. But there was something a little rougher about him. Beyond, half a dozen burly men waited on the gravel driveway, arms folded. From their size and casual shirts and brown trousers, I guessed they were labourers.

My throat constricted. Attorneys meant trouble. And burly men meant more trouble. Either the official kind or the kind that hoped to find a woman home alone. I'd sent Horwich on an errand, and Morag was hearty for her age, but I wouldn't duck behind her for protection.

Home was usually safe—away from society, somewhere I didn't have to play by its rules. But this? This was decidedly *not* safe.

I clasped my skirts, wishing my fingers were fastening around the butt of my pistol, but that was upstairs in my bedroom. No way would I outrun these men to reach it.

Politeness was my only protection. My back straightened, and it was shocking how easily I slid back into that old mould —ladylike and poised. "How may I help you?"

"Morning, miss." The suited man nodded. "We've come to execute the warrant. Has Lady Fanshawe...? Sorry, it says Ferrers on here." He glanced down at a sheaf of papers in his hand. "Has Lady Ferrers left the keys for us?"

"*I'm* Lady Ferrers." Yet my brain clamoured with questions. *Warrant? Keys?*

His eyes went wide and his face grew maybe a shade paler. "Oh. I was..." He gripped the papers with both hands now. "I thought you would've vacated the estate by now, milady."

"Vacated the estate? Why would I do that?"

He shuffled uncomfortably and cleared his throat. "Well, because of the warrant." He paused and when I didn't reply, raised his eyebrows. "The one served on Lord Fanshawe three months ago?"

"A warrant for what?"

But I knew. Deep down in the ice creaking through my bones, I knew.

"To seize the estate."

My breaths were too loud, blocking my ears. *Seize the estate. Seize the estate. Seize the estate.*

The sentence went round and round in time with the drumming of my heart, a jumble of sounds I couldn't make sense of.

The man's mouth was still moving, but I didn't hear a word.

Seizing. Warrants. No more estate. No more home. Not safe. Not safe *at all*.

I blinked and found myself clutching the doorframe, the world spinning slowly, sickeningly.

"Milady, are you—?"

"What has he done?"

The bailiff explained. I took in half of what he said; it was enough.

The foetid cesspit I'd been married off to had secured a five-thousand-pound debt against Markyate Cell—the estate I worked myself to the bone to keep afloat. The estate that hadn't made that much money in any of the years I'd been here.

And, being a useless bag of bones, he'd failed to pay the debt *or* respond to the warrant he'd been served three months ago.

"Three months." The words scoured my throat. He'd known all that time, and he hadn't even sent a letter to warn me.

The bailiff shifted his weight, lips tightening as his fingertips traced the edge of the warrant in his hands. "You knew nothing of this until I appeared on your doorstep, did you?"

I shook my head, though it took far more effort than it should've, as if my bones were suddenly heavier and my muscles had forgotten how to work.

He swallowed and glanced down the steps at the men waiting. As though coming to a decision, he leant in closer, shoulders blocking them out. "Look, madam... they don't like us telling anyone about this, and normally I wouldn't, but it seems unfair on this occasion. There's a clause on the final page of the warrant." He flicked through the papers and held one up, but I couldn't take in anything more than a jumble of ink. "If you pay one tenth within a week, we'll accept that as part payment, with another tenth due a month later, and so on, until the debt is cleared. As long as you keep up payments, the estate won't be seized."

Five hundred pounds. That was still a huge sum, ten times what I paid Horwich in an entire year.

"I'll do it." I heard my voice as if it was from very far away. As if someone else had spoken.

His shoulders sank a fraction of an inch as though *he* was relieved. Putting the papers back in his briefcase, he promised to return in seven days' time. He handed me a card with the address of his offices and bowed his head before leaving.

Face tingling, I slammed the door and fell against it.

How the hells was I going to raise that much money in a week?

"A week!" My hysteria-edged voice bounced around the hall.

There was only one way I stood a chance. Despite the danger of being on the road so often, I had to ride every night.

Even that might not be enough.

A whole set of gold jewellery—necklace, earrings, brooch, bracelets—would bring in perhaps two-hundred and fifty. That was without the taint of stolen goods. I'd be lucky to get two thirds of that from my fence if she was in a good mood... a really, *really* good mood.

My stomach churned as I walked through the halls, no particular destination in mind. There was no space in my brain for anything other than what had just happened.

Five thousand pounds. *Five thousand*! That was a year's income, even for a wealthy gentleman.

At last, I stumbled outside and threw up everything I could. The mouthful of honey cake wasn't sweet coming back up. I could only taste bitter, sour bile as I heaved and heaved, tears gathering at the corners of my eyes from the effort.

When I looked up, the roses still watched.

How I used to love tending them.

Once upon a time, I'd read every book I could on the subject. I bought every different variety and fertiliser I could get my hands on, testing them in different beds to see what gave the best results. I wrote notes on the outcomes. I even started breeding different varieties together, seeing if perhaps I could create something new. But my project ended before they had a chance to flower.

Because I found out the truth about my husband's debts and the floundering financials of the estate.

What a foolish girl. Such frivolous concerns. It had been an utterly pointless way to spend my time. Roses were pretty and they smelled divine, but they were useless.

Vegetables, though—they were entirely practical. They'd kept us going these past few years.

And with the bailiff breathing down my neck, we would need to grow and hunt all our food for the foreseeable future.

Before I even consciously thought about it, I was approaching the nearest rose bed. The soil crumbled under my feet, still clayish after all this time. The soft sensation made me want to sink to my knees and clip the tangled stems to ensure I'd get the fattest flowers. For a moment, I paused, weight on my toes, so close to succumbing.

But only for a moment.

I didn't bother to dig, I just grabbed close to the base. Dry bark cracked in my grip as I pulled. The stunted bush came out easily—too easily. Its roots had been half dead for a long while. I threw it to one side and started on the next.

Thorns tore at my palms. Pinpricks of beautiful, useless pain.

I didn't stop.

Their twisted branches tangled in my hair. They scratched my face.

Teeth gritted, I yanked out that one and the next and the next.

I needed food more than I needed this reminder of past beauty.

Maybe that hot liquid trickling down my cheeks was blood from the scratches. Perhaps it was tears.

I'd killed for the sake of survival. I'd fucked a husband I hated for the sake of *survival*. Tears were as useless as the roses I ripped up, but blood? Yes, I would bleed for survival.

Whatever it took.

4

The gods weren't on my side, judging by the rain pouring in a constant drizzle. But fuck them if they thought a bit of weather was enough to put me off.

I didn't love Markyate Cell the way some aristocrats might love their estates. It didn't belong to me; it was *his*.

Part of me would've been perfectly happy to watch it all burn—the angry, seething part that was all thorns and no flowers. But without it, I had no home. And Morag and Horwich needed it just as much. She refused to move away, and since his accident, he relied on a walking stick and would struggle to get another job.

So despite my stupid husband frittering everything away on his grand tours and terrible "investments," I'd spent ten years trying to clear up his financial mess. And I faced losing it all anyway.

Fuck him, too.

Selling a parcel of land from the estate's edges would've helped when the debts were smaller. Every time I'd asked, he'd refused—that was back when he bothered to reply to my letters at all. Being a woman, by Albionic law, I didn't even own the land myself: I needed his permission to sell it.

Fuck the law, especially.

So I rode and peered through the drizzle.

And I found nothing.

No coaches. No riders. Not even a fox's screams on the breeze. Just the splatter of rain rippling through puddles and spiking Vespera's fur in black tufts. Her ears bent forward and she kept her head down, as fed up with the weather as I was.

But come winter, the weather would be far worse, and if the bailiff took the house, we wouldn't have a roof, never mind fuel or food. So I clicked my tongue and urged her on.

"I'm sorry." I stroked her powerful shoulder, every muscle in my body aching from the day's work. "I'll let you come in and lie in front of the fire—promise."

She huffed, breath misting in the cool air before it disappeared in the drizzle's constant grey.

I couldn't tell if the sun threatened on the horizon yet, because the clouds blocked out everything. It felt late enough for that to be a real possibility. My tired shoulders sank as I turned Vespera on the road home and fixed my gaze between her ears.

Another night, another failure.

I only had a week. I'd ride out every night if I had to. Yes, I could sell the last of the furniture, but that wouldn't come close to five hundred pounds. Robbery was my only chance.

The weather had kept people off the road tonight, but last night had been clear: there should've been more than just that one carriage. Maybe the Wicked Lady's reputation had scared people from travelling far after dark. If they stayed with the hosts of their parties or at nearby inns, they'd be indoors and safe before I had a chance to reach them.

If they kept that up...

"Shitting hells."

Despite the rain, Vespera's ears pricked. She lifted her head, and her nose twitched, steam puffing out.

My heartbeat sped. "What can you smell?" Urging her to the edge of the road, I peered ahead. It was long minutes before I spotted a figure in the drizzle-haze.

A lone rider.

My breath caught, and I steered into the forest's edge. Pickings wouldn't be as rich as with a carriage, but a lone rider was more vulnerable. I'd take whatever I could get.

Still, what would drive someone out in this weather? Desperation like me? Or something else?

We waited, and I chewed my lip. They had a sabrecat, so they probably weren't poor. But what if the cat was borrowed or stolen? The Wicked Lady's fearsome reputation came from preying on the rich—after all, they had the most to take, and they screamed loudest to the newspapers when it was taken. But most of all, they could afford the loss.

I wouldn't take from those who had too little.

I drew my pistol and cocked it, watching as the figure came closer, closer. Like me, he wore a hood. Broad shoulders and a sure seat despite his cat's swift canter. He knew how to ride, and he was large enough that I wouldn't want to face him in a toe-to-toe fight.

But that was what my pistols were for.

I drew the second one, eyes burning as I stared, waiting for details to resolve themselves and tell me whether he was a have or have not.

He was five sabrecat lengths from where I needed to step out if I was going to stop him, and I still didn't know.

I strained forward, holding Vespera still with the butt of my pistol on her shoulder. My heart thundered, and I couldn't hear anything except for that and the constant rain.

Please. Please, gods.

His sabrecat took another stride. Slate grey, powerful flanks, elongated canines gleaming. No decoration on the saddle, but its cut was so sleek it had to be made for his cat, not second hand. His hooded coat was plain, too, but dyed a rich, pure black. Darker than any simple farmer could afford... or was it just so sodden, it looked that dark?

I swallowed, caught between lifting my hand from Vespera's shoulder and letting the man pass.

What to do?

Then the dim light gleamed on something that wasn't just another puddle or the wet fur of his sabrecat.

A small metal sphere chained to his belt.

Not just metal, *gold*.

I didn't have time to work out if it was gold or brass. Two more strides and he'd be beyond my ambush point.

I lifted my hand, and Vespera surged forward.

5

"Stand and deliver." Sometimes the old lines were best, and this one worked a charm, bringing the rider to a splashing halt. Or maybe it was my pistols that did the trick. One glinted back at me, its cogs marking it as fae-worked, the stag on its butt bright.

The rider's breaths heaved. I swore I caught a glimpse of bared teeth in the shadow of his hood, but he looked over his shoulder before I could be sure.

It gave me a chance to survey him properly. His thighs were muscular around his sabrecat, and I guessed he stood a head taller than me, maybe more. Not difficult, since I was short. That was part of why no one suspected me of being the Wicked Lady. Underestimation had its benefits.

Satisfied no one was behind, his attention returned and he took me in before cocking his head.

A beat of silence and then he laughed.

He fucking laughed.

"You're..." His voice was low, like it wasn't meant for me to hear. "The gods have a sense of humour after all." He shook his head, and my grip tightened, making my leather gloves squeak.

"Money," I said through gritted teeth. "Though I'll also take valuables, like *that*." I dipped my fae-worked pistol towards the golden ball. "Or if you're going for the 'your life' option, just tell me, and I'll take it off your corpse while it's still warm." I grinned and although I couldn't see myself, I knew it was a rigid thing, all full of the hard edges of my anger where he'd *laughed* at me.

I, Kat, couldn't indulge my rage at having a useless husband who'd left me in such a desperate situation, but the Wicked Lady could. Anger scared prey, making her job easier. She'd killed a man, after all.

The rider stiffened, gripping the reins. Perhaps he hadn't taken my threat seriously until he saw my pistol was cocked.

"Which will it be?" I twitched the second gun towards his belly, letting him see that one was ready to fire, too. "I don't recommend trying anything stupid—it'll only make me shoot you somewhere that leaves you to bleed out in a slow death." I tilted my head back and gave him a bright smile, knowing he'd be able to see as my hood shifted.

He tried to just give me a pouch of money. I took it, of course, but I'd seen the orb. If I was right and it was gold, it would go a long way towards paying that debt.

"And the rest."

"I assure you, this is a terrible decision." All trace of laughter had disappeared from his voice, and something about the set of his broad shoulders told me I had his undivided attention.

"And I assure you, I only have terrible options left."

Another twitch of my pistol. "Now, give me that pretty trinket."

There was a beat where he weighed up his options. Fight, run, or obey. I prayed he chose the last of those. Though Vespera was as fast as the wind, I didn't fancy a chase through the rain, especially not this late.

And a fight? Well, I might've killed before—it had been him or me and I always chose to survive—but I still carried the nightmares. I didn't intend to repeat it unless I had to.

With that strong physique, if he went for a weapon, he'd leave me no choice but to fire.

My finger eased against the trigger, and I fixed my aim on his head.

His shoulders lowered in an exhale, and I knew I'd won. If he was readying for action, he'd have drawn a breath, not blown one out. He was giving in.

Sure enough, his long fingers went to his belt and unfastened the orb's chain before he held it out.

I swallowed, trying to mask the relief flooding through me as I secured the money in my saddlebag. "A pleasure doing business with you." I gave him a charming smile as I placed my hand on the etched surface of the ball.

But he didn't give it up right away, grip tightening as I pulled. "I promise you," he ground out as he finally let me yank it from his fingers, "I will get this back."

As I dropped the orb into my inside pocket, the hairs on the back of my neck prickled, but I couldn't say why.

Wrong.

Something was wrong.

The way the air shifted when he made that promise. It...

It felt like magic.

Vespera must've felt it too, because she backed away, ears flicking.

As if in response, a breeze kicked up, pressing on my shoulders like it would push me towards him, catching in his hood until it fell back.

The first thing I saw was a pair of straight, dark eyebrows drawn together in absolute fury. It was the kind of look that promised I would die, and the chill running through my sodden body believed it.

Somehow, in the shadows of those brows, his eyes glowed like the silvery moon. I froze, only able to blink at the impossibility.

A trick of the light. Nothing more.

But even without that, his face would've struck me still and stupid, because, good gods, he was fucking gorgeous. The dim light loved his sharp lines—the hard angles of his cheekbones, the proud set of his jaw, the curved edges of his lips where they met in a cruel line. It carved him into something statuesque.

A thin, pale scar cut through his mouth and chin. Without its jagged line, he might've been beautiful, but with it he was handsome. The kind of handsome that made you stop mid-step, mid-breath, mid-thought.

Except, no, he wasn't the carved stone of a statue, I realised, as he slowly smiled.

Because that smile was sharp and without any hint of the safe shelter that stone could offer.

This was a smile of metal and edges. This was a man whose beauty cut.

He was a thing forged from steel, not carved from rock.

I couldn't breathe, even though my heart slammed against

the cage of my ribs. It wanted to do the same thing my bones screamed at me to do: escape.

Maybe it knew an instant before my eyes roved over his black as coal hair and landed on...

Pointed ears.

As sharp as the dagger at my belt.

He was even more deadly than steel.

Because he was a fae.

A fucking fae.

And I'd just stolen from him.

6

Fae were not known for their kindness. They rewarded good turns that were done to them with the gift of magic, but that was payment—a transaction. And they liked to elevate skilled craftsfolk, again by gifting them with magic. But that was so they could use their creations or tempt them to work for their fae courts.

They were not kind.

And they were not forgiving.

Before my brain could even calculate a next move, my thighs squeezed around Vespera. One shifted forwards, the other back, urging her into movement and steering away from him.

Oh gods. No wonder he was so furious.

What had I done?

What had I fucking done?

As we charged into the forest, my heart raced with the beat of Vespera's paws. It was all I could do to duck close to her back and suck in piercing breath after piercing breath.

My fae-worked pistol was no longer in my hand. I had no idea if I'd dropped it or slid it into its holster in a movement that had become automatic from years of practice. I just knew Vespera was running as hard as she could and I gave her all the rein she needed to do that.

A fae.

I'd stolen from a fae.

And he was going to kill me.

This was beyond unsafe. This was spectacularly, stupidly, life-endingly dangerous.

My insides roiled, liquid, as Vespera pounded through the trees. Breathe. I just needed to breathe and stay on... and ride faster than he did.

He was so going to kill me.

After what might've been moments or minutes, my heart quietened enough that I could hear more than just it and Vespera. There was movement behind me—the pound of a sabrecat's great paws, the crash of undergrowth.

The stories said fae could move silently, but it turned out that wasn't true of their sabrecats. Lucky for me. Though the stories also said fae rode deer, so maybe they didn't get everything right.

Dragging in several deep breaths made the tingling in my face fade. *Focus, Kat.*

I needed to get away.

I gathered Vespera's reins, brushed them over the right side of her neck and whiskers, and pulled my left leg back, guiding her into a tight left turn. Obeying my signals, she took us deeper into the forest.

Branches and brambles whipped and slashed at my legs, but they were nothing compared to the way the rose bushes had sliced my hands.

Vespera was fast, but I wasn't sure we could outrun a fae all night. Hiding was our only chance. Maybe somewhere above his eyeline.

In moments, she had us up a tree and for the first time tonight I thanked the rain, as it chose that moment to open into a downpour. Its patter on the canopy drowned out the sounds of us panting.

Still, I bit my lip, trying to keep as quiet as possible.

Below, the fae's dark shape emerged from the undergrowth, shadows thick around him. His grey cat blended into the darkness well.

I covered my mouth. Under me, Vespera tensed as though she wanted to leap down and rip his throat out.

That would only get us both killed.

Only two things killed fae: iron and aconite. The first of those was banned in Albion, and as for the second—I didn't carry poison.

So I clung to Vespera's reins and waited. My torn hands cried out in pain. I'd sworn to survive, but that seemed laughable now.

Especially when the fae drew to a halt.

Wild Hunt take me. He knew. He knew I was up here. Any second now, he would peer up at me with those silvery eyes— those silvery eyes that really did glow, because he was a fucking fae.

I bit my knuckle.

Please, gods. Please. I know I said "fuck you" earlier, but please. Make him ride on.

He cocked his head, listening.

Vespera crouched as though trying to make herself smaller, and I hugged tight against her, screwing my eyes shut. Her fur tickled my cheek, soft and familiar.

At least I was going to die with that small comfort.

Please.

Then the pounding of large paws on the ground sounded below me, and the undergrowth rustled. He was taking a run-up, ready to leap up this tree after us. I squeezed Vespera tight and whispered an apology for getting her killed, just like I'd got my little cub Fantôme killed all those years ago.

I waited.

And I waited, but the tree didn't shake as another sabrecat leapt up it.

In fact, the sound of galloping paws grew *quieter*.

When I dared to open my eyes, the forest floor below us was empty.

He'd ridden on, thinking I'd continued into the forest.

I wasn't about to hang around and see if he came back. In seconds, Vespera had us on solid ground, and we fled in the opposite direction.

Normally I rode home in a circuitous route just in case one of the Night Watch's constables spotted me and tried to follow, but not tonight.

Tonight I wanted to get under a roof and away from the forest and that fae as quickly as possible. He was a far worse danger than any officer of the law.

At last, at long blessed last, I rode into the stable yard. There was no sign of pursuit.

I had walls. Around the estate and the stable yard. They meant safety. With a shaky breath out, I sagged against Vespera.

True to my word, with saddlebags slung over my shoulder, I led her inside. We took the hidden entrance tucked in the shadows between the main house and the arcade linking it to the stables. She just about fit through the secret passage, her paws silent now she was only walking rather than running.

We emerged in the entrance hall with its bare floors and faded oak panels. Someone—Horwich, most likely—had left a lantern for me, though I'd walked these halls enough times to know them by heart. The lantern highlighted the dark rectangles of wood that remained where paintings had hung for centuries as the panelling faded. Those I'd been able to sell.

I couldn't feel the cold, though I knew it must've leached into me through my drenched clothes, which left a trail of water through the corridor. My hands shook as I set a fire in the drawing room for Vespera. Somehow, I managed to light it. Thank the gods for muscle memory... and for rain.

Vespera butted into my shoulder before stretching out on the tatty rug before the fire.

"I'm the one who should be thanking you." My voice was distant and raw, almost not my own. I scratched behind her ears as she rumbled and pressed into my touch.

Like an automaton on a rail, I made my way to the study. It had once been my husband's, but he had no use for it since he hadn't seen the inside of this house in years. Still, it didn't feel like *mine*. None of this did. It was just a safe place.

Before it was only Morag and Horwich left, I was sure the servants thought I left the master suite empty out of respect for him, ready for his return.

Respect? For *him*?

If every muscle hadn't been so heavy that my feet plodded along the floor, I would've laughed at the idea.

No. That room was his. And that bed was just as hateful. It was the place he'd taken me on our wedding night and a handful of times since.

I'd sooner watch it burn than sleep in it.

The study was free of any such associations, thankfully, but it was still only a place of practicality. I barely saw it as I passed the worn old desk, pulled open the cabinet, and unlocked the safe. I threw inside the pouch of coins. I was too tired to count it, but from the weight I knew it contained a lot of money. Maybe even enough to cover the bailiff's first payment.

With the safe locked, I staggered upstairs, thighs burning from that frantic ride, muscles giving out now the danger had passed. I had to crawl up the last few steps.

I didn't remember getting to my room, just that I dropped into my bed, fully clothed, and kept falling, falling, falling into a sleep where shadows crawled across the floor and up the sides of my bed.

7

I woke up to something creaking outside and the crunch of gravel from the driveway.

The fae. He'd come for the orb—for me. Gasping, I was upright in an instant. "Shit."

Sunlight hazed at the edges of my curtains, and the clock on the mantlepiece read nine o'clock. It was a stupid, faint comfort that I wouldn't be facing him at night this time.

I could die in the sunshine. Great.

Swallowing, I forced myself to cross the room. Perhaps if I gave the orb back, that would be enough to send him away. Except, the fury I'd seen on his face wasn't the kind to be satisfied with a simple return and apology. It was the kind that demanded revenge. The kind that demanded blood.

Mine chilled in my veins.

I steeled myself and opened the curtains a crack, squinting at the morning light that speared my eyes. Once I blinked away the glare, I had to blink some more. Because there was no slate grey sabrecat or an enraged fae outside.

35

Instead, with the jingle of harness and creak of axles, a huge carriage and four pure white sabrecats were trundling onto my weed-strewn drive.

That wasn't the vehicle of a tradesperson or debt-collector. That belonged to an aristocrat—a very, *very* rich one. The kind that hadn't been seen at the estate in years.

Despite exhaustion making my muscles leaden and fretful dreams that left my eyes sore, I threw a dress on and ran downstairs and out the front doors. If they just turned around in the driveway, they'd taken a wrong turn. If they stopped, they were here for me.

Was this who my useless husband had got into debt with? I didn't recognise the vehicle, hadn't stolen from it, so it couldn't be one of the Wicked Lady's victims. Still, my bones knew this kind of visitor couldn't be safe.

As the carriage turned and stopped, its glossy white door came into view and on it, a gilt crest gleamed in the morning sun. A lion and a dragon, both rearing, and between them a shield showing a white rose, a red rose, and three lions.

I skidded to a halt on the gravel, knees threatening to give out.

Because that was the queen's crest.

What the hells?

I stood there dumbly, my highway robbery gear under the dress, while the carriage door swung open.

Thank the gods a man perhaps a decade older than me got out, rather than the queen herself. Still, in velvet trimmed with fur and an ornate gold necklace featuring an emerald pendant, he was dressed no less richly than Her Majesty. And since he'd arrived in her carriage, he represented her.

So when he stood before me, an expectant look on his face, I did what I'd been told to do since I was a girl. I bowed.

"Ser, welcome to my estate. Please excuse me for receiving you in such..." I didn't even have words for my outfit, especially since my dress now featured at least two holes from tearing up the roses. "Well, in *this*." I gestured to myself with an apologetic smile. "To what do I owe the pleasure of a visit from the palace?"

He kept his expression guarded for the most part, unsurprising for a courtier, but even that couldn't prevent the slight flicker of his eyebrows as I said *my* estate.

He inclined his head politely. "Lady Katherine Ferrers, your country has need of you."

I blinked at him, at the letter he held out, at the gold seal upon it bearing the queen's crest. Almost as surprising was the fact he'd got my name right. I'd changed it back legally years ago, but most still called me Lady Fanshawe out of irritating habit.

It was an honour to serve—a duty. It would elevate my family, which was sorely needed since my parents never ventured out of their estate and my husband spent all his time (and money) gallivanting around Europa. Then there was Uncle Rufus. The very thought of him tightened my chest. He schemed and insinuated himself with powerful folk. Last I'd heard, it hadn't got the family further titles or lands.

Even so, I wasn't a soldier or a general who could fight for my country. I had no great skill the queen could use. I had no magic gift that might serve her.

He twitched the letter towards me, impatience etched in the tightness of his lips. "You are summoned to the palace."

My heart stuttered in my chest. Summoned. By the queen.

Did that mean she knew? It had to. That was the only reason she might want me there—to face her justice.

Her representative huffed a sigh and cracked the seal on

the letter himself before holding it up and reading. "Her Majesty, Elizabeth the Fifth, Queen of Albion, requires the presence of Lady Katherine Ferrers at court as her lady-in-waiting."

His lips kept moving, but I could only hear a high ringing.

By some miracle, I wasn't being punished for my crimes.

The queen had summoned me to the palace.

I TRIED TO DECLINE—POLITELY, of course. But this wasn't an invitation. I had two weeks to prepare before I was expected to present myself to Her Majesty. He made it clear in that way courtiers had, all controlled smiles and what they *didn't* say as much as what they did, that I had no choice in the matter. Failure to appear would be considered an insult to Her Majesty.

But I couldn't afford to go to court. I could barely afford to feed my household, never mind pay for gowns fit to be seen at the palace. I needed to be here finding some way to pay off that damn debt. I probably had the first payment from last night, but I still needed to conjure another five hundred pounds each month.

Maybe I could anger the queen just enough to be dismissed. Except, no. Not safe. There was a fine line when it came to pissing off a monarch, and the wrong side of that line led to an appointment with the axeman.

Would being incredibly boring get me sent home without the risk of execution?

I wondered as I watched the carriage drive away. Even

though Her Majesty's representative was gone, I couldn't shake the feeling that there was someone else here. I glanced around, but there was no sign of Horwich or Morag at the windows or anyone lurking in the overgrown mess I'd let the front gardens become.

"Lurking." I scoffed at myself and turned back to the house. Still, the back of my neck prickled like I was being watched.

Between the bailiff and this summons from the queen, of course I felt out of sorts. Add the fae from last night and it was no surprise I was imagining things.

As I went inside, I pulled his trinket from my inside pocket. This was my first time getting a good look at it in the light. Last night I'd seen it was gold and about an inch across with some sort of pattern engraved in the surface. Now I could see they were more than just engravings. Deep grooves crossed its surface. Between the lines spread stars and constellations, and when I turned it over, I found the moon and even a shooting star.

It was too heavy to be hollow, but perhaps it wasn't entirely solid—not with the way those grooves cut through the surface. It looked as though the ball was made of separate sections. I tried to pry one out with my fingernail, but it didn't budge.

What the hells *was* it? Just a pretty trinket, or did it have a practical use? The only things I knew for sure: one, it was definitely real gold; two, it was fae-worked.

And that, in turn, meant two things. One, it was worth a great deal, and two, I couldn't bloody sell it.

Fae-worked items were rare enough that as soon as it went on the market, even through shadowy channels like my fence's, it would cause a stir. That would risk leading the fae right to me. And the moment my fence caught the faintest whiff of wealth or a threat, she would sell me out. No hesitation.

That left me with little choice but to prepare for court.

After my encounter with the fae, I didn't dare go out on the road at night. Thankfully, my assessment was correct and his pouch of money covered the bailiff's first instalment, which I paid the next day. I even had enough left for Horwich's and Morag's wages.

The following weeks, I spent working in the gardens, getting as many seeds sown as possible, so they'd have food in my absence.

As I kept my hands busy, a question dragged on my mind. Why had I, of all people, been called to court?

Usually ladies-in-waiting were women who'd gained the queen's favour or whose husbands had pleased her in some way. I was pretty sure the queen wasn't aware of my existence beyond a name on a record of noblewomen. And there was no way in the universe that arsehole I was married to had done anything to please her. He pleased only himself.

Even though it didn't *seem* to relate to my nighttime activities, the summons left me uneasy. What if it was a trick to bring the Wicked Lady to justice publicly and make an example of her?

Of *me*.

8

Regardless of my fears, the days ticked away, and although I put it off as long as possible, the time came when I had to ride for Lunden. Vespera and I arrived at dusk, when the palace walls were nothing more than deeper darkness spreading left and right, studded with torches. When I showed the summons, the guards nodded and let me through the huge gates. I smothered a disappointed sigh—if they'd turned me away, it would've been a good excuse to go home.

Lanterns lined the drive that wound through the gardens, but beyond their pools of golden light, I could only see indistinct shapes and shadowy masses. The faint scent of greenery wafted past the lantern smoke.

Ahead, the palace itself was a series of turrets and crenelated walls that looked black against the violet sky. I held my breath as I passed through an archway and tried not to think how much it looked like the gaping maw of some fairy tale monster.

The courtyard was well lit by gas lamps, so it was easy to see the road dirt on my riding habit and the hair pulling loose from my braid. Maybe the state of my appearance would be just enough to get me sent home if word reached the queen.

But while servants gave me odd looks—a lone woman arriving in the in-between of twilight—and the looks got odder when I presented my summons.

I smiled politely at the chamberlain, who greeted me and showed me through the winding corridors of the palace. But he only gave me a cool look and a nod before pointing out the library and the corridor to the throne room.

I winced as I realised he wasn't being cruel. He was just doing his job. He was a chamberlain and I was a lady. However faded that line had become at Markyate Cell, the rest of the world still scored it afresh every day. Servants. Aristocrats. Never the twain shall meet.

My heart sank, aching for Morag and Horwich, missing them already. I hadn't gone this long without seeing them in years. And here at court, I knew no one. I didn't have a single ally of high rank or low. That thought made my stomach twist.

Living on our estate so long had insulated me from the world, and that insulation had brought a kind of protection. There it didn't matter if I wore muddy clothes or even (gasp) trousers. I could slump at the kitchen table and eat a honey cake with no one to rap my knuckles and remind me of posture. I didn't need to follow all those rules of etiquette that had been drummed into me as a child.

But the outside world meant compliance. Safety required me to blend in, to mask up, to obey the rules and be whatever people in power wanted.

It was a part I'd been moulded into by my father, my

uncle, and, when he'd been around, my husband. I just had to remind myself how to fit into it.

I pulled my shoulders back and folded my hands—the perfect, neat Lady Katherine Ferrers.

When we arrived in my suite, I found it was luxurious and decorated in dove grey, albeit a little sparse. I supposed most ladies-in-waiting brought whole carriages full of belongings and made their quarters homely. I'd sent a small chest ahead by stagecoach. It now sat in the living room as though the servants hadn't quite known what to do with the sole piece of luggage. Perhaps they thought it was a mistake and that I'd arrive with a dozen more.

I had a small sitting room, a large bedroom, and a private room off that with a toilet and sink. The chamberlain told me I could call for a bath at any time, giving my muddy hem a lingering look. Any embarrassment I might've felt was eclipsed by the idea of a bath that maids would fill, rather than one where I had to lug buckets from the kitchen stove.

Maybe I could get sent home *after* that.

"Since you have no retinue, we can recruit a lady's maid on your behalf. Unless they're arriving separately?" He raised an eyebrow.

It was silly, but my cheeks heated. I'd gone without a lady's maid for years after the previous one had fallen pregnant and married. It didn't bother me to dress myself and, when I had the energy, to brush my own hair. Yet standing here in a palace, in front of a chamberlain whose velvet jacket and shiny shoes were newer, smarter, and richer than any garment I owned, made me shift uncomfortably. "No. No retinue."

He inclined his head with a soft sound. Again, it wasn't unkind, just... efficient.

He explained I'd be presented to the queen tomorrow and that although I'd missed dinner, he'd have some food sent up. Of course I wouldn't be expected to hunt through the kitchens for supper myself, I knew that. But it would take some time getting used to this business of being served again.

Moments after the chamberlain left, a servant came with my saddlebags. I'd barely put my small selection of clothes away when another appeared with a tray of cold meats, cheese, bread, and pickle, apologising for the simple fare. It was the largest meal I'd had in weeks and more meat than I'd seen in months.

I polished off the lot and fell into bed.

But sleep wouldn't come.

Because tomorrow, I'd be presented to the queen, and I was sorely out of practice at playing this part.

I tossed and turned, and my stomach twisted, until eventually I had to run to the toilet and throw up everything I'd eaten.

Bathed in cold sweat, I sat on the cool stone floor and stared into the darkness.

Lady Katherine Ferrers. Noblewoman. Married (however much I loathed the fact). And now a lady-in-waiting to the queen.

Across more than a decade, my father's words came to me, reminders of everything being a lady meant.

Obedient. Dutiful. Silent.

I had to be exactly that.

9

My stomach churned as I stared at the throne room doors. I'd slept maybe an hour or two. Not that I'd found any relief there, drifting into dreams where I stood before the queen in rags and she set the Wild Hunt on me as punishment. At their front, riding a huge, half-rotten stag, was the fae I'd encountered on the road, his eyes glowing in the darkness, fixed on me with murderous intent.

I needed to get my hands on some wine or gin—something to help me sink into sleep and avoid more nightmares.

Truth be told, the jade green gown I wore, while made of silk, wasn't many steps above rags. I'd cannibalised another moth-eaten dress and taken the lace and trim from that to hide the marks and holes in this one. But even the flounce I'd added to cover the worn hem couldn't disguise the fact its style was a decade out of date.

Much as I hoped to get sent home, the prospect of facing a room full of courtiers who wore fashion so cutting edge it bled while I wore *this* was a different matter.

At some signal I didn't catch, the guards swung the great double doors open. I straightened my back, tried to control my breath, and entered.

It was a blur. Sky blue and dawn pink. Midnight, black, and purple. Silver and gold.

At the far end of the room, the queen was a smear of golden throne, mourning black, and crimson hair. Such an impossible colour had to be a mark of her fae ancestry. The black gown was for her mother, who'd died towards the end of last year.

It was like my eyes refused to acknowledge that the queen was a reality and I was standing in her presence in such shabby attire. Finally, I managed to blink away the blur and instantly regretted it. Too many people stared back.

They watched, eyebrows rising, corners of mouths twitching. A woman muttered behind a fan to her neighbour, who tittered.

I hadn't eaten, so I could only guess the lurch in my torso was my stomach itself. I couldn't blame it for wanting to leap from my body and flee.

But I kept up a sedate pace, stopped when the chamberlain announced me, and bowed deeply, waiting for the queen to call me back upright.

The tiniest speck of pride glimmered in my chest at the precision of my bow. Exactly as I'd been taught. I couldn't present myself in the most beautiful outfit, but I could at least do that well.

It eased my hammering pulse and churning stomach and allowed me to take in the people closest as I waited. In the periphery of my vision, the woman who'd whispered to her friend wore a floaty lilac gown with a slit that ran from the hem up to—

Thank the gods my head was bowed, because I couldn't keep the shock from my face. The gown revealed the bare skin of her thigh.

I didn't think I'd seen any woman's thigh except for my sister's, and that was because we would swim in the lake on our family estate.

But a lady's leg revealed in public?

Unheard of.

I blinked and checked her companion. Her legs were covered, but again she wore a floaty dress, not layers upon layers of skirts like I did. The pleated bodice dipped in a V so low it revealed her belly button.

They had to be here from a foreign court. The first, the whisperer, kept tugging the edges of that slit, trying to close the skirt around herself. Maybe she was realising her country's fashions didn't suit Albionic weather.

"Arise," a clear, female voice said at last, ringing out over the whispered conversations that had erupted upon my entrance.

I obeyed, though part of me registered surprise that it was out of choice, rather than any compulsion. Descended from Elizabeth I and her fae husband, the queen should've inherited magic and fae charm that could compel me to do as she wished. And yet...

My brow tensed as I met her brown eyes.

And yet I felt none of that. Perhaps the rumours about her not having magic were true.

I didn't dare linger on the comments I'd once heard with those rumours. In a quiet corner of the marketplace when the speaker thought no one but their friend was in earshot, they'd said, "No magic. No right to rule."

I stamped the thought down. Even if the queen had no

gift, who knew what other fae-blooded or fae-touched folk might be in her court? One of them might be able to sift through thoughts. I'd heard stories.

The way those dark brown eyes surveyed me, evaluating, calculating, gave the impression that even without magic, the queen saw everything. At last, one corner of her mouth rose, cool and considered. "Well, here she is at last: the elusive Lady Katherine Fanshawe."

I bit my tongue against correcting her.

At her side, a brown-haired man in sleek black clothing bent and whispered in her ear. Golden light from the chandeliers lined his sharp cheekbones. He didn't so much as look at me, which was how I liked it. A low profile—that was safe. Maybe he had important news for the queen that would get this presentation over nice and quickly.

Around me, the room leant in. The woman who'd laughed at me murmured to her friend and I caught one word. "Spymaster."

I clasped my hands tighter to suppress the shiver that wanted to pass through me now I knew I was in the presence of Lord Thomas Cavendish. His reputation preceded him in every room in the country. But then, with his network of whispers, he probably knew that. Even closeted in the estate, I'd read about him in the news. Many an execution went ahead on his say so alone.

Was he talking to her about *me*? Did he know? Was *I* about to be executed on his say so?

My chest practically vibrated with how fast my heart was beating. Cold sweat beaded on my back.

The queen's eyebrows rose as her gaze stayed on me.

Shit. Bringing me here on false pretences, closing a trap on me while being presented to the queen—that was exactly the sort of thing he'd do.

But if he didn't know, any unladylike reaction from me might arouse suspicion.

I planted my feet to the floor, but good gods, I wanted to bolt.

At last, the queen nodded and Cavendish straightened. She smiled. But it was the coldest thing I'd ever seen—worse than a frozen lake in the icy heart of January. "I understand it's actually Lady Katherine *Ferrers*." She arched one eyebrow, and the look was so sharp, I might as well have corrected her out loud in front of the entire court.

"Your Majesty"—I bowed a little more deeply than earlier and stayed there—"I apologise, I wasn't aware—"

She raised a hand. "That's quite enough, Lady... *Ferrers*." She said it with a little raise of her eyebrows and the hint of a smirk, like it was a joke. "Perhaps we should simply call you Lady Katherine and save everyone the embarrassment. For gods' sakes, get up."

When I dragged myself upright, that arched eyebrow was back, and it reminded me of a bow drawn, ready to fire. "I suppose we should count ourselves lucky that we'll have the amusement of your *old* name and your *old* dress." She gave a low chuckle, and the rest of the room followed her cue, erupting into laughter.

It burned.

Good gods, it burned like ice.

Not just in my cheeks, but my chest, my arms, my back, my legs. Slick sweat coated my palms, and my heart hammered so hard I could barely breathe past it.

I was meant to be blending in. Obedient and safe—that

was the best way. But here I stood, marked as old-fashioned and as near as damn it divorced. And although I'd been at court for less than twenty-four hours, I already understood these were dangerous things.

A single clap snapped the room back into quiet, and the queen rubbed her hands together. "I believe my ancestors had jesters to make them laugh—I never expected to end up with one of my own standing here in such *motley* attire."

The room laughed again, and I smiled, though my teeth gritted behind my lips and retorts burned on my tongue. But I needed to not get myself executed, so I spread my hands and inclined my head like I was in on the joke and not its butt. "I came to serve Your Majesty, though I confess that wasn't the position I expected."

At that, she chuckled again, eyes glinting as though I really had amused her. "Yes, I think you'll make a *most interesting* addition to my court. Welcome to Riverton Palace, Lady Katherine."

With a wave of her hand, my audience with the queen was ended.

Or at least, I thought it was. As I took a step back and went to turn, she raised one finger and cast a meaningful look from head to toe. "In future, I trust my little jester will present herself to me with a more pleasing appearance."

"Of course, Your Majesty." Gods knew how I got the words out past the dryness of my mouth.

Then, with a nod from her, I really was dismissed.

Somehow, I made it out of the room. I didn't remember anything other than the intense pressure at the back of my eyes and the even more intense desperation to not let it out.

Because there was no mistaking it: this had been a

complete, total, and utter disaster. It couldn't have gone much worse if I'd tried.

And I hadn't even got myself sent home.

10

Once the throne room doors were shut and out of sight, I cranked my sedate glide up to the fastest walk I could manage, breaths coming in short, sharp bursts.

It was stupid to want to cry.

Crying didn't achieve anything. It didn't *do* anything other than leave your eyes sore and swollen.

This, being at court, wasn't even something I wanted. What I *wanted* was to be sent home so I could try to make some money. But somehow the humiliation had scratched my skin open and the horror of getting this so wrong worked its way underneath.

I was a practical woman. I got things right. Always.

Because if I didn't, then someone would die, whether that was me getting captured during my night jaunts, one of my robbery targets, or Morag or Horwich starving.

I didn't give a shit about dresses and prettiness or any of

that. I was too busy worrying about fertiliser and seeds—useful things.

And yet, when I reached my rooms, I slammed the door and leant against it. I pressed my palms and forehead into the solid oak, like that could hold the world out as I failed to keep the tears in.

"Ahem."

I whirled and found I was too late to hold the world out. A pretty girl of maybe fifteen or sixteen with blond ringlets was lounging on the settee, legs hooked over its arm. She grinned and gave me a little wave. "Got a message for you."

It took a moment of staring at her before I registered that she was wearing the sombre grey and white linen of a servant. But other than Horwich and Morag, I'd never seen a servant behave so casually.

I dashed away my tears and pulled my shoulders back before making for the door to my bathroom. I'd get rid of her and splash my face with cold water. "You can leave it on the side."

She flipped to her feet like she should've been capering at the circus rather than delivering messages in a palace. "Begging your pardon, madam, but it isn't written." Much as her manner was *technically* polite, amusement edged her tone as though the idea of a written note was ridiculous. "You're to meet my master at the seventh door on the left in the north corridor. Quick as you can." She finished with a bow, as if to soften the flippant delivery of that last line.

I took a long breath and smoothed my skirts, buying myself a moment to formulate a response. I mean, how the hells did I reply to such an odd request? "And who is your master?"

"That was the only message I was asked to deliver." She

shrugged with an impish smirk that made her look suddenly older and much less like an obedient servant. Maybe she was more woman than girl. "You'll have to go to find out." Her ringlets swung as she turned to leave. Pausing with the door open, she tossed me a look over her shoulder. "I wouldn't hang around. He doesn't like to be kept waiting."

Before I could ask anything more, she'd disappeared.

Master. My only clue. And with enough influence to have a messenger sent to me right away. Probably some high-ranking courtier who wanted to debrief me about my presentation to the queen—what I'd done wrong, what to do next time. As though I didn't know already.

I paused at the dressing table to tuck a loose lock of hair back in place. And I saw—really *saw*—what the queen and her entire throne room had.

Russet waves fought against the chignon I'd tried to pin them into. No surprise my hair was so unruly: it looked more like straw than the "silken locks" poets wrote about.

Despite the red hair and green eyes from Papa, I'd inherited Mama's tanned skin, passed down from her foreign mother. Between tending the vegetables and riding to the palace, my nose and cheeks were red, flecked with even darker freckles. Blueish circles underlined my eyes.

I looked like I should be working in a field, not standing in a palace.

I swore and tore the pins from my hair before braiding it over my shoulder and coiling that into a bun. Something caught on the strands as I worked and when I looked down at my hands, I realised it was their rough skin. The reddened knuckles, the calluses from holding various tools, the dryness: these were working hands, not a lady's.

What the hells was I doing here?

On paper I was Lady Katherine Ferrers, but that identity felt just as flimsy as the paper my change of name was written on.

However, my summoner didn't like to be kept waiting, and I'd already pissed off the most powerful woman in the realm today. So with a deep sigh I set off for my mysterious meeting.

II

I reached the door the messenger had directed me to and knocked.

A deep voice responded, "Enter."

I obeyed but stopped short when I saw the brown-haired man seated behind the desk, fingers steepled over a notebook as he gave me an appraising look. The queen's spymaster. He must've come straight here from the throne room.

At these close quarters, I could tell he was several years older than me, edging into his late thirties. With those sharp cheekbones and lean body, he was still handsome. That didn't explain what he might want with me, though.

"Ser." I gave a quick bow, nowhere near as deep as the two I'd given the queen. "I believe you sent me a message?" Unless someone was playing a nasty trick on me. The blond messenger seemed the type to do something like that.

He nodded, even as his hazel eyes continued their slow path down my body. It was the most thorough look I'd been given in a long time, and I had to fight the urge to fidget under it. "You're no doubt wondering why you've been summoned to court so suddenly."

"The question had crossed my mind."

"I understand you have need of something. And luckily for you, I have the means to procure it." A self-satisfied smile inched across his face.

Despite only spending minutes in the throne room, I'd had my fill of courtier life, and his vague comments made me bristle. Would it kill him to just give me a straight answer?

Still, he was a powerful man, so I had to play the part. Acting out only led to worse trouble, like it had for Fantôme and my sister Avice.

The thought of them was enough to sober me and keep my tongue civil as I replied, "What is it you believe I need?"

His smile grew wider as he finally met my gaze, apparently satisfied he'd assessed every inch of me. "Straight to the point. You really are new at court, aren't you?" Scoffing, he stood and gave the book another glance.

Now I could see it wasn't a notebook, but a diary—dates marked with meetings and events. Before I could see much more, he closed it. Slowly, he circled the desk. "Money, Katherine. That is what you need. It's the starting point of what anyone needs. First money, then power." He leant back against the desk and shrugged. "What else is there?"

Money. There was only money.

I'd spent so long focused on getting just that, keeping our heads above water, I hadn't even considered anything else. How could I think of power when I was drowning in debt?

I raised an eyebrow at him. "And the means?"

He stood with a sigh, shaking his head. "You have so much

to learn." Tapping his forefinger to his chin, he circled me. I could *feel* the weight of his gaze—or maybe it was that I could feel how he was weighing me. Against what, though?

I clasped my hands together against the urge to cross my arms. I couldn't react. I had to consider my actions, place every step perfectly, and at least play the part of the obedient lady.

My breath stilled.

Unless I'd been right in the throne room, and he knew my secret.

That explained how he knew I needed money. Though it was probably clear from my clothes and the fact various parts of the estate were in obvious need of repair. A man with a network of spies didn't have to dig deep to get that tidbit of information.

But perhaps that network had discovered the Wicked Lady and the elusive Lady Katherine Ferrers were one and the same.

The room spun slowly. I held still and forced breaths in and out, just as I had whenever Papa lost his temper with Avice. Just as I had when his brother had come charging across the stable yard towards us.

I flinched from the memory.

Even breaths. Calm. There was a chance he didn't know. I couldn't give away that he had me spooked.

He finished one circle, and the next brought him closer, closer, until his strides rustled my full skirts and I could see the gold chain disappearing under his collar. Too close. I planted my feet and didn't lean away, but I wanted to. Gods, I wanted to.

At last he stopped in front of me, the toes of his boots disappearing under the hem of my skirts. He didn't disguise the way his hooded gaze trailed over my face.

Again, that slow smile. "Though perhaps your lack of guile means you'll do perfectly." He reached out.

I stood there, trapped between instinct that said I should step away and ladylike obedience that said I should stand still and fold my hands just so and endure. But there was another, deeper part of me that helped back me into a corner. That part *yearned.*

It was a traitor.

Because it was only a little, but I swayed towards those fingers. It had been so long since anyone had touched me. So, so long.

It was pathetic, but that deep part of me didn't care; it only wanted.

Cavendish's fingers closed on a lock of hair that curled over my shoulder. He picked it up and turned it in the light, hazel eyes fixed upon it as though it were a jewel to be checked for flaws. This jewel had plenty.

"You've no doubt heard that the fae courts have sent suitors to bid for the queen's hand." His voice was a low thrum in the air between us, intimate. He cocked his head in question, though his gaze didn't leave my hair, which he now rubbed between finger and thumb.

I raised my eyebrows at his choice of subject. From his behaviour so far and the mention of money, I'd half-expected him to propose I become his mistress. "I've heard the rumours. I suspect everyone has."

"They've sent two contingents. That many fae after so long, I'd be surprised if there *weren't* rumours. They claim it's diplomacy. I call it spying." He frowned, at last replacing the lock of hair. One finger hooked under my chin, the touch firm and so, so warm as he tilted my head back until I met his gaze.

I tried to suppress my shiver, but this was the first time in years I'd felt someone else's skin. The last time had been that idiot Fanshawe's fumbling attempts in the dark. He'd been so drunk, I'd fooled him into thinking we'd fucked, when really he'd just spilled himself on my belly.

Queasiness at the thought warred with the sheer physical shock of Cavendish's skin upon mine. It held me still as he gave me such a stern look, I once again wondered if I was in trouble.

"I do not take kindly to being spied upon, and I do not trust Dusk Court."

Although the fae of Alba had been elusive for centuries now, I had a vague understanding that they functioned with two courts. Dusk and Dawn, ruled by a Day King and a Night Queen, respectively. How that worked, I had no idea. Seemed highly impractical.

I couldn't blame the spymaster for being suspicious. It seemed odd that they'd suddenly resumed contact after all this time.

Expression tightening, Cavendish tilted his head back. "You will gather information on Lord Bastian Marwood, the Night Queen's Shadow."

"What?" My eyes might've popped out of my head, they opened so wide. "You want me to be a spy?" This had to be another joke at my expense.

But he didn't laugh, his frown only deepened, forming dark creases between his eyebrows, shading the green flecks in his eyes.

No joke. My throat tightened.

At last he sighed and turned away, pacing the room's length, fingertips trailing the bookshelves that lined that wall. "Did you know the fae consider red hair the most beautiful trait?"

Another flip in topic. Did he do that deliberately to keep me off balance? Still, my hair wasn't going to enable me to spy on a fae lord. "I don't see how that helps. 'Beautiful' is not useful."

Cavendish snorted and shook his head, tapping the spine of a book. "On the contrary. Beautiful can be *very* useful indeed. You are an attractive woman, Katherine, but with that hair, you are irresistible to fae." He turned to me, expression hardening. "Use it. First, gain Marwood's attention, then work your way closer to him. Get me information on him and his companions. I want to know where he goes, who he speaks to, what he thinks about Albion and Her Majesty. Ultimately, what he is planning."

My eyes widened with each demand. He had the wrong person. He had to think I was someone, something I wasn't.

His expression tightened. "Be in no doubt: he plots against this court, just as his kind plots against Dawn."

A fae plot against Albion. That could be dangerous for everyone at court—hells, everyone in the country, if it was a precursor to war. Nowhere would be safe.

Still, I shook my head, not even able to scoff at the insanity of what he was suggesting. I couldn't be presented to the queen without making a fool of myself. I was no spy.

"I don't know if you'd noticed, but I've hardly made a good first impression. I don't have the right clothes. I don't know the right people." Now I did laugh and it was as bitter as a frozen winter night. "I certainly don't have any allies. I'm not the person you're looking for."

"See, you doubt yourself. And yet there are many reasons you're perfect for this little mission." He sauntered closer, like a hunting sabrecat. "Your hair will draw him in like a moth to a flame. The fact you're a married woman, not a debutant who needs to keep her reputation. And you're estranged from your husband, so he won't be an issue."

"My reputation? My husband?" It was a miracle I didn't refer to him by one of my more inventive names. "What have they got to do with anything?"

"Come now, Katherine." His voice was low and soft again, his toes back at the hem of my gown. "You're no innocent maiden. I'm sure you understand." He gave a faint smirk as his gaze slid to my mouth, then down to my bodice. His shoulders sank a fraction as though he was disappointed. "I expect you to do whatever is required to get close to your target and gain his trust."

Ah. Not a proposal to be *his* mistress, but to become Bastian Marwood's. That broke the rules—an affair wasn't an appropriate pastime for a lady. If anyone found out...

"But you mustn't tell him you're married." A stiffness entered his smirk before it faded. "You already behave like a widow—let him believe that's what you are. As to the rest"—he gave a dismissive flick of his hand—"I can give you all that. You'll have an allowance for gowns and jewels; I'll get you a maid. And you'll know *me*. I'm the only alliance you need. As part of my network, you'll be privy to all kinds of information, including the sort people don't want getting out." He smiled, cool and calculated. "Everyone will want to be your friend when they see the alternative."

I held still at the reminder: this was a man whose wrong side was very dangerous indeed.

But if I got on his *right* side, he'd make an invaluable ally at court. Since it looked like I was stuck here, I needed one, and with him, I wouldn't be cast adrift in its currents as I was now.

"And let me spell it out." He said each word slowly with a

vicious intensity that stole any objection I might've voiced. "I will pay you a large sum of money." He drew a piece of paper from his inside pocket and held it out.

£1,000.

I blinked at it, tried to speak, couldn't. That was what the estate, in its pitiful condition, might bring in over an entire year. Last year it had been less.

I had to clear my throat before I could form a coherent reply. "You'll pay me a thousand pounds for spying on him?"

"Per month."

The world tilted. Somehow, I didn't stagger.

Just five months and I'd be able to pay the bailiff in full. Five months. That was nothing after all these years.

Hells, with Cavendish as an ally, maybe I could even persuade the queen to grant me a divorce. Her mother had denied me, but she was dead now, and this new queen might be more sympathetic, especially with a few whispers from her spymaster.

"Plus"—Cavendish folded the note in half before tossing it on the fire—"an even more outrageous bonus on top of that if you get me the information I want."

The paper crinkled and curled before singeing at the edges and finally surrendering to the lick of orange flame.

Money to save the estate. An alliance that might free me from that arsehole husband.

It was no choice at all.

As for the price. Well, I'd already slept with my husband. I could deal with fucking another man I didn't care for.

If it saved the estate, I could endure anything.

Squaring my shoulders, I looked up at him. "What do I need to do?"

This smile spread even more slowly than his earlier ones, like he'd won.

But with that sum of money—more than I'd ever dreamed of laying my hands on—it was definitely *me* who had won.

12

I would meet the Night Queen's Shadow at a ball in two days. In the meantime, Cavendish had given me a necklace to make me immune from fae charm's intoxication and said one of his "network" would visit shortly to prepare me.

He ended the meeting with a stern warning not to, under any circumstances, approach him in public. "No one must suspect you of working for me, especially not your target. Your appearance of unworldliness will be your cover—mixing with me will ruin that." My only way to contact him would be to leave a note behind a loose tile in the west corridor showing a dragon. I had to return the tile with the dragon on its side, so he'd know he had a message. Otherwise, he would tell me when and where to meet him.

The delicate silver necklace sat in place now. He'd told me to keep it in contact with my skin at all times while he'd fastened it at the nape of my neck. My heart still beat a little too fast at the intimacy of that action. He wasn't a man with boundaries. And that pathetic, deep part of myself was greedy for touch, so I didn't set any. Not that I realistically could with a man of his status.

I touched the necklace, running my fingernail over the tiny pearls. In folklore, pearlwort was reputed to ward against fae charm. Whoever had made this had taken it literally, using seed pearls to form the five-petalled flowers that now clustered against my collarbone.

As for the visit, he wasn't exaggerating about the "shortly" part. When I returned to my rooms, she was already sitting on the settee, waiting. Apparently Cavendish's network didn't believe in things like keys or privacy.

When I entered, the woman's charming smile revealed perfect white teeth. From her carefully curled hair to her perfect little feet in dainty jewelled slippers, she was beautiful. Captivatingly, achingly, unattainably beautiful.

"And this must be the lady herself." When she looked me over, for the first time since I'd arrived at court, I saw approval. "Oh yes, I see why he picked you. Such potential." She nodded as she completed a circuit around me, caramel-coloured curls bouncing. There was something softer in her appraisal, and her eyes sparked with excitement rather than cold calculation.

"And you are?"

"Oh my"—she touched her chest, giving a chuckle accompanied by an elegant toss of her head—"I'm sorry, darling, I quite forget myself. Lady Eloisa-Elizabetta-Belladonna Fortnum-Knightly-Chase." She spread her arms as if presenting herself to an audience. "My parents couldn't agree on just one name, and when I married, I picked up yet another." The briefest shadow crossed her features before she went on. "But you can call me Ella, because life's too short for all that, eh?"

She winked and bumped shoulders with me before placing a hand on the small of my back. She steered me towards a full-length mirror that had appeared while I'd met with the spymaster.

I couldn't help but smile. There was something infectious in her manner. That had to be why Cavendish had recruited her.

I felt even more of an anomaly.

She cocked her head at me in the mirror. "This is when you're supposed to say I can call you Kathy or Kitty or Kate, or something like that."

"Kat."

"Oh, perfect." Her eyes and smile widened. "They'll like that. A little kitty reminder always goes down well."

My reflection's face screwed up enough to spell out my confusion.

Another infectious chuckle and Ella squeezed me close, one arm around my waist. "Dear heart, are you an innocent? Oh my! That's a twist I hadn't expected. I thought you were married?"

The woman talked in code as though half the conversation was with herself and it didn't matter that I didn't understand. Still, I chuckled along with her as I held up a hand and explained, "I'm married. And not innocent." In more ways than she meant, too.

"Then you know men like a certain kind of cat very well indeed." She raised her eyebrows meaningfully.

"Please," I groaned, rubbing my head, "enough courtly skirting around what you're trying to say. Just spell it out."

"Well, where's the fun in that?" She huffed a playful sigh. "Fine. I *mean*, your name being Kat will serve as a good trigger for any man interested in you to think about your pussy."

If I'd been drinking, I'd have spat it out.

"I... my..." I blinked at her, trying to regain control of my mouth that had fallen slack. "That's what men do when they hear my name?"

"Well"—she lifted one shoulder—"I daresay *some* do." She grinned at me in the mirror. Then there was a knock at the door. "Ah, perfect. Come in," she called. "I hope you don't mind, but I've taken the liberty of summoning a designer to help us." She propelled me out of the way as a tall woman with short, sharp jaw-length hair entered. A retinue of servants followed, carrying various boxes, sketchbooks, and bolts of fabric.

I could only gape as they all piled in.

Ella squeezed my shoulder as the designer directed a foot stool to be placed before her for me to stand on. "I hope you don't think me unkind for saying," Ella murmured, "but after your presentation, I figured you could use the help." She gave me an apologetic smile.

Even though she read as genuine, I grimaced. My gown, once the height of fashion, felt like a dirty sack, marking me as a penniless outsider. At court, that painted a target on my back. Replacing it wouldn't only help me spy for Cavendish, it would help me blend in. It would keep me safe.

"You're right. No offence taken."

Still, when the designer, known only as Blaze (one word, no surname, undoubtedly made up), had her assistants unroll sheer silks and open sketchbooks with drawings of low-cut bodices and backless dresses, I balked.

I wasn't petite and slight like Ella or tall and slender, like the woman who'd whispered to her friend in the throne room.

Short and rounded, with wide hips, full breasts, and thighs made for riding. That was me.

But Blaze waved off my concerns and made me strip to my chemise so she could get a proper look at me.

"Do not question my creations. If you wore Ella's garment, then yes, you would look like a potato in a sack, because it wasn't designed for you."

I enjoyed the soft edges of her Frankish accent, which reminded me of the summer I spent there.

She circled me with yet another appraising look. "Just like those old fashions don't suit you either—full, stiff skirts." She tutted and shook her head. "No, for you, we want delicate gathers, not adding too much volume. Let the sheer fabric pool around you, hinting at what's beneath."

She clicked her fingers and one of her entourage hurried forward with a large tome that Blaze flipped through. Inside were dozens of swatches of fabric. I didn't see which one she finally thrust her finger at, but the assistant flitted back to their stack of supplies.

As if none of that had happened, she continued. "Vertical lines, and... hmm..." She narrowed her eyes at me before snatching the neckline of my chemise to one side. "Ah, yes. It's as I suspected—look! She has beautiful shoulders. And with that décolletage..." She nodded, then flicked a glance at Ella. "You agree, no?"

"Quite beautiful, certainly, and..." Ella wandered to another chest I hadn't noticed before, with *E.E.B.F.K.C.* written on the lid in a gilded script. "Hmm, yes, I think I have a few things that will help." She rifled through the chest, but before I could see the contents, Blaze stepped in the way, eyebrows raised.

"And how are your thighs?"

"My..." I blinked at her. "My thighs are *just fine*, thank you."

With a twitch of her finger, she canted her head. "Show me, then."

"Good grief. I don't think I've had a doctor this thorough."

But the look she gave me said she wouldn't be put off, so I raised the hem of my chemise and let her see.

Blaze nodded, black, straight hair bobbing. "You ride... and I'd say walk, yes?"

"Oh my." Ella's eyes widened as she turned back from the chest, arms full of jars made from smoked glass. "Kat, you are... yes, *yes*, you definitely need Blaze's touch. They"—she shook her head at my thighs, and I went to drop my hem, but Blaze caught my hand before I could—"*they* need showing off."

The skin between my shoulder blades crawled under the scrutiny. Being *looked at* like this, being *noticed*... they weren't safe things. They weren't things I wanted. I cleared my throat as Blaze pulled the hem from my hand and started fussing with my chemise, gathering it at my waist, tugging it lower at the front.

"I noticed the change in dress in the throne room." I eyed the blush pink gown Ella wore, which scooped low at the front and back. Fashions hadn't changed that dramatically in centuries, going by all the ancestral portraits I'd seen at Markyate Cell and my parents' estate. "What happened?"

Ella lifted one shoulder and scooped some cream from one of the jars. "Fae happened, darling." She took my hand and rubbed the cream into my skin.

She did it so casually and yet so unexpectedly, I sucked in a breath and had to hold it. More touch for me to lean into as she massaged my hands and arms with firm sweeps.

Either she didn't catch my reaction or chose to ignore it,

because with another shrug, she went on. "They arrive in their daring outfits and suddenly everyone wants to copy."

With a hiss, Blaze shot her a look. A capital *L* Look. "Copy! La! It is *not* copying. It's merely that the opening of patrons' minds has allowed us to create. No more stiff layers and covered skin. Now we are free." As if to illustrate, she slid my chemise off my shoulders and let it pool on the floor. "See? Much better, no?"

With a strangled gasp, I clutched my breasts and tried to cover myself, but... none of the assistants so much as glanced. Ella's cheeks and nose were pink, perhaps. But she only met my gaze and held out her hand, waiting for me to let her continue working the cream into my skin.

"You see, my little diamond in the rough..." Blaze narrowed her eyes at me. "Ah, with this hair, make that *ruby*." Her nose wrinkled as she gave a little satisfied grin. "You just need some polish." Her assistant arrived with a bolt of deep teal silk, which Blaze grabbed the end of without taking her eyes off me. "And then..."

She draped a length over my shoulder and matched it on the other side, forming a deep V between my breasts. One-handed, she gathered it at my waist and pointed. "Pin there, there, and there." With another tug on the bolt of fabric, she wafted it around my middle and had her assistant pin it in place. A twist at my back, more pinning, then she stood back and nodded. "Yes. *Yes.* Mirror!" She gestured, and it appeared behind her, an assistant scuttling away the only sign she hadn't summoned it magically.

Shoulders back, she gave a deep sigh of satisfaction and stepped out of the way. "*Voilà.*"

I blinked in the mirror and turned left and right. Slits hidden in the gathers of the not-quite-a-gown opened as I moved. Sleeveless, slitted, and the low, low V that ended somewhere between my breasts and belly button... I'd never shown so much flesh, but... the shape suited me. The skirt skimmed my hips. The fine gathers emphasised my waist, making it look narrow without the need for a corset. And the colour brought out both the red of my hair and the green of my eyes.

"Oh yes," Ella breathed. "That should get his attention." She bit her lip and shook her head. "Kat, if I wasn't already working on someone else, I'd be making plans to seduce you at the first opportunity."

I went to laugh, but the look she gave me was serious, making my cheeks warm instead.

"Of course, we'll add a little something here"—Blaze wiggled her fingers and passed them down that daring neckline—"and here." She indicated the skirt. "Perfect." When she nodded, it must've included some other signal for her assistants, because they gathered the bolts and boxes and loaded everything up.

"And for the ball?" Ella cocked her head.

"Not this." Blaze pulled her eyebrows together, mouth flattening. "This requires more time. I have her measurements. I have some items part-made—an off the shoulder number..." She squinted at me as one of her assistants peeled the pinned fabric off, somehow keeping it intact. "Yes, it will be perfect, and ready in time for the ball. She needs the lingerie also, yes?"

Naked once more, I scoffed and pulled my chemise over my head. "Lingerie? What can I wear under a dress like *that*?"

Ella and Blaze laughed. Even the assistant stifled a giggle behind her hand as she wafted away the teal silk.

"Oh, my sweet darling." Ella draped an arm over my

shoulder and gave me a squeeze. "You are a *delight*." She nodded to Blaze. "Yes, to the lingerie. Something... dark and daring, I think."

"I have just the thing." Blaze winked and bowed her head before gathering up the last of her assistants and striding out without so much as a wave.

"Ah, Kat." Ella chuckled softly and patted my shoulder. "The lingerie is not to wear *under* your clothes, but to wear *instead* of them."

I blinked at her, and I must've looked stricken, because she laughed again and took another scoop of cream from the jar.

"Not in public." She massaged the cream into my other arm. "But when you're with Lord Marwood in private. If you're going to seduce him and extract information from him, you'll need to use all the tools at your disposal. A little alcohol, some underwear that will have his eyes popping out of his head, and plenty of my potions." She winked and held up a jar.

"You make these?" I peered at a tub labelled *Hair Masque*.

"Don't worry, I may have the name Belladonna in my collection, but there's no poison in these. Promise."

I laughed at the idea and took mental note as she explained what each jar was for and how to use it. Meadowsweet and rose moisturiser—that was what she'd applied to my hands and arms with the assurance that the dry skin would be gone in no time. A bottle of lightweight oil to use on my face in the morning and evening had a faintly nutty scent, almond perhaps. And the masque was to apply to my hair, wrap in a towel, and leave overnight before washing off in the morning.

"We'll get these tresses shiny again." Eyes warm, she smiled and handed over the collection of jars and bottles, including bubble bath and shampoo. "They say poison is a woman's weapon, but I think these are, really. Make sure you use them to best effect." With that and a promise to help me get ready for the ball, she adjusted a lock of my hair and left.

Suddenly the room was quiet and empty, with no one appraising or touching me, no chatter, no smiles or laughter. I huffed and plopped onto the settee, not entirely sure I didn't miss it.

13

True to his word, Cavendish sent me a maid (the blond messenger, Seren, much to my annoyance) and an allowance for everything required to look the part at court. Ella wrinkled her nose when I chose to buy paste jewellery rather than the real thing, but she didn't try to stop me. It meant I could send a good chunk of cash back to Morag and Horwich to tide them over until I received my first month's pay. It wasn't enough to solve all our problems, but writing to them to say I'd be sending money regularly felt good. For the first time in a decade, I could breathe where money was concerned.

For my part, I made a much better impression at my second meeting with the queen. She took tea and biscuits in a parlour with her ladies-in-waiting. After eyeing my outfit when I entered, she finally inclined her head with the smallest smile, and flicked her gaze to an empty chair. It was an improvement.

When I wasn't entertaining the queen, Ella brought me up

to date on the key players at court and the suitors who'd come for the queen's hand. She showed me more ways to flirt than I knew were possible. Lingering eye contact over the rim of a glass. The touch that seemed casual but was not. Biting your lip while looking at your target's mouth. I catalogued them all and practised.

As well as that, I obeyed her instructions and moisturised twice a day, as well as using the hair masque before the ball. When she arrived to help me get ready, my hair wasn't quite as glossy as hers, but the condition had improved. Once she cut off the split ends, I looked...

I blinked at myself in the mirror, at the long layers framing my face. "And you're sure it isn't frowned upon to wear your hair down anymore? It's... allowed?"

"Darling, it's positively *encouraged*." She flicked her caramel mane over her shoulder and flashed me a grin. "With Blaze's creation, it isn't your hair people will be staring at, anyway."

My heart skipped at the thought of the gown one of her assistants had dropped off earlier. Midnight blue velvet that sheened purple in the light, it hugged my body and swept from my shoulders to my cleavage in a deep V. That wasn't the part that had my pulse playing such a fast tune. Even without trying it on, I could see it had a high, *high* slit on one side.

"I suppose you're getting your wish to have my thighs on display."

"Well"—she sighed—"one of them. Oh, speaking of which, I spotted this and just *had* to get it for you." She produced a small jewellery box. "I think you should wear it tonight—the only piece of jewellery, so it gets all the more attention."

"A gift? You didn't—"

"No, I didn't *have* to—that's the point of gifts, Katherine! Just open it."

Inside was a series of fine gold chains and a twisting serpent pendant. The way its etched scales caught the light made it look like it was moving, really alive. "It's... beautiful. You shouldn't have." But when I picked it up, I couldn't work out how it was supposed to go around my throat—the way the chains connected didn't make sense.

"It isn't a necklace." She winked. "Come on, get dressed, and I'll show you."

I ENTERED the ballroom with thigh on display and the gold chain around it like a garter, showing off the snake charm. That was a sentence I never thought I'd ever need to utter or even think in my life.

Then again, I never thought I'd be a lady-in-waiting to the queen either, but here I was.

Arm looped through mine, Ella led me through a ballroom so huge I could barely see the far end through the throngs of people. Aristocrats, yes, but also servants who saw to their every whim with drinks and canapés so exquisite they rivalled items of jewellery I'd once owned.

Overhead, the chandeliers chimed softly, twinkling. Fae-worked, they'd been a wedding gift to Elizabeth I from her fae husband. It seemed appropriate they'd oversee tonight's ball where her several-times great-granddaughter would entertain suitors of her own, including fae from Dusk and Dawn courts.

Ella had explained the politics behind it all. The rumours were true—our new queen, Elizabeth V, hadn't displayed any signs of a gift, despite her fae blood. Magic and money meant power, at least for our royals, so she was under pressure to marry to shore up her rule. Cue the couple of dozen suitors who'd descended upon court to present themselves as the "perfect match."

"You've come to court at an exciting time." Ella bent closer, but her gaze swept the crowd, and she nodded greetings to one person, then another. "With the suitors gathered, there's so much going on. Balls and garden parties. A flotilla down the river. The annual sabrecat race looks set to be bigger and with tougher competition than ever. Not to mention..." Her voice dropped to a low murmur, though with the noise of so many people speaking and an entire orchestra playing, I'd have been shocked if anyone had heard us. "I *hear* the fae have been hosting their own parties that are much more... *interesting* than tea and biscuits." Her eyebrow twitched meaningfully.

This time I caught her meaning—I'd heard of debauched parties, after all—but I gave her a wide-eyed look instead. "Card parties? I do so *love* a game of cards. So exciting."

Her eyes widened, but when they turned to me, they soon narrowed. "My darling, was that a joke?" She chuckled and nudged into me. "Oh, you dark cat. Yes, we'll make a fine courtier of you yet. As for the fae parties... Let's just say there's a reason for their gowns being... *easy access*." Another twitch of her eyebrow, this time followed by a wink.

I couldn't help but chuckle, infected by her amusement, even as my head spun with the noise and colour that surrounded us. I hadn't been around so many people in years, and I was grateful to have Ella's arm to anchor me.

"I must say, I'm glad the fae have sent suitors. Their presence has certainly livened things up around here."

She'd explained a bit more about their odd system with two royal courts. From dawn until dusk, the Day King ruled, then as the sun set, he fell into an enchanted sleep. That left the Night Queen ascendant, waking and ruling from dusk until dawn. Two monarchs, one country, but never able to speak to one another, since they were never awake at the same time.

It sounded like something from a fairy story, but Ella assured me it was quite real.

She squeezed my arm. "Now, see there"—she inclined her head to one side—"the gentleman with mousy hair and a long nose."

As our course through the room turned, I spotted the man she'd indicated. Around forty, he had a crescent-shaped mark on his neck just below the ear. So precise, it had to be a fae mark—one of the odd, not-quite human features that said he had fae magic. That could either be through fae blood in his ancestry, making him fae-blooded, or because a fae had gifted him with magic, making him fae-touched.

Sometimes the most skilled craftsfolk were given magic in that way—a sign of fae approval. Other times no one really knew what they'd done to win the boon or whether it was just fae caprice. Yet another reason the fae were unfathomable.

I glanced at Ella. "Let me guess, one of the suitors."

The corner of her mouth rose. "Yes, but that's obvious, considering the context." She took two glasses from a footman's tray and passed one to me. "What else?"

"Since he's fae-marked, he must be Albionic." The only part of the world where the fae remained was Alba, which formed the northern part of our island. There were rumours of other pockets, but that was folklore and superstition. So, the humans gifted with their magic lived almost exclusively in Albion.

"Obvious," Ella sing-songed in my ear.

I lifted my glass and used it as another opportunity to glance at the man in question. Lines bracketed his mouth, and he frowned towards the far end of the ballroom, where I could finally see Her Majesty sitting on an ornate chair, watching couples dancing. "He's not in favour. And he isn't happy about it. My guess is he's one of the lower ranking suitors—an earl, most likely."

I ran through the list in my head. I'd been surprised to hear we had so many foreign princes and dukes courting the queen. Visitors to our island nation were rare since we had sea witches protecting our seas. However, I could discount all of them at once. Most of the local suitors were dukes, and I trusted my guess that he wasn't—there was something about the way he stood that didn't say ducal arrogance to me—which left...

I flashed a triumphant smile at Ella. "The Earl of Langdon."

Her eyebrows shot up and she squeezed my arm. "She's got it." A laugh laced her words, and she raised her glass in salute before taking a sip. "I have to admit, when I heard I was going to have a new colleague to train, I feared it would be terribly dull, but you're... unusual, Kat... and amusing." She grinned and clinked her glass to mine before drinking more.

Except, I wasn't here to be amusing. Or to enjoy myself.

I lowered my glass and looked away. I was here to do a job and earn some money.

"What's that?" Ella nudged into me. "Guilt?" She raised an eyebrow when my gaze jerked to hers. "You aren't the only one who can read people, darling. Let me guess. You're worried you shouldn't be enjoying yourself while you pursue our line of work?"

I clenched my jaw, and my grip on the wine glass tightened. It was one thing reading others—it was another matter entirely to be on the receiving end. "I have a duty." To my estate, to my family, to Morag and Horwich.

She scoffed, but on her it was as ladylike as all her other actions, rather than a raw, snorting guffaw like I'd done at the estate. "To queen and country? My dear girl, Her Majesty doesn't give a damn about you, and the country is a lump of rock and earth. It is incapable of caring, like most men." She lifted one shoulder and beckoned over another footman. "So long as you're not harming anybody, why not do what you want? And"—she took a gilded lemon tart from the footman's platter—"where's the harm in a little fun?"

Head canted, she held out the tart, leaving it inches below my nose. The zesty, fresh scent filled my nose, making my mouth water. Morag made the best lemon tarts, but it had been a long while since we'd been able to afford citrus fruit. I swallowed, and Ella raised the treat another inch.

As long as I did my job and met my target tonight, did it matter if I had this one bit of enjoyment?

I took the tart.

Ella's smile was triumphant.

The smile I returned was rueful. "I never could resist sweet treats." At least this was one I didn't have to pay for.

I took a bite and savoured it, where Ella put hers into her mouth in one go. The pastry melted on my tongue, and the lemon was just the right side of sharp and sweet, making me salivate even more. Good gods, it almost rivalled Morag's.

As we circulated (and grabbed another couple of tarts),

Ella pointed out various important folk, the suitors as well as factions within court. She also gave me little tidbits about them. This viscount was having an affair with that earl. This duchess was rumoured to have given birth six months ago, even though her husband had been away for the past year. Lady such-and-such had sold a portion of her estate to pay for her eldest son's gambling habit.

The eldest Miss Ward had been caught having an affair and sent away from court. Or a rival had set her up, if you believed certain whispers. Her sister remained, but she stood alone on the side of the ballroom, tarred by association and the fact this was her third time wearing the same dress to a ball. Rumours abounded that the family had been forced to gather a huge dowry to marry off her elder sister, leaving her finances precarious. No one came within three feet of her, as though they feared her bad luck was catching.

That was the risk. Shunned like this, she was alone at court with no allies. If anyone wanted to act against her, she would be an easy target. Fish in a gods damned barrel.

If the true depths of my financial woes came out, it would be me standing there. And if I managed to lure Marwood to my bed and word got out, well, I might not be sent away like her sister, since I was married, but any lady who wished to protect her own reputation would treat me like a leper.

With a shiver, I pulled my attention from the unfortunate Miss Ward. As well as Ella's commentary, I heard snatches from the crowd. A pair of blond fae from Dawn Court referred to Marwood as the Bastard of Tenebris and muttered about how ruthless he was.

Others, humans, speculated on who would win the queen's hand. One man had his money on Dawn's suitor, another on Cestyll Caradoc's. Surprising that they'd sent a representative—the kingdom to the west was almost as private as the fae. But the mousy-haired man who thought Cestyll Caradoc would win said it was down to his fae blood. Plus he was a prince rather than a mere duke.

I made mental note of it all.

As we gathered our third round of drinks from a passing footman, I eyed Ella sidelong. "The Bastard of Tenebris?"

She lifted one shoulder. "Everyone has a nickname or two." Her blue eyes trailed over my shoulder. "Ah, speak of the very devil and he shall appear. Lord Marwood, so pleased to see you."

The moment I'd been waiting for.

"Allow me to introduce Lady Katherine Ferrers."

I drew a quick breath, folded my hands, and lowered my eyes demurely before turning.

It took an age for my gaze to trail all the way up his black-clad legs—good gods, he was tall. And well-muscled, with broad shoulders.

Then I reached his face and froze.

Not because of how gorgeous he was. Not this time.

But because I knew the cruel line of his lips, the pale scar running through those lips down to his chin, the hard angles of those cheekbones.

Lord Bastian Marwood was the fae I'd stolen from.

14

Not just my heart, but the whole world stuttered as I met a pair of silvery eyes that took me in with... Wait, was that *indifference*?

I watched him, unable to tear my gaze away, even as my body took over and dipped me into a neat bow.

But, no, I was right—this was him and he looked at me with disinterest. Not recognition.

"A pleasure." It was even that same deep voice. He inclined his head. Then Ella introduced the blond woman at his side as Lady Lara Granville, the human liaison who'd been allocated to help him integrate.

With his attention off me, I finally managed to breathe. But my face tingled and his presence a few feet away blazed in my awareness, like I stood right next to a bonfire.

Now we weren't both sodden from rain, I could see his hair wasn't just as black as coal. It was also as flat, not reflecting the slightest hint of light from the chandeliers above. It created an odd effect, as though his hair were made of darkness itself. His clothes amplified the effect, all deepest black, with silver snakes embroidered on the collar of his jacket, and black embroidery on the shoulders, like scales. His sigil was the serpent, as Ella had told me during our briefings over the past couple of days, and he was clearly leaning into that.

As was I with the serpent chain-garter. *Well played, Ella, well played.*

I bowed at the right point in my introduction to Lara, who was slender, stunning, tall. I'd had enough compliments to know I was pretty, but she was... Well, she could've been fae herself: she was as beautiful as one, as not-quite-real-looking as one. Where Ella was warmth and perfection, this woman was cool, detached elegance.

Ella and Lara broke into light conversation as I tried to remember the normal rhythm for breathing and Marwood looked bored.

I sipped my drink, though I wanted to down the lot, followed by at least five more.

But I forced myself to give him a proper look. Mouth relaxed, gaze flicking between Ella and Lara before drifting to one side. He made an idle comment. He was definitely bored. No sign of any interest in me. And no sign *at all* of that murderous look he'd given me as I'd taken his gold orb.

It was locked in a chest under my bed, and my awareness of that fact shone like a beacon in my head. I'd toyed with the idea of burying it or keeping hold of it for a while, then selling it when the fae had probably given up. But now here he was.

As the conversation turned to tonight's ball and how many guests were here, I caught Ella giving me a Look. I was meant to be making an impression on my target, not reeling from the fact I'd already royally pissed him off.

Except, he didn't recognise me, and we were miles from the road where I'd stopped him. Realistically, he had no reason to suspect the lady before him was the highwaywoman from weeks ago. That knowledge was mine alone.

I had to stamp down my fears and get on with the task at hand. After all, I had an estate to save.

So when Lara commented on the elegance of the dancing couples nearby, I found my voice.

"But not enough of them. I think the suitors don't want to be seen dancing with anyone but Her Majesty, which has created a shortage of male partners." I blinked up at Marwood, all innocence. "And yet, Lord Marwood, you're not dancing."

Lara watched my mouth as I spoke—a habit I'd noticed throughout the conversation, which gave the impression that she paid close attention. When I'd finished, she gave an indulgent smile. "Oh, he never dances."

Then he wouldn't be easily tempted, and pity wouldn't work, not with a fae. Maybe pride would push him. "Well, it's nothing to be ashamed of."

His attention snapped to me, and he arched one eyebrow. "Ashamed? Of what?"

My pulse sped now I was under his scrutiny. *He doesn't know.* To make myself seem nonchalant where I was very much *chalant* (even if that wasn't a word), I took a sip of wine. Rich and deep, like the velvet of my gown. The taste and the alcohol centred me and I shrugged, gesturing with my glass as I gave him a wide-eyed look. "Of not being able to dance."

Where moments ago he'd seemed so disinterested, now his attention narrowed until it was a sharp point driving into me. A muscle in his jaw feathered, but it was only for a moment before he gave a soft sigh and held out his hand.

"Lady Katherine, kindly do me the *very* high honour of a dance."

Hook, line, and sinker.

Honestly, I hadn't expected him to fall for my ploy so easily, but I blinked at him as though surprised that he'd offered rather than the fact he'd done it so quickly. "I wasn't fishing for an offer, Lord Marwood."

He only flexed his fingers, giving a pointed look at his offered hand as if wondering why it was still empty.

His arrogant assumption tempted me to decline. But that was pure impertinence and would get me nowhere. I'd been instructed to get close to him and eventually seduce him, and many a seduction began on the dance floor, so I took his hand.

I tried not to react to his touch, but...

One finger traced ever so lightly across my palm, ticklish, teasing, and there was a flicker of something I couldn't quite read on his face. Not surprise, but... confirmation, perhaps? I tried not to squint at him, at the frustration of not being able to read him as effortlessly as I did most people. I wasn't sure I was entirely successful.

"You won't be needing *that*." He plucked the glass from my hand and passed it to Ella, a twitch at the corner of his mouth. That I *could* read: amusement.

Great, he thought me an idiot already. Or perhaps struck stupid by his looks. I doubted I was the first.

As he led me to the dance floor, I swallowed, suddenly all too aware of the necklace at my throat and grateful for its protection. Without it, would I be a blathering fool throwing myself at him?

On a gilded chair a little smaller than the one in the throne room, the queen idly watched as a dance ended. At her side, Cavendish murmured something in her ear, casting his gaze over the room. He didn't so much as glance this way as I took to the floor with the target he'd assigned me. He gave no reaction at all, in fact. No wonder he was a spymaster: he was damn good at keeping his secrets.

Marwood felt my palm again and narrowed his eyes before releasing me and bowing.

Shit. I knew what that was. I'd used Ella's moisturiser religiously over the past couple of days, and my skin was much softer. However, it hadn't completely erased the signs of hard work from my hands. He'd noticed.

Throat tight, I bowed in return.

As he stepped close, I could only think how he had to be wondering what kind of lady even knew the meaning of hard work. After the way I'd tricked him into dancing, he was surely going to ask. He seemed the type to want to strike a verbal blow like that in punishment. I'd have to make up something about not liking gloves when I rode. Reins might explain the persistent calluses.

I swallowed and forced a pleasant smile on my face as I took his hand. The other, I placed on his shoulder, right next to the silver serpent embroidered on his collar. Unsmiling, he took hold of my waist and pulled me closer.

I'd never appreciated before how the full skirts of older fashions formed a kind of boundary. No one was meant to cross that line into a lady's space (Cavendish apparently hadn't got this message). But fae fashion left women without such protection, and Marwood manoeuvred me so our hips were only inches apart.

There was no time to react, though, because the music started and he swept me across the floor. With the gliding steps, the slit of my skirt fell open, exposing the garter chain Ella had given me... not to mention my bare skin.

My stomach tightened at the thought of how I must look. This much flesh, this close a dance—these things didn't fit the mould for what it meant to be a lady. They would've earned me a slash of birch across the palm. *Obedient, dutiful, silent.*

And yet, obedience was part of my job. A job that would pay off my syphilitic ball-bag of a husband's debts. Despite Papa's lessons, I had to remember that.

I lifted my chin, but Marwood wasn't even looking at me —he gazed off over my shoulder, bored again. I didn't know whether to give him credit for not staring at my exposed skin, or if I should be affronted that he *wasn't.*

Still, this was meant to be the start of a grand seduction. I'd never seduced anyone before, but even without Ella's instruction over the past couple of days, I knew attention was the first step.

"My lord, why is it you never normally dance?" I canted my head at him, eyes wide and innocent again. "You're clearly good at it." I might've been stating it to ingratiate myself with him, but it was also true. He led us well, cutting through the other couples, every step smooth and measured, his movements economical like a hunting sabrecat's.

Yet his eyebrows twitched in irritation. "Don't call me that."

I blinked. "Lord Marwood, then. I—"

"Not that either."

He really was making this impossible. How was I meant to seduce a man who was so irritating?

"Why not? It's your name, isn't it?" It was a battle to keep the frustration from my tone.

He finally met my gaze, and I tried not to shiver at the way his silvery eyes glowed. This close, I could see the darker grey edge of his irises—a steely colour to go with the sharpness I'd noted at our first meeting. But there were also lighter flecks near his pupils—not just lighter, but *light*, as though they were glowing motes of moon dust.

"Other than the queen and king, we don't use titles in everyday talk. It's just Bastian."

My stomach fluttered, part-surprise and part something else. Whatever the rules in his homeland, in Albion, ladies didn't call gentlemen by their first names.

Yes, I was meant to be seducing the man, but that was all bodies mashing together, his hands wherever he wanted, me on my back, gritting my teeth through it all. There was nothing intimate about it.

But this felt far closer than any of that physicality ever had.

Still, the job. And the money.

So, I fluttered my lashes and glanced away. "I'm not sure I should." Calling him Bastian might be the perfect start for drawing him in, but I should at least pretend to resist.

He gave me a look that was every bit as sharp as the one he'd given me on the road. Though perhaps there was an edge of amusement rather than cruelty to the curves of his mouth.

And damn, it was a perfect mouth, even with the scar tracing through it. Full. Kissable. Expressive, if you knew how to read people as I did. Now the edge of it quirked.

Because I was staring. At his mouth, imagining how it might feel on mine, on my throat, on... well, any part of my body, frankly.

Cavendish had chosen well. My isolation had me practically throwing myself at Marwood's—*Bastian's* feet already. I licked my lips and pushed my eyes up to meet his. Yes, they definitely glinted in amusement. My self-conscious laugh wasn't faked. "Very well, *Bastian*. But you didn't answer my question."

"No, I didn't."

And that was it. No elaboration. No flirtation. He just held eye contact as we danced in silence.

Maybe not such a good start after all, since he wouldn't even engage in small talk. How was I going to seduce him, never mind get any information out of him?

His gaze slid over my shoulder and that bored look returned. "Is it worth asking whether you still have my orrery, or have you already sold it?"

15

My heart lurched to my throat. My lungs forgot how to work. My feet stopped moving.

But he was prepared, because his hands fastened around my waist and he lifted me across the floor as if that was what he'd always meant to do. Gasps came from the onlookers.

When he returned me to my feet, his grip at my waist was tighter, anchoring me closer. Now each step brought our thighs together, his sliding between mine, the fabric of his trousers brushing my bare skin, making the chain clink softly.

My body practically hummed at the shock of what he'd just said, coupled with sheer sensory overload. My head spun. What was he doing? What had he just said? What was I meant to say?

When I tried to measure my steps to put a little distance between us, to allow myself to catch my breath, his grip was unyielding. I stared up at him, trying to force my staggered mind to work.

Deny it. He's fishing for information. Don't give him any. Blame your reaction on surprise and confusion at his odd question.

At last, he blinked and returned his gaze to mine. Slowly, lazily, he smiled. Sharp canines glinted, revealing that apparent ease to be the biggest lie of all.

And to think they said fae couldn't lie.

This wasn't just a guess. He knew. He bloody well knew, and I wagered he had from the moment we'd been introduced. Not the slightest doubt shadowed the look he gave me.

Shitting hells.

There was no point denying it. Fine.

"How did you recognise me? I was wearing a mask."

He laughed darkly, the sound a low thrum in the air. "Humans never fail to amuse me with their stupidity and limited senses. You think a person can only be recognised by their appearance?"

I gritted my teeth. Could the man not give a straight answer to anything? "Then what gave me away?"

He leant closer still, and for an insane moment, I thought he was going to kiss my forehead. Instead, he murmured, "Early narcissi. A stream rushing fast and clear with snowmelt. The first sunny day of the year. The promise of spring."

What the hells was that supposed to mean? That wasn't an answer. That was a list of—of *things*.

The corner of that stupid, perfect mouth twitched. "Your *scent* is what gave you away."

"My..." I blinked up at him, lips parted like they'd forgotten how to work. Somehow my feet kept up with his, though I didn't doubt he'd have swept me through the air again if they hadn't.

My scent had given me away. Fae were... They weren't just

pretty humans with pointed ears and magic and a complicated relationship with the truth—they were something else entirely.

"And"—he cocked his head like the hunting sabrecat toying with its prey—"I hear the Wicked Lady has haunted those roads some years. It isn't your first transgression."

It was like someone poured a bucket of snowmelt over me. I was surprised my teeth didn't chatter at the cold that consumed my body. He didn't just know it was me, but he knew the bigger picture—the years of highway robbery.

Shit, shit, shit.

His eyebrows lowered. "I was puzzled as to why a woman with a well-kept sabrecat and a fae-worked pistol would turn highwaywoman. Did you steal that necklace and the gown or just the money to buy them for yourself?"

I flinched, jaw cranking tight. "It's not for me, it's—"

I managed to gather enough control over my body to bite my tongue before I blurted anything more. After a deep breath, I went on, more quietly, "I don't do it for the sake of pretty dresses."

He watched me closely through several steps. "It's for your home, isn't it? It's in a sorry state."

"My home..." Realisation bloomed in me. "You were there. When the summons came."

He lifted his chin, and that was confirmation enough.

That feeling of being watched—I'd been right. I dragged in a few shaky breaths as we swept past the queen. She was a smear of gold, black, and crimson.

There was just one question left for me to ask. "What will you do about it?"

He smiled. It would've been charming if not for the fact it

was too wide and showed off those long, sharp canines. "Remind me what the human punishment is for one who's stolen as much as the Wicked Lady." He narrowed his eyes and pursed his lips as if trying to remember. "Hangman or axe?"

I choked on whatever words I might've said to that. A threat. To my life. He was going to have me killed.

I glanced over at the queen, who spoke to one of the other ladies-in-waiting. If Bastian revealed my secret, would Cavendish be able to save me? Would he even care to, since I wasn't yet valuable to him?

The fae scoffed softly. "No need to look so stricken, Katherine. Whichever execution awaits the Wicked Lady, it would be a shame to mar that slender neck." His gaze on my throat was a caress, lifting the delicate hairs on my arms. The intensity in his eyes left me with no doubt that he spotted the way my pulse leapt at the threat he dangled over me. "But there is a price for my silence."

Of course there was. My face tingled and my limbs were suddenly heavy. Gods, please don't let me faint.

"A favour from you to be called in at a time of my choosing."

A bargain with a fae. That was folly. Worse than folly—pure fucking stupidity. But what choice did I have?

Maybe one. "I—I can give it back."

He shook his head. "Too late for that. The insult is done. Do you accept my bargain or must I enquire with your queen whether it's noose or axe for the Wicked Lady?"

Yes meant owing him, the fae I was meant to be spying on, a favour of his choice.

No meant execution.

There had to be another answer.

Except... we spun and spun, gliding across the floor and I realised.

There wasn't.

So, shoulders sinking, I nodded my agreement to his bargain, the words too bitter to force through my mouth. "And my financial difficulties—you'll keep quiet about those, too."

"Very well. It is so," he intoned the words I'd read in a hundred stories. Words of power that would seal our bargain. With a dip of his chin, he indicated it was my turn.

"It is so," I muttered.

"No need to look so sullen about it. Consider yourself lucky I'm not calling in your other debt."

"What other debt?"

He shrugged. "You tricked me into dancing, didn't you?"

"You knew." I squeezed his hand, letting my nails dig in just a little. He only smirked and pulled me closer. Our hips bumped, and my breasts brushed his chest. Heat—from irritation and the physical contact—flooded me, washing away my earlier cold dread. "Why agree, then?"

"Better to knowingly fall for your manipulation than let you make out that there's a version of the universe in which I can't dance."

Arrogant fucking bastard. I ground my teeth to keep from spitting the words at him.

He shook his head, tongue clicking like I was a wayward child. "You make a fae do your bidding, and you're not even prepared to pay the price. Foolish, Katherine, very, very foolish."

"Though not as foolish as stealing from you in the first place."

His smirk turned into a devilish smile. "You're bound to me by a favour. Just be grateful it's not two." He leant in, mouth close to my ear, and his voice dropped. "The things I could demand in exchange for a debt that size..." His words tickled my ear and the side of my neck, sending a shiver through me.

The Bastard of Tenebris. How accurate a nickname. I didn't dare voice it, though, so instead I gave him a bitter smile. "And here I was thinking the rumours about you were exaggeration."

His expression flickered, gone so quickly, I couldn't quite read it. "If we were in Elfhame, I'd remind you that nothing is as it seems. Though perhaps in your court, that's still true."

The music swelled, each note holding on longer, until there was just one fading into silence.

Thank the gods this dance was over.

As I took a step back, he kept hold of my hand and bowed over it, not breaking eye contact.

"I will collect your debt, Katherine. You may count on it."

16

The next day, I was sitting in a parlour having tea and biscuits with the queen and her other ladies-in-waiting, when a note arrived. I recognised where it was sending me—seventh door on the left, north corridor—so I made my excuses and headed to Cavendish's office.

After the dance with Bastian the Bastard, Ella had congratulated me. "You two looked very cosy out there. I can't believe he held you so close."

I'd only managed to give her a faint smile back, queasy at the thought of *why* he'd pulled me against him like that. All to toy with me for stealing his orrery.

Now that queasiness made a return. Spying on a man who knew my secret. This was the very definition of dangerous. If he had the slightest inkling of what I was doing... Well, he couldn't tell anyone, since he'd sworn silence, but now I owed him. And what was to stop him just quietly disposing of me once he realised I'd crossed him twice?

I had to tread lightly in trying to get information from him. He already knew I wasn't just an aristocratic lady; he was sure to get suspicious if I poked into his business too deeply.

I also couldn't tell Cavendish that I'd changed my mind about the job. That would only lead to questions and an answer I couldn't give. I was sure he didn't mind his spies breaking the law as part of their work, but outside of that? I didn't picture him being the forgiving type.

Besides, I needed his money. Which meant being useful so he didn't replace me. After the ball, I'd stayed up with a candle and noted who Bastian had spoken to, what I'd heard about him, and anything else of interest I'd learned. On my way to this meeting, I stopped in my rooms to grab my notes from the locked chest under my bed.

I refused to look at Bastian's orrery and poked it to one corner of the box.

When I entered Cavendish's office, I found him behind the desk again. He didn't offer me a chair. Instead, he watched me over his steepled fingers and nodded. "You got Marwood to dance. Well done—very well done. That's a good start, considering he's refused to dance with anyone else."

The praise drifted over me, a warm, heavy blanket that stilled all the fears that had haunted me on the way here. Praise was good. Praise meant safety.

"And I wrote these." I handed him the notes, which he flicked through, expression flat. Unimpressed.

I bit the inside of my cheek. "It's just a start." I folded my hands. "I'm trying to put him at ease." Not entirely a lie—after last night, he probably saw me as too incompetent and too attracted to him to be a threat.

Cavendish nodded, stacking the papers and placing them

on his desk. "A wise course of action. And I have just the thing that will help you get closer to him."

He stood and circled the desk, eyes on me in that calculating way he had. "You've met his liaison."

"Lara. Yes, she's—"

With a flick of his hand, he waved me to silence. "Beautiful, yes. But hers is not the kind that's useful." He stalked closer and smoothed a lock of my hair between finger and thumb, as though testing its new lustre.

I held still, though once again I was caught between backing away and leaning towards him. My skin flushed warmer, like I couldn't get enough of contact now I had a taste for it, no matter who that contact came from.

He sighed, deep and weary. "She's unmarried. A poor choice, but it wasn't my decision. Sometimes in chess, a piece needs to be sacrificed so another can take its place. Get her removed from the position, and I'll ensure you're her replacement."

"Removed? Can't you just have the queen replace her?" He had Her Majesty's ear, after all.

He made a low grunt as his fingers continued toying with the lengths of my hair. The movement transferred along the strands to my scalp, where it was a whisper of touch that set the hair at the nape of my neck on end. "She's one of Her Majesty's favourites. Even I can't outright tell a queen what to do." The way his nose wrinkled said he wasn't happy about that fact.

"And how am I meant to get her removed?"

He huffed out a breath, dropping my hair. "Must I spell everything out? I'm starting to think maybe *I* chose poorly with you."

His look speared me and all the warmth his praise had raised vanished with a chill. He couldn't dismiss me so soon, surely? And just for a question. I'd made a good start, he'd said.

But I couldn't argue, could I? Not when he held all the cards, and I didn't even have a seat at the table.

So I clenched my jaw and waited.

Eventually, he nodded, as though approving of my silence. "Undermine her, and she'll lose her position, leaving the way open for you."

Undermine her. He meant ruin her. As an unmarried woman, she had a reputation that could be destroyed and get her dismissed.

My stomach swirled, curdling the biscuits I'd enjoyed earlier.

There had to be a way to get close to Bastian without harming an innocent woman. "Why not just recruit her, since she's already close to him?"

Tension flickered around his eyes, and his lips tightened.

"Oh." My eyes widened, and I bit back a chuckle. "You already tried, didn't you? But she said no."

This time, the tension wasn't only around his eyes—it made his eyebrows clash together, his neck cord, his shoulders flex.

I knew that look. I'd seen it on my father before plates smashed, but it had been a while.

Maybe that was why I only managed to gasp and take half a step back before he had hold of me. My heart slammed into my rib cage as my back slammed into the wall. I swallowed my surprise, barely breathing as I stared up at him.

He gripped my chin, other hand splayed across my chest,

just below my collarbones. "Do not presume to fucking read me, Katherine. You are here because I chose you to do a job, but do not mistake that for need. There are other women with red hair I can send to Marwood's bed. You are nothing special."

I wanted to cry.

I wanted to laugh.

Because he thought this was news. I wasn't special. No one was. I was just trying to get through life. I was just trying to survive. That was all we had.

And what he'd done? This ache across my back? Papa hadn't hit me, no, but after my sister had been born, he'd ruled our house with fear. Shouts that could split my ears. Crockery shards across the floor. Locking Avice in the cupboard when she didn't obey, which was often. I'd lived that.

Most importantly, I'd survived it. I could get through whatever he threw at me.

I reminded myself of that as I dragged in shaky, shallow breaths, and memories crowded the edge of my mind, threatening to break through.

"Hmm." He raised an eyebrow, watching me. "There's a little steel in you. Interesting." The pressure on my chest increased as he pushed me into the wall. "Even so, I pay you to do a job. Do you understand what that is? Who you're meant to be gathering information from?"

Obedience. That was the way to survive moments like this, men like him. I nodded.

"Good." He smiled like nothing had happened, then straightened my hair and the neckline of my gown. "Recruiting the Granville woman is off the table. Removal is the only option. Get her disgraced. Uncover an illicit affair, seditious ideas—you know the sort of thing."

I swallowed past the tightness of my throat. "What if she's not having an affair?"

"Good gods, Katherine, do you think the truth matters?" He rolled his eyes and turned to a chess board set up by the fireplace.

It was partway through a game, and by the number of pieces left, it looked like white was winning.

"You're at court now—you have to play the game." He picked up a black pawn and pointed it at me. "Manufacture reality to suit your agenda. Manipulate the woman into a difficult position. Forge letters that prove her treasonous plans. Frame her for a crime. I don't care how, but you will see to it that she loses her position." He replaced the pawn and straightened, fixing me with an imperious stare. "Consider it your first test as the newest member of my network."

With a jerk of his chin, I was dismissed.

Stomach roiling, I left and wandered through maze-like corridors, not entirely sure I was heading the right way to return to the queen. Not entirely caring.

I should've known Cavendish would be like this. It was a plague amongst powerful men—I wouldn't be surprised if all of them had it.

Power through fear.

Obedience through intimidation.

Gain through the work of others.

My brain buzzed with it, over and over. I needed his work. I needed to keep him happy. If I didn't...

I reached an empty hallway and allowed myself to fold my arms. It was safe now I was out of sight. Though, a corner of my mind whispered, was anywhere at court really private?

Still, I needed this—nothing else would still the trembling of my arms and breaths, only the pressure of hugging myself. Pausing at a set of windows, I pressed my head to the cold glass and closed my eyes.

"You're safe." I whispered it again and again, a litany, finishing with, "You'll get through this. You know what he is now. You know how to manage him."

Agree with him. Obey him. Please him.

After a few minutes, my pulse had calmed to something like normal, and I could open my eyes to the clear summer day outside.

The gods had a sense of humour, because in the gardens was Lara with Bastian and another fae with dark hair. She laughed, all controlled and elegant.

She knew nothing about Cavendish's plot against her. As an unmarried woman, her marriage prospects and thus her future would be ruined if she was involved in a scandal.

Treason would see her executed in the worst possible way. I'd seen illustrations of Elizabeth I's former favourite being hung, drawn, and quartered. All because he'd spilled a few secrets to a foreign spy he'd let into his bed.

The turning of my stomach started afresh.

Outside, she pointed away from the house and when I squinted in that direction, I found the dark green hedges of the palace maze.

It felt like I was stuck inside it, and every way I turned led not to a dead end but to the one fact I couldn't escape.

I needed the money.

To get it, I needed to get close to Bastian.

That was what Cavendish was really asking of me. That would appease him and earn my pay. I didn't need to become

Bastian's liaison to become his lover. Lara didn't need to be involved. I just had to do a better job of luring him in.

I glared at his distant figure. Even in the sun, his hair didn't reflect the slightest gleam, and he moved with an ease that irritated me, though I couldn't say why. My hands balled into fists.

I wouldn't ruin Lara. I would do this my way.

17

I spent the next week working out exactly what "my way" would look like, driven on by a brief letter from Morag. She did an excellent job of keeping our books, but she wasn't the most forthcoming. Still, I could read the cautious hope between her words, even as she asked how I was getting this money. I stuffed the letter away, not sure how to reply. Bastian's orrery eyed me from the corner of the same box. I tried opening it with no luck.

There were plenty of things other than letters and fae mechanisms to keep me busy. When I wasn't with the other ladies-in-waiting entertaining the queen, I grilled Ella about the art of seduction and practised everything she showed me. I needed to get into Bastian's bed. The sooner the better.

My hair and skin continued to improve with her concoctions, too. I had to confess, I grew a little vain about the rich red of my hair, experimenting with new styles, asking Ella if she thought I should wear it up or down.

We settled on up for the next ball, exposing my neck. This

event was hosted by the Frankish ambassador, seeking favour for her suitor, Prince Valois.

This time, I arrived alone—Ella said it might encourage Bastian to approach me. I couldn't voice why I thought it unlikely. "Oh yes, probably not, since I stole from him when we first met. Ha. Ha. Ha."

Inwardly, I grimaced as I entered the ballroom—a different one in a guest wing of the palace. I wasn't sure exactly how many ballrooms this place had or why it needed more than one, but here we were.

I counted my paces, keeping them steady and lady-like, as I approached a table that groaned under the weight of a tower of drinks. The way the glasses had been stacked on top of each other had my nerves fluttering until I couldn't stand it any longer and had to look away.

The queen stood in conversation with the Dusk suitor, Lord Asher Mallory—the dark-haired fae I'd spotted with Bastian in the gardens. Beyond them, half a dozen other suitors watched, some in silence, some muttering to their companions.

But it wasn't jealousy lighting their eyes. It was avarice.

They didn't want to marry the queen. They wanted the throne for themselves; she was merely their means to get it.

When I turned back to her, I realised just how stiff her smile was, how studied her laugh. She was queen of Albion, yes, but even she walked a tightrope. And falling would see her fed to so many wolves.

Or maybe she was more like the top glass on this huge tower, which I'd just reached and now squinted up at. How the hells was I meant to get a drink? Was this ridiculousness just for show or—?

"You must've heard he killed his father." A woman's voice came from the other side of the tower.

"Of course. Hasn't everyone?" I could hear the eye-roll in her voice.

"Then what reason under the sun would you have to be making eyes at the Serpent like that?"

My body went taut at the mention of Bastian's sigil.

"*I'm* not his father." The eye-roller made a dismissive sound. "But I'd certainly let him *and* his serpent run amok with me." She giggled, and maybe I'd spent too much time around Ella, but I had to cover my mouth to smother my own laugh. "Besides, I hear the unseelie make the best lovers."

Unseelie? The laugh died in my throat. The fae of Alba were bad enough—and they were seelie. Selfish. Pitiless. Viewing humans as brief lights in their centuries of existence.

The unseelie were so much worse, they'd been banished from, well, *the world*, sent to some other plane of existence.

"*Half* unseelie. Still, that's enough for him to tear you apart with his bare hands," the first one said, voice low and tight.

"Yes," the second woman said, voice edged with a groan. "But think of what he'd do with those bare hands first."

And that's what my fool mind did. Just for a second before I dug my nails into my palm. I would let him do whatever he wanted with his hands, for the sake of my job. That was all.

Still, I was curious who was speculating about his sexual prowess... and who seemed to think he was half unseelie. Did Cavendish know about that rumour?

I peeked around the tower.

Two fae women stood close together, one biting her lip, the other scowling. They both had pale, rose gold hair that fell over their shoulders in waves. That and their matching, narrow noses suggested they were sisters, and the sun pendants hanging between their breasts said they were Dawn Court. That explained the first one's disapproval.

Her violet eyes turned to me, and her scowl deepened, making her nose wrinkle. She nudged her younger sister, who turned dawn pink eyes on me and hissed—*actually* hissed.

I only kept my feet planted because the table shielded me from her.

"Listening in, are you?" the younger one spat, baring her teeth. Her lithe arms flexed, and she took a step as if to circle the table, but her sister grabbed her and murmured something. The pink-eyed one huffed out a breath and sneered, "Of course you were. Your kind get everywhere."

They spun on their heels and walked away, but I caught the tail end of one more sentence: "... a blight."

I blinked after them. "Delightful."

Then, thankfully, something delightful did appear—a footman offering me a glass of wine. Apparently, the tower was just for show.

Taking a long gulp to soothe my nerves, I started in the opposite direction from the two Dawn women.

She'd *hissed* at me like an angry cat. I scoffed into my glass and drank some more. Her court had to be very different from ours. Alba, the fae realm, bordered Albion, but at that moment, it felt like a world away.

Despite my unease, I wore my cool, calm, collected outer appearance like armour. It was the only protection women like me had. In Albion, strong passions like hers, like my sister Avice's—they got you in trouble.

A little wit was fine, a little flirtation, too, but ultimately those in power wanted the rest of us to not take up too much space. By "those in power" I meant men. And by "the rest of us" I meant women.

Not taking up too much space meant being quiet and polite, smothering inconvenient feelings. It meant obeying.

"Good gods," I muttered at those gloomy thoughts and drained my drink before stalking across the room to find a fresh one.

"There you are." Ella emerged from a knot of people, leaving more than a few admiring glances in her wake. "Have you *made contact* yet?" She glanced around as though disappointed to find Bastian not on my arm.

"I haven't seen him tonight, but..." I bent closer, jaw tightening. "You didn't tell me he'd killed his father." The other comment, that he was unseelie, seemed too outlandish to entertain for even a second, but this? The murderous look he'd given me when I'd taken his orrery—I could believe that man had committed patricide.

"*Pfft.*" Ella waved off my concerns. "That's just a rumour. And an ugly one at that."

"Then you *knew*?" Some part of me had clung to the idea that perhaps it was only known amongst the fae contingents.

She exhaled through her nose. "I'm here to gather information, just like you are. Of course I'd heard it, but from Dawn. Do you really think the Day King's court is going to have anything good to say about the man they call the Night Queen's Shadow? Frankly, I wouldn't believe a word they say about any member of Dusk."

I bit the inside of my cheek. She had a point. Maybe I'd been too eager to believe the worst of him, despite the source.

"From that look, I'd wager you heard it from Dawn, too." She squeezed my shoulder. "I'm sorry, Kat. Maybe I should've warned you, but I figured there was no point in scaring you

senseless over something that probably isn't even true. But"—
she gave me a little shake and caught my eye, smiling—"if I
hear anything about it from a credible source, I'll tell you right
away."

I sighed. "I'm the one who should apologise. That makes
sense. Dusk and Dawn are opposites—both in the turning of
the day *and* in their courts, it seems."

She chuckled and gave me a quick hug that I couldn't help
but lean into. I could get used to this business of being
touched. It was a shame it would be over when Bastian left or
Cavendish had enough information out of him, whichever
came first. I was under no illusions that I'd be kept at court a
moment longer than necessary. He would send me home once
the job was done.

Was it better to shy away from touch and not get used to it
or swallow it down greedily while I could, like an animal
putting on fat before the lean days of winter?

Before I had a chance to decide, a familiar voice broke
through my thoughts. "Katherine."

When I looked up, I found Bastian standing over Ella and
me, wearing another black outfit. This one's snakes were a
darker shade of black, as though made from the night sky,
with only their eyes in silver, like stars.

Ella made a soft sound and inclined her head to him, but
I could feel her eyes boring into the side of my head. It took
me a moment to realise why. *Katherine.* Not proper address
—even Lady Katherine as the queen, and thus the rest of
court, had taken to calling me would've been more
appropriate.

Not that Bastian seemed capable of *appropriate.*

"Ser." I smiled at him, making it as sweet and placid as all
the smiles I'd given my father and uncle.

There was the flicker of a frown, but he held out his hand. "A dance?"

Ella cleared her throat and eased the empty glass from my fingers as she took a sip from her own, all while looking the other way. The queen of discretion.

"I'd be *honoured*." As I took his hand, I couldn't help the edge of sarcasm in my voice. The bastard had used our last dance to get me alone and extort a bargain from me—I was entitled to at least a little sarcasm. That was safe.

Perhaps it was better than safe, because it won me a smirk that was warmer than all his others as he led me to the dance floor.

18

"You shouldn't call me that," I told him as we stepped out from the crowd and he led me to an empty space.

He arched one eyebrow. "It's your name."

"First names alone aren't appropriate. You might use them back in Alba, but here it's not..." I shook my head. "It's too intimate."

I didn't look directly at him, but out of the corner of my eye, I couldn't miss his widening smirk. "Maybe I want to be intimate, *Katherine*. And the way you look at me—I'd say you do, too."

I should've known staring at his mouth at the last ball would come back to bite me in the arse. But I didn't need to inflate his ego any further by addressing how attractive I found him, so I cleared my throat. "Call me whatever you like when there's no one in earshot, but around others, you should have some pretence of propriety."

"Whatever I like?" He sounded far too excited at the prospect.

As we faced one another, I shot him a wide-eyed look in the hopes he'd understand how serious I was. "That's how court life works."

"In your court, perhaps," he muttered before bowing.

Again, he took my waist and hand, and again, I hated myself for liking it, just a little.

"I noticed you haven't danced with anyone else," I pointed out as we set off across the floor.

He cocked his head, one eyebrow rising. "Are you keeping tabs on me? *Kat*, I didn't know you cared."

I pursed my lips and gave him a flat look that was only a step away from an eye-roll. I suppose I'd given him permission to call me that, since no one could hear as we swept by.

"I've danced with you now—the seal has been broken. Besides, how else will I get you to myself for long enough to tease you about your secret identity?" His teeth flashed in a devilish grin. "Tell me, how *did* you come up with the name 'Wicked Lady'? It's deliciously dramatic and suggests you get up to *all kinds* of things other than highway robbery."

"The newspapers came up with it. It was nothing to do with me."

"Shame. I think it suits you."

"I'm not wicked." That would be a dangerous reputation to have following me around—almost as dangerous as an association with an infamous highwaywoman. "Aside from that, I'm very well behaved."

He chuckled, soft and low, then leant closer. "Aside from that? That one tiny little transgression that will get you killed if anyone finds out? Stars above, Kat, you are practically a saint."

My throat tightened like someone had hold of it. Transgressions weren't safe, especially not ones that others knew about. I'd only survived my crimes because I'd kept them secret. "I obey."

"*Do* you, now? That's good to know." As he spoke, one canine showed, like he was fighting a lopsided smile.

I swallowed, the grip on my throat loosening a fraction. His tone and expression said it was a double entendre, but I didn't grasp the specifics. How did obeying relate to sex?

"And is that every order without question?" His eyes narrowed at me. "Every rule? Even the foolish ones that are only there to control you?"

I frowned up at him. "Control or keep safe?"

"How does making you small keep you safe? Laughing quietly, folding your hands, letting the men talk. Are they matters of your safety or just keeping you manageable?"

I took the next few steps in silence. Maybe he understood my need to process what he'd just said, because he spun me away, keeping me tethered with a strong grip on my hand.

Had he been watching me so closely as I'd circulated with Ella that he'd seen my behaviour with other men? Was that what he really thought or was he just trying to get a rise out of me?

With a tug, he pulled me back, wrapping his arm around me, so I ended up with my back to his chest. Far too close, touching the length of my spine, my shoulders. Even my backside was against him. My heart sped out of time with the music. I had to take deep breaths to try to steady myself, but the air was full of citrus-fresh bergamot and deep, woody cedar, like an old cigar box. It was full of *him*.

"Well?" he murmured against my hair.

I had to swallow before I could reply. "Ladies who don't obey those rules are... punished harshly—by society and fate." Like Avice. She'd broken more rules than I could count, and now she was dead because of it. If I'd made her stay...

"Social punishment. Is that why you added the state of your home to our bargain?"

"If anyone found out about my finances, I'd be shunned. Just look at Miss Ward." No dowry, no allies, and a dwindling supply of money—she hadn't danced all evening.

"Hmm."

Only the music filled the silence between us. His warmth spread into my muscles, and his free hand planed up my bare arm to my shoulder.

This wasn't just part of the dance. The other couples weren't doing this. But I couldn't work out whether it was that he wanted to touch me or just keep me off balance, like he seemed to so enjoy.

His arm around my waist tightened, pulling me closer still. He was all hard surfaces and angles, just like I'd observed on the road—more a thing forged than a man. But he fit against me well, and my pulse throbbed harder, faster at that fact.

"Rules and consequences aside"—his fingers trailed to my neck, pausing at the necklace, and my breath caught both at the touch and the idea that he might yank the charm-protection away—"you're much more interesting when you're trying to manipulate me into dancing than when you're giving the ladylike act."

Again, he spun me away, keeping me bound with that grip on my hand. I reached up and checked—the necklace was still there. When he turned me back, this time so we were face-to-face, my head kept spinning.

Somehow, I managed to scoff. "Trying?" I raised my chin

and met his silvery gaze with more steadiness than I felt. "I'm pretty sure I succeeded."

"But I knew what you were doing."

"And yet I still got my way. And now we're dancing again, so I'd say I won doubly."

"Oh, you think you won, do you?" He huffed, and his hold tightened, pulling me flush against him. There was barely space for our separate steps: they merged together as his thigh pressed into mine, making me glide back as he did. My breasts crushed into his chest. My stomach pressed against his pelvis and I tried not to think about exactly what part of him.

This was scandalous. Was I imagining the quiet that fell across the onlookers? I couldn't tear my gaze from him to check.

His hand spread across my lower back, clamping me in place.

I wasn't sure I wanted to pull away.

I should have.

This was my job, yes, but it was meant to be done in secret. I shouldn't be here on a dance floor before all of court, so perilously close to him. I certainly shouldn't be enjoying it.

And yet his warmth, the solidity of his muscles, the scent that came off him—it all filled my senses, shooting pleasure through my nerves, making the world shrink down to just those things. I drank it in, greedy for more, storing it away for the inevitable drought that was to come.

Then his thumb took up a soft stroke at the small of my back and I was lost.

My breaths heaved against him, and I suspected it was only his strong lead that kept me moving across the dance floor.

"Katherine." He said my name slowly, voice a low rumble

that spilled into me like a sabrecat's purr. "What did you do with my orrery?"

I couldn't even summon a surprised reaction at the shift in subject. My body was too busy swimming in sensation, especially as he shifted and it brushed a button on his jacket across my nipple. It sparked through me, bright and hot, making my breath hitch.

Eyes hooded, he watched, and the edge of a smile curved his lips. He was doing this deliberately, using his body and my attraction to him to get this piece of information out of me.

I wasn't sure I cared.

Though a distant part of me laughed at the irony, when that was exactly what I'd been employed to do to him.

I hadn't written off the idea of selling his orrery in a few months. The fact he'd go to these lengths to get it back... It had to be more than just a pretty trinket. If I could get it open, maybe it would reveal something interesting. Something I could use. Something Cavendish would pay me for.

Pulse throbbing low in my belly, I managed to lift my chin. "I sold it."

His jaw feathered. His shoulders sank. Irritation coupled with disappointment, perhaps? But he didn't loosen his grip.

"If you wanted it so badly, why didn't you just take it back when you followed me home?" My voice came out breathy.

"I didn't need to." He shrugged, all dismissive arrogance. "I heard your summons to court, so I knew I could just sit back and wait for you to come to me. And here you are."

It took me a second to realise we'd stopped dancing and the music had faded.

"So, please tell me again, Katherine, how it is *you* have won."

I have your orrery, and you think I'm just flustered by your

118

good looks and the fact I stole from you, you arrogant prick. You have no idea I'm here to spy on you.

Thank the gods I bit my tongue against blurting all that. But damn, was it tempting.

Tempting and foolish.

Just like missing the warmth and feel of his body as he finally released me and stepped back. I composed myself just in time to bow and take his arm as he offered it. He escorted me from the dance floor in silence.

My brain buzzed and my body thrummed like an angry wasp trapped in a jar. The former wondered what might be so special about this orrery. The latter wanted more, frustrated by the heavy tightness in my thighs and belly.

He slowed, head cocking, and for a horrifying moment I thought I'd voiced one of my many, many thoughts out loud, but then I caught what he'd heard.

"... close to that Ferrers woman."

"She's the only one he's danced with, you know. My guess is they're at it."

"Of course they are... or if they're not, they soon will be. I didn't expect a fae to be so easily captured."

My skin burned, and I dared a glance at Bastian. He'd gone very still.

Clearing his throat, he disentangled his arm from my grip and inclined his head. "Katherine. Enjoy your evening."

With that, he was gone.

And I had no idea whether I'd made progress in my seduction or if I was the one who'd been seduced.

19

My confusion was anything but eased over the next fortnight. I saw him at a party and a play the Caradocian suitor's retinue put on. At both events, I approached him and we chatted briefly, but there were always others in the group. He kept it all cool and polite, albeit a little sarcastic. I suspected sarcastic was his default.

The only sign of the man I'd danced with was that every time we spoke, he managed to get the words deal, bargain, or favour into the conversation. But after a short while, he'd make his excuses and disappear.

I wasn't just failing in my attempts to get close to him—I was actively getting *further* from him.

As I walked Vespera back from a ride through the Queenswood, I huffed. The man was infuriating. One minute he held me against him in front of a whole ballroom, the next I could barely catch him for a few words and a bit of idle flirtation. He had to be avoiding me.

My scowl deepened and my grip on the reins tightened.

Around us, preparations were under way for a garden party. I slowed, listening out for conversations that might interest Cavendish. I wasn't getting anywhere with Bastian, but maybe information from other sources would help keep my job.

To the left, a host of burly carpenters and labourers heaved on ropes, erecting a large marquee overlooking the gardens. After all, you never could be entirely sure of Albionic weather. Rain could come at any time of year, and aristocrats hated getting wet. Even now, clouds gathered overhead, suggesting we might be in for a rainy afternoon.

Frustratingly, the workers quietened when I came close. An aristocratic lady walking with a large, black sabrecat wasn't exactly subtle.

To the right, gardeners weeded the flower beds and trimmed the lawns, ensuring everything would be perfect for the event. They were doing a wonderful job—roses and sweet peas brightened the overcast day with deep velvet red, pale yellow, and hot, sunset orange.

I dismounted Vespera and walked her along the path so I could get closer to the damp, fresh scent of grass cuttings and mingled florals. The sweetness eased my tight jaw and loosened the knot of irritation that I'd grown tangled in.

Even if Bastian was avoiding me, that wasn't the end of my work. I could still salvage this.

Perhaps all my talk about obeying the rules had given him the impression I was *too* well behaved to take a lover. Maybe if I was more flirtatious next time I saw him, made it clear I was open to such things...

I nodded to myself and scratched Vespera behind the ear. "See? There's always a solution." Pushing into my hand, she looked more impressed by the scratches than my brilliant solution to the Bastian Seduction Problem.

When we turned onto a path leading to a pretty arbour seat covered in rambling honeysuckle, I stopped short.

Ahead stood a rose bush covered in the brightest coral pink blooms I'd ever seen. The colour was so rich, it seemed to glow, even on this overcast day. The green foliage gleamed without a hint of black spot, and its straight branches spread evenly, rather than twisting upon themselves from neglect.

It was everything the roses on my estate should've become.

I left Vespera on the path and crept closer, as though I feared I'd scare away the beauty. It was a ridiculous thought. I was well aware of that, and yet I had no other way of explaining my caution. Maybe it was simple, stupid reverence.

The nearest gardener, a young man with chestnut brown hair, straightened from his work and approached. "Can I help you, milady?"

I clasped my hands, which had been so close to touching the petals of the nearest flower, my face heated. How stupid I had to look, gawping at a damn flower, about to touch it. But my traitorous eyes skipped back to the roses. "What variety are they? That colour is incredible. From the shape, I thought they were Lady Greys, but I've never seen them in that colour. That's more like a Devonshire pink."

His eyebrows shot up, and a slow-dawning smile lit his face. "Well, milady is clearly an expert. They're a hybrid between the two. Most people guess Devonshires on account of the colour, but the Lady Greys give a longer season."

"Ah, yes! Hence them being out still." I bent closer to the bush, unable to keep my fingers from the velvety petals a moment longer. Even softer than I remembered healthy roses being. Salt coated the back of my throat and I had to give a slight cough before I could go on. "That also explains the lush foliage—Devonshires are usually bronze, no?"

"Aye, exactly that. When they came on, the leaves were a pleasant surprise."

"You bred them yourself?"

His tanned cheeks flushed, and he bowed his head. "They're out of my greenhouse, milady."

"How did you get around the problem of drop?"

"Well..."

And that was how we got on to the intricacies of rose hybridisation. Challenges, successes, good combinations and doomed ones. After his initial stiffness, Webster as he introduced himself, relaxed, lighting up to be discussing something he was clearly passionate about.

With the sun hazing behind pale cloud, I lost track of time as our conversation turned to pruning and soil type, then fertiliser. "Guano's best," he said, crouching and crumbling a handful of rich earth, watching it break up with something that looked a lot like pride. "I've never seen roses grow so fast or so well as they do in that."

I sighed at the soil, just the right side of clayish, and at the roses, which were probably the most perfect things I'd ever seen in my life. "Best, but expensive. And even if I could get hold of it, I'd have to use it on the vegetables."

He blinked up at me, a frown pulling his brows together.

Because a lady-in-waiting wasn't supposed to grow vegetables or prioritise them over roses. She certainly shouldn't worry about the expense of guano. My heart tripped over a beat.

A quick glance confirmed no one else was on the path, just us and the arbour further along. Only he had heard me slip.

That was marginally better than a courtier catching wind of just how bad my money worries were.

"Or... rather..." I chuckled, though even I had to admit, it sounded strangled and nervy. "That's what our head gardener always tells me." My cheeks hurt from the smile I forced in place.

From the palace's clock tower, the great bell chimed twelve.

"Goodness, is that the time?" I took a step back. "I could talk about roses and fertiliser all day, but I'm keeping you from your work. I'm so sorry."

That made him tilt his head, a bemused smile on his face.

Because I wasn't treating him like a lady treated a servant. She wouldn't have apologised, just told him to get back to work or been oblivious to the fact she was keeping him *from* his work. Damn it, I'd lost myself in all this talk of roses and forgotten I wasn't on my estate with its safe buffer from the rules of society.

Flustered, I excused myself. He just bowed his head and wished me a good afternoon. I called Vespera to me and hurried along the path, with her following.

If I had money left over from paying off the bailiff, maybe I could get hold of some guano, or at least bone meal. For the vegetables, though, not the roses—they were a lost cause. I mulled over the idea, tugging off my gloves as I reached the arbour.

From its shadows, just a pace away, a pair of glowing eyes watched me.

I gasped and stopped dead, dropping my gloves.

But I knew those glowing eyes, silvery like the moon, and the stupid, gorgeous face they belonged to.

I waited for my heart to calm from the surprise and

waited, too, for his inevitable smirk. He liked to put me off-balance—he would *love* seeing me so shocked by his appearance.

But the smirk didn't come. Not even an amused twitch of his lips.

Head cocked, he just looked at me with such intensity it was as though it peeled my clothing away. There was something evaluative there, but not in the way Cavendish had weighed my usefulness, more... like he was seeing me afresh.

Oh shit, had he heard me wittering on at Webster about gardening? Had I made a fool of myself? I gripped my hands together, picking at the side of a nail, frantically running through the conversation. He already knew about my poor finances from seeing the estate, but was there anything else I'd spilled that I shouldn't have?

Finally, he broke from his stillness and swept to the floor, retrieving my gloves. When he righted himself, he stood a little too close and held them out in the space between us. His silvery eyes roved across my face, lingering on my cheeks, and there was maybe the shadow of a smile, but it wasn't anything like his usual mocking one.

I'd be damned if I knew what it *was*, though.

I should use this moment. I was meant to be drawing him in with more flirtation.

But his silence and that look emptied my head of everything Ella had taught me. What had he overheard to make him act this way? I must've said something while I'd been so unguarded.

Maybe it was just another way for him to unnerve me, this time with something that looked like sincerity.

I reached for my gloves, braced for him to tighten his grip so I couldn't take them as he had with the orrery, but...

he didn't. I squinted at him before slowly saying, "Thank you."

He inclined his head, took a step back, and turned down another path.

I squeezed my gloves, letting out a long breath. What an odd encounter.

It was a good reminder: I had an agenda of my own, but so did he. And I had no idea what it was.

I needed to find out, for the sake of my wages, but also for the safety of the people I cared about.

And maybe, with the look he'd just given me, for my own sake, too.

20

The day after the encounter in the gardens, a large pot with a rose bush like the one I'd admired was delivered to my rooms. At first, I thought it was from Bastian, but when I read the wooden marker planted in the soil, it said,

To Lady Katherine. Hope this beauty brings you some pleasure. Webster.

I wasn't disappointed, not when it was such a bright splash of colour in the sedate decor of my suite. I placed it by the window in my living room and checked its soil.

Shortly after, Ella arrived, but instead of her usual easy smile, she came through the door tight and agitated. Before I could ask, she made a beeline for the rose. Ever the spy.

"An admirer?" She raised her eyebrows at me, though there was still a lingering tension in her expression. "Bastian?"

"Just a kind gift from an acquaintance. What's got you so irritated?"

She gave a rueful tilt of her head. "The lingerie hasn't been delivered yet, and I was planning to make use of mine tonight."

"Oh?" I sidled closer to her and widened my eyes in question.

She wouldn't tell me exactly who Cavendish had her spying on, but I had a few guesses. One was the Frankish ambassador who'd thrown the recent ball. Since she had no necklace to protect her from fae charm, I was confident her target was human. Whoever it was, she hadn't yet slept with them, but it sounded like her seduction was going far better than mine.

"*Oh.*" She nodded enthusiastically, and there was a ghost of her usual good mood. "I'm hoping they *and* I will be making that noise a lot tonight."

She didn't speak of it like it was a chore or a thing to be endured. In fact, her enthusiasm had me smiling. "Well, I can go and collect it. I don't mind."

"No, I couldn't ask you to—"

"You're not asking. I'm offering. On Vespera I'll move more quickly through the streets than a carriage, and besides, I haven't had a chance to see any of the city since arriving."

Plus, it would make me feel useful. Sitting with the queen and swanning around social events didn't feel like work. That together with my failure to make progress with Bastian had me feeling as useful as a tissue paper fire guard.

With a sigh and a bit more prodding, Ella agreed and gave me the details for Blaze's atelier.

The sun came out for my ride, and I had to admit I enjoyed it. The streets bustled with folk on errands, hawkers selling all kinds of wares, and extravagant carriages that I would've been glad to see on the highway at night. The city felt... *alive.*

I reached Blaze's atelier, a glass and gilt storefront that attracted passersby with the undeniable air of glamour. It only took ten minutes to stack the boxes of lingerie on Vespera's back. I tried not to dwell on the fact that a number of them contained items for me to wear. In front of Bastian.

But I wasn't thinking about that. No.

I shoved the thought away and led my laden sabrecat the long way back to the palace, exploring the city. Theatres and huge town houses set back from the road. Restaurants and lush parks. Squares with market stalls and gushing fountains. There was so much here, so much movement, so many people. They paid no attention to the gallows that darkened one end of the largest square I passed through. I couldn't keep my eyes from it, throat tight.

Hangman or axe?

My head was still heavy with thoughts of the punishment for my crimes when we arrived in the stable yard. In my riding clothes, I blended with the stable hands grooming the other cats, so I took Vespera to her enclosure, unfastened the boxes, and removed her tack.

But I didn't blend in for long—no sooner had I started brushing down her coat than a stable girl appeared and took over. Another took her saddle and bridle away to the tack room, while a young man loaded himself with the boxes and whisked them to my suite.

There was nothing left for me to do.

I bit back a sigh and headed towards the palace. But as I entered a courtyard that was usually quiet, the low hum of a familiar voice drifted across the gravel. Bastian.

Not yet able to make out any words, I paused behind a privet hedge and peered around.

A dark-haired woman stood with him, hand on his arm, green gown a little too garish to be fashionable, but still finely made. When my gaze reached her freckled face, I half-fell into the hedge.

Because I knew her.

Dark hair, blue eyes, and an impish grin. It was, of all the people in the world, my fence, Winifred. Also known as Win, the woman I'd sold stolen goods to for a decade. I'd never seen her in such fine clothes, but there was no mistaking—it was definitely her.

Talking to Bastian.

She was meant to be in Verulamium, where her shop was. Not here. Not in the palace. Not *speaking to the man I was spying on.*

My heart thundered as though the clashing of those two parts of my world was happening in my chest and not in the middle of Riverton Palace.

Face tingling, I stared at the pair of them.

If Win was here in Lunden, in the palace, that risked people discovering our connection and thus uncovering my secret. And the fact Bastian was speaking to her... There could be no other reason. I told him I'd sold his orrery. Somehow, *some-fucking-how,* he'd found Win and had to be asking her where it now was.

He wasn't just toying with me. He was poking into my affairs. Aggressively.

When I bumped into him in the gardens, had he been spying on me? Or was I just being paranoid?

Good gods, *I* was meant to be spying on him, not the other way around.

Shitting hells, this was such a mess. I'd only been at court five minutes, and I'd already screwed it up.

A weight pressed on my chest, and I sucked in air, searching for a closer hiding spot where I might hear Win's reply. There was none.

She nodded, eyes lighting up in the way they did whenever I brought her something particularly expensive. Excitement, avarice, her thrill at the promise of a particularly good payday. She was selling me out. Had to be.

I closed my eyes and held my breath, desperate to catch even a word.

"... So happy with the gown you sent." She smiled up at him and touched his arm again.

Something ugly that I didn't have any right or wish to feel slithered through me. But I stamped it down, because it wasn't important or useful.

So he'd sent her the gown, which made sense—I doubted anything she owned would be suitable for the palace. But why bring her here at all? Why not go to her?

She tossed her head as they walked across the gravel, out of earshot. Chin up, shoulders back, swaggering, she was loving every second of playing the part of a lady, albeit she did it poorly.

I waited, and they spoke for a minute or so more. I couldn't quite see Bastian's face, but he shook his head several times before finally nodding and gesturing towards the entrance I'd used. I ducked behind the hedge, muscles tight, but he didn't appear and demand to know what the hells I was doing.

When I dared to peek out again, he was leaving through another archway and Win came strolling this way, whistling. So much for the ladylike act.

Bastian was well out of sight by the time she reached my hedge, and I grabbed her arm, yanking her to a stop.

"Kat!" She stared at me for a second, then laughed. "I was just talking about you."

"I guessed. What the hells did you say?"

"Oh no, you don't get to be pissed off," she hissed, scowling. "Not when you've been holding out on me. Who did you sell it to?"

Bastian had asked about the orrery. Shit.

Though that did give him away. To go to the trouble of finding Win and bringing her here—even sending a gown so she could blend in... He was desperate to get the orrery back. What would he do if he found out I still had it? If I gave it to Cavendish, would he find it useful enough to keep me safe from Bastian's ire?

It was too much to think about now. I needed to learn more about the object... and right now, I needed to deflect Win. "I didn't have a chance to visit you, not with all the preparation for coming here."

She sniffed, still scowling. "*And* I didn't know you were in Lunden. I'm hurt you didn't tell me yourself. And at court!" She eyed our palatial surrounds, then me. "Just look at you!" I could see the cogs in her mind working as she eyed my simple but smart riding gown, the pearlwort necklace, the combs holding my hair from my face.

She'd caught a whiff of money.

Sure enough, she leant close. "Rich pickings, Kat. Rich pickings indeed. Maybe I can forgive you for that business with the fae." She waved in the direction Bastian had disappeared. "After all, this will be a great moneymaker for us."

I flinched and glanced back down the archway. No one in

sight to hear her careless talk. "I can't steal from these people. I'll get caught."

She snorted, as unladylike as it got. "That's never bothered you before. Unless..." Her head tilted; her eyes narrowed, and I braced myself. "You have another way of making money now? Yes, you must to afford that gear." She took in my outfit with a nod. "So what's the gig, then? Come on, share with Winifred. We've been friends how many years? You can tell me."

I folded my arms. "We're not friends, just business associates—*former* business associates."

Her eyes widened. "Former? You're dumping me? Ouch, Kat, I'm wounded." She clutched her chest and I might've felt more sympathy if not for how over-exaggerated her look of hurt was. "I thought we were buddies—comrades in arms, a team! All for one and all that."

"Comrades in arms?" I raised an eyebrow. "I must've missed you riding out on the road all those nights, risking your neck with me."

"Hey, I risk my neck handling your goods. I risk plenty. But, fine, I understand." She spread her hands. "You have some other gig now. You don't need me. But we can still be friends, can't we?"

Why the sudden interest in friendship? I watched her for some clue, but Win's dramatics and the chaotic way she flicked from emotion to emotion made her hard to read.

"I mean"—she fixed her large, blue eyes on me—"we're not *enemies*, are we?"

That was easy to understand. A veiled threat.

She knew enough to hurt me. I didn't trust her as far as I could throw her, but it hadn't been easy to find a fence, especially not one who'd speak to an aristocrat. I gave her that placating smile I'd learned so well. "No, of course not. Never."

She smiled brightly, eyes lighting again. "Good. *Good.* You just let me know if any exciting opportunities come about in your new life." She stared up at the palace again. "And be sure to invite me to any interesting events, won't you? Just because you don't want to make use of this opportunity, doesn't mean I can't." With that, she clapped me on the shoulder and left.

I followed at a discreet distance to make sure she did indeed leave. It was only once she exited a side gate that I allowed myself to sag against a tree and rub my face. The first sneaky meeting I caught Bastian at, and I couldn't even tell Cavendish, because it was with *my* fence.

What a fucking mess.

21

That night, as I was getting ready for bed, another note came from Cavendish. This one instructed me to "wear quiet clothes" and gave directions to the centre of the maze.

What quiet clothes were, I wasn't entirely sure, but I put on breeches, soft leather boots, and a simple black shirt. The kind of gear I wore on the highway. I could sneak easily in the dark wearing those, and just about pass as a man if glimpsed in the shadows with my braid tucked into my shirt.

Guards patrolled the walls and gates around the palace grounds but tended to leave the grounds themselves alone, so it was easy to creep out an unguarded door. Torches and lanterns dotted the gardens. Shadows pooled between them, and I slipped through the darkness.

I'd learned to move quietly through woods and gardens as a child. My sister Avice had somehow been preternaturally good at it, so she'd won far too many games of hide and sneak. What had come naturally to her, I had to practise, practise,

practise. It eventually paid off because I learned to win as many games as she did, and now I placed each step in silence.

As I set foot in the yew hedge maze, I frowned. This was the first time Cavendish had asked me to meet him anywhere other than his office. Although it was the middle of the night, the maze could be accessed by anyone within the palace. It wasn't exactly private.

But he'd made it clear it wasn't my place to question him. So I followed the directions I'd memorised, able to see in the moonlight spilling between the dark hedges.

Not far from the centre, a noise made me stop. Just a soft one. So soft, I wasn't entirely sure what I'd heard. I paused, ears straining.

A sigh. A woman's sigh. And... a gasp shortly after.

I kept my breaths quiet and padded around the corner. At a break in the hedges stood a waist-high wall with a trellis above. Weaving through the trellis grew the deepest, darkest velvet red roses I'd ever seen. Their scent hung in the air, redolent of summer warmth and the pleasure of hard work towards a driving passion.

A foolish passion.

"Oh!" Followed by a lower sound—a man?

Heart beating just a little faster, I crept closer. The rose's lush leaves were full and thick, but didn't quite hide everything beyond.

On a stone table at the centre of the maze lay Lara, blond hair cascading over the edge. Her eyebrows peaked and her lips parted in a look that you didn't need to read people to know was pure pleasure. I swallowed and forced my eyes to move from her face.

The moonlight bathed her bare skin, and her breasts

bounced as she arched into the pounding rhythm of the man standing between her legs.

I should look away.

I couldn't.

My mouth was dry, my skin too hot. My cheeks burned, despite the cool night air.

I found myself gripping the trellis, leaning against it, hungry to see more.

Her lover's shirt hung open, revealing a muscled chest that flexed as his stomach tightened and he thrust into her again and again. His trousers sat at his knees as though he'd been in too much rush to fully undress.

She clung to the edge of the table, biting her lip, and I found myself biting my own, body throbbing.

That arse of a husband had never made me feel like this. He'd certainly never made me bite my lip and whimper as Lara now did.

Was this what lit up Ella's eyes when she spoke of her sexual conquests?

As a girl, I'd known what was expected of a "good wife." The moment I'd learned I was being married off to a vile man ten years my senior, I'd resigned myself to duty. Fighting it would've got me nowhere.

But I did allow myself one rebellion on the matter of marriage.

I vowed I wouldn't go into it with my virginity intact.

On our family estate, there weren't many options, but I let Avice in on my plan. She'd just started to learn about sex and had some idea of my plight. She pointed out the stable groom with a strong nose and easy smile. It took me weeks to gather my courage. Weeks of dress fittings and the gathering of my wedding trousseau and all the other nonsense that had gone into my marriage to that man.

It was only when I reached the day before, still horrifyingly virginal, that I finally forced myself to do it. I was sure the young man didn't know quite what was going on... or maybe he did. He understood I was to be wed. He had to know what that meant for a girl like me.

I came in from a ride and ensured we were alone. It hadn't taken much. A smile and a request for help in one of the stables, followed by a touch of his arm, the upward tilt of my chin, inviting him to kiss me. Once that had started, I'd felt the hardness in his trousers as I'd rubbed against him, determined to make my body say what I couldn't bring my mouth to. *Fuck me.* That's all I'd wanted from him. It didn't even have to be him, just not Lord Robin Fanshawe.

I got my wish. It had hurt. It had almost felt good at one point, but then it was over.

After, we'd lay there in the straw, panting, and he'd asked me, "What does this mean?"

I laughed. Even then, I must've had some measure of cynicism, because I sat up, gathered my clothes, and shook my head at him. "This? There is no *this*. It means nothing. Just that I don't go to my wedding bed a maiden." I wasn't sure if he'd thought it the start of some grand love affair. After I dressed and strode from the stable, I never saw him again.

The moment with him that had felt almost good—it was a single raindrop against the torrent of pleasure I watched Lara losing herself in.

My husband could've treated me like that, maybe made me feel like that. Had he realised I wasn't a virgin, and that was why he didn't bother? Because I'd failed in my wifely duties?

Lara didn't appear concerned in the slightest. She normally seemed so sensible, so straight-laced and restrained. The perfect lady. But here she was, writhing on a stone slab in the centre of the palace maze while this man fucked her to within an inch of her life.

Cavendish had sent me here. Not to meet him, but to see this. To find out who her lover was, to get ammunition against her, either to spread news of her secret affair and get her dismissed or to blackmail her into leaving.

I should go. I didn't want that kind of knowledge.

I should go back to bed. I should forget I'd seen this.

And yet...

The way his hand planed her thigh. The little gasp she made as it slid higher and dipped between her legs. The way he bent over her, brows peaked with pleasured concentration as he kissed her in a way I'd never been kissed.

I hung on every breath, on each whimper, on every point of contact my greedy eyes could take in.

It took a long while before I really registered his long nose, his thin lips, the dark eyes that drank in the sight of Lara even more greedily than I did. The Earl of Langdon—one of the queen's suitors. Somehow, that made this all the more wrong.

And yet I still couldn't look away. He gripped Lara's thighs, pushing them up as a fierce smile lit his face. When his mouth opened, I found myself straining forward to hear. "That's it, darling. You come on my cock again." He bent over her and his teeth flashed in a fierce snarl. "Again."

Her eyes screwed shut and she cried out.

Just as a low voice spoke in my ear. "My, my, my."

22

It was just as well a hand clamped over my mouth, because with my body so tight, I might've screamed. Instead, I made a muffled sound into someone's palm as a warm body pressed against my rigid back and pinned me to the low wall. He was strong, one arm looping around my waist and arms, holding me flush against every hard plane of his chest, thighs holding mine still. I tensed in his hold but couldn't do more than wriggle uselessly.

As the scent of bergamot and cedar filled me, I realised I knew the voice. My eyes bulged as Lara's cries faded.

"My dear Lady Katherine," Bastian murmured in my ear, voice hot. "I don't know what game you're playing, but I didn't imagine it would involve spying on people fucking in a maze."

Shit, shit, shit. Did he realise I was spying? Or did he just think I was some kind of pervert? Which was worse?

His grip over my mouth eased, and I panted against his skin, which tasted ever so slightly of salt.

In the centre of the maze, Lara also panted, her breasts heaving as Langdon pulled out of her. His cock glistened with her wetness, still hard. Gripping her hips, he turned her onto her front, so she was bent over the marble table, and stood back a moment to enjoy the view.

My breath caught as he plunged back inside. I tried to hold still, to not lean back into Bastian, as I realised our position wasn't so different to the one they were now enjoying.

"Interesting." Bastian pulled me a little closer, and I fought the urge to arch into him. "I didn't have you down as a voyeur. An exhibitionist, perhaps, given the right nurturing, but never a voyeur. And standing here in the middle of the night in clothes your kind consider so scandalous for women..." His face came into view at the edge of my vision as he peered down my front. "In this shirt that betrays just how much you're enjoying the show."

He pulled the shirt taut over my chest, and the way the linen chafed my nipples told me they'd peaked against the fabric. No surprise, I'd been practically trembling with want before he'd arrived, and now the throbbing between my thighs grew harder and wetter.

But he knew. He knew I wasn't just watching by accident or for the sake of gathering gossip. He knew why I hadn't been able to turn away.

And now he was torturing me with my embarrassment. He didn't need his fae ability to see in the dark to know I must've gone bright red—he had to feel how hot my skin was.

I didn't know what to do, what to say. I could only stare at Langdon screwing Lara and try my best to keep still.

Bastian's arm loosened around my waist and his fingers trailed over the curve of my belly. The muscles there twitched at his light touch. It was as ticklish as it was teasing, and he must've heard my breath catch, because I felt him smile against my ear. "It doesn't feel right to call you Lady Katherine, not when you're imagining yourself there, someone doing that to you, aren't you?"

I inhaled, shaky, and whispered against his hand, "Please." I didn't know why that was the word that came out, just that it was the only one my tongue could form. Maybe I wanted him to put me out of my misery and call out to Lara and Langdon that he'd caught me watching.

"Is that 'please release you' or 'please give you release'?" At last he took his hand from my mouth.

I gulped in fresh air, focusing on that rather than what he'd just asked. Cool, fresh, but saturated with his scent and the faint salt that still tinged my lips.

Which one was it I wanted?

My tongue had known the moment it had formed its plea. The pounding in my body knew it, pulling me against him. The roses weren't too thorny: I could've leant into the trellis if I didn't want to be pressed against him.

But I did.

I'd found release in my bed, alone. Many times. But I wanted it now, and I wanted him to give it to me.

Pathetic, but I burned for it.

Not that it was really an offer. I could feel he wasn't hard against my arse, even as he continued to trace spirals over my belly. Sometimes he drifted higher, stopping just below my breasts. Sometimes he dipped lower, stopping at the waistband of my trousers. He just wanted me to admit I wanted him for his own amusement.

He made a low, thoughtful sound as his fingers splayed across my stomach. "I feel you arching back into me, Kat. I see the pulse at your throat leaping harder. I hear your breaths heaving faster. Why not take the satisfaction you desire?"

Why not?

Like it was that easy. Like I could just ask and he'd grant my wish and there would be no consequences.

In the maze, Langdon took a handful of Lara's hair and pulled her back onto him. Neck arching, she cried out, but not in pain, only with more pleasure.

"Unless... ah..." Bastian pulled my braid from the neck of my shirt and wrapped it around his hand. "No lover has ever made you make those sounds, have they?"

My face burned, though I couldn't have said if it was with shame, humiliation, or desire.

Shame that he was right? Humiliation that he could see through me so clearly? Or stupid fucking desire for him?

There was a twitch against my arse, and he pressed against me more firmly. I pushed back, body not entirely under my conscious command.

"You turn such a pretty shade of pink, it clashes with your hair."

I squeezed my eyes shut and hung my head, rose leaves fluttering against my brow.

He stopped playing with my stomach, stopped pressing into me, and took my chin, lifting my head and turning it so I could finally look him in the eye.

Moonlight edged with darkness, he held my gaze, and it felt less guarded than I'd seen it before. "There's no shame in sex, you know, Wicked Lady. No shame in bodies. No shame in pleasure. That's some strange idea humans have drummed into their own minds."

That perfect mouth was perhaps an inch from mine. His

words brushed my lips. He stroked the sensitive skin behind my ear, adding to the stacked overwhelm of sensation, making me shudder.

"And yet... you deny yourself, don't you?" His eyebrows lowered, but it was a gentler expression than the glare that had promised to kill me for stealing from him. "Such a pity. Such a waste."

Every nerve in me strained, wanting, needing, pitiful, and denied, just as he said.

"If I had water and you were dying of thirst, I would give it to you. This is no different. So, I ask again"—his voice lowered and the look he gave me intensified—"was that 'please' begging to *be* released or begging *for* release? Answer and I'll do it."

I could only stare back, mouth dry. Was he really offering...?

I'd been trying to get closer to him. Seduction was part of the plan. My stupid, touch-craving body had made me forget that fact, too caught up in shock and lust.

Was he really offering it to me on a plate?

And yet if I said yes, it wasn't only for the sake of spying— he was right, I wanted, *needed* release.

"I said answer me, Katherine. I won't ask again."

"Yes." It came out on a breath, as though scared out by the prospect of losing my chance. "Give it to me."

I swore there was a flicker of a smile, but he turned my head away with the hand knotted into my braid before I could be sure.

"Good," he said in my ear. "Hands on the trellis. Keep them there."

Thorns or none, I obeyed. This was worth tearing my

hands open for. The command in his voice already had the throb at my centre spreading.

That space he'd left me earlier, where I could've chosen to press into the wall rather than him—now he took it away, crushing me against the stone. "Watch them and imagine it's me fucking you."

It wasn't only a twitch anymore. Now his hardness ground against my arse. It wasn't difficult to imagine it sliding between my thighs, between my folds, finally pushing into me, in the same way Langdon pushed into Lara.

I surrendered my battle. I let my back arch like it had begged to earlier. I circled my hips, meeting him, tilting further and further back until I could feel his hardness against my softness.

"You said when we were alone, I could call you whatever I wanted. Now I call you my ember."

Maybe he was right to, because I'd thought myself on fire earlier and I'd been wrong. That was barely lukewarm compared to this. My skin tingled, too hot, too tight, covered in too many gods damned clothes.

But I'd been told to keep my hands on the trellis, and if there was one thing I was good at, it was obeying. So I gripped tighter, when all I really wanted to do was pull my shirt open and get some cool night air on my skin. The very idea should've shocked me.

But this wasn't real. It didn't count.

Or this was for the job. It was just to get close to him.

Or I wanted it, but only because of what I watched at the centre of the maze. Not because I wanted it for myself. Not because I wanted him.

The excuses tripped over each other. I wasn't sure if I believed all of them or none.

Then they seemed a lot less important, because Bastian's lips feathered over my neck, tracing upward, before he bit my ear, firm but not quite painful. I tightened at that solid, hard shred of sensation that promised so much. When I tried to turn and capture his lips, he gripped my braid and tutted in my ear.

"I said watch them."

So I pressed my tongue to the roof of my mouth and obeyed.

"Good."

Wild fucking hunt. Even that word flushed me with pleasure. I'd pleased him. That was safe. But he was pleasing me, too, and that was dangerous.

Apparently satisfied that I wasn't going to turn, he released my hair and planed his hands to my breasts. With a gasp, I leant my head back on his shoulder, still dutifully watching Langdon and Lara. But with Bastian grinding against my arse and kneading my breasts, I found what they were doing much less interesting than I had earlier.

If I didn't fear any disobedience would've made him stop, I'd have let my eyes drift shut and let myself drown in this sea of sensation.

He ran his thumbs over my pebbled nipples and gave a soft sound that didn't seem entirely deliberate, as though my heightened state gave him pleasure, too. Then his fingers closed with his thumbs, pinching, and I bucked with a soft cry.

His hand clamped over my mouth. "You're lucky it's humans you're spying on—my kind would've heard that."

Him saying the word "spying" broke through the haze he had me under and woke my mind from its fog. He hadn't guessed what I was really doing, but it was a step too close.

As he soothed my nipple with a circling caress and his other lowered from my mouth, I found my tongue. "Is this your favour?"

He gave a low, dark chuckle that buzzed along my nerves and thrummed in my bones. "I rather think I'm the one doing you a favour, don't you?"

I wilted and bit my lip as he scraped a nail over the tight point of my breast. "Does this mean I owe you?"

"You already do, Wicked Lady. But don't worry, when I choose to collect, I'll make sure I get my pound of flesh." I felt him smile against my ear as he squeezed my breast and placed one hand around my neck.

The world flickered. I flinched.

Soil. Night darkness. And something I couldn't see. Something I could never see—a blank surrounded by fragments of old memory.

"Not that." My voice wavered, like it was shaken by the frantic throb of my heart.

He released my throat at once. "Of course." He held still for several heartbeats, then placed both hands on my shoulders and just held me, cheek leaning against mine. "Anything you don't want, any time you want me to stop, any moment you want this to end, say the word and *I'll* be the one who obeys. No hesitation. No questions asked. Do you understand?"

I nodded.

"Do you want us to stop?"

I shook my head.

"Say it."

"No. Don't stop. Please. I... I want to keep going." The tension in my body demanded it. It might break me if we stopped whatever the fuck this was.

He inclined his head, stubble abrading my cheek.

"Remember, any time you say, we stop. Any time." He kissed my cheek, so gentle it stole my breath.

We held still for a long moment and the momentary fear in me dissolved, leaving only desire.

"I haven't told you how exquisite you are, have I, Kat?" He stroked my hair and pulled the ribbon that secured my braid. "This flame hair"—he ran his fingers through the braid, undoing it—"so thick, so glorious. Your green eyes, glinting with far more intelligence than you let on..." He brushed his lips down the side of my neck. Finally he returned to my breasts, capturing my nipples between his fingers and squeezing.

I bit back my whimper at the unbearable pressure building deep inside.

"With a wickedness even I hadn't realised, drinking up those two fucking in the dark." Again, that laugh that was as soft as the night. He gripped my hair and turned my face to his.

I let my head tilt back, waiting for the kiss I knew was to come.

"And these lying lips, so sweet, so troublesome." But instead of kissing me, he pulled my lower lip from between my teeth, and slid his thumb over it and into my mouth. The way he watched, I knew he was imagining it wasn't just his finger, like he'd ordered me to imagine it wasn't Lara and Langdon fucking.

I flicked my tongue over the pad of his thumb. He rewarded me with a shaky exhale and the glimpse of his teeth as they flashed in a grin that was part pleasure, part surprise. With a low groan, he resumed his grind against my arse, just edging my pussy.

The shadows around us seemed to throb and heave with

my pulse, with our breaths, like they were a seething mass, alive.

"Much too troublesome," he murmured, pulling his thumb out, letting it tug on my lower lip, tracing over my chin, then lightly down. He paused before reaching my throat, eyebrows rising in question, asking permission.

I nodded. "It's only holding."

"No holding you there. Understood." He nudged his nose to mine as he let his thumb continue down my throat, touch so light, it set the hairs at the nape of my neck on end.

His breaths came faster now, though nowhere near the heave mine had become. It was like I couldn't get enough air in my lungs, like I couldn't get enough of his touch, which now toyed with the waistband of my trousers.

He teased my mouth, not quite touching it with his, keeping always a hair's breadth away. "Little ember, who did you sell my orrery to?"

If I hadn't been fighting so hard to breathe, I would've laughed. That was the real reason for all this. He didn't give a damn about my desire except for how he could use it for his own ends. But my body was so taut with more pleasure than I'd known at someone else's hands, I couldn't complain.

"Why would I tell you that?"

He brushed his lips over mine, not quite a kiss but enough to whisper along every nerve ending. "Why wouldn't you?"

"You'll kill them to get it back."

His gaze flicked to my lips, as though promising the kiss he was withholding. "I haven't killed you."

I scoffed, but it became strangled as he pinched my nipple again. Gods knew how I managed to reply. "Because it would cause a diplomatic incident."

"That's not the only reason." He lifted one shoulder and

tilted my hips back until his hardness made contact with my sensitive pussy, separated only by fabric.

I gritted my teeth against a groan as the pressure inside me built.

"You're not going to tell me then?" Again, that graze of his lips over mine.

"No." I breathed the word out, disappointed to be saying it.

His actions spelled it out: if I told him, he would claim my mouth and slide his hand into my trousers.

If the orrery was this important to him, it could be useful to me. "However, that was an excellent attempt at distraction."

One canine showed as he smirked, watching my parted lips. "You can't blame me for trying."

He kept watching, kept grinding against me, kept kneading my breasts, teasing my belly, and all the while I braced myself for it to end.

My insides were molten, and I was sure I'd left a damp mark on my trousers by this point. "Aren't you going to stop, then?"

He pulled back with a frown. "Why in the world would I do that?" He mimicked my earlier tone, albeit octaves lower.

"I thought this was just to get information out of me?"

He made a thoughtful sound. "Is that what you want?"

Maybe I wanted it to be true. It would be simpler than the reality that I didn't want him to stop. I shook my head.

"Then burn for me, my ember. I want to see you become a flame." With one hand, he unbuttoned my trousers.

My grip on the trellis tightened, thorns pressing against my skin, threatening to break through. He was going to continue. I was going to feel him against my slick flesh, without stupid fabric getting in the way. He was going to give me that release he'd made me ask for.

With no buttons left, his hooded gaze stayed on me as his hand slid down my belly.

Lower.

Lower.

The thorns pierced my flesh, pinpricks of pain forcing a gasp through my lips. I would endure them to get this.

He tensed, breath held, fingers maybe an inch from the bundle of nerves that delivered pure, sweet pleasure. "Quiet."

Then I heard it, too.

The rustle of someone approaching.

He exhaled and withdrew his hand. "Bastard timing, little ember." He gripped my shoulders for a fraction of a second, and I could feel the tension against my back, as though he were wrestling with himself. "You might want to slip away. My reputation will fare better if I'm caught here than yours will."

Langdon let out a hoarse grunt, reminding me of how this had all started.

Bastian took a step back, leaving me cold and tight and empty. "Quickly."

The scuff of a foot on paving. Louder. Closer.

I dragged in a breath and turned to him. Just one second. I took him in for that briefest moment; I needed to. I needed reassurance this had really happened, or had almost happened, and that it wasn't a fantasy I'd conjured as I'd watched Lara and Langdon.

But no, he stood there, chest rising and falling a little too fast, a little too deep, a bulge in his trousers.

Head spinning, I turned and fled into the maze's shadows.

This had happened, and I wasn't entirely sure what it was or what it meant.

But one thing was sure: I had Bastian's attention.

23

I had to find my own satisfaction when I got to my rooms. I lay in bed thinking of Bastian, imagining he had me bent over that marble slab, fucking me, making *me* cry out. Twice I came, but I was still heavy and frustrated rather than tired and sated. When sleep finally claimed me, shadows invaded my dreams, with silvery eyes in their depths. My dream self was even more desperate than my waking self, because she plunged headlong into those shadows, chasing what those eyes promised.

The next day, I took a turn around the gardens with the queen and the other ladies-in-waiting. As we passed the arbour, another note arrived from Cavendish. I flinched when I saw it, like I'd been caught doing something wrong. It was ridiculous to feel guilty for thinking of Bastian as I'd touched myself last night. On a logical level, I understood there was no way Cavendish could know, but the unease that gripped me was anything but logical.

When I arrived, he stood over his chess set, back to me.

"Katherine." He drawled my name. "I hear you had an *interesting* evening." He turned, eyebrow raised, a smirk teasing his mouth. "Though you were interrupted before matters could proceed to everyone's *satisfaction*."

How did he know? And how would he react if he found out I'd taken my own satisfaction and thought of my target as I'd done it? I clasped my hands together against the urge to cross my arms, but I couldn't stop my cheeks burning. The small cuts on my palms from the roses smarted, helping my self-control.

"I'll ensure you're followed at more of a distance in future."

That doused the fire under my skin. "Follow... me?"

"You didn't think I'd leave you to wander the palace alone at night, did you?" He gave an indulgent smile as he stalked closer. "A beautiful creature like you, with this hair that's like a beacon." He shook his head and stroked his fingertips over a lock, following it down over my shoulder. "You never know what kind of dangers you might attract." His fingers, still following the wave of hair, passed my collarbone and crossed the expanse of my chest, getting closer to the swell of my breasts.

I'd seen how he reacted when displeased. If I pulled away, he'd surely do the same, or maybe worse. So I held my breath and kept dead still.

Somehow, I managed to swallow around my thick tongue. "Well, it's safe to say I have his attention." After what we'd done last night, we were practically lovers, and it was only a matter of time before we sealed the deal. The next time I had him alone, I wagered. As per my plan—no need to disgrace Lara.

His fingers stopped their progress, and his gaze snapped

to mine. "His attention, yes, but not his secrets, and not an assured path to them, either." Mouth flat, he turned his finger, wrapping my hair around it until it went taut and pulled me slowly closer. "This is the time, Katherine. Becoming his liaison will secure your place at his side, and where better to learn what he's plotting?"

"But I can get to his side—to his *bed* without becoming his liaison. Please, just give me a couple of weeks and it'll be—"

My scalp shrieked in pain as he grabbed a handful of hair and yanked until I fell against his chest. Tears prickled my eyes, but I gritted my teeth against making any sound.

Crying out would either anger him and earn further punishment or please him in some perverse way, so he'd make me do it again. The outcome was the same—he'd hurt me more.

My pulse roared, though, making all the sound I could not.

He pulled my head back, forcing my body to arch into his until I met his gaze. His was cold fire. "You"—he yanked my hair—"will"—he did it again—"become"—again—"his"—again—"fucking"—harder this time, so I had to bite my tongue to not whimper—"liaison. Do you understand?"

Each breath seared my lungs as I choked it down. It took several before I could speak. "Yes."

"Yes, what?"

"Yes, ser."

"You'd do well to remember your place, Katherine. You work for me. You are but a piece on my board. You can be replaced, those wages paid to someone else. Is that what you want?"

My face tingled. If I lost the house, I had nothing. No roof. No hope. No safety. Next time I saw my husband, I'd stab him in the eye for all I'd gone through to pay his debt.

Except I wouldn't. I'd just fantasise about it.

"No, ser." He wanted me to call him ser; I would oblige. I learned quickly.

"Good." He released my hair. "Sabotage her, blackmail her, kill her. Frankly, I don't care how you do it, just get rid of the girl. I'll take care of you succeeding her."

He said it like it was a kindness, like he was taking the lion's share of the work and I had just one simple task.

"If you don't deal with her, I will, and I guarantee you won't like my methods." He took a step back, but still held me pinned in his gaze. "You have one month."

24

I didn't raise Cavendish's behaviour with Ella. Maybe it was that I didn't want to make her dwell on anything he'd done to her. He'd employed her for longer. Surely she'd faced worse than I had, yet she worked with a cheerful smile.

Or maybe it was that I feared he *didn't* do it to her, that it was just me, because he saw some failing there, some flaw that needed correcting.

No more disagreeing with him or answering back. Head down, get the job done, and give him no more reasons to be angry with me. There was no point dwelling on those moments of aggression: I'd make sure there wouldn't be any more.

The days after that meeting passed quietly with no summons to Cavendish or encounters with Bastian. Even the weather drizzled, grey and bleak from dawn until dusk, keeping us cooped up indoors. That and my lack of progress with Bastian or my attempts to open his orrery had me restless with no outlet.

The one bright moment was my first payday. A thousand pounds in notes. And earned by working *for* the crown instead of by breaking its laws. I separated what I needed to return to my allowance. The rest I sent to Morag, together with a cagey letter explaining that a lady-in-waiting was a paid position. With a little luck, there would be no more difficult questions.

Thankfully, the day of the queen's picnic dawned bright and clear. Everyone important at court was invited, the Night Queen's Shadow included, and I took special care over my appearance. Blaze designed leather goods as well as gowns. When I'd complained about wearing floaty skirts for riding, because they left my legs bare, her answer had been to send an exquisite pair of thigh high leather boots.

I wore those today with a black gown made of several layers of sheer fabric that glittered darkly. It covered me from collarbone to wrists and ankles, though of course, she'd added slits to the skirt to allow me to ride easily... and show off those boots.

Somehow she'd constructed the layers so everything that needed covering remained hidden, but they shifted as I walked, becoming gauzy enough to reveal flesh here and there. It gave the sense that as I moved, you might catch a glimpse of something you shouldn't. But I'd tested it in the mirror, running, jumping, bending over, and dancing—not once did the dress fail me.

I had to give it to Blaze: she was something of a genius when it came to fabric.

When I reached the outer courtyard where everyone gathered, I was satisfied to see all the other ladies wore summer colours, sky blues, pale pinks, sunshine yellows. I stood out among them, like someone had torn through the day to reveal darkest night.

If my outfit didn't catch Bastian's attention, nothing would.

The courtyard bustled. Servants loaded carriages with cushions, blankets, and baskets of food, while us nobles readied and mounted our sabrecats. The ladies stood in small groups speaking quietly, while the men gathered with loud voices and even louder laughter.

I readied Vespera, checking the saddle, mentally preparing myself to see Bastian again. I wouldn't be embarrassed by what we'd done or nearly done; I had to secure my place as his lover.

Saddle and bridle fastened, I stood back and patted Vespera's shoulder when the queen emerged from the palace.

My body seized as Cavendish trailed behind her. His sharp eyes skimmed over the courtyard, expression a study in neutrality. He didn't so much as pause on me, and there was no flicker of *anything*. No sign of the fact he'd almost yanked the hair off my head the last time I'd seen him.

My blood boiled. I gritted my teeth and allowed my hands to ball into fists. No one was looking at me; this little reaction was safe.

When he disappeared into the crowd, I mastered myself, exhaling long and hard, before adjusting Vespera's bridle, even though it didn't really need it. Anything to keep my hands busy.

It was lucky I did, because past her, I caught a glimpse of hair unnaturally dark and flat, like it was a hole in the universe. Bastian.

Standing by his sabrecat, he spoke to Asher, who nodded and slipped away into the crowd.

Alone. Perfect.

I headed in that direction, as though walking past on some imaginary errand. I felt the moment he spotted me, like his gaze was a physical force that pushed my pulse to a dull throb.

I made it seem like a glance that just happened to land on him, stopping me in my tracks. I made it seem so casual, I should've been an actress on stage at one of the city's theatres. This was the height of coincidence.

What bullshit.

What I didn't have to fake was the way my skin flushed, suddenly warm despite the morning chill that clung to the air.

His silver eyes, somehow all the paler in the bright sunshine, skimmed over me, hard and sharp like a freshly honed blade. No surprise, he wore black. But the gods must've been smiling on me, because his jet buttons glinted and the black piping on his jacket gleamed, making it look like our outfits were coordinated.

Maybe it was a sign. I was pretty sure I didn't even believe in signs, but right now, I'd take anything that suggested I'd succeed.

"Bastian." I inclined my head. But instead of approaching him, I went to his sabrecat—the grey one he'd ridden when I'd stolen from him—and let the creature sniff my hand.

It chuffed, breath tickling my skin, as Bastian appeared at my side. "Kat." His voice was low, almost lost in the general chatter bouncing off the courtyard walls.

Court gave few opportunities for privacy, instead only allowing odd, half-private moments, like murmured conversations while dancing. This, bracketed between his sabrecat and Asher's, our voices soft, was one of those moments.

"It's good to see you." I kept my eyes on his cat, who

apparently accepted me, because it butted into my hand. "Though I almost didn't recognise you in daylight." *As opposed to pinning me against a wall in the dark, grinding against my arse.* Like that thought didn't have my thighs clenching, I gave him a sidelong look, laced with the slightest smile.

His expression remained neutral, but he placed one hand on his cat's shoulder. It wasn't quite a pat or a stroke, but it might've been for reassurance or a gesture to steady himself. After a beat of silence, he raised an eyebrow, gaze flicking to where I scratched his cat behind the ear. "How are your hands?"

He knew I'd left blood on that trellis. Two small cuts on my palms and one at the base of my finger. The wounds were small, red lines by now. One of Ella's concoctions had helped them heal without infection.

It had been worth it. Or at least it would've been if we hadn't been interrupted.

I held both palms up for his inspection, though it was also an invitation.

He craned over, hand leaving his sabrecat's shoulder, twitching in my direction, but it stopped there, then lowered to his side. A frown flickered between his brows and he nodded. "You heal quickly." He took half a step back. "I'm glad they won't get in the way of your ride today."

It was a battle not to let my shoulders sink. He should've taken my hands, looked more closely, maybe traced a line across my palm. *Something.* It would've been far less than he'd done on the dance floor.

This wasn't going to be as easy as I expected.

I pressed my tongue to the roof of my mouth in a bid to avoid the bitter taste of disappointment. I went back to fussing his sabrecat, whose eyes closed as he pushed into my touch. At least *someone* was enjoying my attention. I made my excuses and returned to Vespera.

Our encounter in the maze should've been a sign of progress, but here he was, acting even *less* flirtatious than usual.

Shit. I'd been so sure this was the start of an affair.

Skin prickling, I finished getting Vespera ready, mounted her, and went to find Ella. Her bright mood, pink cheeks, and slight hint of tiredness around the eyes told me that she had been making great progress with her target. Great fucking progress. All night.

I squirmed with the envy that slithered through me and told myself it was just that I wanted to be successful on my mission.

We set off quarter of an hour later, with the queen leading. Bastian rode at the back with Asher Mallory and Lara, who waved to Ella and me, giving us the perfect excuse to circle back to them.

Bastian caught my eye and held it, but continued his conversation with Asher. Maybe his grip on the reins tightened a little.

Maybe that was wishful thinking.

I fell in beside Lara, leaving Bastian with a lingering look, and let Ella lead the way in idle chatter. I tried to ignore the sour flavour coating my tongue, reminding me of what I needed to do to Lara. That, coupled with the position she'd been in the last time I saw her, made my side of the conversation stiff at first.

Ella had told me the reason for Lara's close attention. She didn't watch people's mouths in order to seduce them, but because an illness some years ago had affected her hearing. Now she relied on lip-reading to help her follow conversation. I tried to make sure the few times I did speak, I faced her.

As we left the gardens and reached the Queenswood, the men grew louder—the dukes especially. There was much talk of who was the fastest rider, whose cat was the strongest. They weren't measuring the speed of their mounts but the length of their dicks. I noted Bastian and Asher didn't get involved with that nonsense, neither did the men from Dawn Court.

Eventually, two dukes got into an argument that their friends decided could only be settled by a race, which of course the rest placed bets upon. The queen watched, eyebrow cocked in passing amusement, and placed a bet on Lord Eckington.

He was one of her suitors and he'd spent a lot of time with her at the last ball. Did her backing mean he had her favour? Or was it just about the race? I made a mental note to mention it in my next report to Cavendish, since he seemed interested in who she might choose.

Eckington's cat, a male, was tall with long legs. Most of those betting seemed swayed by that, putting their money on him. But his cat lacked the muscle definition of his opponent's. Lord Winthrop's female was a little smaller, but over the distance they proposed, her stronger muscles would win out. Maybe I could gamble my way out of debt where that idiot Fanshawe had gambled us into it.

Quietly, I placed my bet on Winthrop. It wasn't much, but it matched what everyone else had put in and only two others had wagered on him. I'd get a third of the prize pot when he won.

When. Not if.

Eyebrows rose, and a number of the men gave me patronising smiles. "Welcome to the game, Lady Katherine." A couple wished me luck before looking away with smirks that said they thought I'd need it.

Eckington led the way for the initial sprint, but, of course, Winthrop won. As I collected my money, a number of the dukes congratulated me on my "chance win."

But Winthrop just inclined his head to me with a private smile. He'd known his sabrecat was faster, and that smile said he realised my choice was no mere chance. "Maybe you should back me at Her Majesty's race. There are sure to be plenty of opportunities to wager for someone with a keen eye for a sabrecat."

Eckington scoffed as he drew level with us. "You may have won today on a simple flat, Winthrop, but there will be dozens on the field and the course is a complex one. You'll need more than the favour of Lady Katherine to help you even reach the top ten."

"And what about the favour of your queen?" The woman herself said as she joined us, eyebrow arching. A handful of the other dukes veered over, more interested now she'd arrived.

Winthrop's back straightened. "With that, I could win anything, Your Majesty."

"Oh, really? Perhaps I can make the race more interesting, since you're so sure you'll win it. As well as the prize money, I'll grant the winner a boon. Anything within my power to bestow, so long as it doesn't damage the nation, I will grant to the winner." With that, she rode on ahead, leaving me surrounded by half a dozen dukes and their cronies.

And thus began another argument.

I left them to it and circled back to Bastian, who was off to one side as Ella and Lara explained the forthcoming race to

Asher. Perfect—no one would be blocking his view of my outfit this time.

Out of the corner of my eye, I watched him watching me approach. He shifted in the saddle as his gaze snagged on my leg, and I bit back a triumphant grin. I owed Blaze a thank you.

"Those are interesting boots."

"Do you like them?" I flexed my leg and made a show of looking down at it. "They're new."

"They're..." His throat bobbed in a slow swallow. "I noticed them."

Make that a *big* thank you I owed the designer. Perhaps I could spare the money for a gift.

Straightening his back, he cleared his throat and turned to Lara. "And what's the prize for this race?"

My grip on the reins tightened, making the still-healing cuts sore. Gods bloody damn it. What the hells was he playing at? I'd seen the way his lips had parted when he spotted the boots hugging my thighs. He'd practically drooled.

And now he rode at my side, the back of his head to me.

More games to keep me off balance. It had to be.

Maybe that night had just been about getting information, and now I'd refused, he had no use for me. He could be attracted to me, but that didn't mean he'd pursue it.

"Every year it's the same," Lara said with her serene smile. No hint of the wanton woman I'd seen moaning with Langdon's cock in her. "Three thousand pounds."

I almost choked on my own tongue, barely disguising it as a genteel cough.

Three thousand. I'd heard about the race, but maybe that figure didn't mean anything to the other nobles I knew, because they'd never even hinted at the prize being so huge.

Schooling my expression to calmness, I didn't hear the rest of the conversation as we rode. I just stared ahead, wondering that people could win such a sum in the space of an hour and that the queen could so easily give it away.

The servants had gone ahead in their carriages. By the time we reached the meadow, they'd set up a circle of blankets and large cushions, plus a low, gilded chair and parasol for the queen. Tiered stands held cakes, sandwiches, and bite-sized pastries, savoury and sweet. Bottles of wine sat open, ready to be poured into crystal glasses, alongside teapots with steaming spouts.

The sight of the cakes filled me with a little flutter that was part pleasure, part relief. No need to feel guilty about spending on sugar, since these were made by the palace, with the bill footed by Her Majesty.

I said a silent *thank you.*

As the group spread out across the blankets, I dawdled at Vespera's saddle bags, putting my gloves away and retrieving my fan. All the while I covertly watched where Bastian sat and planned my path to him.

What better way to show off my new boots?

Perhaps today I'd throw *him* off balance.

25

No sooner had I taken a step in Bastian's direction than Lara called me over and patted an empty space between her and Ella. They sat a dozen feet from Bastian, Asher, and two other men who'd come with them from Dusk Court.

My smile was gritted as I made my way to her and took the offered seat.

"We'll leave them to their chatter," she said, bending closer to me as if sharing a secret. "I'm sure it's terribly dull."

Fanning myself and taking ladylike bites from insipid cucumber sandwiches, I made small talk with her and the other women in our little circle. At least Bastian and I were facing each other, so I made sure I draped myself over the cushions in one of the elegant poses Ella had shown me. Of course, my skirt just *happened* to part and reveal one of those boots he'd struggled to tear his eyes from.

I wondered what they'd made him think of, and my mind

enjoyed ambling in that direction while I pretended to listen to Lady Ponsonby's tales of her travels in Frankia.

While she regaled us, using her walking stick as a prop, Langdon, in the group behind me, passed over a platter of salmon and cream cheese sandwiches. His gaze lingered on Lara. I smothered my smirk by taking a second helping. His attention snapped to me as he arched an eyebrow, though I couldn't tell if it was at my expression or choice of food. I frowned and turned away, fighting the urge to fidget.

"Don't all turn around at once, ladies"—Ponsonby lowered her voice, leaning in—"but Lord Marwood keeps looking over here. And I don't think it's to check whether we have any sandwiches left." She raised her eyebrows. Though it was a delicate movement, the way her eyes widened gave it all the meaning of one of Ella's winks.

I took a sip of wine and glanced over the brim of my glass.

Sure enough, I found a pair of silver eyes pointed this way. He lay back, propped up on one elbow, one leg straight, the other bent, apparently at ease, but the way he watched me was anything but easy.

People always said, if looks could kill...

This was more a case of, if looks could fuck.

I'd have been in a lot of trouble. Delicious, trembling, whimpering trouble.

I gulped down my wine and reached for my fan, cheeks suddenly hot.

"Poor Lara," Lady Ponsonby went on, "I don't know what Her Majesty was thinking, putting you in his path. He's looking at you like he wants to... Well!" She shook her head, clutching her emerald necklace, which clashed nicely with how red her face had gone. "Do *unspeakable* things to you. And right in front of us all!"

Unspeakable things. Yes, please. I bit my lip.

Lara laughed and waved off Ponsonby's concerns. "He's never been the slightest bit improper with me. I'm sure you're mistaken." But she gave me the quickest glance out of the corner of her eye. Lady Ponsonby was mistaken about who Bastian was fucking with his eyes, but from Lara's angle, she had to realise it was me.

I kept my attention fixed on Lady Ponsonby as though she was suddenly the most interesting person in all the world.

She went on, "Thank goodness, that's all I can say. Have you *heard* his terrible reputation? Who he is? What he's done? A ruthless murderer."

It was a challenge to fight the sigh that wanted to blast from me. More Dawn Court nonsense about Bastian.

The two younger ladies sitting with us widened their eyes and leant closer. These were the two who'd whispered and laughed at me in the throne room. Sweet girls, if a little easily led. And Lady Ponsonby was only too glad to lead.

In an effort not to roll my own eyes, I grabbed the nearest cake from a stand and sat back, taking a bite.

"He killed his own father, don't you know?"

Yawn. I'd seen that one coming. I shared a smirk with Ella before finishing the little cake. Lemon and poppy seed—one of my favourites. Delicious and much less sour than Lady Ponsonby.

Lara's lips thinned. "I'm not sure we need to repeat such idle gossip. We've all heard that one by now."

"Yes, but did you hear how he followed it up by beheading a woman?"

Lara's eyebrows shot up, and though she smoothed her expression, it wasn't quick enough. She hadn't heard that, just as I hadn't. I shared a look with Ella, who gave the subtlest shake of her head.

"Not just any woman." Lady Ponsonby balled her little hand in a fist and shook it in the air, clearly thriving on our undivided attention. "But a *princess*."

One of the young ladies gasped. "What?"

"No! Surely not." The other stared at Lady Ponsonby, clutching her chest.

"I have it on good authority. It was the Night Queen's own daughter he murdered *in the palace*. A coup attempt some years ago. His father was involved somehow"—she waved her hand—"I don't know how. But this Lord Marwood executed him and then the princess. He would do anything for his queen. *Anything*. You mark my words"—she held Lara's gaze and nodded solemnly—"that man is dangerous. Merciless. The very worst kind of creature to walk this earth. You keep any relationship with him strictly business, or I fear where you will end up."

The beheading, the princess, the coup. Those details made it sound less like spiteful gossip from Dawn Court and more like it could be true. A tingling sensation that bordered on numbness spread across my cheeks.

Had he really done those things? It was a sobering idea.

And I didn't want to be sober.

I gulped down the last of my wine and topped up the glass, almost to the brim, before offering the bottle to Lara. She'd gone so pale, she looked like she could use it. Had my cheeks gone similarly ashen?

More sugar would help. I reached for a small, round coffee cake on the stand between me and the group behind us.

Langdon caught my eye and arched his eyebrow again, just as my fingers closed around the mouthful of caffeinated deliciousness. "Are you sure?" He drawled the question, like the answer was obvious.

I blinked, looked at the cake, in case there was a fly on it or something else that I'd missed. "What do you mean?"

"Well, all that cake on top of the sandwiches and pastries you've already eaten." He chuckled and I couldn't miss the way his gaze flicked down to my body—to the curve of my belly. "If you want to wear fae fashions, Lady Katherine, you can't have your cake *and* eat it. Though I daresay, by the look of you, you don't agree."

I stared. I blinked.

I had no idea how to be composed and ladylike. It was only when I clamped my mouth shut that I realised it had been hanging open. My chest tightened like all that earlier food was stuck there, and I kept swallowing, trying to force it down as my neck burned.

The chatter further away continued, but the fact I could hear it meant all conversation nearby had dried up. They had to be staring at me, thinking how Langdon was right.

Meanwhile, he'd shrugged and returned to quaffing wine.

My lashes fluttered as I looked down at my plate and placed the cake on it. It suddenly seemed less delicious.

There was a tinkle of something breaking.

Bastian sat up, shards of glass in his fist, red wine dripping onto his lap. But the look he directed at Langdon could've cut far deeper.

It wasn't a glare. It had none of a glare's heat.

It was pure cold, like ice. Like a promise not to kill someone here and now, but to plot and plan and execute the most perfect, the most exquisite revenge the world had ever seen.

Next to him, Asher sat with all the appearance of calm,

except he gripped Bastian's shoulder. The way his neck corded, I could tell he was having to hold him down.

I must've been having an odd reaction to the intense embarrassment that held me in its grip, because I could've sworn...

It looked like Bastian's black clothing was running into the picnic blankets, like ink spilling into water.

"Bastian," Lara gasped. "Your hand."

He finally broke away from staring at Langdon and blinked at Lara as though he'd forgotten about her existence and couldn't make sense of her words.

"You're bleeding."

He looked at his hand, finally straightening his fingers. Several pieces of glass fell from his grip, and it was only then I realised it wasn't red wine dripping—it was too deep, too crimson, too thick.

It was blood.

Apparently, that was of no concern, though, because his nostrils flared as his cold stare returned to Langdon.

And I needed smelling salts or a glass of good, strong brandy or *something*, because those black tendrils were still there, slithering across the blankets, coming this way.

Asher's knuckles went white on Bastian's shoulder, and the muscles in his jaw twitched. He muttered something, and Bastian finally exhaled and busied himself pulling shards of glass from his palm, fixing that with all the seething attention he'd speared Langdon with.

The tendrils of darkness stopped advancing, just swirling between cake stands and plates, pooling and eddying.

Could anyone else see that? Was I losing my mind? Had I drunk too much wine? But everyone else was transfixed, staring either at Bastian or Langdon.

Asher finally released his shoulder and gave Langdon a smile that carried all of politeness's cool distance. "Lord Langdon, I've heard that peculiar human phrase before. But I confess I don't understand it. What is cake for, if not eating?"

Langdon chuckled and opened and closed his mouth a few times before forming any actual words. "I... Ah... Well... It's..."

The conversation further along the picnic blankets died out, and more eyes turned our way. I wanted the shadows I was hallucinating to consume me—anything to avoid the attention.

Apparently unaware or unconcerned, Asher cocked his head, eyebrows twitching together as though genuinely confused. "What do you propose Lady Katherine does with cake, if not eat it? Or any of us, for that matter?"

Langdon cleared his throat. "No, I... it was only to say... I thought perhaps..."

Long seconds of silence opened up as he rubbed his cheek and tugged at his collar and failed to tell us exactly what it was he thought.

I sat very still, my own embarrassment forgotten as I drank up every moment of his squirming uncertainty.

Good gods, it was delicious. Even better than cake.

At last, Asher lifted his chin and looked down his nose at Langdon, eyes narrowing as his pretence of innocent enquiry faded. "How is it wrong to want to eat food? How is it wrong to want to enjoy small pleasures like a sweet morsel on a sunny day? Should we all be ashamed of wanting to have our cake and daring to have the audacity to"—he gave a mock gasp—"eat it too?"

Shaking his head, Langdon laughed, the sound strangled. "No, of course not. I only meant that Lady Katherine is—"

"Is what?" Bastian bit out those two words.

Langdon's eyes bulged at the picnic blanket, at the dark tendrils snaking across it, knocking over tea cups as they came this way.

They were real.

Others stared, too, now, mouths dropping open.

The shadows split and swirled around obstacles, including me. One brushed my skirt on its whispering way past.

Langdon babbled something incoherent, a bead of sweat trickling down his temple as the shadows—*Bastian's* shadows converged once they'd passed me.

"Lady Katherine is *what?*"

"L–lovely," the man spluttered, backing from the advancing darkness. "Beautiful. I didn't... She's—"

"She's far above you, Langdon." There was a flash of sharp canine as Bastian spoke. "Keep her name out of your mouth."

Langdon's head bobbed up and down over and over before he found his voice. "Yes, yes. Of course."

The shadows stopped, and it was only when Bastian nodded that they dissipated.

Silence rang out across the meadow, as though someone had a magic bell that cancelled sound and had struck it over us.

Lips pursed, Asher took Bastian's injured hand. He passed his fingertips over the torn flesh and a silvery glow lit up the point of contact. The skin around Bastian's eyes tightened as though it hurt. I'd heard rumours that one of the Dusk Court fae had the gift of healing, but hadn't realised it was Asher.

As they worked, people began to draw deep breaths and blink from Bastian to Langdon and back again. Several threw furtive glances my way but quickly ducked their heads, as though afraid to be caught looking at me.

"Well." Ella shook her head and went to take a sip from

her glass, then blinked down at the fact it was empty. By the time she'd rectified that, I'd downed mine in one go and held it out for a refill.

I wasn't sure whether I should kiss Asher and Bastian for shutting Langdon up so thoroughly or slap them for bringing so much attention my way. Much as I'd enjoyed Langdon's uncertainty and borderline terror, I also wished I could just dissipate into nothingness as Bastian's shadows had.

And those shadows.

Good fucking gods.

What the hells was that?

The Night Queen's Shadow. I'd thought it was because he extended the reach of her influence, acting as her eyes and ears. But this...

Who exactly had I been tasked with seducing?

Or should the question be, *what?*

26

It took a while for chat to resume, but eventually Lady Ponsonby shook her head and huffed. "And this is why they aren't allowed to leave the palace. Can you imagine *that* let loose on Lunden? On *Albion*? No one would be safe!"

I couldn't find my tongue, so I busied myself with the wine. It was the closest thing I knew to disappearing like Bastian's shadows had.

By the time we rode back to the palace, I was, I confess, a little tipsy. But I'd been riding long enough to ignore the way the world spun slowly. It also loosened my tongue. "What did Lady Ponsonby mean earlier? About leaving the palace?" I raised my eyebrows at Ella and Lara.

"The Dusk and Dawn delegations aren't allowed to leave the palace grounds. It's part of the terms of their visit. For... their safety."

The way she hesitated—she read the same thing into the rule that I did. It wasn't for their safety, but for ours. And that was exactly what Lady Ponsonby thought. *No one would be safe.*

Yet I'd seen Bastian on the road, not just outside the palace grounds, but miles outside Lunden. I bit back a laugh at the hypocrisy. To think he'd extracted a bargain from me to keep my secret, when I knew one that could also get him in trouble. Bloody bastard.

Lara shrugged, elegant even in that gesture, and carried on. "That's part of why they're allocated a human liaison like me. As well as helping them integrate with our court, I can procure anything they might need from the city."

Anything... or anyone. Did that mean she'd helped him bring Win to the palace?

But another idea batted that one out of the way. If Bastian had extorted a bargain from me in exchange for keeping my secret, maybe I could do the same to him.

It was time to give Bastian Marwood a taste of his own medicine.

We rode on in quiet before I excused myself and circled back to find the sneaky bastard. I smiled sweetly as I approached him, and his eyes narrowed as he broke off from his conversation with Asher. Maybe his inner alarm bells were ringing.

"A word." No niceties. Maybe that was what made him circle around to the back of the group with me, a discreet distance from anyone else.

He gave me an appraising look. "Are you all right?"

I blinked at him. He'd never asked me how I was before. I had to be misunderstanding his meaning.

"After Langdon." His jaw feathered.

"Oh. *That.*" I exhaled, not quite laughing at the unexpected turn. There was nothing I could do about the likes of

Langdon. Arseholes were always going to be arseholes. Dwelling on him wasn't going to help anyone or anything. It certainly wouldn't make me slim. "The fact I'm larger than most other ladies at court isn't news to me." I gritted my teeth and met his gaze. I didn't need pity. Pity wasn't useful.

Except the look he returned wasn't pitying. I couldn't quite place what it *was*, but there was no pity in the way it penetrated me. Reminiscent of his look by the arbour, perhaps.

But I hadn't ridden back here to get distracted by his silver eyes. I cleared my throat. "I have a bone to pick with you."

A flicker of surprise before he mastered himself and cocked his head. "Oh?"

"You lied to me."

"That's impossible."

I gave a low hum. Trust a fae to be into semantics. "Fine, then you misled me. Deliberately. You blackmailed me into owing you a favour when all the time you were breaking the law yourself. You aren't allowed to leave the palace grounds, but that first time I saw you..." I finished the sentence by raising my eyebrows.

It was a triumph to see his fingers tighten around the reins, even if he scoffed, shifting into that amused arsehole mode he so adored. "And, what? You're going to tell your queen that while you were out robbing folk on the highway, you found me slipping curfew?"

"But what if I didn't see you while stealing? What if I saw you while I, an aristocratic lady, was on my way back from a ball?"

Those perfect lips of his pressed together. I didn't dare drop eye contact, but I fancied that on the edge of my vision, shadows ghosted around his hands and feet. "What if you did?"

"I don't think the queen would be very amused. I imagine it would put a dampener on your attempts at diplomacy. Perhaps even get you sent home." I narrowed my eyes and pursed my lips, the perfect mirror of that expression he'd worn when he'd mused *hangman or axe* at our first ball. "I wonder how *your* queen would react to that."

His nostrils flared, and I couldn't describe the pleasure coursing through me at getting such an obvious reaction from him.

Gods, he was *so annoyed*.

And it was fucking glorious.

"And you're willing to risk me revealing the truth about you in order to get me sent home."

I smiled sweetly again. Because, damn, this *was* sweet— even better than the coffee cake I'd returned to my plate uneaten. "We already made a bargain, Bastian. You promised to keep quiet about my crimes in exchange for me owing you a favour." My smile shifted to something sharp. "You can't tell."

He exhaled, expression flattening to the bored one. "What do you want, Katherine?"

"A bargain, since you extorted one from me." My pulse grew heavier. Another bargain with a fae. Folly, perhaps, but I was already deep into that territory, and at least this time *I* was the one dictating the terms. "I don't tell. And in return, you pretend we're in a relationship."

His remarkable eyes widened, and for an instant, I could see the whites all the way around. "What?"

Cavendish was adamant that becoming Bastian's lover alone wasn't enough—I still had to replace Lara. But I hadn't entirely given up on my solution. Maybe, just maybe, if he heard I'd bedded my target, he'd give up on that awful idea of ruining the girl.

And even if he didn't, pretending to be Bastian's lover would give me plenty of excuses to be close to him so I could work on making it the truth.

Of course, I couldn't say any of that. Instead, I tossed my head as though what I was about to say was difficult to admit. "I have precious few allies at court. I don't have money, power, or influence. If people hear rumours about us, they'll think twice before they act against me."

Low-level rumours were safe, and although it wasn't my reason for doing this, they *would* give me some measure of armour. It was being caught in a compromising situation that might get me kicked out of court. A tricky tightrope, to be sure, but I lived on those.

His jaw worked for a moment before he spoke. "People like Langdon."

Langdon? I could've laughed. If he thought men like him were even in my top five worries, he was sorely mistaken. Not trusting my voice, I just lifted one shoulder.

"And rumours? *Really?*"

I nodded once. "Rumours. People have been hanged based on nothing more than whispers in the right ears."

"Hmm. What will this entail?"

"Then you agree?" I kept tight hold of Vespera's reins. He hadn't yet exhaled as he had on the road when he'd given in.

"I'm asking what I would need to do if I did." His shadows thickened, emphasising the irritation in his voice. "You want me to fuck you over the throne or...?"

I gasped, and Vespera took a step sideways at my sudden jolt. "Bastian! Good gods, this is still court—*Albion's* court. I want to start rumours, not a riot."

A flicker at the corner of his mouth told me I'd reacted just as he'd hoped. I could've sworn the darkest shadows swirled around his thighs, and I couldn't help but glance down at the thick muscles. *You want me to fuck you over the throne or...?*

Mouth suddenly dry, I cleared my throat and shifted on Vespera's back. "No, just... things that will make tongues wag. Dance with me. Spend time with me. Pretend the next piece of jewellery I buy is a gift from you. Let yourself be seen in the corridor where my rooms are. Maybe... Um... You could... touch my hand or something when we're in public." It was the first time I'd invited him to touch me. Considering the way he'd ground against me in the maze, it was ridiculous to be suddenly coy about it, but no one had told my tongue that. Damn wine, making my words clumsy. "Something that's not scandalous but also not entirely appropriate."

That perfect mouth spread into a wicked grin. "Not entirely appropriate." He said it slowly, like he savoured each word and the fact I'd said it. "You've just described my entire existence. Fine, Kat, you have a deal. I'll play your lover and ally and keep you safe from court vultures."

We said the words of power, sealing our bargain, and rode on a few more paces in quiet.

Quiet, that was, except for the pounding of my heart. I'd got my bargain. I'd bought myself time to spend closer to him so I could work on *actually* seducing him. It was a small victory, but then wasn't life made of those?

"I suppose I should call you Kat, even in front of people, shouldn't I? That would be *not entirely appropriate*."

When I looked up at him, he was wearing a look that was part sinful smirk and part... Well, the skin around his eyes tensed as he stared off into the distance.

Oh gods. *Thoughtful*, that was the other thing in his expression.

Yes, I'd made progress, but I'd also actively encouraged him. Calling me Kat in front of others was only the beginning.

What else might Bastian the Bastard of Tenebris class as *not entirely appropriate*?

27

The next time I saw Langdon, at the garden party, he had a broken nose. It shouldn't have filled me with a sense of satisfaction. And yet it did.

Especially when his eyes widened at me, and he strode off in the opposite direction. It seemed he had a knack for pissing people off. Well-deserved. I hoped whoever he'd angered this time had felt good watching him clutching his nose as it bled.

I filed it away to report to Cavendish. After the picnic, I'd told him about Lady Ponsonby's rumours of a coup attempt in the fae capital, Tenebris-Luminis. Maybe he'd also find it interesting to know some of the so-called gentlemen at court weren't entirely *gentle*.

Speaking of which...

I scanned the crowd for Bastian, but there was no sign of that blackest black hair amongst the folk lounging on cushions and low settees. Beyond the fire jugglers, an aerial performer spun slowly in a hoop suspended from a timber frame. She gleamed in the sun and for a moment I paused, unable to tear myself from her gold-painted skin, her compact, muscled figure.

You can't have your cake and eat it. Though I daresay, by the look of you, you don't agree.

The performer didn't look like she had her cake *or* ate it. Maybe she didn't even know what cake was.

I envied her muscles, but more than that, I envied how others looked at her. She was a marvel.

"A beauty, isn't she?" Ella appeared at my side, eyes fixed on the woman, who now tipped from the hoop, making my heart pitch. But she caught herself by the back of one bent knee and held an elegant pose that made it look like she was flying.

"And brave." I might've called it foolish, but the flex of her thighs as she held herself aloft told me she had every reason to believe in her own body. That we had in common—hard work had made my body strong, even if men like Langdon underestimated it.

"Bravery isn't only reserved for folk who throw themselves into physical danger... or off hoops." The corner of Ella's mouth twitched. "I saw Bastian receive a note a little while ago, then he headed inside. Maybe you can catch him on his own."

I laughed at the unsubtle change in topic. "Thanks. You're the best." I bumped my hip into hers and set off towards the palace.

Almost everyone was outside—all the courtiers and most of the servants, anyway—leaving the halls quiet. Motes of dust drifted past windows, lit by shafts of afternoon sun. My footsteps were a solitary *tap, tap, tap* across the stone floors, muffled only when I reached a thick rug. I checked the library, but it was dark. The billiard room, too.

When I turned onto the corridor that led to a small parlour, a tall grandfather clock was my only companion, its *tick-tock* forming an off-beat counterpoint to my feet.

I hadn't seen a servant or another soul in quarter of an hour, maybe longer. Living on the estate with just Horwich and Morag, I'd once been used to the quiet of a large, empty building, but now a shudder swept over my shoulders.

Someone had spilt water at the parlour door. Except, no, the curved shape suggested a footprint. In the palace, I'd never seen any sort of mess stay in place longer than a moment, but the servants were all outside keeping drinks topped up.

With a secret smile in place, ready in case Bastian was inside, I stepped over the water, opened the door, and entered.

Broken glass littered the wet floor, interspersed with crushed hyacinths and scattered petals. Their strong, sweet scent filled the air. Someone had knocked over a vase. I was already crouching down to pick it up when I saw feet peeking out from the other side of the coffee table. Dainty feet in pretty silk slippers.

"Hello? Are you—?"

But when I stood, I saw she wasn't all right.

Lara lay on the floor, staring up at the ceiling, hands fisted.

I hurried to her side. "Lara?" I tapped her cheek. Warm, but no response. "Lara? Can you hear me? Wake up." Shaking her shoulders did nothing, either. She didn't even blink.

And that was what set the dread creeping down my back. I held still.

She held more still.

No rise and fall of her chest. No fluttering pulse at her throat. Blueish marks ringed her neck.

I felt her pulse point. I found nothing.

She was dead. And those marks... Had she been strangled?

My lips and cheeks tingled, and breathing was suddenly an effort. The broken vase. There'd been a struggle. She'd been murdered.

Her hands rested on the floor up near her shoulders, fingers bent, and I understood now. She'd fought back.

Gold glinted from between her fingers. Had she managed to grab something in her struggle? Did it belong to—?

The doorknob turned.

The killer?

Come back for the item she'd grabbed. A clue that might lead back to them.

The door opened.

No time to pry whatever it was from her lifeless hands. No time to think.

I flung myself behind the floor-length curtains.

Breath held, I waited. No footsteps, but the door had to be wide open now. Whoever it was, they moved silently. Was that how they'd snuck up on Lara? But her expression hadn't been one of surprise, more... confusion. *Why are you doing this to me?*

Was it someone she knew?

My pulse thrashed through my throat in the place where I'd failed to find hers. I could barely swallow. I tried to listen, to get some idea of where in the room they were, but I could hear nothing beyond my thundering heart.

My lungs burned. I needed to breathe. But in the quiet of this room, that risked them hearing.

"Who's there?" The voice seemed to come from very far away, distorted like I was underwater.

I bit my lip, pressing myself into the wall. Why didn't I have a weapon? I didn't carry one at court. Not because it was

186

a safe place, but because its dangers weren't the kind to be solved by a dagger. Not usually, anyway.

I squeezed my eyes shut. *Please, gods. Please. I'll be good. I'll pray in the grove every day. I'll give you libation upon libation. I'll give you my blood. Just... please.*

The curtain twitched open.

I inhaled, ready to call for help. Maybe someone would hear. Please, gods, let someone hear.

"Shh." A large hand caught my breath before I could shout, and silver eyes looked down at me, wide for a moment.

Bastian.

He'd killed her.

And now he was about to kill me.

I panted against his palm. Maybe I could persuade him I'd keep quiet. Maybe I could—

"Kat? Did you do something? Do you need this to go away?" He glanced back at Lara's body.

I stared at him, taking a while to understand his meaning. He thought I'd killed her. And was that an offer to help? I swatted his hand away—he dropped it easily. "What? No! You..."

And then I remembered. He usually carried a dagger at his belt. I wasn't armed, but I could be.

It was shockingly easy to grab it and get the blade to his

throat. He didn't back away or try to stop me, just stood there, frowning.

"Did you do this?" I stared up at him, ready to catch the smallest, briefest reaction that might give him away. "Answer me straight—none of your fae twisting of the truth."

He exhaled, eyes closing. "I didn't kill or hurt Lara. I didn't in any way influence anyone else to kill her. I knew nothing about it until I walked into this room thirty seconds ago. And" —his shoulders sank—"I am sad at the waste of life, at the fact she won't smile or laugh or explain the finer points of human society to me ever again."

I'd been expecting a simple "I didn't do it," not a confession of mourning. I tried to flip the pieces of what he'd said, see how they might fit together differently. His lengthy answer made sense—it left no space to hide a lie between words that were only technically true.

"Why are you here, then?"

"I got a note that I *thought* was from you, but..." He huffed. "I'm guessing it wasn't. It even smells of you. Check my inside pocket—it's there."

Not taking my eyes off him or relaxing my grip on his dagger, I felt my way into his inside pocket and found a small piece of paper. In looping handwriting, it said, *Yellow parlour. Now. K.*

"I thought it was part of this fake relationship of ours." The corner of his mouth flickered when he said *ours.*

I bit the inside of my cheek. It made sense that he'd think the note was from me. It was a very specific prop to have in his pocket otherwise; he couldn't have known he would find me in here.

And yet, lowering the blade meant surrendering some measure of safety. It meant trusting him.

"Kat." His gaze skipped between my eyes. "I could've stopped you drawing my dagger, could've grabbed your hand before you got it anywhere near my flesh. But I let you take it."

"Why?"

"I knew you needed the reassurance that I'd tell the total truth, on pain of death."

"Pain of death? Hardly. It might hurt, but it won't kill you. I may be human, but I still know I'd need iron or aconite to kill your kind." Hence the purple flower's other name: faebane.

"Or a fae-worked weapon." The corner of his mouth rose, the picture of sardonic humour. "How do you think we go about killing each other?"

The filigree hilt peeking out of my grip showed stars and ivy in a design so elegant it couldn't be of human origin. Fae wove magic into fae-worked weapons. I'd always assumed that was just to make them better. A sharper sword. A gun that resisted the damp, like my pistol.

"This could kill you?"

"Yes. Just as easily as any dagger could kill you. Stab my heart. Cut my throat." He lifted his chin, letting the dagger touch his skin. "If you don't believe me, you may as well do it now."

Hand shaking, I lowered the blade. "I believe you."

He didn't snatch it away but caught my upper arms as I sagged back against the wall. "Are you all right? Not hurt?"

I shook my head, face still a little tingly. "There was something in her hand." I returned his blade and kneeled beside Lara, my eyes burning as the full weight of this hit me.

Dead.

Her unseeing stare was an accusation. But against who?

If we could find out, it might give her some peace. Hells, it might give me some. "I'm sorry this happened to you." I closed her eyelids, but that stare was etched in my mind.

Bastian crouched at my side and placed his hand on her brow. He murmured something in a lilting language I didn't recognise, head bowed. I didn't need to understand the words to know it was a prayer for the dead. Some things transcended language.

I waited for him to finish before retrieving the item from her hand. Her still-warm fingers pulled open easily, revealing a gold pendant in the shape of a seven-pointed star. At its centre glinted a brassy-yellow gemstone streaked with brown. The loop a chain would pass through was missing.

"Tiger's eye. And that star. It's a fae symbol for magical strength." His eyebrows pulled together, and his jaw hardened. "One of my kind did this... or someone working for one of us." He swept to his feet, dagger in hand, sharp gaze flashing around the room.

I couldn't keep mine from his pointed ears. He'd told me he hadn't hurt her, but he was fae. Then again, he didn't have to tell me where the symbol came from. He could've kept that quiet and left the field of suspects wide open.

A fae or someone working for them... or at least someone who had access to fae-worked goods. And Bastian brought here at this very moment by a message that *wasn't* from me.

"That note... Do you think it was luring you here?"

"I do." Tension coiled in his shoulders and thighs, ready to spring. "But was it to frame me or attack me?"

I shivered and slipped behind him. "I hadn't thought of that." But there were no large cupboards in the room—the only hiding place was behind the curtains.

He checked the others with a deft flick of his blade. No one.

His nostrils flared. "The flowers..." He frowned at the smashed petals. "Someone trod on them."

"The footprint outside. The killer left it on their way out."

"Hmm." He strode for the door but stopped short and turned back to me, mouth compressing. "I need to get you somewhere safe. They can't be far. Even if it was just a lone attacker after her, he might come back for that pendant and find you. Come on."

I took a step closer, ready to obey. And yet...

I bit the inside of my cheek and planted my feet, chest growing tight at my small rebellion. "No. Maybe those footprints carry on. With your sense of smell, you can follow the scent of hyacinths, right? But if you waste time taking me to safety, it will fade and you might never pick up the trail."

He watched me for long seconds, evaluation and something else in his gaze. Finally, he exhaled in defeat. "It wouldn't be time wasted," he muttered. "But... otherwise you're right."

He reached under his jacket and pulled out another, smaller knife, then offered me the hilt. "Do you know how to use one of these?"

"Hmm, I can't remember." I screwed up my face and took it between finger and thumb as though it was something I'd found on the floor. "Which end do you poke them with again?"

"Didn't think you'd be the type to joke at a time like this."

His judgement made me wither, and I muttered, "I'll take any distraction I can get."

After a long look, he nodded once. "Just because you know which end is sharp, doesn't mean you know how to use it. I need to know how much I should prioritise protecting you if we do get into a fight."

"Pistols are more my thing." I held the dagger properly. "I'll give this a good go, though."

"Understood. Stay close." He led the way, sharp eyes on that wet spot in the doorway.

I lingered and looked back at Lara.

"There's nothing we can do for her here." His voice was soft. "She's dead; we aren't. I intend to keep it that way. But we might be able to find out who did this." When I looked up, he held out his hand.

I took it.

It was easy at first—wet footprints led down the corridor in the opposite direction from the way I'd come. If I'd taken a different route, I might've bumped into the killer. I swallowed, grip on Bastian's hand tightening.

He looked up and down each hallway we came to, paused at corners, tension etched in his corded neck.

The thunderous quiet of the palace pressed on my ears. "Do you think there will be a fight?" I asked in an attempt to distract myself and beat back the silence. "Won't they give up when you find them?"

"If it's just one person, perhaps. But... even then, I doubt it. Not with the punishment from your queen—both against them, but also their court."

Of course. If the murderer was fae, their guilt would taint whichever court they'd come from.

"And if it's an attack on Dusk or an attempt to frame us for an attack on your court, they might've sent a strike team from Elfhame. Half a dozen, perhaps. All fae. All trained. All faster than one of your kind could hope to be. It's what I would do."

With that cheery thought, we crept on further. There weren't any more obvious footprints, and he paused at intersections, nostrils flaring as he sniffed the air. The palace's emptiness brought goosebumps to my flesh.

They'd planned this. Whoever it was had used the garden party to get Lara utterly alone.

Had she cried out, hoping for help? We'd all been outside, drinking and laughing, watching the acrobats and selecting the tastiest canapés.

While she died in there, someone's fingers fastened around her neck.

Just as I realised I was trembling, Bastian stopped at a corner and tugged me against the wall. He pressed a finger to his lips. "I hear something," he breathed in my ear.

I held my breath. Nothing. Too quiet for my human ears.

He peeled away from the wall.

Except, he was also still against it.

I screwed my eyes shut, opened them again, but there were two Bastians. One strode around the corner.

"I think I'm having an episode," I whispered, massaging my temples.

"You're not. You saw what you saw." He squeezed my hand.

"Two of you? How does that work? A twin? An illusion? Or... something else?"

"Something else. Another part of me that can be separated sometimes. He's as solid and real as I am here." He threaded his fingers through mine, thumb brushing over my knuckles. He hadn't let go since we'd left the parlour.

I hadn't expected Bastian the Bastard to be quite so reassuring in a crisis. Useful, yes. But not reassuring.

"He'll—*I'll* draw out anyone planning to ambush us."

I peered at the corner but didn't dare look around it.

"Don't you need to keep an eye on him? What if he gets attacked?"

"I can see and feel what both parts of me are doing, a bit like you can feel both hands. Admittedly, it's easier to focus if both parts of me are in the same place. If he's attacked, we'll join him and give the enemy a nasty surprise." His teeth flashed fiercely.

"Won't they expect it, though?" His reputation did tend to precede him.

"I find it beneficial to keep this a secret. I'd appreciate it if you did, too." He angled his head like it was a question.

"Of course." I glanced at the corner again. There had been no sound of an attack. Not yet, anyway. "I bet having two of you is useful in a fight."

He smirked, eyes glinting. "And other times."

I frowned. With all the work that needed doing on the estate, I'd have found it useful to have two of me, but I suspected that wasn't what he meant. "Like when?"

Fingers laced with mine, he tugged me closer, so only an inch separated us. His warmth crossed the gap, chasing away the goosebumps that had plagued me all the way through this empty palace. "I wouldn't want to scandalise the terribly proper Lady Katherine." There was a flash of canines in a wicked grin.

My breath caught as I understood. Two Bastians. The only thing that might be better than one.

He opened his mouth as if to say more, but his gaze went off to one side, distant, and his grip on my hand flexed.

Shoulders sinking, he huffed. "A bloody house cat. It's clear." He bent and whispered in my ear. "I hope that little distraction helped. Come on."

I'd joked in a crisis. Now he'd flirted in one. We were both damned.

We continued along the corridor and caught up with his second self. The Bastian holding my hand stepped into the same space as the other. For a second I had the dizzying sensation of seeing double before their bodies aligned and there was only one.

We threaded deeper into the palace and the moments he had to pause at intersections grew longer and longer. The tension in his shoulders wound proportionally tighter.

After five minutes at the foot of a staircase on the second floor, I touched his arm. It was the first time I'd initiated any contact between us, and it wasn't for anything to do with my mission to seduce him. "Bastian, do you think they're gone?"

His head bowed. "The trail's faded. I can't…" He shook his head, deep lines scoring between his eyebrows.

I wanted to smooth them away with my fingertips, with a kiss. It was a ridiculous, fleeting thought, no doubt brought on by the unbearable apprehension of creeping after unseen intruders and the horror of finding poor, sweet Lara.

"That's it. They got away, and we've found nothing."

"Not nothing." That word 'intruders' stuck in my mind like a burr. "The trail… it didn't lead us to the nearest exit. This wasn't someone trying to escape."

He lifted his head, eyes widening. "Not out of the palace but deeper into it."

This wasn't an attack by an outsider—a stranger in our midst.

Someone at court had killed Lara.

29

Despite the trail going cold, Bastian was intent on doing his own sweep of the palace before finding the guards. Since I would slow him down and we were already near his rooms, he insisted on leaving me—and the pendant—there. "It's the safest place in the building."

I eyed the double doors leading into his suite while he fished out a key. "They don't look sturdier than any other doors."

"Didn't I tell you before? Nothing is as it seems." He turned the key, then placed his hand on the door and paused. The air hummed like distant conversation, making the back of my neck prickle. Then he opened it.

"So, magically safe."

He only gave an enigmatic smile and ushered me in.

As a diplomat from a foreign realm—especially one with powerful magic—it was no surprise that Bastian's suite was much larger than mine. Still, its lavishness slowed my steps.

Huge windows looked west—where the sun would later

set, I noted. Someone had chosen this suite not only for its size but with care for Dusk's affinity with sunset.

Thick carpets muffled my footsteps. Three more sets of double doors led elsewhere—a bedroom, bathroom, and a private dining room, perhaps. We'd entered a sitting room with gilded and lacquered furniture, not too much, not too little. At one end sat a large, ornate desk, which Bastian stood over, tidying some papers. Making sure I wouldn't find any state secrets?

I exhaled, shoulders sinking. That's exactly what I was meant to be doing.

After everything with Lara, I still had a job to do. And maybe that job had something to do with her death. After all, hadn't Cavendish said he didn't trust the fae and suspected them of plotting against us? Perhaps this attack was an attempt to drive a wedge between Dusk and Albion and keep their suitor out of the running.

Speculation, all of it. But it was worth considering, worth seeing whether I could find any evidence to support or disprove it.

Bastian crossed the room and prodded the wood in the fireplace, scowling.

"I thought you were going to check the rest of the palace and raise the alarm?"

He gave a low hum, swiping a box of matches from the mantlepiece. "Are you warm enough, though? I don't want to leave you—"

"I'm fine. It's a warm day."

His scowl deepened, fixed on the matchbox he fiddled with. "But humans feel the cold more than—"

"Not that much more." I crouched and placed my hands over his, stilling them. "I'll be fine. You said this was the safest place in the palace. It's a sunny day. I'll be safe from attackers *and* freezing to death."

"I thought it was you." A certain roughness in his voice scraped over me.

"What do you mean?"

His throat bobbed before he looked up. There was something in his eyes I hadn't seen before. I couldn't quite place it, but it wasn't sharp or soft. It was as though, rather than his usual piercing gaze, something had pierced *him*.

"When I walked into that room and saw Lara's feet and caught your scent, I thought it was you."

"Oh." It came out of me, barely more than a breath. I could've sworn it looked like he cared. Which was preposterous. But...

"I didn't want it to be *her*, either. And I hate that I failed her. But I really thought..." With a shake of his head, the vulnerability vanished and he pulled from me and stood. "Don't get killed, Kat. I don't want to have to continue our lovers' act by throwing myself into your grave." He took a step back. "It would be inconvenient to clean the dirt off my best trousers."

I raised an eyebrow. "You'd wear your *best* trousers? I'm touched."

He laughed. "Keep finding those distractions where you can. I have a feeling we're going to need them."

Before he left, he pointed out a couple of decanters and a tin of biscuits and told me to help myself. The door closed. The lock clunked. For a second, the air hummed with magic. Then I was alone.

First, I poured myself a brandy. A large one. My breaths were still a little shaky, and the rhythm of my heart hadn't quite settled back to normal. This would help.

Then I tested the doors. The ones he'd exited through didn't even rattle, as though magic held them fast against the frame. Another set was the same. The other set of double doors opened to a small dining room. The rich, dark colours and the intimacy of its round table made the space feel private. I could imagine sitting in here, chatting over dinner, putting him at ease, then sitting in his lap and bringing his arms around me...

I sucked in a breath, took a warming gulp of brandy, and strode out to check the final set of doors. They led to a huge bathroom with a sunken bathtub that could fit four people comfortably.

"It pays to be a diplomat." I snorted into my drink and trailed around the bath. "Or at least the Night Queen's Shadow." Somehow I doubted the other suitors' companions had a bath big enough for me to float in, arms and legs outstretched without touching the sides.

If... *when* I snared Bastian, I would make sure this got used, with him or without. My muscles ached with longing.

Back in the sitting room, I circled, sipping brandy, looking for signs of him rather than the palace's hospitality. On one end table, I found a pile of books on Albionic history. Amongst them sat a lone volume on etiquette with a scrap of paper in the front.

Thought you might find this useful. Do try to obey the rules. Lara.

It made me pause and hold my breath as I fought a terrible pressure at the back of my eyes.

I drained my brandy and hurried across the room to top it up.

In a fruit bowl, I found shards of a broken vase. The blue and white ceramic design was one I knew—an import from the east, commonly seen in stately homes. Expensive for most people, but not something a wealthy aristocrat would consider special. Certainly not something that could stand up to the impossible elegance of fae designs. Besides, why keep it when it was broken?

The locked door had to be his bedroom—there would be more personal touches in there. If it didn't have the same magical closure on it as the main doors, I might've tried to pick the lock. Not that I could, but maybe I'd get lucky jiggling a hairpin in there. I scoffed and swirled my brandy. I'd have to ask if Ella knew the trick and could show me; it seemed like a useful skill for a spy to have.

Finally, I checked the desk, which seemed my best bet for finding something of interest to Cavendish. A few papers sat on top—all invoices for boring things like books and sabrecat hire. Lore said the fae rode deer rather than sabrecats as we did, and this was confirmation he'd hired this one to blend in with us. If I'd seen him riding a stag that night on the road, I'd have known straight away he was a fae. And it would've given him away as he'd left the palace.

"Hmm. Sneaky, Bastian. Very sneaky."

He must've tidied away anything more exciting. But the top drawer sat not quite flush with the front of the desk, as though it had been closed in a hurry.

"Maybe not so sneaky."

Inside sat a note. Simple, nondescript handwriting said:

New drop location—last is compromised.

Cavendish had called the loose tile where I was to leave him messages a "drop point." So, Bastian was spying, feeding information to someone.

Below the text was a crude drawing of a map. It showed a series of cloud shapes that looked like trees, a branching road, and a star marking a point inside a rectangular building.

Except... I blinked at it. There was something familiar in the layout.

Not trees, bushes. Not roads, but paths. And the rectangle was... "The arbour."

Glancing at the doors, I bit back a laugh. At last, information I could use. Bastian had helped me today, yes, but I still had a job to do, especially if I wanted to keep it. Losing it meant losing my home. Not an option.

And... this was bigger than me. Bigger than my estate. If Bastian was gathering information on our court, he might be planning to use it against us. Even if he wasn't, the person he was giving it to might.

I found a sheet of paper and copied the note and map carefully. I was fairly sure I'd identified the correct location, but there might be something else hidden in the message that I hadn't spotted, but the spymaster would. If I did well, he'd promised me extra money.

And if I pleased him, there would be no more yanking on my hair or slamming me into walls.

There was nothing else of interest under the note, so I replaced it and left the drawer as I'd found it. The others were locked, and the rest of the room revealed nothing more about Bastian.

So, I paced and drank brandy until my limbs were too heavy to keep it up, when I curled up on the settee and watched the doors.

For all my earlier bravado, it grew a little chilly as afternoon approached evening, so I took a coat from the stand by the door and pulled it over myself. Of course, I took the opportunity to top up my drink before settling back in my spot, surrounded by the scent of cedar and bergamot and warm, rich brandy.

The next thing I knew, I blinked, groggy, finding myself hugging the empty tumbler. The room was dark, but a deeper shadow stood over me. Glowing silver eyes pierced the darkness.

"Bastian?" I sat up, rubbing my face. "What's the time?"

"Almost midnight. I didn't mean to leave you locked up so long. There were more questions than I expected." I could hear the edge of a rueful smile in his voice. He offered his hand and I let him help me up.

"Did you find anything?" I held out my makeshift blanket. "Sorry, I did get a little chilly after all."

He made a dismissive sound and took the coat. "Nothing. No sign of forced entry, intruders, or any other attack. I told them about the pendant, but they haven't asked to see it. I find their incompetence... irritating." He paused and shook out the coat, then swept it around my shoulders. He took a long while pulling the edges together, eyes fixed on that simple task. "I suppose you want to go back to your rooms."

I raised an eyebrow. Since he could see in the dark, it didn't feel like an entirely wasted gesture. "Where else am I meant to go?"

"You could stay here. I'd prefer that; I know it's safe."

It took some time for my tongue to remember how to

work. Would he let me stay in his bed? *With him?* Or would he be hit by a sudden attack of uncharacteristic nobility and insist on sleeping out here on the settee? That would give me a chance to investigate his room... and then I could use the opportunity to...

I swallowed, face warm. For all that Ella had shown me the little touches and loaded looks that were the tools of seduction, I somehow couldn't fathom piecing them together to use on Bastian. Coming out here and sitting beside his sleeping form on the settee. Saying his name in a low, seductive voice. Cupping his cheek with my palm. It seemed clumsy. Ludicrous. Too much. Not enough.

Not when I wanted to stretch along the length of his body, taking in every hard muscle, absorbing his warmth, letting his hands plane up my back as mine reached into his hair.

Shit. I wanted that.

Not just as a means to the end of getting information from him. But just for the sake of it, the feel of it, the delicious luxury of it, as intoxicating as the fine brandy from his decanter.

And that was dangerous. As far past safe as it was possible to get.

I needed some space, some air. To get my brandy-addled self away from Bastian and his silver eyes that rested on me with far too much intensity.

And I needed to get this copied note away from him, too. Its stiff, folded shape was a reminder poking into the sole of my foot. With the lightness of fae fashions, my shoe had been my only hiding place.

"Kat, are you—?"

"I can't stay here." I laughed like he was ridiculous to even suggest it. "That's *too* inappropriate. It's bad enough that I've been here all afternoon, but at least we can blame that on... on..." But I couldn't bring myself to reference Lara's murder.

Which I'd used to get into his rooms and gather information. Practical. So very practical of me.

A weight settled in my stomach and I started for the door, pulling his coat from my shoulders.

"I'm walking you back." He appeared at my side, tugging the coat back into place.

Knowing him even as little as I did, it would've been a waste of breath to object.

I led the way in silence. The corridors were as eerily quiet as before, but every candle and wall sconce had been lit, leaving the hallways blazing.

He didn't try to take my hand as he had earlier, but he walked close enough that his arm kept brushing mine. A reminder that I wasn't alone, even as Lara's eyes swam into my mind. This time, the accusation in them was on me.

You used my death.

You used me to get information from him.

You want to use me to get close to him, to drape yourself over him, to give yourself to him.

I couldn't lie. I wanted distraction even more than I had earlier. If I'd stayed in that suite a moment longer, I might've thrown myself at him. Not for my job, but just for the numbing nothing of my body being used however he wished. Then I'd have downed the rest of that brandy and thanked the gods for the oblivion.

I wasn't sure I deserved distraction though. And I wanted to know...

I swallowed down the salt in my throat. "Is she...?"

"There's a mortuary nearby. I made sure they did it

respectfully. Your queen has said she'll pay for a lavish funeral."

The word *funeral* settled over me, cold and light, like a death shroud. It would be final. Concrete. Marking the end of Lara's last journey.

My eyes burned, and the corridor blurred.

When we reached my suite, he insisted on sweeping the rooms to check for danger. I didn't have the energy to argue. He checked in cupboards, the bathroom, under the bed, behind the curtains. He lingered by the rose in its pot, then drew the curtains and set about lighting every candle and lamp.

I watched all of it, leaning against the bedroom doorframe.

"It's clear," he announced at last. He said nothing about the tears on my cheeks, but his gaze followed their trails and his eyebrows clenched together. He produced a handkerchief from his pocket. After a few seconds, he pressed it into my hand and backed away.

"Good night, Kat. Sleep well. Dream of nothing."

30

Maybe it was my subconscious obeying his instruction, but I didn't dream that night.

My relief only lasted that long, though. The next day the palace was a strange subdued place. When I walked down to the drawing room where the queen had summoned all her ladies-in-waiting, everyone fell silent and watched me pass. Even the servants slowed their work and let their wide eyes follow me.

In the drawing room, I found the other ladies-in-waiting gathered around the queen, everyone dressed in the black of mourning. It made their faces look paler when they turned and stared. The queen had me sit next to her—unheard of since I'd arrived—and had the others bring me brandy and cake, even though it was still morning. I didn't turn either down.

Alcohol and sugar. Just what I needed.

She took my arm and looked at me with something approaching kindness as she asked about yesterday and my "ordeal." The others crowded round, eyes wide. Their looks weren't only full of curiosity, the kind that swarmed around gossip like flies around shit, but behind that, hidden beneath their folded hands and the appearance of calm obedience...

Fear.

Lara had been killed. But we knew nothing of the culprit or their motive.

It could have been any one of them—of us.

Court wasn't just an intriguing game—it was a deadly one. It had cost Lara her life, and she was one of the queen's favourites, with Langdon as a powerful ally. How could I even hope to survive? I had no allies. I didn't know the rules or how to play.

Knowledge was power, so some old philosopher had said. So I gave them the knowledge I had—everything that was safe to share, anyway. I kept secret the pendant I'd found in her grasp. If the rest of it could save any one of them from the same fate, it was worth reliving my fear.

The world continued to be strange over the following days. All events were cancelled. A nine o'clock curfew was put in place by the palace guard, even though she'd been murdered in the middle of the afternoon. Maybe Bastian was right about their incompetence. Or maybe they just wanted to reassure us by doing *something*.

Everyone treated me with varying combinations of sympathy, suspicion, and curiosity, and that watchful silence followed everywhere I went. Only Ella behaved with something approaching normality, though her cheeks were pale. When she agreed to show me how to pick locks, she hugged me tighter than usual.

I didn't see Bastian.

But there was a glimmer of good news in the form of a

reply from Morag. The palace's increased security delayed its delivery, but she reported that the books were at last moving in the right direction. She'd sent an overpayment to the bailiff, and Horwich had started working on various smaller repairs to the estate.

Meanwhile, the queen kept us ladies-in-waiting close. All meals were taken with her. We attended her in the bath. And she developed a deep fascination with a series of romance novels recently translated from Frankish.

Of course, as soon as word got around, the work of the author Madame Sergeanne became something of a craze. We were all gifted copies and ordered to read so we could entertain Her Majesty by discussing them. "It will be a club," she announced, eyes bright as she handed me the book tied with a lush black ribbon. We were still in mourning, after all.

She caught my hand before I turned away and leant close. "Katherine." She cupped my cheek, and I had to keep the shock from my face at the gentle intimacy of that gesture. "You look tired. I hope this is a distraction for you. Go and read and enjoy. *Memento mori.* Take pleasure while you can."

Her mood didn't last, though. By lunchtime, she'd snapped at Ella, snatched the teapot from Lady Ponsonby and poured her own drink, and told a younger girl to begone from her sight. At last, she dismissed us all.

I couldn't say I was sorry. We'd been cooped up for a week with no events to break up the monotony of each other's company.

New book in hand, I hurried to my room, grabbed my copy of Bastian's note, and made a beeline for the garden. Between the queen's demands and our curfew, there'd been no chance to check his drop point, and Cavendish hadn't responded to my message saying I had news. I shouldn't fish around for a package or note at the drop point, not without instruction, but I wanted to check the diagram matched. It would make my information more useful to him.

Whether it was information I should be passing him was something I tried not to think about too closely. Not after the way Bastian had seemed so keen to keep me safe the day of Lara's murder.

When I stepped out into the sunshine, I took the deepest breath I'd drawn all week. It tasted of damp earth and growing things. Fresh mint and rosemary. Savoury thyme and sage. The woody, sappy scent of cedar that tugged my mind to the borrowed coat still hanging in my rooms.

Birdsong drifted on the air, and squirrels darted up tree trunks as I passed, their red fur almost the same colour as my hair. I crossed the grassy paths, wishing I could take my shoes off and walk barefoot as I would on my estate. But that wouldn't do, even if there was no one around to see.

While I loved being out here with life to combat the death choking the palace's halls, maybe others avoided its contrasting reminder. I only glimpsed one other person on the far side of the gardens.

I reached the arbour and dared a quick look at my copied map. Yes, the angle of the paths was the same, the location of the rose bush fitted. This was the spot. Sweet honeysuckle and rose hung thick in the air, lulling me. I could enjoy it after I'd done my work.

I checked again for anyone nearby before reaching under the wide bench. A crossbar beneath the seat formed a nook where a package or message could be left. Empty for now, though.

Smiling, I re-folded the paper. The need for black clothing had me re-wearing the shimmering, layered gown from the picnic. However, its lightness left nowhere to hide the note, so I slotted it in the back of the book and settled down to read.

By page three, my eyes had grown round.

Smut. The queen was obsessed with *smut*.

Already the heroine was splayed out on a staircase with a prince's head between her—

A shadow passed over me, and someone plucked the book from my hand. "What have we here?"

It took me a long and stupid second to realise it was Bastian standing there, holding the book, gaze raking over its pages.

Oh, good gods, no. Not this book. Not with the copied note nestled in the back.

I dived at him, but he caught my wrist without looking away from the pages. His eyes widened and flicked to me, then back to the book as a smirk dawned on his lips.

I grabbed for it again, but he spun me around and pulled me against him, both arms pinned to my sides, as easily as he had on the dance floor. He backed us into the shade of the arbour, and I fancied his shadows thickened the darkness.

"*Katherine.*" He spoke with his cheek pressed to mine, stubble prickling as he held the book open before us.

The note hadn't slipped out. Yet.

"First I catch you spying and now you're reading smutty books."

"It was a gift from the queen." I wriggled in his grasp, but that only pressed me harder against him. "Please give it back."

"'Please'?" His voice dropped an octave. "You know I love it when you say please."

I was right back in the maze, flooded with the feel of him, the scent, the idea that he might fuck me then and there. I sucked in a sharp breath, chest suddenly too tight.

But this wasn't the maze in the dead of night. We were out in the gardens, the sun high. Anyone might see.

Besides, he didn't mean this. He just loved to watch me squirm. Literally.

And my incriminating copy of his note was one jolt away from falling out of that book.

"What do you want, Bastian?"

"You look tired." The teasing tone disappeared from his voice as it went quieter, as though it was an admission he didn't want others to hear. "Like you could use a distraction. And besides..." He brightened, right back to the smirking bastard of moments ago. "I'm curious about what you're read-ing. Hmm. Let's see..." He cleared his throat and turned his mouth to my ear. "'The prince laid her upon the chaise longue, pushing her skirts up, all the while claiming her mouth with his, drinking up her very essence with the depth of his kiss. "*Ma chérie*," he whispered, causing her to feel quite sweet and heavy and wet with longing...' Blah, blah, blah, talking, talking, talking." He flicked the pages with his thumb. "Ah, here's the good stuff. 'His fingers played her until she cried out in glorious completion, and at last, he unleashed his—'"

"Stop it."

"'—throbbing member.' Stop it? Oh, Kat, I can't. This is just too delicious. *Throbbing member.*" His dark laugh rumbled into me. "It isn't Kat I've found in the gardens today, is it? It's the Wicked Lady." His grip around my waist tensed, and he made a low, thoughtful sound. "Or," he whispered against the side of my neck, "is it my ember?"

A shiver ran away with me at the reminder of how he'd promised to make me burn.

His lips trailed over the tight, sensitive skin of my neck,

leaving a blaze in their wake. My back arched, as involuntary as the shiver, bringing me achingly close to finding the friction I sought.

I counted my breath in and out, trying to quench the unbearable heat of my cheeks. "Why are you torturing me?"

"Torture? You asked me to pretend to be your lover. I'm only doing as you wish."

"Our fake relationship is meant to be *subtle*, not you rubbing up against me in the gardens."

"You're doing your fair share of rubbing right now." He chuckled and loosened his grip as though to prove it. My body stayed against him, though I could pull free. "Not that I'm surprised after you've read this. Remember what I said before, Kat. You say stop, I stop. That can mean stop right now or for all time. Your choice. I'll never tease you again, if that's what you ask. Do you want me to stop?"

I couldn't say yes because it was a lie. And I lied all the time, but this was one my body wouldn't tolerate. It would've been a betrayal.

Yet neither could I say no. That wasn't allowed. Not for Lady Katherine Ferrers. Even if she was being paid a princely sum to seduce this man. Her need for cash couldn't blot out what she'd been moulded into.

Obedient. Dutiful. Silent.

I wasn't cut out for this. I couldn't play the perfect lady and then fuck a man in the centre of the palace maze as Lara had.

Eyes screwing shut, I let my head drop back onto his shoulder in defeat.

There was a flap of paper and a thud. Then his fingertips grazed my jaw, turning my face towards him. I couldn't bring myself to look. It would be an admission. It would make this real. And if it was real, then I should be telling him to stop.

He touched his forehead to mine. "Are you ashamed?" His voice was gentle.

The only answer I could give was opening my eyes.

"Your pretty pink cheeks say you are." He stroked one cheek, then kissed the other. "You shouldn't be, though. Do you want the things in that book?" He nodded to the floor, where it lay discarded.

No sign of the note. I let out a breath. "Why do you do this to me?"

"Do what? This?" His fingertips trailed down my throat, feather light, and circled the hollow at its base, just above the pearlwort necklace.

"Everything in your power to put me off-balance."

"Oh, this isn't *everything* in my power, sweet ember. But it's everything you've consented to. I could go much further, if you wished it." His hand ventured down, passing over the swell of my breast, winding my body tighter until he grazed my nipple.

I couldn't help the groan he dragged from me or the way my head dropped back, this time in something closer to surrender.

"That's it. No shame in pleasure. No shame in your body."

"But why?" It mattered. He hadn't asked me about the orrery this time, so he wasn't using my pleasure against me. And yet it still felt dangerous, control slipping from my grasp.

Maybe it was more dangerous because I didn't know what game he was playing and that left me a piece for him to move across the board.

He made a thoughtful sound. "I'm trying to work you out. The first time we met, you pointed a pistol at me and forced me to choose between my money and my life." He circled my nipple, a little harder this time, but it was still a tease. "The second time, I met the perfect lady, studied and stiff, blushing because our thighs touched on the dance floor."

The irony of him being confused by my behaviour wasn't lost on me, but I was too occupied trying to keep hold of my sanity as he teased me closer and closer to its edge.

"Where's the line between obedience and law-breaking?" He asked it against my skin, like it was a lover's poetry. "I can't tell where you draw it or how you leap between the two, but keeping you off-balance makes you slip, and I catch such tantalising glimpses when you do."

I wasn't just on the edge, I walked a tightrope. My plan was to use desire to make him careless enough to spill secrets, but he endangered me with the same ploy.

"My turn for a question." He kissed the nape of my neck, the point between it and my shoulder, his touch drugging. "Why were you prepared to let me give you release in the maze, but now you fight your desires?"

It took several gasped breaths before I could reply. "Some things are possible in the dead of night, but not in daylight."

"Hmm." His shadows deepened around us, licking at the afternoon sun until it was just a dim disk in a grey sky and the gardens faded to nothing. They thickened the air, making the smell of roses and honeysuckle heavier, mingling with his cedar and bergamot.

As the scent filled me, he held tighter and finally gave the friction my arched back was seeking, the growing hardness of his cock rubbing my needy flesh. Then it was his turn to groan, a rumble against my spine that had my hips tilting further back.

I wasn't meant to be doing this. I shouldn't want this. I

dragged my body away from this dangerous desire and straightened my spine. *You should be mortified, Katherine Ferrers.*

He sighed. "And there go the rules chiming in your head."

He said it like it was a bad thing. But rules kept me safe.

"Your body calls for pleasure, for touch..." He dipped closer to my ear, grinding my arse and pinching my nipple at the same instant, making me shudder. "And I must say, responds to it quite beautifully. And yet you deny yourself... Or is it the circumstance you find yourself in? A woman alone at court with no husband in a society where that is the only sex allowed."

I clenched my jaw, unable to answer.

His fingers splayed across my stomach and he leant his head against mine. "Sex is like good food or drink—it's something we need and it's something to be shared with whoever the fuck you want."

Such an easy thing to say when he could do anything he desired. When he was in charge of this moment. When he could whip me up like this and then act so indifferent the next time he saw me.

So fucking easy.

He held every card in the game and every piece on the chess board, and I had nothing. I could only try to get through court, buffeted by him and the other powers swirling through its murky waters.

My hands balled into fists. "Why do you care, Bastian? Why bother to work me out? *Why?*"

With a low sound, close to a growl, he spun me to face him. "Because yours is a life half-lived. You're constantly on guard, holding back, and I can't work out why. I certainly can't stand to see it." He bared his teeth, voice dropping. "And

I can't stand that Langdon stopped you eating a piece of damn cake."

My breath caught, and I would've stepped away if not for his hold on my shoulders.

"It's men like him who made the rules that keep you bound up with your folded hands and polite smiles, isn't it? It's voices like his you hear when you stand there torn between what your country says a lady should be and seeking the pleasure your body craves."

I rubbed my chest. A direct hit.

"If you don't want me to touch you, Kat, that's fine." He shook his head, frown as deep as his shadows. "This isn't about me having you. It's about you doing what you want, rather than following the rules someone else has imposed on you that aren't even for your own good." He bent closer, gaze so intense I couldn't look away. "No one else gets a say in who you share your body with or what you do with it. No one. So I'll ask you again: do you want the things in that book?"

My body ached, yearning, even as my mind whispered that I could say yes and it would just be part of the job, part of spying. A way to get closer to him.

I almost—*almost* believed.

His eyebrows rose, prompting.

"Hello there? Is everything all right?"

The man's voice broke the spell that had me burning and truly considering my answer—that had me thinking I had a choice.

Beyond Bastian's shadows, there was a world. With judgement and cruelty. Both worse for women.

"Show yourself or I'll call the guard!"

Bastian exhaled and the shadows dissipated.

Several feet away stood Webster, his eyes wide, another

gardener behind him. He brandished a spade like he might use it to smack Bastian into next week.

Which would end badly for Webster.

"A conversation between friends." I tried to make my smile reassuring, even though my voice came out hoarse.

Bastian hadn't so much as glanced at him and now came closer. "Didn't Lara's death remind you how damn short your life is?" He spoke with a low ferocity. "Too short to deny yourself. Too short to spend it locked up in other people's rules." He released my shoulders. "Consider that next time someone offers you cake. It's there to be eaten. Just like life is to be enjoyed."

With that, he turned and strode away, shadows seething in his wake. Webster watched him, spade still over his shoulder. I gulped like that might make my chest less tight and heavy.

"I thought, with the terrible news about the lady..." Webster shook his head. "I was afraid it was another attack. Are you sure you're all right?"

Bright smile, straight back. "Of course. But I appreciate you looking out for us. And... on a different note, I appreciate your gift." I hadn't seen him since the rose had arrived. "Thank you so much. It's beautiful."

He blushed and ducked his head, then asked if I was well, if I felt safe after the attack. Even as I answered, my traitorous gaze skipped past him to where Bastian strode away.

Wreathed in shadows, he was a force of nature or magic or something else just as powerful. And if I wasn't careful, I would be lost in his maelstrom.

31

Clouds blotted the sky the day of Lara's funeral, making all the gathered faces look pale. Even those with skin darker than mine looked ashen, as if the world held less colour today. The grey stones around us didn't help—dozens and dozens of granite markers for those who'd died with their king or queen's favour over the centuries. The graveyard sat beside the palace's sacred space —a dead, stone counterpart to the life in the oak, yew, and elder trees of the grove.

The Watch hadn't found any further clues, but they'd finally shown up at my door a couple of days ago and taken the pendant.

It could've belonged to one of these solemn courtiers in black silk.

Langdon's nose was no longer swollen and bruised, and he stood there, jaw and brow tight, expression the same as the other gentlemen. No one could've guessed he'd been involved with her. Apparently, the Watch knew, but they were keeping things discreet for Lara's sake.

Langdon had crossed my mind as a possible culprit. The look frozen on her face had been one of betrayal and the killer had got close enough to strangle her. It could be him.

Beside the queen, Cavendish watched the druid leading the rite as he spoke over her grave. The spymaster's expression was perfectly flat. Was he really paying attention or was his mind on his network of spies? He'd finally summoned me to his office two days ago, and I'd given him the note copied from Bastian's desk. His praise still hummed in me, an odd reassurance after the way Bastian had left me so off-balance in the gardens.

The man himself stood a few places away from the queen, Asher beside him—the closest of the suitors to Her Majesty. It seemed Bastian's actions the day of the murder had moved Dusk up the rankings.

I still didn't know what the hells to make of Bastian or his behaviour towards me. I knew I should be thankful. The sensible option would be to accept his advances and use them as part of my plan to get close to him. And yet...

It wasn't so simple. And maybe not so sensible.

His behaviour in public was totally inappropriate and could cost me more than it gave. Even worse, he made *me* inappropriate. To do my job, I needed to maintain control. I needed to be ready to capitalise on any momentary weakness I brought out in him. Instead, whenever he held me too close and touched me the way he did, I was weakness incarnate.

And weakness was dangerous.

Was that why someone had gone after Lara? Using her as a weakness to go after him...

I thought it was you.

I clasped my hands. That admission had been a moment of weakness in him—a tiny chink of vulnerability in his armour.

Perhaps his insistence on sweeping the palace until so late had been an attempt to... What? Not fail her in death? I wasn't sure, but from the way he'd behaved that night, it was clear that he saw himself as a protector of sorts.

The druid sprinkled lunar water and placed a yew branch on her casket before the grave diggers filled it in. I couldn't look away from the tumbling soil, crumbling and brown. I felt like it was falling over me, like I was the one at the bottom of that hole, slowly being crushed by the weight of earth.

Dark. Cold. Damp. Soaking through my nightgown...

I blinked, sucking in a shallow breath, skin prickly like it didn't fit right, heart trying to pound its way out of my rib cage.

The grave was filled; the rite finished. Half the mourners had already left. How long had I been standing here?

That half-memory again. Not even half, really. Just shards I didn't know what to do with. Queasiness rolled through me, bringing a cold sweat. I couldn't say if it was because of the pieces I could remember or the yawning gaps.

As the remaining people filed away in twos and threes, I stood there waiting for my pulse to calm.

It was right that I should be the last one here, when I'd been the one to find her.

"I'm sorry I wasn't there a few minutes earlier." Would that have been enough to save her? Would I have seen the killer? Or would I have just become his next victim?

I couldn't help thinking of the murderer as "him"—it seemed like it would need a man's strength to overpower and strangle her with bare hands. The Watch had confirmed they were finger marks I'd seen on her neck.

I swallowed, tugging on the high neckline of my gown. "And I'm sorry someone did this to you."

There was no answer. I hadn't been expecting one, of course, but for some reason I waited there a long while. Maybe it was simply guilt and some part of me thought I could atone for it by standing vigil.

The Watch had the pendant now. That would lead them to the killer. For all I'd spent the past decade evading justice, when it slipped a noose around her murderer's throat, I'd cheer it on.

Eventually, I turned and strode across the graveyard, a determined smile in place.

"Well, if it isn't my favourite niece."

The determination died. The smile died. Inside, *I* died.

I couldn't move as he stepped into my path. Red hair, lighter than my own. Eyes the colour of ice that smothered the lake on our family's estate in the depths of winter. Tall—well, taller than me, but not as tall as I remembered. Maybe I'd grown used to craning my neck so much to speak to Bastian. Maybe it was just that he'd grown in my memory over the years since I'd last seen him.

"Well?" He spread his hands. "Aren't you going to greet your uncle?"

I plastered a smile on my face and bowed my head, movements jerky like I was a marionette under someone else's control. "Uncle Rufus. So good to see you." The hollowness of my words was only matched by the hollowness of my stomach as breakfast lurched up, threatening to make a reappearance.

"Yes." He nodded and said it again, drawing out the word.

"My friend Langdon said you were here at court. And when I said I was your uncle, the chamberlain was only too happy to admit me. But how appropriate that I should run into you in a *graveyard*, of all places."

I kept the smile in place, even though I didn't understand. Shuffling through my memories brought up no reason a graveyard would be relevant.

His eyebrows flashed up—a warning. "Though I suppose the stable yard would have been just as appropriate."

My face tingled, and the world spun, as though all the alcohol I'd consumed last night chose this moment to hit me afresh. Fantôme. The sweet little cub. My first sabrecat.

I was fifteen when Mama and Papa gave her to me, and so proud. I taught her tricks, using Frankish, since I'd just spent the summer there with my aunt. White fur, a peach nose, and ghostly grey eyes—that was why I'd picked her name. Clever, too. So clever.

When Uncle Rufus had found Avice and me playing with her and she'd failed to obey his commands, he hadn't agreed. His face growing redder and redder had been almost amusing at first. Almost.

But then his movements had gone jerky. Eyes bulging, spittle on his lips, he'd bellowed the commands to her over and over—in Albionic, even though I told him to use Frankish. He hadn't listened. What use had he for listening to a fifteen-year-old girl?

He'd said, "An untrainable cat is a danger to everyone." And then he'd closed his hands around her neck.

The seconds after were a blank space in my mind. Maybe just as well. After that day, Avice would always flinch whenever she heard a sharp crack, even if it was only a twig breaking in the woods. She remembered and it haunted her.

I only remembered blinking, and suddenly Fantôme wasn't moving. She never moved again.

Here and now, Uncle Rufus was still talking, and my body had taken over, nodding, staring at him, smiling, smiling, smiling.

What was he doing here? He had no position at court. No one had mentioned him since I'd arrived.

My mouth moved and words came out, asking how he was, how his wife fared, like this was a lovely catch-up with family.

How fucking lovely.

Sweat poured between my shoulder blades, and my toes scrunched up inside my shoes. Those secret ways were the only outlet for my shock at seeing him here.

Then again, should I be surprised to find him at court? He'd always held lofty ambitions for our family—that was why he'd worked with Papa to arrange Avice's marriage to the Villiers heir.

"Well, I'll let you run along." His smile was bright as he looked down at me. "I'm sure you have the wake to get to in such a fine dress. I hear you're a lady-in-waiting now." His smile widened—too wide, too bright, showing too many teeth. "Look at you, my clever little niece. All these new friends you've found in *such* high places." He stepped back, opening up my path again. "I'll see you very soon."

I ducked my head and said something polite. I couldn't hear it over the roaring of my pulse pressing, pressing, pressing on my ears, painful there and in my chest.

One step. Two steps. Three. I left the graveyard at a normal pace, but as soon as I was around the corner, behind the hedges, I broke into a run.

I didn't look where I was going. I just needed to be away. I just needed—

I ran into something hard, something that caught my upper arms, stopping me from falling back. *Someone,* a still coherent fragment of my mind told me.

I blinked, finding silver eyes on me. Frowning. A frown meant they were displeased. Angry. That meant danger.

"Kat?" His voice broke through my fog. Bastian's voice.

I'd been tearing up the path between the grove and the palace like no lady ever should. Now I stood here, staring up at him, breaths too fast, unable to speak.

His gaze passed from one eye to the other, then roved across my face. His frown cranked tighter, but it wasn't anger, not entirely—more like confusion.

A light mist of shadows curled up around us, thickening until I couldn't see anything else, just him outlined in the dim light that crept through. Which meant no one else could see me reacting.

It wasn't a lady's place to react. Obedient, dutiful, silent. Cool, calm, collected.

"What's wrong, Kat? Who frightened you?"

I was too busy fighting to bring my breathing under control to reply. What the hells could I say, anyway? I couldn't tell. It would only make Uncle Rufus angry.

"Slower, slower. That's it." Bastian's thumbs took up a slow, rhythmic stroke on my shoulders. "Was it Langdon again?" He glanced past me. "Do you want him dead or just so terrified that he's a gibbering wreck for the rest of his days?" The low darkness in his voice was even deeper than his shadows.

Dead? Surely he couldn't mean that. It was a joke. Something to jolt me out of my state.

Then again, his tone wasn't exactly amused, and the way he'd looked at the picnic...

Shit. Yes, he needed to know this wasn't down to Langdon. If there was the possibility Bastian *might* kill the man on my account, I had to nip that in the bud.

I shook my head. "No. Not him. I'm not... I'm fine." To demonstrate, I swallowed and took a step back, pulling out of his grip. It left me untethered though, the air around me a void that I wanted to combat by hugging myself. But that wasn't appropriate for a lady. Neither was standing here in Bastian's shadows.

His lips pressed together. "Kat, I can—"

"I'm fine. I just remembered I need to get back to my rooms. Thank you." His dark veil had at least stopped anyone witnessing me quite so out of control and given me a moment to remember myself.

With an exhale, he withdrew the darkness.

Even overcast, the day was too bright without it. But thankfully, there was no one in sight. Gods willing, nobody had witnessed this. Stiff and straight, I walked away, hands clasped so tightly my knuckles ached.

I'll see you very soon. Rufus had said that. Promised it.

He would be back.

32

Even though the wake continued elsewhere in the palace, I hid in my rooms until I could trust myself to behave correctly. By the time my heart had recovered, I didn't have the energy to face people. Instead, I lay on the settee drinking brandy from a bottle the queen had sent me the day after Lara's murder.

But Ella had missed me at the wake, and declared that I shouldn't "languish like a dying seal and drink yourself into oblivion alone." Then she plopped into the armchair opposite me.

"Fine," I sighed. "I'll share." I held out the brandy, and she poured herself a generous slug. Eyeing the bottle, she fetched me a glass, too, and refused to give me more than that.

"Spoilsport," I muttered, though I was starting to feel fuzzy and somehow half the bottle had disappeared already.

"I'm protecting my hard work." She grinned and raised her drink in my direction. "Too much alcohol will ruin your complexion and make your eyes bloodshot. Speaking of which." She pulled a tiny cobalt blue vial from somewhere on her person and tossed it to me.

It hit the padded back of the settee. I didn't even get close to catching it.

"As I thought. You've been lying there too long with only the bottle for company." She arched one eyebrow. "Those are eyedrops. They'll help with the gritty tiredness."

"What tiredness?"

She tilted her head in a way that asked if we were really going to play this game.

Maybe I was feeling playful, because I just repeated, "What tiredness?"

"My darling, it's written all over your face. You've barely slept since Lara was... Well, *you know*. And I know it isn't because you're too busy entertaining a certain Dusk Court fae in your bed."

I grunted. "I hate that you find me so transparent."

"You had a traumatic experience. If you walk away from that with a few sleepless nights, you'll be remarkably lucky." Her mouth twisted as her eyes narrowed. "Though I daresay it isn't your first time."

I sank into my glass, unable to bear the weight of her scrutiny. Especially not when she was right.

Fantôme's death had been horrifying, worse than anything Papa had done. He was all bluster and threats, where his brother... He was a man of action.

But I couldn't shake the feeling that there was something else. Something in that blank space amongst my memories. Another piece between the shards.

I didn't want to know what it was, so I drained my glass, barely registering the fire that licked down my throat, and gave Ella a beseeching look.

Her mouth flattened. That was a no.

"What happened to the breezy Lady Eloisa-Elizabetta-Belladonna Fortnum-Knightly-Chase?"

Her eyes softened, and in answer, my chest tightened. "She was worried about you, so she sent me."

Worried about me. I bit my lip to keep it from trembling. "I think... right now, I need *her*." I hated how desperate I sounded, how much my voice wavered.

She inspected me from across the coffee table, then one side of her mouth lifted. "You do, don't you, darling? Well, I'll be breezy if you have no more of this today." She sloshed the contents of the bottle. "Deal?"

It was safer than either of the bargains I'd struck with Bastian. I sat up, ignored the room spinning, and held out my hand. "Deal."

We shook, and she nodded. She wasn't as powerful as Cavendish or Bastian, but her silent approval still felt good. Warmer in a less hollow way than the brandy.

We chatted about the latest gossip at court. There wasn't as much as usual, with the lack of social events and the curfew. The queen had stated it again this morning: *No one but guards in the corridors after nine o'clock on pain of death.* I doubted she'd really meant the last part, but I didn't fancy testing that theory.

I wasn't sure I felt even marginally safer knowing no one was prowling the corridors at night. Not when they could strike just as anonymously by day. But Ella must've caught a hint that my thoughts had turned that way and steered us towards brighter topics.

Eventually a companionable silence fell between us, and I sipped elderflower cordial—non-alcoholic, so not forbidden. "Ella... Have you ever wanted one of your targets?"

229

I didn't have to look at her to know she raised an eyebrow at me. "I want most of them. And it makes it all the more enjoyable for both parties."

Enjoyable. I stared at the ceiling, shaken by the word.

Ella didn't just lie back and endure the people she seduced. She didn't even fake pleasure to lull them into the kind of security that would make them slip up and reveal something they shouldn't.

She *enjoyed* it.

"Buuut," she said, drawing the word out, "it doesn't tend to bring me the angst I can see on your face. What are you really asking?"

Clearing my throat, I went and fiddled with the wood arranged in the fireplace. Technically, Seren did everything I asked, but her skills as a lady's maid... left something to be desired. The kindling had been arranged haphazardly, the matches discarded on the hearth. I scooped the wood off the grate and started again.

As I worked, I managed to loosen my jaw and explained to Ella what had happened between Bastian and me. Not the parts where I'd stolen from him or he'd left the palace grounds or anything that seemed better kept a secret, like his ability to split himself in two. But the way he teased me and toyed with my body, making me burn for him.

When I'd talked myself out, she didn't reply, and I looked up to find her staring at me, wide-eyed, rosy-cheeked. She opened and closed her mouth, swallowed, then shook her head slowly. "Oh my." She huffed a shaky laugh and gulped her brandy. "And... then what?"

I blinked. I'd stopped at Webster interrupting us in the gardens and left out Bastian finding me fleeing the graveyard, since that wasn't relevant to my attempts to seduce him. "That's... it."

"You mean you haven't...?" Her eyelashes fluttered as she shook her head. "I knew you hadn't fucked him, but I assumed you'd done *something*. And with all that lead-up!" She sounded more shocked than I had the first time she'd told me about straddling a duke's face in his carriage while waving out the window. "Why haven't you ridden his hand all the way to the bloody Underworld? Or his tongue? I'd take either."

Somehow, conversations with Ella always went in this direction, and my cheeks no longer burned at it. But part of me was still *a little* scandalised to hear her speak of sex in such a candid way.

A bigger part of me enjoyed it, though, like it was an antidote to some poison I'd taken long ago.

"Seriously, Katherine—yes, I'm using your full name, because I'm that shocked and horrified by what you've just told me—*why* haven't you taken this further? You know it's your job, right?"

"It's my job to get information from—"

"Yes, yes, of course." She waved that off. "But that comes with the, uh, *coming*." She grinned at me, eyes glinting with pleasure at her own pun. "You still haven't answered the question, though."

"Hmph, you noticed that, then?"

"I haven't got all day, Kat. Curfew's at nine, but don't think you can ride this out until then. If you haven't told me by then, I'm staying here for the night and badgering you until you answer." Even though she smiled so sweetly, I didn't dare hope it was an idle threat.

I slid open the box of matches, closed it again. "I... I want him. I want him to touch me, to do the things I've read about, but... that feels dangerous."

"Oh, my darling." She gave a heavy sigh. "Everything is dangerous. The things that feel safe are the worst of all. But this whole business of living is dangerous. Sometimes you just need to dive in anyway."

"If I can just make it safe..." There had to be a way. Something I could do to insulate myself from the risk of wanting him so much it addled my mind and risked revealing too much.

She sighed and shook her head. "Did you not hear me? Life is dangerous. The threat of losing it makes it all the sweeter."

I must've given her a blank look, because she came over, knelt on the hearth, and gathered me to her.

I loosely looped my arms around her waist, but couldn't work out what I'd said that was worthy of a hug. Or the kiss she now planted on my brow.

"What am I going to do with you? What nonsense lies live in this pretty head of yours?" She stroked my hair and held me a long while.

I didn't deserve it, but I also didn't pull away.

Just as I sank into a doze, head in her lap, she spoke again. "I'll help you unlearn it all."

33

In the days after Lara's funeral, social events around the palace started again. I slept a little better after Ella's visit, so I didn't look too ghastly for them. As my nerves steadied, my attempts to pick locks improved, too.

Cavendish remained oddly quiet. Either he was busy dealing with the aftermath of the murder, or he'd heard rumour of my fake relationship with Bastian and was satisfied I was doing my job. I heard nothing from my uncle and dared to hope it had been only a fleeting visit to court.

One afternoon, I was returning from a ride with Ella and a couple of other ladies-in-waiting when I found the door to my room open a crack.

"Bloody hells, Seren," I huffed, throwing it open, striding in. "Can you not even do a simple...?"

In the middle of the settee, legs wide, arms spread over its back, sat Bastian. I stopped in my tracks and he gave me a dazzling smile, like he was welcoming me into my own suite.

I glanced out into the hall. Empty. Hopefully, that meant no one knew he was in here. Being seen on this corridor was one thing, enough for a rumour, but being in here alone with me was a step further. I gritted my teeth and shut the door.

"How did you get in here?" I held up the key, which was apparently useless in keeping my rooms secure.

"You think a locked door is enough to keep me out?"

"What a sinister thing to say when you've broken into a woman's rooms. Are you trying out for some sort of creepy villain tournament?"

His chuckle wouldn't have been out of place at such an event. "And here I was thinking you'd be pleased to see me." He sighed and stood, pouting as though hurt. "We *are* meant to be keeping up appearances, remember, *darling*?"

Some days, I regretted the decisions my past self had made.

Make that most days.

"Speaking of which, I got you a gift." He nodded to the coffee table. There sat a package wrapped in shimmery turquoise cloth.

I narrowed my eyes. It felt like a trap. To be fair, when it came to Bastian, a lot of things felt like traps.

But it didn't do to anger a fae, and they were big on manners, so I inclined my head. "Thank you."

He bowed with a flourish. "You're welcome, *my love*." For all his tone dripped with sarcasm, there was a flush of genuine pleasure in his grin.

I folded my arms as he stalked around the room, touching the mantlepiece, the frame of the mirror, the small trinket box Ella had given me to keep jewellery in. It felt uncomfortably like he was cataloguing me, just as I had done when left alone in his suite. Except he'd been in here alone for gods knew how long and there was no magical lock on my bedroom door.

He must've already gone through everything, so this little tour of the sitting room was all a show.

Everything. Like the drawer of indecent lingerie from Blaze. My heart somersaulted and then plummeted as I realised what else "everything" included.

The chest under my bed. Was the lock on that enough to keep him out? Had he found his orrery and discovered that I was lying about selling it?

I took a small step closer to the door, making sure he didn't get between me and it.

But... he didn't seem angry. And he wasn't wearing that bored look he fell back on to mask other emotions. He appeared content busying himself with poking around the room.

I sucked in a deep breath and tossed my head like I was irritated. "You've delivered your gift, and yet you're still here. What do you want, Bastian?"

As though he hadn't been absorbed with straightening items on the dressing table, he spun on his heel, that dazzling smile in place again. "I'm so glad you asked. That favour you owe me. I'm calling it in."

I straightened, steeling myself for whatever it might be. In the maze and gardens, he'd made a point of giving me a way out of his touches, so it didn't seem likely it would be a *sexual* favour. But I struggled to think of anything else he might want from me.

"You draw attention wherever you go."

I raised an eyebrow. I wasn't sure what reality he lived in, but in mine, I kept quiet and actively *avoided* attention.

"And you keep your head, even under shitty circumstances." Tension flickered at his jaw and brow. "You also aren't above a little manipulation—"

"Is this favour listening to you list my character faults? I'm not saying I won't do it, but a little warning would be nice."

"Faults?" Frowning, he crossed the room, and I thought he was going to pull me against him again, but he stopped just out of arm's reach. At his side, his fingers flexed. "Everything I've just said is something I... It's something that's useful."

Useful. Another woman might've found that choice of word insulting, but for me it was praise. It suffused me with as much warmth and pleasure as if he'd caressed my cheek.

"And that's why I need your help. Go to the east corridor where Dawn's rooms are and distract anyone who tries to enter Caelus's suite. I need ten minutes uninterrupted."

Caelus, Dawn Court's suitor. That didn't sound too dangerous. "To do what?"

His mouth tensed.

"Fine, fine. You're not going to tell me. When do you need these ten minutes?"

"You'll do it, then?"

"I'm not sure I have a choice."

"You always have a choice." He left the sentence hanging in the air, heavy, as he held my gaze.

Swallowing, I resisted the urge to rub my chest, where my heart beat a little faster. "We made a bargain. You're calling it in. I'm honouring our deal. When do you need me?"

"Now. I left Caelus with your queen, and the rest of Dawn is all there. It's the first time they've been occupied in days, but I don't know when one of them might slip away."

I nodded and went to the mirror, smoothing the front of my emerald green dress.

"You look perfect." From behind me, he met my gaze in the mirror, his closeness and yet more praise working together to make my breath catch. "Exquisite, in fact." He reached out like he was going to touch my hair, but stopped a few inches short.

He let his hand drop. "Come on."

34

I followed Bastian's directions to the correct corridor
while he took a different route. To do what, I didn't
know, though I might tell Cavendish he'd snuck into
Caelus's room. Stealing something, perhaps. Gathering information. Leaving an anonymous note. It didn't feel like too
major a secret, since I didn't have any details.

I found an alcove with an alabaster statue of a naked
woman. Cloth swirled over the apex of her thighs and around
her, as though she'd been caught mid-dance with the wind
itself. Across the corridor, a painting depicted a feast in
honour of Elizabeth I and her marriage. It made the perfect
spot for me to wait, pretending the art had captured my
attention.

Minutes ticked by and the corridor remained empty. This
was going to be the world's easiest favour. I'd got off lightly.

Just as I was smiling to myself at the fact, a low, private
voice sounded behind me. "Lady Katherine, what brings you
to this end of the palace?"

Spinning around, I gasped and clutched my chest like I'd been completely absorbed by the sculpture.

Just two feet away stood Lord Caelus. Damn fae and their silent feet.

His chestnut brown hair glinted and gleamed like sun poured upon it, but there were no windows on this stretch of corridor. Bright blue eyes, as clear as a summer's day, pierced me, carrying a barb of suspicion.

"And so close to my suite, too." He arched an eyebrow, though his gaze skimmed to my hair as though distracted by it.

Considering the rumours that had to be circulating about Bastian and me, I couldn't blame him for his suspicion. He had to believe I'd aligned myself with Dusk and thus against his court.

Now he'd pointed it out, blaming simple coincidence became too flimsy an excuse. I needed something more believable. If he thought me complicit in some action against him...

I swallowed, pulse a little too fast.

Time to try a different tack.

I let my eyes lower and took a deeper breath than was necessary, well aware of the way it made my breasts heave at the low neckline of my gown. "You've caught me out." I bit my lip like Ella had taught me, releasing it slowly so it would glisten, now moistened. "I confess it's no accident." The best lies contained a grain of truth, after all. "I was hoping to bump into you as if by pure coincidence. But you've seen through my ploy."

Make them feel clever, Ella had told me.

Well, here I was, making him feel like the cleverest man in all Lunden.

When I looked up from below my lashes, his chin lifted

fractionally as though trying to disguise his pride. He'd have to do better than that. "And why would you try such a trick?"

"Am I not allowed to want to see you, my lord?" The huskiness of my voice surprised me. The way I slipped so easily into flirtation, too. And, most of all, the way he seemed to be buying it, greedily drinking up my every movement.

I tilted my head, an apparently innocent gesture, but it exposed my throat, and sure enough, his eyes flicked to it, settling there. Did he see the speed of my pulse fluttering against my skin?

"'My lord'?" He made a soft, dismissive sound, but his gaze didn't shift. "I think you know my kind well enough to know we don't use such titles. Call me Caelus or don't call me at all."

"And what occasion might I have to call out your name, *Caelus*?" I drew out its two syllables, licking my lips after, and now his gaze was trapped there. It was a battle not to grin in victory.

Perhaps I was getting the hang of courtier life after all.

His throat bobbed slowly. "I can think of a few."

"I'm not sure I catch your meaning." Though I let the corner of my mouth twitch to signal that I knew exactly what we were skirting around. "Perhaps you could explain."

"I could show you." He came closer, backing me into the alcove, though really I was the one luring him there. In the alcove, he wouldn't be able to see down the corridor if Bastian left his suite.

"*Could* you?" As my back hit the wall, the breathiness in my voice wasn't entirely feigned. Flirting was one thing, but I was getting closer and closer to having to act.

He stood over me, one hand coming up to rest on the wall

above my shoulder. He bent closer, and I caught the scent of freshly cut grass on a sultry summer day. "Are you collecting fae, Katherine?"

"Would it be a problem if I was?"

There was a flash of his teeth as he smirked. "Not one bit. I'm happy to share." He edged closer, stirring the hem of my gown, gaze intent on my mouth.

Bastian had asked for a distraction. If it meant kissing Caelus, so be it. I lifted my chin like it was an invitation.

Footsteps echoed down the hall, and I flinched. Caelus's eyes narrowed before he straightened and turned, just in time to see Bastian draw to a halt, looking daggers at us. My heart thudded harder at that than at Caelus's proximity.

"Katherine." Bastian's voice could've given me frostbite. "I was just looking for you. But it appears you're *busy*." Jaw tightening, he swept away down the corridor.

Oh, he was good. Looking for me gave him the perfect excuse to be in this corridor, and his appearance told me he'd finished his secret mission, so I was free to go. He could move in silence, so he'd deliberately let his footsteps sound to get our attention.

Very, very sneaky, Bastian.

Caelus gave an amused smirk. "Apparently not everyone is as eager to share as I am." He backed away a step and inclined his head in mock formality. "Lady Katherine. I appreciate your visit. Feel free to call upon me again when you're *available*."

I edged past him and into the corridor. At the far end stood a red-haired fae I didn't recognise, pointed face and lithe form not quite male, not quite female. They didn't move, just watched me with dark eyes as Caelus stepped out from the alcove.

A shiver running down my spine, I hurried away as though chasing after Bastian. All the way down the hall, though, it was their gazes that chased me.

35

Heading back to my suite, I couldn't shake the feeling that I'd either made a new ally or an enemy. With what I'd offered through my flirtation, I wasn't sure Caelus was the kind of ally I wanted. The way he'd said *available* had hung thick with meaning and expectation.

There would be consequences with Dawn after this. Either because of my actions or Bastian's. But that was something to deal with another day.

I closed the door behind me and leant on it, heaving a sigh. Afternoon had slipped into evening, but the lamps and candles around the sitting room had already been lit. That was uncharacteristically efficient of Seren.

Now I was alone, I could put on a nightgown and curl up on the settee with a book. I'd promised Ella I'd only have one drink a night, but I'd savour it... and maybe I'd make it a large one.

Smiling to myself, I wandered into my bedroom.

By the windows, a tall shadow uncurled.

A gasp tore through me, and the next second, I registered that it wasn't a shadow, but Bastian, straightening from an inspection of the rosebush.

"Wild fucking Hunt, would you stop doing that?" I clutched my chest, which was about to break from the pounding of my heart.

He blinked. "What?"

"Appearing in my rooms. You scared the life out of me."

"I thought you'd realise I was here, since I lit everything."

"You..." I heaved a sigh and my heart slowed a little. "Of course you did." That was more believable than Seren doing her job. "Did you manage to do what you needed to?"

"I did. Thank you." He gave me a long look. "You did your job... very thoroughly."

Was that tension around his jaw? I couldn't be sure when he was on the other side of the room.

I raised one shoulder. "I don't think it would've gone well for you if he'd found you in his suite."

A cruel smile exposed his teeth. "It wouldn't have gone well *for him*."

That look wasn't a million miles from the one he'd given me on the road, the one that had promised to destroy me.

It was a reminder.

For all Bastian looked human, he was not. He was fae. Ruthless. Dangerous. With shadows that obeyed his command.

"Well, I'm glad I could keep him safe, if not you." I started back into the sitting room, suddenly aware that I was alone with him in my bedroom. I busied myself, unpinning sections of hair I'd pulled back from my face, waiting for him to get the hint that it was time to leave.

"You didn't open your present yet." He stood in the doorway, half in my bedroom, half in the sitting room, as though he didn't quite want to leave my private space.

Unwrap the gift, thank him, then show him to the door. That would be a perfect way to end this impromptu visit. I went to the coffee table and hefted the parcel. "A book?" I cocked my head at him.

"Open it and see." He stalked closer, gaze so intent it was like he hunted me.

I cleared my throat and looked away, grateful to have the gift as an excuse and distraction. The shimmering turquoise silk kept unfolding and unfolding where it had been wrapped many times. In itself, the fabric was beautiful. Sheer and glittering.

"It's from Tenebris," he murmured. "I thought the colour would suit you. Perhaps your dressmaker could make something from it."

"Then this is the gift?"

"The thing inside it is." He lifted one shoulder, the tiniest hint of bashfulness in the curve of his lips. "This is just an extra."

As the last length of cloth fell away, caught by Bastian before it hit the floor, it revealed a book bound in the deepest, lushest green leather. A gold debossed rose decorated the front, with an elegant border formed from thorny stems that trailed over to the spine and back cover. I turned it over three times, savouring the softness of the leather, running my thumb over the gilded page edges. "This is beautiful, Bastian."

"It does open, you know."

"I know how books work."

"I was wondering, since you keep fingering that cover like it's the point of the thing. *Open it.*"

I huffed but obeyed, flicking to a random page in the middle. The scent hit first, so heavy and rich it staggered me, and Bastian had to catch my shoulder as a low "Oh" fell from my lips.

Classic rose, sweet and heady, freshened with a dash of dew like I'd come across it in the early morning.

I had to blink before I registered the illustration on the page—the flower itself, in a delicate blush pink. A caption read *La Ville*. An old damask rose variety I'd once grown.

"How? How does it *smell*?" I shook my head, unable to tear myself from the illustration. Not just every petal, but every hint of texture, had been captured by the artist in sheer perfection.

"Wait until you touch it."

I blinked up at him, wondering what that meant, but he only nodded towards the page.

Feeling quite silly and like this might well be a trap to make me look stupid, I touched the paper.

"I meant a part with the rose on it, Kat."

"Fine." I traced my fingertip across until it hit—

"Oh!" I froze. Because my finger wasn't on smooth paper anymore but the velvet softness of a rose petal. It even had that slight damp sensation that hinted at the oils and moisture held within, like I could crush the flower and it would stain my hand with scent. As I pressed, the illustration itself moved, petals bending as though I were touching a real rose. A shiver chased through me. "What...? What is this?"

"Yours."

I flicked to another page. It showed a tea rose in rich apricot, wafting a spiced aroma with undertones of fruit and just a hint of violet. Each page showed a different variety, capturing not just its appearance in perfect detail, but the individual scents and textures.

Fae magic. Potent and yet used on something so frivolous.

"I can't..." I shook my head and slammed the book shut, holding it up to him. "This is too much. It's only meant to be..." I swallowed, throat thick. I didn't deserve this. It was too beautiful. Too special. It must've cost so much. "We were only meant to pretend you bought me gifts."

He placed his hands over mine, holding them around the book, and gently pushed it back towards me. "I'm pretending very hard. Besides, I don't know anyone who'd appreciate it more than you."

I swallowed again, but pulled the book against my chest, some part of me keen to see what other varieties were inside. "Thank you. I'll return it when our fakery is over."

"No, you won't. I want you to have it." He bowed his head and stepped back. "Gifts work the same in Albion as they do in Elfhame—it is yours to do with as you wish."

Squeezing the book, I had to turn away. He'd heard enough of my conversation with Webster to know I'd once been obsessed with roses. What else had I let slip? What else had he worked out? I suddenly felt like I was standing here naked.

Clearing my throat, I set the book down on a side table and bustled to the doors. "Well, thank you again." Was that three times now? Flustered by a book. Really? It was just pages bound in dead animal hide. "So, that's one bargain complete." I gave him a wide smile and opened the door.

From down the hall drifted low voices, so I peeked out. Guards at the end of the corridor. And when I turned—yes, more at the other end.

I eased the door shut, one hand planted on it. "Bastian... What time is it?"

"Your clock says quarter past nine."

"Shitting hells."

"*Katherine.* That's the second time I've heard you swear and both of those tonight." He added in a lower tone, "I think I like it."

I whirled on my heel and shot him a glare that stopped his approach. "I'm not joking around. It's past curfew. You can't go."

He snorted. "A little curfew isn't going to stop me—they'll move along soon enough. I'm sure you can entertain me until then." He raised one eyebrow suggestively.

I gritted my teeth, since he apparently hadn't got the message about this not being funny. "They won't. Because I found her, they've been stationed at both ends of this corridor every night, worried I might be in danger."

"Fine." He shrugged, all nonchalance. "Then I'll just explain that we're having a very much not fake relationship, but you've kicked me out because—"

"Because you're an idiot." I pointed at him, stalking closer. "Don't you understand? That note supposedly from me was designed to lure you to the murder scene. Therefore, it had to be from the killer. If you'd been found there, everyone would've thought you'd done it. They were trying to frame you, right?"

His eyebrows inched up in slow-dawning surprise. "Rii-ight. Why do I feel like your point doesn't end there?"

"That means someone here is working against you. Either your court or you specifically. If you're seen breaking curfew, the Watch might start to wonder if you're guilty after all and I'm covering for you. And even if that doesn't happen, the killer could take advantage of it to do gods know what." I set my jaw and folded my arms. "I won't risk you walking the corridors past curfew."

He narrowed his eyes. "Are you trying to protect me? That's... why, that's almost *sweet*, Kat. What do you propose I do instead?"

"Stay."

36

"You're asking me to stay with you?" He said it slowly, like he enjoyed each word.

I scowled in the hopes it would scare him off. "Not like *that*."

But he just continued as if I hadn't spoken. "The obedient Lady Katherine is asking me to stay in her room. Aren't you just a walking contradiction?" He smirked, making me want to punch the smugness clean off his face.

Instead, I clenched my jaw. He wanted a rise out of me and I refused to give him the satisfaction. I sighed and pulled the same bored expression he loved so bloody much. "Are you staying or shall I unlock the door and shove you out there in front of the guards?"

"Oh, I'm far too intrigued not to stay." His teeth flashed as he came closer, stopping just a foot away. "Will you have me sleep on the floor? In front of the fire, perhaps?"

He was making it very difficult not to punch him. "No," I bit out. "I'm a better host than that."

"Then on the bed?" He batted his lashes in mock innocence. "But where will milady sleep?"

The low sound in my throat was worryingly like a growl. "I'm not giving up my bed for you. There's plenty of space for both of us. Besides"—I gave him a sweet smile—"if you're this irritating on a normal day, I don't want to know what you're like after a sleepless night."

He bent close, bringing the waft of cedar and bergamot. "Oh, I function very well after a sleepless night. Don't you worry."

I went hot, thinking about the ways he might spend such a night. Maybe... tonight?

It hit me. Bastian was actually staying in my bed. I needed to finally make good on my mission to get close to him. All those times he'd been so inappropriate were leading to this.

I swallowed and licked my lips, using what Ella had shown me. "Well, I suppose we'll see. Help yourself to the books on the side. I'm going to ready myself for bed." *For bed with you.* My throat clenched as I backed away to my bedroom, a fluttering sensation in my stomach.

It took all my self-control not to slam the door behind me. I selected a nightgown from the lingerie I'd collected from Blaze's workshop. Backless, with a scooped neckline and billowing sleeves, all made of fine black silk that was ever so slightly sheer. I had outrageous lingerie, of course, but that felt too obvious. This would hint and tempt without making him suspicious about why I'd changed my tune so quickly.

Still, I didn't want to be *too* subtle. I added the gold chain-garter Ella had gifted me, putting it on the same side as the slit in the nightgown, so it would peek out as I walked.

I applied perfume to my pulse points and, as per Ella's

instruction, the tips of my breasts and stood in front of the mirror in my bedroom, brushing my hair.

The woman who looked back at me was not the same one who'd arrived all those weeks ago. Her skin was still darker than most ladies' at court, but the freckles had evened out with Ella's clever oils. Perhaps she looked a little tired, but above the slight shadows, her green eyes were clear and determined. The nightgown draped over her curves, accentuating all that was there rather than making it seem too much. Most strikingly of all, her hair shone, fiery in the candlelight.

She was... beautiful.

I had to lower my pointed chin and watch as the reflection did the same to truly believe it was me.

When I raised it, the pearlwort necklace winked back. I was in control. Bastian couldn't use fae charm to make me his mindless toy. He didn't know I was a spy. He just thought me a prim, sex-starved widow with unusual habits like highway robbery and skulking around mazes at night.

Tonight, he would make some sort of advance, building on all those teasing touches before. And this time, I wouldn't even pretend to resist.

I finally brought the hairbrush to a halt. I was ready.

With a nod, I wrapped the nightgown's matching robe around myself and tied the oversized satin bow neatly. It was an invitation for Bastian to imagine untying it, and a fun piece of theatrics for me to pull loose at the perfect moment and unveil what lay beneath.

Heart rate higher than usual, I smoothed a couple of drops of oil through my hair, bringing out the lustre all the more, and padded barefoot to the door.

The instant I eased it open, he looked up from the book in his hand as though he'd been waiting for me to return rather than really reading it. I paused in the doorway, letting him take his time as his gaze passed over my face and hair. Did his chest rise and fall a little deeper as he took in my nightwear? I couldn't be sure. But the knot of his throat definitely moved slowly, like swallowing was an effort.

It rippled through me: the first warm flush of victory.

"I was going to complain that you took your time, but now I see it was time well spent." The corner of his mouth twitched with the threat of a roguish smirk, but his cheeks were perhaps a little redder than their usual tan.

My preening smile wasn't fake. Foolish, perhaps, but not fake. Maybe I hungered for his praise as much as I did for him. "I'm glad you think so," I breathed, knowing his fae hearing would still pick it up.

When I crossed the room, his gaze snagged on my thigh and the chain there. I needed to thank Ella properly for the stroke of genius that had inspired the garter. He moved over when I arrived at the settee, giving me space to sit. Too much space, annoyingly. And, even worse, when he finally tore his eyes away, he went back to reading the book.

What the hells? That was not how this was supposed to go.

What book could be so damn interesting that he'd ignore a woman with his sigil on her thigh who'd asked him to stay in her bed? I peered over and skimmed a few sentences. One of the history books Ella had lent me—this one focused on what little we knew of Cestyll Caradoc. Their suitor was still one of the queen's favourites and had danced with her three times at the last ball.

Exhaling, I forced the irritation out of my tight muscles. "Can I get you a drink?" That would loosen him up.

He lifted one shoulder, apparently casual, but his eyes did

flick up from the book, getting as far as the gold garter. "If you're having one, I'll join you, but don't trouble yourself on my account."

"Oh, I'm definitely having one," I said with a chuckle as I went to the decanter that contained the last of the queen's brandy.

I needed it to get through this. Right now, my promise to Ella of one drink a night felt like another of those actions I regretted my past self taking. Maybe this could be an exception. It would certainly help put me at ease over what I was about to do.

When I returned with the drinks, I curled up on the settee and leant closer, ostensibly to clink glasses, but also to give him a great view of my tits.

He fell for the bait, attention straying there before he took a sip and held my gaze over the rim of his glass. But it was short lived, and he was soon back to his book.

I tried to strike up conversation. I asked about himself, about Elfhame, about Asher—anything I could think of. But he barely glanced up from the book and kept his replies vague and short.

It took all my willpower not to huff at his disinterest or grab his chin and make him look at me.

All this time, he'd taken every inappropriate opportunity in public and semi-public places, and now he had me alone—nothing. Maybe he wasn't as interested as I thought. Maybe that had all been for his own amusement—watching me squirm, keeping me off balance, trying to get information about his orrery.

Over another two drinks, I continued my attempts to engage him, and he continued his reading.

I had to content myself with letting my mind wander as I

stared into the fire. Its gold and orange flicker reminded me of the tiger's eye pendant Lara had seized from her murderer.

News had got out about her affair with Langdon (thanks to his boasting), but of course, society wasn't punishing him for his indiscretion. Meanwhile, the whispers about her seemed less... sympathetic somehow. Like her involvement with him meant she deserved her fate.

I squeezed my glass, jaw clenching so tight it hurt.

The back of my neck prickled and when I looked up from the fire, I found Bastian's attention on me rather than the book. He tilted his head in question.

"The pendant we found on Lara." I frowned, turning back to the fire, conjuring the exact image of its shape. "You said the symbol was for magical strength. What does it do, exactly?"

"Magic doesn't just come out of nowhere. Humans tend to have a limited pool—more a puddle, really. But even most fae have to... siphon it from somewhere. That symbol increases the power the wearer has access to."

"So it could belong to a human..." I pressed the rim of the glass against my lip, not wanting to voice the idea forming.

"It could." The settee shifted as he leant closer. "What are you thinking?"

"Langdon is fae-touched." I'd seen his fae mark—the crescent on his neck. "You don't think he did it, do you?"

"Hmm." Another shift. I didn't dare look up—I didn't want to see the look on his face that said he thought I was mad for even considering it. "Strangulation is very... personal."

I swallowed and gave him a sidelong glance. His brow was creased in thought as he now stared into the fire.

Slowly, he nodded. "And as a method, it requires the killer to get close to their target."

"Exactly. And I can't explain it, but... her expression... I just can't shake the feeling she knew the person."

"As her lover, he could've easily lured her there. I suppose he could be working for a fae who gave him the necklace."

I pressed my lips together. "Why would a fae need a human to work for them?"

"In Lunden, you can go places we can't. Blend in. Be trusted with things we wouldn't."

Was he suggesting Langdon could be a spy? I bit back a laugh. He'd spilled about his relationship with Lara; he couldn't keep a secret to save his life. Or did that mean he'd make the perfect spy no one would suspect? After all, hadn't Cavendish chosen me because of my apparent lack of guile?

We fell back into a thoughtful silence, and when I next looked up, I found Bastian back in his book.

Finally, as the clock ticked to eleven, I gave up and rose from the settee. The room spun slowly—I'd spent too long with only one drink a night and now the three generous doses of brandy hit me all at once. "Well, I'm going to bed."

I was about to wish him goodnight, assuming he'd come through when he'd finished reading his *terribly* interesting book. But he slammed it shut the instant the word "bed" was out of my mouth. Dropping it on the settee, he flowed to his feet, leaving him standing a little too close.

"Lead the way, Katherine."

37

The husky tone of his voice did things to my insides that I couldn't describe.

He followed me around the room as I blew out candles and turned the dial on each lamp, extinguishing those, too. He didn't help or stray further than arm's reach, like he was nothing more than my shadow. The sudden attention left my stomach tight and that—or perhaps the brandy— had my head spinning even faster. He maintained that slightly too close distance when we entered the bedroom.

While he closed the door behind us, I escaped and crossed the room. I took my time blowing out the candles in the candelabra, letting that seem like my reason for fleeing.

When I turned, he was peeling off his shirt, and the sight stopped me in my tracks. His bronze tan continued under his clothes as though it maybe wasn't a tan at all, but his natural skin tone. Well-packed muscles flexed as he pulled the shirt over his head. Shadows wisped around each movement, light and hazy. If shadows could have feelings, I'd have said they were content.

A voice in my head, the one that was still stuck in those well-worn tracks that were all a lady *should* be, said I should look away.

Of course, I couldn't.

Not when my eyes could follow the ripple of those muscles or get caught by the flash of silvery-pale skin on his chest. From his left shoulder, a scar crossed his torso, narrowly missing his nipple, finishing by his belly button. It must've been a terrible injury. Life-threatening. From battle, surely.

He seemed only a few years older than me. Early thirties wasn't young, no, but too young for such a scar. Other than our unofficial naval conflict with Hesperia, Albion hadn't faced war in many years. The only people with such wounds were old men who told their tales by the fire and fascinated small children with the scars.

True, as a fae, he could be much older than he appeared, but it made me wonder.

What battles had he faced in Elfhame? Who did they fight? Dawn Court, perhaps? But the Night Queen and Day King were officially co-rulers. And I'd heard their followers smiled across the throne room, all the while stabbing each other in the back with subtle intrigues. Not outright war.

He tossed the shirt on a chair and pushed the hair from his face, arm flexing. No wonder I hadn't been able to wriggle from his hold. All those muscles.

I worked my tongue around my suddenly dry mouth.

When he rolled his shoulders, as if glad to be free from the restriction of clothing, the light caught on something at his nipple. Was that metal? How did it just stay there? I peered closer. Sure enough, two small spikes sat either side of his nipple, pointing left and right. Wait, was it a *piercing*?

"Go on." He lifted his chin, watching me with amusement glinting in his eyes.

I yanked my gaze away, face hot. "What?"

"You're wondering about it." He gestured to the metal I'd been staring at. (Yes, I was going with the lie that it was only the metal and not any part of his flesh that had held my attention for so long.) "Ask what you're thinking." He said it lightly, like my wondering about his body was the most natural thing in the world.

Maybe it was the brandy, but I approached, letting my attention return to those two little spikes.

It was *definitely* the brandy that had me reaching out once I was close enough. I'd be able to feel whether they were just stuck on or if they dug into the skin somehow.

He caught my wrist, and I gasped both at the speed and the fact it reminded me of what I'd been about to do. "I said you could ask. I didn't say you could touch."

My cheeks burned, part-brandy, part-embarrassment. "Sorry, I just... Do they go *through* your skin? It is a piercing?"

His thumb stroked the inside of my wrist, slow and soft, perhaps an absent gesture. "Yes. A curved bar runs between them." He didn't seem annoyed about my attempt to touch, even if it was apparently not allowed.

I could've said something about the hypocrisy of that—how many times had he touched me uninvited? And wasn't he still holding my wrist, still stroking, stirring the hairs on my arms to rise?

But curiosity ate at me.

Now we were toe-to-toe, I could see the hint of a metal bar

at the back of both spikes, disappearing into the brown skin of his nipple. "Does it... hurt?"

"When it was first done, yes. Not anymore, though. It's long-healed, just like your ears." He pushed the hair back from one pierced ear, and I shivered at the cool air hitting it.

"Why get it done if it hurt so much?" My breathy voice was soft, like I was losing the power of speech.

He scoffed. "Why did you get your ears pierced? That hurt, didn't it?"

"I didn't choose. It was done when I was a child."

A shadow passed over his face, and he made a low sound. "Well, I suppose I'm lucky I had a choice." He traced the edge of my ear. "I like how it looks, and it makes the nipple more sensitive."

I think I stopped breathing. My hand flexed in his grasp. How sensitive? How might he react to me touching him there? Licking him there? Biting there?

"Katherine?"

I sucked in a lungful of air like I'd surfaced from a deep and maddening dive. "Can women have it done?"

The corner of his mouth rose slowly. "They can."

Not that I needed it. My body already reacted too strongly to the slightest touch; I didn't need to be *more* sensitive.

After a long while, a flicker of a frown crossed his face, and he released my wrist. "Who's Webster?"

"What?"

"That rose." He jerked his chin towards the potted rose bush. "You moved it to your bedroom. You're keeping it close to yourself. The tag says it's from 'Webster.'"

I laughed and his frown deepened. "Webster's the gardener."

He shook his head, still not looking amused.

"The one from the other day—I talked to him about roses and he... interrupted us."

"Hmm. And now he's giving you gifts. That you keep in your bedroom." He nodded and took a step away. "I see."

"He was being kind. I know that's probably an alien concept to you, but other people do do it sometimes." Inwardly, I winced as soon as I said it. He'd just given me that book, hadn't he? Still, he was being ridiculous. "I'd commented on the bush in the gardens, so he gave me one of my own. And it's in here rather than the living room, because the light's better. It's too direct in the living room—it'll scorch over the summer."

His mouth flattened and he shot the plant a glare.

"Good gods, Bastian. Even if there was something more to the gift, I don't see that it's any of your business. You don't own me."

He flinched, shooting upright like I'd pricked him with one of the rose's thorns. "No, I don't. Nor do I wish to."

Did that mean he didn't want me? Or he just didn't want to *own* me? I'd managed to gather a little information about fae society, but it *seemed* like their marriage laws didn't grant a husband effective ownership of his wife as Albionic laws did.

Still, he stood too many paces away now—the moment of closeness between us was broken. This seduction really wasn't going as planned. I needed to get him into bed.

"Well." I gave a delicate (and fake) yawn behind my hand. "Time for bed." I busied myself folding down the blankets.

When I turned, I found him unbuttoning his trousers.

"Keep those on," I blurted. I'd so readily reached out to touch his nipple, I needed to recover some control. I would let him make the first move, let him think it was his idea. That was what I told myself, anyway.

In truth, I didn't dare be the one to cross that line. It felt like contemplating a leap into a bottomless pit.

"As you wish." He inclined his head, then slid into bed.

Into *my* bed. Lords and Ladies. Fuck. Shitting hells.

I went and blew out the remaining candles, hyper-aware of his gaze on me the whole while. I pulled myself together enough to pause in front of the last candelabra, and slowly, slowly pull the tie of my robe. He sat up, drinking in every gesture. Maybe he saw the slight tremble of my hands, too.

Swallowing, I shrugged off the robe and let it fall, knowing the candles would shine through my semi-sheer nightgown.

Hopefully, that suitably dramatic disrobing would repair the distance that had opened between us.

You need to do this for your job. It's just another task, like sowing seeds or digging up potatoes.

That in mind, I slid under the covers. "Good night, Bastian." I didn't dare look at him, just blew out the final candle on my bedside table and lay down.

My face tingled as I waited in the dark. When my husband had come to our wedding bed, I'd lain there, waiting, equal parts afraid and disgusted at what I was expected to do. Duty really fucked over women far more than men. The only positive thing in my mind was gratitude that I'd let the stable groom take me in the hay first. That had been my one thought as he'd clambered across the bed and onto me.

I swallowed down nausea and clutched the silk of my nightgown. This wasn't Robin. This was Bastian. This was a different bed on a very different night, with a different man.

You need to do this for your job.

When I dared to look up, I found the dim glow of his eyes up at the headboard.

"Good night, Katherine. Sleep well." The bed jiggled, and I

tensed. But he didn't come closer or touch me. He just lay down, and the glow of his eyes disappeared.

I waited for him to roll this way and pull up my nightgown... for the clumsy fumbling... for the pawing at my thighs, pulling them apart.

My heart thundered. Surely he couldn't sleep with that much noise.

Maybe I shouldn't have tried this in bed in the dark, when it held too many unpleasant memories.

I waited and waited until the slow steady rhythm of his breaths whispered through the darkness.

Still I waited.

I must've fallen asleep, because the next thing I knew, light crept at the edges of the curtains, and tension coiled through my body. Sweet, delicious friction came from something between my thighs.

And then I realised.

I had one leg draped over him, my cheek and hand on his chest, and his arm around my back, hand on my waist. I sucked in a breath, skin burning as I realised I'd woken rocking against him. That was the source of the friction that had my clit tight and tingling. Swallowing, I forced myself still.

He was right. My body did yearn for touch, for pleasure, for *him*, and it had sought those things out even in sleep.

The hand on my waist tightened. "Kat?" His voice was soft, a little sleep-groggy, but also edged with something raw and hot. The thigh between mine flexed, increasing the pressure against my pussy, so I had to bite back a gasp.

I lifted my head and met his gaze. In this half-light, it was dark, his pupils so wide, they left only narrow rings of dim silver.

"Kat," he said again. It wasn't a question this time, but... maybe a reassurance, given the way he paired it with his hand cupping my cheek. Beneath me, his chest rose and fell more heavily, and I could feel the hardness in his trousers against my thigh.

It wasn't only my heart that throbbed, but my whole body, like a constant cry for *more*.

Maybe he heard it, because he didn't let me look away when his leg rubbed again, and a sound came from my throat.

"You like that, my sweet ember?" He pulled me tight against him and angled my face up like he was going to kiss me.

Three knocks sounded from somewhere in the distance.

I blinked at him, like I'd drunk too much and couldn't entirely understand the world. His touch was drugging, delicious, and I arched into it, gripping with my thighs.

Three more knocks.

Not so distant.

The world swam into some sort of sense, and I didn't like it.

The knocking was coming from the door to my rooms.

Oh no, I did not like it at all.

Shit.

He must've realised the same, because his eyes went wide.

I swept from the bed. Fuck. What was I doing? Inviting a man to stay in my rooms, rubbing myself against his leg...

The accusations blazed through me as I grabbed my robe and pulled it on, face on fire with shame upon shame.

Except. This was my job, and I was a married woman now. An adult. Not a girl whose papa had spent a mind-boggling sum on a fae-worked pistol and given it to her so she could "protect her honour."

Like that was the most important thing I had to offer the world.

I dragged in a long, shaking breath and rubbed my face. Even though it was my sleeping self that had draped over Bastian and begun whatever that was, it was right. My unconscious mind didn't have the same ambivalence about seducing him as my conscious one.

Three more knocks—faster, louder.

I took a step away. "You need to—"

"I know." He was already on his feet, gathering his shirt. "I've snuck out of a lot more rooms than you have." Before he pulled on the shirt, he gave me a slight smile, but tension edged it. "Tell them you'll be right there."

Right. Yes. Thank the gods one of us still had their head. I hurried out into the unlit sitting room and called, "Coming! Who is it?"

"Who else calls for you most days?" Ella's voice.

Not quite as bad as if it had been Seren or someone else. I let out a breath and looked to Bastian for direction. Much as I didn't want to admit it out loud, he was right. I had snuck a grand total of zero men out of my rooms.

He grabbed his jacket and shrugged it on. "Open the door, then distract her, and I'll slip out." He eased into the space behind the door and gave me a firm nod as the shadows around him darkened.

I swallowed and ran my fingers through my hair, as though its state might give away what I'd just been doing. I opened the door with a wide smile in place. "Ella. You're very early."

She frowned. "No, I'm not." She nodded at the clock on the mantlepiece. Almost ten o'clock. Time for brunch with the queen. Her frown deepened, and she glanced over at the sofa.

"You haven't even opened the curtains. What're you doing still in bed at this t—?"

I pulled her into a hug before she could turn and see the shadows behind the door and the man contained within them. "I'm so pleased to see you. I was having the strangest dream."

She raised her eyebrows at me. "Oh? Tell me more." Ella was one of those rare people who enjoyed hearing the odd things that happened in other people's dreams rather than finding them terribly boring.

Bastian slipped out of his hiding place, and I'd never been so grateful for the silence of fae feet.

"It was so horrible." I made my eyes wide, like I'd been trapped in a terrible nightmare. "I'm just glad you woke me from it." The biggest lie I'd ever told.

Bastian arched one eyebrow at me as if to ask, "Really?"

No. Not at all. It was the worst kind of dream to wake up from.

With a lingering look, he crept out the door, leaving my body tight in memory of what I'd so nearly had.

Good gods, Ella, you have the worst timing in the world.

38

It was a few days after Bastian had stayed in my room and I hadn't seen him except for a brief glimpse through a window, so I gathered my courage. It was time to take matters into my own hands. Dressed in the midnight blue off-the-shoulder velvet gown that we'd first danced in, I set off in search of him.

I went straight to the corridor where his rooms were, even though I had no business being there—or at least no legitimate business. To the western end of the palace and up a grand staircase... but when I reached the landing, I found myself face-to-face with a dour fae bodyguard. The way he stood at attention, spear in hand, sharp eyes on me, there was no doubt he was guarding the double doors and the hallway beyond.

"Is... I was looking for Lord Marwood." No matter what he'd said about fae formality (or lack of it), it didn't feel safe to just use his first name with someone else. Much too familiar.

The fae didn't answer. He only blinked, eyes swivelling forwards.

"Is he in his suite?"

Still nothing.

I took a step towards the doors, but a spear blocked my path.

Fine.

I smiled at the guard sweetly. "Thank you so much for your help."

Even my sarcasm got no response.

Prickly, I made my way through the usual spaces courtiers occupied. In the billiard room, I found Langdon and a handful of dukes. They smiled politely, but their sudden stillness made it clear this wasn't a space where a woman was welcome. Langdon kept his head bowed the whole time I made up some story about having a message for Bastian. None of them had seen him, but Langdon's discomfort took the edge off my disappointment.

In a drawing room, I stumbled across Caelus, the two fae women I'd overheard gossiping about Bastian, and another man from Dawn. The look Caelus gave me as I apologised for interrupting them had my skin heating. "No need to hurry away, Katherine. Come and sit with me." He patted a tiny gap on his armchair.

I would've needed to sit half on his lap to fit there.

The rose-gold-haired sisters gave me twin looks that promised they'd find new and unusual uses for my entrails if I took him up on the offer.

I stammered a thank you and made up an excuse about being on an errand for the queen, then fled. Consequences. Definitely catching up with me.

I was still wincing when I spotted a familiar green gown at the doorway to the outer courtyard. "Win?"

She turned, freckled face brightening into a huge grin. "If it isn't my dear friend Katherine!" She hurried over, blue eyes sparkling in a way that set off all kinds of alarm bells.

"What are you up to?" I tried to keep the accusation out of my tone. I may not have been entirely successful.

"Well..." She leant closer, eyes darting side to side before she looped her arm through mine and led me outside like we were bosom buddies out for a stroll. "I've found a new and lucrative client base."

My blood went cold. "You're not stealing from them, are you?"

"No!" She clutched her chest as if mortally wounded by the idea. "These courtier friends of yours..." She hissed in a breath. "They have *muh-ney*." She drew the word out, grin getting even wider. "But they still bloody love a bargain. That's where I come in." She preened, lifting her chin.

Selling them stolen goods. I wasn't sure that was any better. But her veiled threat from our last meeting hung in the air, thick like the sappy scent of freshly pruned hedges that filled the courtyard.

"It's a shame you're not doing your night time work anymore. We could've made a killing." She gave me a sidelong look, lashes lowering like she'd learned Ella's best moves. "Are you sure I can't tempt you back to the dark side of life? I'm sure you have access to all kinds of goodies now."

I scoffed. She thought I'd gone legit. Pretty sure I'd gone even deeper into the dark with my current line of work. "If I'm hit by the urge, you'll be the first to know."

"Aww." She squeezed my arm and her smile was so bright

I'd have sworn there was some genuine warmth in it—not just for ill-gotten-gains, but for me.

No... that had to be... I shook my head. Sometimes my reading of people was off.

If the expression was fleeting enough, I could mis-read the cues. There were certain emotions that looked very similar to each other—the peaked eyebrows and parted lips of fear and sexual pleasure, for instance. The pupils were key to reading the difference between those two. Little pinpricks for fear. Wide blackness for desire.

Other times, I could read the right things on a person's face, but my interpretation of *why* could be wrong. In this instance, my reading of warmth was correct, I had no doubt, but that didn't mean it was for me. It couldn't be.

I gave her a tight smile and patted her hand as we walked. When she said nothing more, I steered the conversation to my own ends. "Have you seen Lord Marwood?"

"Lord Mar—oh, you mean Bastian?"

I tried not to let my teeth grit at hearing her call him that. I failed. "Yes."

Her grin gave it away. She'd seen him.

That only made my teeth grit even tighter. "Well? Tell me."

"I sold to him an hour ago."

He was shopping with her now? "What did he buy?"

"I can't tell you that." She touched her chest where a new necklace hung. Clearly, business was good. "I'm the very soul of discretion."

I narrowed my eyes at her.

"Fine," she huffed an instant later. "I can't tell you, but I will say"—she leant in—"what a man like him wants with broken things, I don't know."

Who knew what the hells he was up to? I was supposed to be finding out, and yet I only found him more puzzling than ever.

She directed me to the room where she'd last seen him— one of the palace's little parlours. As I started away, she called my name and tossed me a shiny green apple. Where she'd pulled that from, I couldn't work out. When I cocked my head at her, she only grinned. "To keep your strength up." With that, she winked suggestively and disappeared through the archway.

All of this was rapidly spiralling out of my control. Not just spiralling but gushing down a flooded gorge, bashing into rocks, breaking apart, and then falling down a sky-high waterfall at the end.

Re-entering the palace, I rubbed my head, which now ached as though *I* had been thrown off that waterfall head-first.

"Ah, I recognise that red hair. If it isn't my dear niece."

"Uncle Rufus." A rictus smile creaked in place as I looked up and found him bearing down on me. Where in the grave-yard, beneath the open sky, he'd seemed less tall, now, boxed in by walls and ceiling, he was every inch the giant I remembered from my childhood. I had to crane my neck to keep all of him in sight.

The ache in my head became throbbing pain.

Tension around his eyes belied his apparent easy confidence. "I'm so glad I caught you alone again."

Sure enough, when I glanced up and down the corridor, there was no one in sight. The throbbing grew faster.

"This is a matter of some delicacy." He used his size to usher me into an alcove.

"Did you need something from me, Uncle?" My voice didn't shake, but it was higher than usual.

He smiled, but his eyes were cold where Win's had been so warm, even when thinking of her own self-interest. "You have friends in all sorts of places now. My clever niece." He shook his head as his gaze skimmed over me. "All grown up and friends with the queen herself."

"I'm only a lady-in-waiting," I blurted. It skirted dangerously close to contradicting him, making my head throb even harder.

"No, no," he crooned. "You're much more than that. Rubbing shoulders with Her Majesty and all those powerful men who've gathered to make her offers of marriage. You might've failed in your family duty to provide an heir, but in this, you've done better than I ever expected. Your position honours the Ferrers name. Don't sell yourself short."

Even with the dig at my childless marriage, the praise might've pleased me coming from someone else. From him, it twisted in my stomach like a snake wrapping around some small creature.

I swallowed, staring up at him, back against the wall of the alcove. I clung to the dado rail, needing solidity. The carved edges bit into my fingertips, confirming that this was indeed real. "What do you need me to do?" My voice came out so soft, I barely heard it.

"Introduce me to some of these new friends of yours. The fellows from Dusk and Dawn Courts, especially."

Introductions to Asher and Caelus... What did he hope to gain from that? Or was it that he wanted to meet Bastian and leverage my relationship with him to his own ends? That would be more dangerous to my uncle than anyone else... anyone except me.

If he tried to manipulate Bastian, it would backfire on him... and once he crawled out of whatever pain Bastian left him in, he'd make sure I suffered.

"Fae will make powerful allies for our family, Katherine." He said it softly, reasonably, like he was doing us a great favour and I was foolish not to see it. "If the family is strong, we don't need to worry about scandal or rumour. We'll be able to protect you from your *indiscretions*."

Consequences catching up with me. This time of my rumoured relationship with Bastian. My cheeks burned.

"And wouldn't it be a shame if I had to give you another reminder of the importance of obedience?"

Fantôme's little face swum into view—her white whiskers and peach nose. But there was more; something on the edge of memory. Her unmoving body. The dark of night. The chill of damp soil. His voice, cold and hard.

It seized my throat. I couldn't displease him. I had to obey. Even my thundering heart was a reminder of that—every paired beat saying *o-bey, o-bey, o-bey*.

Like some sort of automaton, I nodded and nodded.

So reasonable. I should be grateful. I should do as I'm told.

"Kat?"

I'd never been so grateful to hear Ella's voice, and for a second, I thought I'd imagined it through sheer force of hope. But footsteps approached, and she called me again. A note of desperation entered her tone.

My uncle's jaw tightened, but he didn't step back.

"There you are." She peered around him, a frown flashing above her smile. "Can't miss that hair anywhere." She turned the full force of her smile on my uncle and blinked in apparent innocence. "I'm afraid the queen has need of her, Lord...?"

"Ferrers." His voice was low and cold, like a biting winter wind.

Her eyes went wide. "Oh, Kat's father or—?"

"Her uncle." He turned on a charming smile of his own and tilted his head. "Katherine didn't tell me she had such a pretty friend."

My stomach threatened to exit my body. I pressed myself harder into the wall, but all I really wanted to do was grab Ella's hand and run.

"Oh, his lordship is too kind." But there was a note of dismissal in her tone. "Kat? Come on, Her Majesty has summoned you." She raised her eyebrows at Rufus, holding his gaze where many a man twice her size would've dropped it after a second.

There was a hollowness to Uncle Rufus. A cold spark in the depths of his eyes that meant few could maintain eye contact with him for long. Ella looked like she was about to set the record.

At last, he stepped aside. It wasn't for Ella's sake and certainly not mine, but even he wasn't going to argue with the queen's orders.

When he gestured, I lurched from the wall. Ella caught my hand and bade him farewell. I think I might've said something, but the throbbing of my head drowned it out.

"Remember what we discussed, dear niece," he called down the hallway. "I look forward to meeting more of your friends."

We turned several corners and walked for a few minutes, my heart slowing, muscles loosening.

Even though Ella remained silent, I could *feel* her unspoken questions in the air. She understood people. She had to know it was abject fear that had held me so still in the alcove. She had to wonder what had happened.

I didn't want to face airing it. I'd closed the door on Fantôme and that stable yard.

Finally, I found my tongue. "Thank you for the lie about the queen. It was the only thing that would've made him let me go." I squeezed her hand, grateful she hadn't dropped it. The pounding of my head abated, leaving me shaky.

"That... wasn't a lie."

When I looked up, she winced. That was the clue that I'd missed under the effect of my uncle's presence.

Her Majesty wasn't just gathering all her ladies-in-waiting. This wasn't just lunch time or a whim where she wanted us to listen to another chapter from one of Madame Sergeanne's books. This was different. She wanted me specifically.

"The queen has summoned you to the throne room immediately."

39

Immediately. The queen's orders were generally to be obeyed at once, but that went without saying. In my months at court, I'd never heard her actually *say* "immediately." That snake in my stomach coiled tighter around its prey.

Trouble.

Not safe. Not *at all*.

Had someone seen Bastian leaving my rooms?

Did the Watch think I had more to do with Lara's death than just finding her?

A chill spread over me like a cloak of ice. There was another possibility.

Had my years as the Wicked Lady finally caught up with me?

Ears ringing, I entered the corridor leading to the throne room.

"Kat?" Ella squeezed my hand. "Are you—?"

"I'm fine." I pulled my shoulders back, swallowed down

the rising panic, and counted a long inhale, then a long exhale. Whatever was coming, I would face it with at least a scrap of dignity. No one else needed to know my pulse skipped along in an erratic rhythm or that my face tingled.

Guards opened the throne room doors, and I dropped Ella's hand. No sense in tainting her by association.

The herald announced us, and the comedy of Ella's absurdly long name eased my shoulders a little.

Still, the ringing in my ears followed us across the carpet on a journey that felt like miles through the hushed throne room. No one tittered at me behind a fan today.

Guards flanked the dais. To protect the queen or seize me? The woman herself sat upon her gilded throne, still in black for her mother, with a black ribbon in her hair for Lara. To one side stood Cavendish, face impassive as ever. I'd stopped being surprised by that.

But on her other side stood Bastian and Asher. It was only sheer force of will that stopped me missing a step at the sight of them.

Had Bastian revealed my secret? Except... no. He couldn't. Our deal.

Unless... There'd been nothing in our bargain about him not telling Asher. He could've told him, and then *he'd* told the queen.

Yes, he'd seemed ready to take our flirtation further in my bed, but that didn't mean a damn thing. Wasn't I using my body against him? He wasn't above doing the same in return or even indulging in a little fun while he destroyed me.

The tingling of my face became a thick buzz, and grey blotches crowded the edge of my vision.

Would he? *Would* he? I forced myself to take a proper look at him.

I couldn't read his expression, but his eyes drilled into me, as intense as they'd been when he'd eye-fucked me at the picnic.

Was this a look that fucked or a look that killed, though? Either way, my skin rose to goosebumps under its weight. At his sides, his hands flexed.

Ella and I stopped at an appropriate distance from the throne and bowed low. The queen dismissed her with a casual flick, but Ella paused for a moment and glanced at me as though hesitant to leave my side. Sweet woman, but self-preservation should've had her scuttling away at once.

I lifted my chin, eyes still on Her Majesty, hoping Ella would get the message: *Leave me to face this alone.*

With another bow, she withdrew.

"Lady Katherine." The queen smiled, but like many of her smiles, it was unreadable. She'd had far too much practice at this. "You have been with us but a short time... and yet you've already made *quite* the impression at court. Not to mention a transformation." One eyebrow raised, she took in my outfit.

Was this "impression" about Bastian and how he'd been seen leaving my rooms? Or was "transformation" a veiled reference to my finances, and she was going to segue to how that had driven me to ride at night?

"I must confess"—her voice lowered—"when you first stood there, I never expected to be calling you before me under such shocking circumstances."

Shock that I was the Wicked Lady?

I swallowed but allowed myself no other outer reaction. The high sound in my ears blocked her next words.

Blinking, I tried my hardest to focus, but the world swayed, those grey blotches eating up more and more of my field of view.

Whatever she said, it had Bastian's and Asher's expressions tightening. Even Cavendish's jaw clenched for the briefest instant. That had to be the revelation.

"... the wicked circumstances. I'm sure everyone will agree you deserve your new place." She raised her eyebrows expectantly.

My new place in jail, awaiting execution. I waited for the guards to come and clap manacles around my wrists.

Long seconds later, I was still waiting.

The queen's eyebrows crept higher. Eventually, she cleared her throat. "Lady Katherine, approach." Almost a bark.

Three paces forward, then up the three steps to the dais. I don't know how my shaking legs managed it, but somehow I stood before her.

She beckoned, and I leant in. "This world sees us women as disposable. Even me. I understand if that makes you uncomfortable, but rest assured that Lara will never be forgotten."

I blinked at her, trying not to let my face screw up. What the hells was she talking about?

"This role is a high honour, and one you deserve. Now"—her eyebrows drew together—"for goodness' sake, woman, turn and bow."

Even as my mind tripped over her words, my body obeyed.

"Presenting Lady Katherine Ferrers," the herald announced as I bowed, "liaison to Lord Bastian Marwood."

Still bent over, I almost stumbled forward, but managed to rock my balance back onto my heels.

Liaison. Me.

I wasn't in trouble. I was safe.

The grey dissolved and my ears popped as the rest of the world rushed back in. The courtiers in their finery were an explosion of colour. Their polite applause thundered against my eardrums. Their gazes, some envious, some assessing, were physical blows on sensitive skin.

I managed a smile, but I clasped my hands so tightly, my knuckles groaned.

With a word from the queen, the throne room's formality evaporated, and footmen appeared with trays of drinks and canapés. Chatter filled the air, battering me. Several people rushed forward, offering congratulations. I nodded and nodded, inane smile in place, while my heart thrashed in my chest like a caged beast, and my skin prickled, ready to crawl off my bones.

I needed quiet. I needed to get out of here. I needed to be alone to purge these reactions from my body, because I couldn't hold them in much longer.

Lost in the crowd, shaking, I shoved my way to the doors.

The instant I reached the hallway, I fled.

40

I burst into the library—it was the closest quiet place. In all my other visits, I'd only found it occupied once with the Dawn sisters. Today, it was empty—everyone was drinking to my new appointment.

Hands pressed into a table, I let the breaths tear through me.

So sure. I'd been so sure.

Disaster. That's what I'd expected in the throne room today.

Dismissal or arrest—either way, it would've been a very public punishment for disobedience, a very public shaming. My reputation would never have recovered. I wouldn't have been able to continue my work for Cavendish. I could've waved goodbye to any hopes of paying off the bailiff.

If arrested, I could've waved goodbye to *life*.

I pushed up from the table and hugged myself, fingers digging into my biceps. "You're safe," I whispered through the shaking. "You're safe."

I'd jumped to such extreme conclusions. That wasn't sensible or useful or practical. It wasn't what I'd moulded myself to be.

Then again, should I be surprised when it had come right after facing my uncle?

"You're safe." I stroked my arms, soothing my breaths to something closer to normal.

At last, my heart calmed, but energy still thrummed through my muscles, forcing me to pace before the large windows with their deep window seats.

As I turned for the dozenth time, the door flew open, and a dark shape swept in.

Bastian, chest heaving like he'd run here. Shadows churned around his feet, looking like he stood in a pool of darkness. He scanned the room from left to right, and the instant his gaze landed on me, he slammed the door and made a beeline this way. More shadows poured off his shoulders, leaving night in his wake.

I stilled. If disaster had struck today, there would have been no more chances with him.

He didn't slow, just charged into my space, cupped my cheeks, and met my gaze.

I read so much in that single moment.

Want. Desperation. Need. Hunger. Desire. The most intense longing I'd ever known.

Or maybe it was just that I saw myself mirrored in his blazing silver eyes.

It didn't matter, because I knew in that second what he was going to do. And I wanted it. Craved it. Tilted my chin up, clutched his shoulders, and invited it.

Still striding into me, scuffing my shoes along the floor, his mouth met mine.

It was the sweetest destruction.

Hot, breathless, claiming, he kissed me, and I bent to it eagerly. Tongues, lips, teeth, his hands angling my face so he could plunge deeper while I clung to him. We kissed with every point of contact.

He lit up my body, so when his unstoppable trajectory bumped me against the wall, it was like an asteroid had struck the very earth. He crushed me into it, and I relished the pressure anchoring me to the moment, banishing every last ounce of fear that had dogged my steps from the throne room. I let his hard and unyielding body direct mine.

No more resistance.

I wrapped my legs around him, seeking more pressure, more closeness, more contact with the solid muscles I'd been unable to tear my gaze from in my bedroom.

And he gave.

Good gods, how he gave. He could've pulverised me to dust against that wall, and I'd have thanked him for it. His hips filled the space between my thighs with something close to perfection, and the pressure upon my centre knotted every nerve.

Drowning in sensory overload, I could barely move, only respond to the command of his mouth on mine.

When I wilted, barely able to think, barely able to contain the devastating storm raging in my chest and my core, he pulled away the barest inch. His breaths heaved over my lips, sparking sensation that licked through me like lightning.

Eyes shut, he pressed his nose and forehead to mine and swallowed. "I haven't been able to stop thinking about you since I left your rooms." His voice was thick and low, rumbling into me. With a ragged inhale, he opened his eyes and stroked his thumbs over my cheeks. "I had to stay away. Regain my control."

I huffed, somewhere between laughter and panting. "Yes, you seem very controlled right now."

But inwardly I crowed. *He* had thought of *me*. The power of his confession was as overwhelming to my powerless self as his touch to my touch-starved body.

One canine flashed. "I waited until we were alone, didn't I?" His fingers threaded into my hair, adding to the layers of feeling my body was struggling to keep track of. "A couple of days ago, I would've taken you over the throne the instant you walked in."

I laughed again, though I wasn't entirely sure it was a joke. In fact, the wideness of his pupils and heat in their depths said it probably wasn't.

When I fell silent, he kissed me again, less hard this time, more considered, like he was mapping my mouth, testing what spots wrung a whimper from me (the roof of my mouth, the length of my tongue) and giving me space to explore in turn. I took his tongue, met it with my own, and I gave, greedy to explore and feel and know.

"In the maze"—he kissed my cheek—"I wanted to make you come as they did"—another kiss on my jaw—"so their cries would mask yours." His hands trailed lower, light upon my throat and bare shoulders, and he followed with his mouth, nibbling and teasing, making my breath hitch and my centre molten. "I'd have licked you from my fingers, Katherine." He lapped at my fluttering pulse as if to demonstrate. "I'd have kissed you hard and deep, so you'd know I wanted to taste every inch of you, so you'd know I meant every word I said about how fucking exquisite you are." He paused, fingers tracing the neckline of my dress, and pulled back to meet my gaze. "But we were interrupted, weren't we?"

I nodded and had to swallow before I could speak. "By some bastard."

Another flash of his teeth. "Some absolute fucking bastard. But now I intend to make up for it."

And yet, he stepped back and lowered my feet to the floor. I blinked up at him, an instant away from asking what the hells he was doing.

"Before we were interrupted in the gardens, I asked whether you wanted the things in that delicious book you were reading. What was your answer going to be?"

I gripped his jacket, body tight and empty, now it wasn't pressed against his. "You know what it was going to be."

A lazy curl of his mouth as he watched mine. "I want to hear you say it."

Hyper-aware of the closeness of his attention, I licked my lips. His parted as if in response, and he took a deeper breath.

"Yes." I nodded, emphatic for once, despite all the doubts and ambivalence that had made me hold back before. "I want the things in that book. From you."

His smile was slow and seductive—as if he didn't already have me exactly where he wished. "That's my ember." Hands on my shoulders, he angled me to one side and propelled me backwards. "Sit."

The command in his voice was a reassurance—I wasn't responsible for what was about to happen. Or at least, I could tell myself that.

The backs of my legs hit the edge of a window seat and I dropped into it.

"Good." He knelt, putting his face level with mine, and

kissed me again and again, pushing me into the cushions resting against the window.

I looped my legs around his hips, using my years of riding to squeeze tight. A low sound rumbled from him as he ground into me and gripped my thighs in place like he was afraid I'd move them.

Not a chance. Not a fucking chance. Not when I was throbbing and wet, muscles clenching tighter with every press of his hard cock.

"Please," I whispered against his lips. Like at the maze, I had no idea what I asked for, but he'd been so good at deciphering it then, I would leave it to him.

He groaned. "You have no idea what it does to me when you say that."

Again, the power flushed through me, hot and fierce.

He kissed my throat, his stubble and lips combining in a torrent of sensation I couldn't pick apart. I threaded my fingers through his thick hair. When I traced the edge of one pointed ear, he pressed into the touch with a low rumbling sound that hummed through every point of contact.

A moment later, he stilled and pulled back, eyes dark. "Hands on the window frame."

It seemed, just as when I'd reached for his nipple piercing, I wasn't allowed to touch today. But, of course, I obeyed, placing my hands upon cold stone either side of the window.

Shadows snaked off him and clasped my wrists, holding them in place. They were cool and dry, like a pillow just flipped over on a hot summer's night.

"There." He drank in the sight of me, the faintest smile on his lips, like he didn't realise he was doing it. "Don't you look stunning?"

I tested the hold. The restraints flexed, more like flesh than solid steel, but I couldn't pull away.

"Remember." He watched me tug on the bindings. "You say stop, we stop. Always."

I nodded and sank back into the seat, letting the cushions and his shadows hold me. "I understand."

"Good." He squeezed my hips, reinforcing the pleasure of that word with a touch. "Now, where were we? Ah, yes." He planed his hands up to the low neckline of my dress and tugged it down, letting my breasts spill out.

I let out a soft sound at the chill air hitting my skin, making my nipples hard.

For a beat he paused, taking me in so intently I squirmed. Then he replaced that cold with the heat of his mouth, taking in one furled bud. My body arched, pulling at his restraints, and I cried out at the streak of pleasure so pure and intense, it was almost painful. As he sucked one nipple and flicked his tongue across it, he toyed with the other, circling with his thumb, kneading my breast, pinching.

Each breath was a gasp as I tried to maintain some semblance of control. This was supposed to be work. Supposed to be... but fuck, the things he was doing to me. My pussy reverberated in time with my pulse. It echoed in my belly, my thighs, my throat and bound wrists.

"I'm your liaison now," I managed to huff. "Doesn't that complicate things?"

He pulled away, lower lip still brushing my flesh as he said, "I requested you." His attention shifted to my other nipple, surrounding it in the wet heat of his mouth.

There was another question I'd meant to ask next, but the sight of him consuming me, eyes shut, brows pulled together in focus, put everything else out of my mind.

He withdrew an inch, eyes flicking up to me before he blew across my wet nipple, making me jerk as a whole new sensation gripped me. "Why? You don't have anyone else, do you?" He cocked his head, shadows seething. "That gardener... Does he mean something to you? I'm sure he doesn't do this to you..." He sucked me back into his mouth, not dropping eye contact.

"No." It came out on a breath, though I could've sworn I *couldn't* breathe anymore. Not when my body was this tight, this achy, this trembling.

He pulled away and the shadows around us eased into content ripples, like the surface of a lake on a calm day. "Good. *Good.*"

As he continued to ravage my breasts, leaving me a molten pool of need, he pushed open the slit of my dress, pausing only to tug the chain garter. "This was an interesting choice. I like it very much. Like you're mine." He kissed me, then, deep, deliberate, slow, making white stars bloom behind my eyelids. When he finally broke off, he sat back on his heels and took in my bare thighs and pussy.

Under his scrutiny, I shifted and bit my lip. No one had ever looked at me like this.

This exposed but also with such a heavy gaze—even without his grip on my wrists, the weight of it would've held me still. The stable groom hadn't paused—there hadn't been time, not when someone could've walked in at any moment. And that arsehole I was married to had always fumbled around in the dark, focused only on his own cock and finding somewhere warm to put it.

Chest rising and falling deeply, Bastian shook his head. "Fuck, Katherine." He placed his hands on my knees and skimmed up, teasing my legs apart. "Is every inch of you sublime?" He kissed the inside of one thigh, then the other, as though he couldn't decide which one he wanted first or more. His shadows shuddered and stuttered, thick and dark. "You could crush a man's head with these." His gaze flicked up to me as his teeth flashed. "And to be clear, I'm volunteering."

I chuckled, but it became a strangled gasp as he pulled me to the edge of the seat and pressed my legs wide.

It was as the cool air hit my aching pussy that I realised we were still in the palace library in the middle of the day. "What if someone comes?"

"Someone is going to come." He nipped the inside of my thigh, working his way higher, scrambling my brain. "*You*. That's the point."

"I mean, through the door." I jerked as his breaths fanned my slick flesh. "I can't have—"

"They won't. The door is mysteriously jammed." He arched an eyebrow up at me, taking the backs of my knees and pushing them up and out as far as they would go, leaving me so open, I thought I might die if anyone saw. "Though I suppose someone could peer through the keyhole. Then again, I'm not sure *you* can lecture anyone on voyeurism."

"I can't have them see me." More than a note of panic entered my voice. "I can't—"

"This seat isn't visible from the keyhole." Shadows flowed from him, forming two hands, which took over holding my legs in place.

I stared at them, fascinated by the way their fingers dimpled my flesh, just as his physical fingers had. Remarkable. And the feeling of being held taut, at my body's limit, pulled the tension inside me tighter.

"Wait"—I dragged my attention from his shadow hands —"did you check?"

He just smiled enigmatically, his corporeal hands sliding along my thighs until his thumbs teased my edges. "I don't remember there being this much talking in that book you were reading."

I squirmed as he teased me and kissed my parted legs, working closer and closer to what I needed.

"Why are you doing this?" Because he was still fully dressed and he'd only mentioned me coming, even though I'd felt the evidence of how turned on he was moments ago. Some part of my mind that was always aware of danger registered all that, even through the haze of pleasure I currently lived in. "What do you want from me?"

"'Why?'" He nipped me, and I gasped at yet another sensation layered in with all the others. "I told you, Katherine. It's a tragedy for a beautiful flame to be starved of fuel and allowed to gutter so low, it doesn't even know it's a flame anymore."

Then he licked. Directly up my centre, hotter and more sublime than anything I'd ever known.

Every muscle in me wound tighter as I arched off the cushions and let out a cry that filled the cavernous library.

He left it there, just that one swipe, but it cleaved through me, making my breaths ragged, as my body pounded in a demanding rhythm that needed release or it would surely kill me.

He bit his lip and exhaled. "Stars above, you taste incredible," he said, so low I barely heard it over the drumming of my heart. "As for what I want from you..." He slid one thumb along the same path his tongue had taken, slipping through my folds, nudging my clit, dragging a strangled gasp from me as I pulled against my restraints. "Right now, I want you to come all over my face, so I can go about the rest of my day knowing I'm responsible for you screaming my name, while the rest of the palace wonders who I elicited that response from."

I had to swallow several times before I could speak. "I know you're lying—"

He returned his thumb to my wetness, circling my entrance, and it felt like I really was an ember as he'd said and about to burst into terrible and glorious flame. "That's impossible."

"Then... then you're not being entirely honest." My words broke as I fought to master my tongue. "Y-you twisted my question to what you want 'right now.'"

Eyes hooded, he gave me a lazy smile and kissed the spot right above my clit, making me ache for him to go just half an inch lower. "Do you really care?" he whispered, thumb pressing that little harder, threatening to dip into me.

It was a threat I wanted. Needed. Craved. Would sell my soul for. Fullness. Pleasure. That deep touch.

"Right now? No."

"Good." He flashed his teeth, devilish and damned and fucking gorgeous, and then his head bowed to my waiting flesh.

From back to front, his tongue burned through me, finishing on my throbbing clit, wringing a strangled moan from my throat. He followed with his thumb, letting that finally sink inside, thick and filling.

I didn't have words for how good it felt, and I had even fewer as he thrust in and out and closed his mouth around my clit.

Touching myself was nothing compared to this. Even the orgasms that had felt like bright peaks were dim shadows of the pleasure raging in my body, like every fibre contained a storm that threatened to break out at any second.

His shadow hands bit into my legs as I wound tighter and pushed at my restraints, pulled on them, not entirely in control... hells, not *remotely* in control. He toyed with my breasts and tweaked my nipples just as his tongue flicked across my tight bud.

I broke.

Each and every one of those storms tore free. Dark. Bright. Nothing and everything. Devastating and joyous. It all ripped through me. Destroyed me. Left me as nothing but fallen leaves drifting on a breeze in the storm's wake.

For one brief moment, the peace was so absolute, I thought I might be dead.

But as I floated down on a long exhale, I realised that outward breath meant I was still very much alive. And the mouth sucking on my over-sensitive clit... Fuck. Yes, I was alive. And winding up again. Surely I couldn't... not so soon, not when...

I did. I came hard, crying out, body arching into the restraints, mind sinking into the comforting darkness of oblivion.

He destroyed me twice more, and I was a quivering, panting wreck, almost afraid of him continuing, when he finally pulled away. My liquid muscles sagged in the grip of his shadows.

With a small, private smile, he met my gaze and stroked my legs. "My ember sparks." There was a triumphant light in his eyes as he kissed my inner thighs. Every part of me buzzed, so sensitised his light touches were almost painful, and I might've flinched away if I'd had any control over my body.

In a haze, I could only watch him and try to remember

how to breathe normally, how to sit up, how to form words... how to *think*.

He sucked my wetness off his thumb and made a soft sound, like it pleased him. I should've been scandalised at the sight, but for the life of me, I couldn't remember why.

"You did so well, ember. So, *so* well." He cupped my cheeks and kissed me, slow and deep this time. There was a musky taste on his lips. My own arousal, some corner of my mind registered, as I met his tongue with my own.

My response must've crossed a line, because the kiss grew heated, consuming and hungry. The ashes left from where he'd set me alight so thoroughly kindled once more. He pressed against me, fingers plunging into my hair, and when he met my quivering flesh, I whimpered into his mouth. I couldn't say whether it was a whimper of desire or one that said I couldn't take any more.

A moment later, he pulled away, rocking back onto his heels. If his wide pupils and breathlessness hadn't been clue enough, his tented trousers would've given away the depth of his need. But with a long rise and fall of his chest, he straightened and took a step back.

Biting his lip, he studied me. In a window seat, dress pulled down and up so it covered nothing that it should. I tried to close my legs, but his shadows held firm.

They let him take his time. The look made it feel like he owned me. Where I raged against my husband's legal ownership, this was... not the same in a way I couldn't explain. It reminded me of how, at a coronation, a new monarch took possession of the realm but in turn vowed to dedicate herself to the nation. It belonged to her but also she to it.

Bastian's look felt like that. Like it was an ownership that went both ways.

"What I wouldn't give for a painting of you like this." His low voice thrummed in the still air of the library. "Sated, splayed open, tits out, clothes and hair and that magnificent body in glorious disarray."

A shiver rippled through me, part fear at the thought of such a painting ever existing and part pleasure at the praise and especially at the word *magnificent*.

Breaths approaching normal, I managed a soft laugh. "I think people might talk."

"Let them."

With care, he worked the neckline of my gown back over my breasts, pausing to plant a firm kiss on one before it was hidden. His shadows released my thighs, and I let out a sigh as my body sank from its taut position.

"So good," he whispered before kissing my temple and pulling my dress over my legs.

My body hummed, sated as he'd said, but also pleased to have pleased him. And all it had taken was sitting back while he devoured me into a state of bliss.

He pushed hair back from my face—it must've pulled loose in all the kissing. "Remember this next time we're before your queen. I like the shade your cheeks go when you're embarrassed, wicked woman."

"Not Wicked Lady?"

"After the things we just did?" He scoffed and shook his head. "I was mistaken—you're clearly no lady."

I gasped, face heating.

Eyes glinting with amusement, he held my chin and stopped me lowering it. "Yes, that colour. It's perfect."

I glowered at him. Apparently, fucking me with his fingers and tongue wasn't going to stop him trying to throw me off balance at every opportunity.

"And so angry, too." His smile widened. "I love it when you spark, little ember."

I opened my mouth to reply, but he fisted my hair, sending a sprinkle of hairpins onto the cushions, and gave me another deep and devastating kiss. For all I'd been about to tell him that I was going to more than spark at him if he kept mocking me, I surrendered to it.

Or at least, mostly surrendered.

Despite not being able to move in his grip—both on my hair and wrists—I wasn't entirely powerless. I nipped his lower lip in warning. But he smiled against my mouth, and a soft groan sounded in his throat.

Finally, he broke off and stepped back, leaving my lips chafed and my scalp tingling. "Katherine." Inclining his head, he turned, and I got a good view of the bulge in his trousers before he strode away. With a gesture, he made the shadows at my wrists vanish before he, too, disappeared through the door.

I sat there, staring after him, body beautifully aching.

His liaison *and* his lover. This month, I'd truly earned my pay.

Yet the feeling running through me, hot and bright *like* victory, *wasn't*. It was something I hadn't felt in a long, long time. Something half-forgotten, so I couldn't quite find the word. But it was green and lush, like new growth.

And it was good.

41

I spent the rest of the afternoon in my chambers, snoozing, grinning... then wondering if anyone had seen. The next morning when I took breakfast with the queen, I spent the whole time on the edge of my seat, waiting for an accusation. The closest thing was Ella's sidelong look, later followed by her murmuring, "You're positively glowing, Katherine. Who knew the position of liaison would have such an effect?" Her enigmatic smile promised she'd ask about it later, which, of course, she did the instant we were alone. I spilled. She listened, biting her lip, squirming in her seat. It was the closest thing I'd seen her to inelegant.

That afternoon, Seren came bouncing into my chambers unannounced.

I raised an eyebrow and sipped my tea. Since Bastian had stayed in my rooms, I'd started drinking the preventative, because it seemed more and more likely I'd have need of it. Honey softened the bitter edge of its various herbal ingredients. "Oh, you remembered your way here." I hadn't seen her in two days. "I was starting to worry."

She snorted and poked around the various jars on the dressing table. "I'm *terribly sorry*, milady. I've been busy." She shrugged, spun on her heel, and came closer, walking on the balls of her feet. She cocked her head at the teapot and sniffed. "He wants to see you. Usual place." She plopped into a seat, leg sprawled over the arm. "Now, of course."

"Oh, *of course*." I sighed and gulped the last of my tea, even though it was a little too hot to do so. I wouldn't be protected from pregnancy if I didn't drink the lot. Being me, I took at least two cups a day. The last thing I needed was to be saddled with a baby as proof of my indiscretion.

From the door, I glanced back. "The sheets need changing." I would've done it myself, but I had no idea where in the palace they kept fresh linen and it really would've blown my cover to go poking around.

She didn't look up from cleaning her nails. "I'll tell someone. Don't keep him waiting." With an impish grin, she waved.

I couldn't decide whether she hated me or found me amusing. She was certainly the most incompetent lady's maid I'd ever known. Cavendish paid for her, though, rather than me having to dig into my own wages, so I wasn't going to dismiss her and hire another.

The stares that had followed me since Lara's murder had ended along with the curfew, but I passed a couple of people I knew on the way to Cavendish's office. Their looks prickled between my shoulder blades. Did they know what I'd done with Bastian yesterday? I bit my tongue and forced my pace even, although I wanted to hurry out of sight.

When I entered, Cavendish stood over his chess set,

contemplating the board, face in profile. His sleeves were rolled up today, and he'd undone the top buttons of his shirt, as though he'd been in here away from public sight a long while. Lips pursed, he rubbed his chin. I waited, not wanting to disturb his concentration.

A strong, sweet scent seized my throat, making me flinch. It was only when I turned, I spotted a vase of hyacinths standing on a cabinet. The image of Lara's body flashed in my mind, harsh and bright.

As I turned from the flowers, Cavendish swept down, moved a white piece, took a black rook and tossed it on the table. A satisfied smile crossed his face.

"Katherine," he said, turning to me at last, "my star operative, the lady of the hour, Dusk's newest liaison."

His praise didn't feel as safe as it usually did. I'd pleased him, but... Maybe it was that something predatory lingered in his gaze from the chess game. I folded my hands and dipped my chin in acknowledgement.

He shook his head as he approached, smile widening to something dazzling. "And I didn't even need to suggest you—I hear he asked for you himself." His eyes narrowed as he stalked closer.

He didn't stop, forcing me to back away until I hit the door. I swallowed, throat clenching as my breaths came quicker. Was he going to yank my hair again? Had I failed somehow? Had I missed something in my task?

He placed his hands on the door above my shoulders, caging me in.

I could duck under his arm to escape, but then what? I was in his office. I was his employee. I needed his money. No, I was trapped in this cage.

"I wonder why that might be." He cocked his head and pressed his thigh between mine.

I froze. I wasn't even sure I breathed.

"How might you have snared his attention, I *wonder*?" He smirked and leant in, gaze turning to the leaping pulse in my throat, pupils blowing wide.

Did he think I'd fucked Bastian at last, and that meant it was his turn to sample me? I could endure it. I would go away in my head and let my body take it. It couldn't be any worse than my useless husband's fumbling.

I pressed into the wall and tore my gaze away from his, ready to let it drift off into the distance.

And that was when I saw, a matter of inches from my face, a familiar necklace.

In gold, a seven-pointed star, a tiger's eye at its centre.

Adrenaline rushed through me, fizzing and bright. It must've been that driving my muscles, because I grabbed the pendant and turned it over. A fresh nodule of gold showed on the back where the loop that the chain passed through had been repaired.

If it wasn't the same pendant, it was a replacement designed to match exactly and fixed to the broken piece.

My heart thrummed. The necklace clinked in my shaking hand.

When I stared up at Cavendish, he watched me, eyebrows raised expectantly.

"You killed Lara." It had crossed my mind as a possibility, but... I'd still had time.

He inclined his head with a faint smile. "I did warn you to hurry up."

"You said a month." Was he really not willing to wait a little longer to see if I managed on my own?

"You had ample opportunity, but you didn't take it. I gave you her affair gift-wrapped, and you didn't use it. I don't like it when my gifts are so unappreciated." His smile turned cold. "And I *really* don't like being kept waiting. She could've survived if you'd just done as you were told."

He'd killed her for the sake of a few weeks. He'd killed her because I'd failed... because I'd disobeyed.

Goosebumps flooded my skin, and a horrible pressure grew at the back of my eyes and throat. If I'd used her affair with Langdon right away to blackmail her into stepping down...

"Why haven't the Watch arrested you? She had your necklace."

"Ah, my dear Katherine—almost a clever question. But do you really think they'd arrest the queen's spymaster? Especially when so many of them work for him. I encouraged them to believe it was planted in an attempt to discredit me and destabilise court."

Even the Watch was in his pocket. Perhaps I shouldn't have been surprised, but... Was nowhere safe from the corruption of powerful men?

My throat shrank to something as thin as a reed. "And the note to Bastian? How was that part of your plan?"

"An opportunity." He shrugged, tossing his head. "I want his secrets, but even more than that, I want him gone. His infatuation with you presented an opportunity too good to pass up. If he'd been found at the scene, it would've been a convenient way to remove him from the board."

I couldn't fathom any sort of response. If he wasn't so calm, so calculated, I might've called him insane. But, no, there was a horrible grand plan behind everything he did.

And if the necklace was his, that meant he was fae-touched, though I hadn't spotted a fae mark on him. It had to be hidden beneath his clothes.

After a long silence, he pushed a lock of hair back from my face and traced a line down my temple. "I'd started to wonder if you truly had what it takes to be part of my network. But here you are, Marwood's liaison and his lover, too." He cupped my cheek and his teeth flashed in a triumphant grin. "I knew you could be counted on to take a practical approach." He angled my face up like he was going to kiss me.

Inwardly, I cringed. Outwardly, nothing.

I'd retreated from my body. Some things in life were better that way.

I watched from a distance as his fingers flexed and he finally backed away, leaving me pinned to the door by my own fear.

He returned to the chess board and considered it. "As for the next phase of your mission..." He went on, but the words were thick and distorted, like I was at the bottom of a lake and he was on the surface.

I caught enough to understand my instructions. Leverage my position as liaison. Cement Bastian's trust. Get him in the palm of my hand and then squeeze for information. Preferably while I literally had his cock in the palm of my hand... or any other part of my anatomy.

I couldn't even bring myself to be shocked at his bluntness —my body was too far away to respond.

His instructions didn't end there. Find more interesting information in his suite, while he's in a sated sleep, and if he was a light sleeper... Cavendish went to a small cabinet, unlocked it, and produced a small bottle of clear liquid. A few drops in a drink would ensure Bastian slept deeply, so my poking around wouldn't wake him.

A million miles away, I accepted the bottle and nodded.

So obedient. So silent. My father would've been so fucking proud.

"There." Cavendish smiled and patted my cheek. "I know you won't keep me waiting again."

With that, I was dismissed.

I lurched from the room, the bottle burning in my palm.

He'd killed Lara. No wonder she'd looked surprised, betrayed. She'd thought the queen's spymaster was here to keep her safe—she was part of this realm, after all.

But... no. He didn't see it that way, did he?

He might be sworn to protect Albion and our queen, but we were just creatures in that domain. We could be useful, like the ducks on my estate had been useful for their eggs and slug-hunting skills. Or we could be in his way, like the slugs and snails I'd squashed. That was how he saw us.

Me included.

I needed to escape this job. I needed to escape the trap he held me in. Working for Cavendish was too dangerous.

And to think I'd considered Bastian the greatest danger to me. A laugh bubbled from my throat as I strode along a corridor. Thankfully, no one was around to hear.

Bastian hadn't murdered anyone, save for in a few rumours. He'd protected me the day we found Lara. He'd tried to uncover her killer. Other than potentially passing information to an unknown person and sneaking into Caelus's suite, I hadn't found him doing anything nefarious.

Cavendish, though... He was a murderer. But he acted with the queen's sanction and that made him untouchable.

I moved through the corridors, chest and throat tight like someone squeezed them, eyes wide and staring as all these thoughts tripped over each other.

I couldn't even tell Bastian I'd discovered the killer. If I did, that would mean admitting I was a spy, and who knew how he'd react to that? Plus, revealing *anything* about Cavendish's operations would count as treason and I had enough crimes to worry about.

Fuck. Fuck! I had to press my fingers to my lips to keep from saying it out loud.

I found myself at the windows where I'd seen Bastian, Asher, and Lara before. I placed my cheek on the cold glass and let my breath mist it. The chill bit through my daze, and I pushed my palm against the window too, soaking it in, sinking back into myself.

Only the gods knew how long I stood there, practically hugging the glass, but eventually I blinked and drew a long breath and straightened. Outside, the sun streamed into the gardens, casting deep shadows on this side of the palace and at the base of each tree and bush. A preening flock of dukes rode out on their sabrecats, laughing and tossing their heads like there were no cares in all the world.

I gritted my teeth as they took off, spurring their cats into a race towards the Queenswood. What must it be like to be one of them? A man. A very, very wealthy man. One with status and power. One who could sleep with a dozen women and face no consequence. One who didn't live in fear of saying or doing the wrong thing, or even the rumour that he had. One whose estate made more money in a year than I'd known in a lifetime.

But, a corner of my mind whispered, *what money could you make in an hour?*

I gasped, finding that my fingertip had traced the dukes' course in the misted glass.

An hour. There was one opportunity to make a *very* large

sum, if I did it right. And... I had the skills. I had Vespera. I had time to train.

The sabrecat race and its three-thousand-pound prize could free me from Cavendish.

It was about the only thing that could.

I would enter, and I would win.

I had to.

42

I started training right away. That afternoon, I took Vespera out for a long ride, testing her endurance. She stretched her legs, loping along at a comfortable speed, sniffing the air as though glad to be out. There hadn't been reason to ride far since coming to the palace, until now.

The queen's race would stretch over ten miles. At a card party that evening, I enquired about the route over the poker table. Most years, it ventured into the city, closing roads and bridges, but this year it would be confined to palace grounds so any fae who wished to enter could.

I bit the inside of my cheek at that idea. Vespera was fast, and I'd back her in any race, but racing against fae? Who knew what tricks they might have up their sleeves?

Speaking of tricks up sleeves, I was fairly sure the Frankish suitor, Prince Valois, was cheating at cards, as he revealed *yet another* winning hand. I chuckled and shook my head like I didn't feel sick about losing another stack of coins. "You have the devil's own luck, Your Highness."

"I am sorry, *madame*, I hate to deprive you, but I do so love to win." His charming smile was the kind it was difficult to stay angry at long.

Across the room, a couple of the younger ladies looked up from their game, watching him. His was also the kind of smile it was difficult to tear your eyes from. I even caught Ella giving him the occasional sidelong look.

As we'd got ready, I'd asked her about Cavendish and his necklace without revealing his connection to Lara's murder. She'd never seen him without it. It had to be important to him —both because he always wore it and because he'd had it repaired after it was broken.

"Perhaps *madame's* luck is about to change." Bastian's low, familiar voice set my body on alert, just in time for his hand to land on my shoulder. An apparently casual gesture, but at my back, out of everyone else's sight, his thumb slid beneath the strap of my gown and lingered there.

The touch shot through my nerves, perhaps heightened by the fact he stood behind me, out of sight. "Lord Marwood." My tongue skipped to formality—a shield against anyone else's accusations... or perhaps to preserve my self-control. "Are you joining us?"

"I prefer to watch. I hear you do too, *Katherine*." The way he said it from over my shoulder was a reminder of the centre of the maze.

My face burned, but I gathered the cards from the table and passed them to Ella. With an expert hand, she riffled the cards, letting them flick and shuffle together.

His grip on my shoulder shifted and hot breath blew over my ear as he bent and whispered, "That's the colour I love so much. So pretty."

Breath hitching, I grabbed my glass.

Ella busied herself with the deck, while Prince Valois watched Bastian and me, one eyebrow rising. He exchanged a glance with Lady Ponsonby.

Bastian's whispering would certainly send tongues wagging, but it remained just this side of the rules. The speeding beat of my heart, though, said *danger*.

Bastian's thumb circled the back of my neck, sliding beneath the pearlwort necklace. His breaths still tickled my ear and I couldn't help but think of how they'd tickled my pussy right before he'd tasted me.

"Did you know that's the colour you go when you come?"

I choked. Wine went down my throat, caught, burned. Somehow I managed to swallow, but I couldn't stop coughing and my eyes streamed. Bastian swept the glass from my hand to stop me spilling it.

"Lady Katherine," Her Majesty called over from the next table, "do *try* not to die... or at least do so quietly." She chuckled, followed by the rest of the room.

News of her brother's death had arrived this afternoon. Accounts varied about who had brought that news, with some saying it was a foreign queen. No matter who'd brought it, she didn't seem exactly grief-stricken—the only sign she was in mourning was her black dress. Ella had told me there was no love lost between the royal siblings, particularly as he'd maintained he should rule after their mother's death.

"Lord Marwood." She inclined her head at him. "Good of you to join us *at last*. I'm glad to see you're getting to know your new liaison."

Weight shifted onto his hand as he bowed, and that gorgeous face finally dipped into view over my shoulder. I had, in his words, "come all over" that face. Please, gods, say I'd have the chance to do it again.

"I'm sure that by the time I'm finished here, I'll know Katherine *very well indeed*." His smile was even more charming than the prince's.

The younger ladies who'd stared at Prince Valois bent their heads together for a whispered conversation. Beyond them, Miss Ward sat alone by the fire. I swore her look, eyes wide, brow furrowed, was one of longing that teetered on the precipice of despair.

As we began the next game, Bastian maintained his distracting position behind my chair. Though that seemed to put Prince Valois off his cheating, as I won the next hand. Maybe he was wary of using sleight of hand in front of a fae and their legendary senses.

Ella clapped and helped gather my money. "It's a miracle! You've broken his winning streak."

"Well done." Bastian's fingertips skimmed my collarbone before he bent to my ear. "When the clock strikes eleven, make your excuses and meet me out on the terrace, so I can reward you for doing so well."

I fought to keep my face neutral at his whisper, but I failed and had to hide it behind another sip of wine.

"That colour again. It's almost as good as when you say 'please.'"

The rest of the game flew by. I wasn't even as excited as I should've been when I won back all I'd lost to Prince Valois and twice as much on top of it. Not with Bastian's promise of a reward of a different kind.

Now the prince's cheating was over, it turned out my reading skills were useful in poker, telling me whether my opponents were bluffing. Eventually, Lady Ponsonby dropped out, as Ella and I dominated each hand, often ending with the two of us locked in battle.

Eye-to-eye, it was a fight waged with body language and subtle expressions.

She had no tells that I could spot. But I deployed my sweet smile, whether I was bluffing or not. The one time I had a terrible hand, Bastian chose that exact moment to whisper something spectacularly filthy in my ear. I couldn't help but react, eyes going wide... and thus spoiling Ella's attempts to read me.

He made a perfect accomplice.

At half past ten, he made his excuses. I spent the following half hour winding tighter and tighter, thighs pressing together as I imagined what he might do to me outside. I lost the last two hands to Ella due to sheer distraction.

At last, the clock ticked to eleven, and I faked a yawn and retired from the table. Ella's eyebrows flashed upward, and she gave me a faint smirk before wishing me a very, *very* deep sleep.

I smothered a laugh behind my hand and tried not to sprint from the room. Skin tingling, I found the nearest door to the terrace and hurried out into the cool night air. No events outside tonight meant few lanterns, and I had to peer into the darkness. Did I chance calling for him? I crept across the flagstones. Over by that pillar, was that shadow—?

A hand clamped over my mouth, faintly salty, and the gasp I dragged in carried notes of cedar and bergamot. An arm banded around my waist, pinning mine at my side. "There you are."

"Bastian," I breathed into his palm as he spun me across the terrace and into an alcove behind a marble statue. Night-blooming jasmine arched overhead, filling the air with its heady scent.

"Of course." Releasing my arms, he pressed against my

back, pushing me into the wall. "Unless there was someone else you were planning to meet out here?" The tone of his voice said it was a smirk I felt upon my ear. "That gardener, perhaps?"

A soft chuckle in the distance, followed by footsteps, froze me. The steps grew louder, crunching on gravel. "I have it on good authority from someone who's seen it with their own two eyes." A woman's voice drifted through the night. Not here on the terrace, perhaps on the lamplit path below. No danger of them spotting us, thank the gods.

Another woman scoffed. "And yet she was at the card table gambling like she didn't have a care in the world."

Their footsteps softened as they moved past us. "Maybe she thinks she can win the money to repair her crumbling estate."

I went stiff, throat closing. The pressure of Bastian's hand softened from my mouth, giving me space to breathe. Were they talking about me?

"Or she thinks she can use Lord Marwood for his fortune."

I sucked in a breath. They *were*.

"Did you see the way he...?" Her sentence faded into the night with their footsteps.

"They know," I whispered against Bastian's skin.

"So what if they do?" he murmured in my ear. "You have me now. No one will dare oust you when you have the Night Queen's Shadow on your side."

The breath eased from me. He was right. Everyone at court either feared or respected him, especially after seeing his shadows going after Langdon at the picnic. Rumours had spread about our relationship, especially after he'd requested me as his liaison.

Ella had been my ally at court from the start, but she didn't have much more power than I did.

Bastian, though? Through him, I had not just an ally, but a powerful one. A player, rather than a piece on the board.

I relaxed against the wall. "Thank you."

"It is my pleasure." The pressure of his body against my back eased, and I feared he was going to step away, thinking I wanted to end this after that momentary shock.

So when he lowered his hand from my mouth, dragging his thumb over my lip, I kissed it, sucked the pad, flicked my tongue over it. I didn't have much practical knowledge of this, but my body clearly had ideas of its own. I let that instinct take over.

"That's sublime, ember." He ground against my arse, and I arched into him as we had in the maze and before in the gardens. "Would you do that to your gardener?"

"No," I said against his skin, then took his thumb into my mouth, curling my tongue around it.

The chill hitting my legs told me he pulled up the skirt of my gown. A moment later, his fingertips trailed up the side of my thigh. "What about if I was watching?"

My skin caught light as he kicked my feet apart and ground into me harder, his cock reaching that sweet spot. I moaned on his thumb.

"Would you arch onto his cock like this if I was watching? If I asked you to?"

Yes. My mind jumped there with horrifying speed.

"How far would you go, Katherine?"

Any distance it took. For an insane moment, I meant it, and that chilled me as much as it thrilled me. I sucked his thumb harder to give myself an excuse for not answering. I was too shaken by his question and the possible answers.

Was this just dirty talk to make my skin blaze hotter, my breaths come harder? Or was he testing me?

If he could drive my desire high enough, what might I let him have?

His fingers reached the top of my thighs and slid between them, and the answer popped into my head.

Everything.

The fear of that mingled with the raw need thundering through my veins and made me clench tighter as he slid along my slick folds.

"You don't answer," he breathed into my ear, making me shiver. "But your wet pussy betrays you. I think you like the idea of being watched."

He took up a slow, torturous circle of my clit, timing it with thrusts of his thumb into my mouth. "Or maybe you prefer the idea of him watching as both parts of me fuck you here"—he sent his thumb deeper and I greedily took it—"and here." He slid a finger inside me, pushing against the clenched muscles. "So tight tonight. I think you like that idea a bit too much." He chuckled softly, the sound rumbling into my back, then used the thumb in my mouth to turn my face to him.

His silver eyes were hooded, fixed on my lips. "Fuck, your mouth looks incredible doing that."

The praise in his words and the lust in his glowing eyes pulled my body tighter. I arched into his thrusts, hands planted on the wall to help me push backwards.

"That's it, love, take your pleasure, chase it, claim it from me." His breaths were ragged now, coming from between parted lips. He slid his thumb out and replaced it with his tongue, kissing me slow and deep as he added another finger inside me.

If not for the wall at my front and him at my back, I

would've fallen by now. All the strength in my body centred on my pussy and thighs and the pulling taut of my back, leaving my legs weak.

He consumed my moans as the tension in me hovered near breaking point, like I was a bending branch about to snap.

"So responsive," he whispered against my lips. "Being touched like this is so new to you, isn't it?"

I nodded, trying to bite back a moan with each thrust, failing when he drove particularly hard.

He placed his hand over my mouth, and I let it catch my cries.

"Including this?" Fingers still thrusting and circling, he slid his thumb between my arse cheeks and let it sit over my back passage.

Eyes wide, I nodded again. I feared he'd try to shove it in, as my husband had almost done once before I pointed out he had the wrong hole. But Bastian just let his thumb sit there, slick from my juices, and that light pressure heightened all other sensation, leaving me gasping for each breath against his palm.

"That's it. You did so well tonight, you earned this." He kissed my neck, my jaw, my ear. "Come for me, ember. Let me see you burn."

I broke. Hard. Loud. Shouting into his hand. Shattering into a thousand pieces, claiming the brief, brilliant nothingness that came with climax.

He broke me four more times before finally letting me sink into his arms and kissing me gently. His hard cock dug into my hip, but he didn't grind against me, just held me until I stopped trembling.

"So beautiful." He pushed the hair back from my forehead

and kissed between my eyebrows. "So perfect." He cupped one cheek and kissed the other. "Maybe next time I'll fuck you with my shadows and just sit back and watch, since you seem to like the idea so much."

I huffed a laugh, though I wasn't sure if he was joking, and I didn't know whether I wanted him to be.

"I would take you back to your rooms now, but I suspect that might cross your personal, unfathomable lines of what's inappropriate or not." One side of his mouth rose. "How what we just did *isn't* inappropriate, but me carrying you to your rooms would be, I have no idea."

"No one saw that." I turned in his embrace, finally facing him, and ran a finger along his jaw, savouring how his stubble dragged on my skin. "In the corridors, someone would see us."

"Hmm." His eyes narrowed, but he pushed into my touch so subtly, I wasn't sure he realised he did it. "Then it's less about obeying the rules and more about being *seen* to obey them."

I bit my lip. It felt raw, vulnerable... dangerous to hear out loud something I'd thought for so long.

And from someone else's mouth? I shivered. They weren't state secrets, but he'd wrung information from me, nonetheless.

While I'd learned nothing from him. And I had a job to do.

I traced his jawline again, drawing a low sound that wasn't *quite* a groan from him. "Why don't you let me touch you, Bastian?"

"Aren't you touching me now?"

"Only until you realise you're enjoying it and pull away." I raised an eyebrow.

The muscles in his jaw feathered against my fingertips. "Oh, you know me so well, do you?"

314

"No. I feel like I don't know you at all. And yet you've just recited one of the rules I live by."

His glowing eyes regarded me a long while. "Does that frighten you?"

"A little. It... doesn't feel right."

"It *is* an imbalance." He sighed. "And I don't want you running away because that feels dangerous. I sense another bargain coming on."

I scoffed, but a frisson rushed through me at the idea. With all I'd got from our fake relationship, I'd come out on top in our bargains so far.

"Any time I want to make you scream like this—"

"I know how fae bargains work, Bastian. You have to be specific."

His chuckle was low and dark. "Fine. Any time I want to fuck you with my fingers, thumb, tongue, shadows, cock, or any other item, I have to tell you something about myself. Is that specific enough?"

It took a while to remember how to speak.

Item. I hadn't even considered that. Thank goodness for his thoroughness. How might he work that *thoroughness* on me?

In the dim light cast by his eyes, I caught a glint of his teeth bared in a grin. He must've realised where my mind had gone.

I cleared my throat. "I think that's sufficient, but... instead of you telling me anything you like, I get to ask a question and you answer."

He sucked in a breath, body tensing. "You ask a lot, Katherine." A warning growl edged his words, making my pulse speed just as it had finally calmed from getting fucked by his fingers.

"Then... You're allowed to veto any question, but I get to ask another in its place."

His eyes narrowed as he looked away. "Fine. You have yourself a bargain, little ember. I look forward to claiming my side of it." In the darkness, I caught sight of both top canines as he grinned so wide, I thought I might've walked into a trap.

But I was already in Cavendish's trap. And even if this was one, at least I got to come *and* ask whatever questions I wished.

I was definitely winning.

43

In the days that followed, I rode out at first light, testing Vespera on flats and hills, through the Queenswood and clearings, in sun and rain. I didn't get information on the full course, but I found out where it would begin and end —by the same marquee they'd erected for the garden party.

I sent a report to Cavendish but kept information back. He'd murdered Lara—he didn't deserve my help, and he certainly didn't have my trust. At least Bastian had tried to help find her killer. With his power and influence and the fact he'd never used violence against me, he made a far better ally than Cavendish. So into my report, I dripped inconsequential details I hadn't bothered to mention before. There was a broken ceramic vase in Bastian's suite. The rumour of a coup included that he'd beheaded a princess.

I only hoped it would keep Cavendish happy while I worked on my escape.

One afternoon, Uncle Rufus found me in a quiet corridor and complained that I hadn't made his introductions yet. It didn't matter that we hadn't been to any of the same events; he was displeased, which had me breaking out in a cold sweat. He suggested a few hundred pounds would help him continue to pay for lodgings in the city and thus keep him patient. Immediately, I hurried to my rooms, grabbed a handful of cash from my lockbox, and raced to get it into his hands.

Although it dented my second month's wages, it was worth any cost to keep him from erupting, and I still had enough to send to the estate.

A couple of mornings later, Vespera and I rode out again. The sun shone, but we left it behind as we passed under the canopy of the Queenswood. Today, I chose a path that looped through the oldest part of the forest. Oaks tangled with ferns and moss covered their trunks and the rocks below, giving the light a greenish quality. The dank air steamed as Vespera and I exhaled, chilly enough to nip through my leather gloves.

To warm up, we'd loped here at an easy gait—one Vespera could keep up over miles and miles—and now I let her slow to a walk. In the distance, wings fluttered, and a bird cawed, soon followed by the clacking cry of magpies. The calls echoed off the boulders, sounding like they came from everywhere at once.

I'd spent many hours in forests, often in the middle of the night, thanks to my work as the Wicked Lady. But the age of this place, the eerie light, and the hollow quality of its sound scratched on my bones—discomforting. Wrong.

Plenty of stories about fae creatures began in such places. Some of them true.

So, when we turned a corner and found a dark figure sitting on a mossy boulder, one leg dangling off the side, I froze. But it was, of course, a figure I knew and one that would normally be welcome.

"Bastian." I huffed out the breath I'd gasped in.

He gave me a lazy smile. His eyes glinted brilliant green in this odd light, as though reflecting the forest. It made them even more disconcerting than usual. His sabrecat lay curled up at the base of the boulder, one eye on me.

"You look like you're ready to collect a toll."

He scoffed and jumped down, landing with feline grace before brushing off his hands. "Waiting for unwary travellers. And, look, I've found one." He glanced at our surroundings. "What are you doing all the way out here?"

I bit the inside of my cheek. Part of my reason for coming out so early was to keep my training secret. Few women entered the race, and those who did rarely won, so I doubted anyone would see me, Lady Katherine Ferrers, as a threat. But if they saw me riding six times a week, steering my cat through tight turns at speed...

At court, threats tended to get neutralised.

"Promise you won't tell anyone else."

His eyebrows rose as he called his sabrecat to its feet. "Oh, now this sounds intriguing." He placed his hand over his heart and inclined his head. "I promise I won't breathe a word."

"I'm entering the queen's race."

His shoulders sank. "Well, that's boring. I was expecting some sort of secret liaison with your fence or a trio of witches over a cauldron or some shadowy spymaster."

I forced my expression flat, even as my pulse spiked. His joke inched too close to the truth. "I'm so sorry to disappoint you." I sounded bored, as intended, but something tight crept into my voice. "I'm serious though—I'm entering that race. I need the money. I don't have time to entertain you right now."

Eyes narrowing, he watched me urge Vespera to resume

walking, then mounted and fell in beside me. "It's a sizeable prize fund, isn't it?"

I gritted my teeth, but there was no room for pride here. Besides, he already knew I had financial worries. "Far more than anyone should be able to win in a bloody race."

"Agreed. And I don't think just anyone should win. *You* should. You stand a good chance, if the way you lost me in the woods is anything to go by."

I shot him a glance, but there was no smirk on his face, just a thoughtful frown. "I'm waiting for the punchline."

He snorted and shook his head. "*I'm* your punchline. Let me help you train."

I opened and closed my mouth, as stupid and staring as a fish on land. "Why would you want to do that?"

"I assume you've been up and out at this unreasonable hour for the past few days—"

"How did you—?"

"Ways and means, Katherine. Ways and means. As I was saying before I was so *rudely* interrupted—the time suggests you want to keep this a secret, which is smart. You have a good chance of winning, and if people realise that..." He pursed his lips, the scar running through them showing silvery pale in this odd light. "Never underestimate what someone will do for a boon from their queen."

Sabotage. He left the word unsaid. I'd feared as much, but it chilled me to know someone else, especially someone who didn't seem as prone to fear as me, thought the same.

His seriousness faded as he lifted one shoulder and canted his head. "If I help, people will assume we're either doing liaison things or fake relationship things." *Now* he smirked.

"Right. That's why I might want your help. But it doesn't tell me why you want to get up at this 'unreasonable hour.'"

Lips pursed, he gave a low hum. "I normally ride deer, not sabrecats. Some things cross over, yes, but I..." His lips thinned even more, and his eyebrows drew low, shading his eyes. "I don't like being at a disadvantage. I like... to master things. And here I have the opportunity to take lessons from the Wicked Lady herself."

The Wicked Lady reference spiked me like one of his usual teasing comments, but coming right after his admission... It felt more like an attempt to distract from his vulnerability.

"I won't have time to teach you or point out all the things you're doing wrong." But teaching him would give me something relatively harmless to report to Cavendish.

"I can learn from observing you. And I'm sure there aren't *that* many things." He gave an arrogant toss of his head, but it didn't disguise the lingering tension at the edges of his mouth. "Besides, having a little competition will push you and your cat."

If he didn't want to focus on the admission that he wasn't an expert at sabrecat riding, I wouldn't force it. Instead, I scoffed and rolled my eyes, playing his game. "You? Competition? Let's see if you are." I squeezed Vespera and urged her into a run.

A moment later, he was on our tail, grinning. I found myself mirroring his expression as I led a course winding through the forest's ancient pathways. Wind whipped through my hair and chilled my cheeks, but absorbing the roll of Vespera's gallop soon had me breathless and warm. I stuck to the established paths, not trusting the rocky ground, and not wanting to lead Bastian onto terrain he wasn't ready for. It wouldn't do to get my pupil thrown off on his first day.

The thought made me laugh into the wind. It sounded wild and reckless and thoroughly not Katherine Ferrers.

I wasn't sure if that thrilled me or frightened me.

At last I stopped in a small clearing, where the morning sun was just spearing through the dense canopy. Bastian caught up several seconds later, grin wide. "Stars above, you're fast."

We caught our breath and chatted about the race before circling back to the palace, trying some tight corners on the way. Vespera stuck to them like glue, but Bastian took them a little wider, as though unsure.

"Could you take that last corner on deerback?" I asked as we entered the gardens at a sedate walk.

"Of course."

"Then your cat can take it. Think of it this way—sabrecats were made to hunt. Their prey takes a corner, they have to be able to do the same. If a deer can take it, so can a sabrecat."

"Hmm." He gave me that thoughtful, assessing look again, the same one he'd worn when he'd heard me speaking to Webster about roses.

"Just stay close to his back and keep your legs firm, but not too tight. You don't want to crush him with your thighs so he can't breathe."

"Ah, but what a way to go." He flashed a grin and a sidelong look. "If I could choose, it would be death by thighs."

I didn't *want* to chuckle—it would only encourage him—but it spilled from me until I had to turn away and smother it.

When we reached the stable yard, he dismounted in a smooth movement, landing lightly. Thank the gods he didn't offer me a hand. Winthrop had done that when we'd returned from the picnic, like it was my first time in the saddle.

When I landed beside him, he inclined his head. "Thank you for the most enjoyable ride, Katherine."

It was only as he disappeared into a stable with his cat, I

realised the double entendre of *ride* and that he'd said it loud enough for others to hear. That would certainly get tongues wagging about our "fake relationship."

Only, I wasn't entirely sure where the line between fake and real was... or if there was one anymore.

44

After removing Vespera's tack, I led her into a quiet stable and stroked her back, smoothing the fur that had been mussed by her saddle. When I turned, I found Bastian too close as always, his silver eyes bright in the dim light. I knew the look he was giving me, but I was still too slow. Before I could grab the lapels of his jacket and some sort of control of the situation, he had hold of my wrists. He pulled them above my head, stretching me back over Vespera, before planting a kiss on my lips.

Throughout our ride, we'd been almost businesslike. Part of me had started to wonder if different rules applied or maybe I'd encountered a changeling out in the forest, rather than the *not entirely appropriate* Night Queen's Shadow.

But this was perfectly inappropriate, his body against mine, his mouth firm, skin soft. Our breaths filled the quiet of the stable, like the rest of the yard wasn't working just outside these doors. Even as I'd focused on training, this was what part of me had wanted.

Just as he teased my mouth open, the door clunked, and we jolted apart. In came a stable hand, eyes lowered, either out of habit or because she was trying to pretend she hadn't seen.

One canine flashed into view as Bastian released my wrists and took light hold of my chin instead. "I'll see you tomorrow," he murmured before turning and leaving.

I was still grinning to myself, still thrumming with the echoes of his touch, when I crossed the stable yard.

"—can't just waltz into the palace willy nilly. You'll have to come back when you have permission." Arms folded, the stable master, Wiley, eyed a young man in crimson livery I didn't recognise.

"But I've ridden all this way." The younger man stood up straight and held out a letter. Its red seal matched his jacket. "By order of the King of Dragons, my message must be delivered the instant I arrive."

I slowed and tugged off my riding gloves. The King of Dragons—that was the Caradocian suitor's father. What could be urgent enough to come so far?

"Well, my boy, the King of Dragons doesn't rule here."

The messenger's shoulders sank.

"If you've ridden all this way, it won't hurt to wait until tomorrow." Wiley nodded towards the ginger sabrecat tethered to one side. "Now, get back on your cat and go. What the guards were thinking letting you in, I have no idea." He stood back and watched as the messenger turned.

I just so happened to be by his steed, stroking the lithe cat's side. "Oh, is he yours?" I smiled and blinked innocently, as though I hadn't spotted the red dragon embossed upon the saddle's leather.

The messenger was younger than I expected, with fuzz on

his cheeks and a hint of roundness as though he hadn't finished growing. Sixteen, maybe seventeen—still a boy, really.

"What a lovely fellow he is." I chuckled as the sabrecat butted into my hand.

"I've changed cats five times to get here." The boy sighed, head hanging. "And I'll have to wait for permission from the chamberlain before I can go inside and deliver my message."

"Oh dear." I frowned and held the sabrecat's bridle as the boy secured the letter in a locked saddlebag and mounted. "Perhaps I can help?"

His gaze flitted to my outfit, a respectable lady's riding gown, with gold braid and shiny brass buttons. My hair was a little messy from the ride, but it still mostly hung over my shoulder in a long braid, tied with a black ribbon. He rubbed his burgeoning beard. "I'm supposed to deliver my message to His Highness personally."

"His Highness?" I raised my eyebrows. "I know the prince. I'm one of the queen's ladies-in-waiting. And..." I leant in closer and winced. "I heard you say you were also supposed to deliver your message the instant you arrived." I held out both hands as if weighing the two options. "It seems you can either deliver it today via me, or deliver it in person when the chamberlain's permission comes through. How long that will take, I don't know."

He pursed his lips, hand going to the locked bag. Considering my offer, but not yet convinced.

"The stable master will vouch for me." I raised my voice a little and gave the older man a winning smile. "Won't you, Mr Wiley?"

He still had his arms folded, watching the boy. "Lady

Ferrers will get that message to your prince quicker than you will, lad."

Biting his lip, the messenger looked off to one side for a few moments before nodding. "Fine." He unlocked the bag and fished the letter out before handing it to me. Fingers still tight on it, he held my gaze. "Please, milady, take it straight to him."

"I promise." It sounded so firm, I almost convinced myself.

He huffed out a breath, shoulders easing. "Thank you, Lady Ferrers. The letter tells His Highness where I'll be staying, should he have need of me." With that, he bowed from atop his cat and rode from the stable yard.

I hurried to the palace, this terribly urgent message giving me an excuse to run.

But I didn't run to the guest wing where the prince's grand suite was... not straight away.

Instead, I went to my own (much less grand) rooms, lit a candle, and heated up a thin butter knife still left on the table from breakfast. For once Seren's terrible work ethic came in handy, as I slid the knife under the seal and eased the letter open.

For speed, I copied it onto a fresh sheet of paper as I read.

... attacks from the water...

"From"? Not "on"? What odd phrasing. I frowned as I scribbled the words as quickly as I could. The whole letter seemed rushed, in fact, with a couple of confusing sentences and other strange word choices. It seemed to be telling the prince about struggles at home, but Bastian's words came back to me. *Nothing is as it seems.*

One paragraph mentioned "otherkin" involvement in the attacks, but gave no explanation of who or what *otherkin* were. Fae, perhaps? And if that meant fae, then were these fae who lived in Cestyll Caradoc, or was this an attack from Dawn or Dusk? They could reach Caradocian shores by sailing south from Elfhame, and we in Albion would never know.

A section of the letter's last sentence made me pause, eyes going wide.

... must return home...

I re-read it, but yes, the message finished by calling the Caradocian heir back as soon as possible.

He seemed nice enough, but I didn't see how he could be so vital in working out the cause of these attacks or ending them.

Aside from being melted off the page by yours truly, the seal looked real, so I had to assume the letter was, too. But the prince had been something of a favourite with Her Majesty since his arrival. Fae blood also ran in his family line, which would bolster her rule and the magic of any future offspring.

His return home would put him out of the running for her hand, though, and that would be a clever trick for an enemy to pull.

In which case, who would be the new favourite? The Caradocian prince had been seated closest to the queen at the most recent formal dinner, but next had been Asher.

Cavendish was positive Dusk plotted against us. Was this their way of ensuring their suitor became our new king?

I didn't have enough information to do anything other than speculate. With his sneaky fingers in so many pies, Cavendish might, though. I felt like a piece on his chess board, only able to see what was directly in front of me, my movements limited, while he looked down upon it all.

As I mulled all this over, I refolded the letter, careful to keep to the original fold lines, and melted the seal's underside before pressing it back into place. The ink on my copy was dry by the time I finished, and I folded it before closing with a blank seal. It would probably never be seen by anyone other than Cavendish, but there was no sense in incriminating myself as the one who'd made the copy.

It took another five minutes to deposit the copy at the drop point, leaving the tile sideways, and reach the guest wing. Thankfully, Cestyll Caradoc's guards were more friendly than Bastian's and let me through. He even bought my excuse that I'd gone searching for the prince, as I apologised for having been waylaid for a few minutes. That would explain any discrepancy between the time I left the stables and got here.

I was still equal parts furious at and terrified of Cavendish, but I needed to stay on his good side, at least until I won the race and could quit. Getting this information so quickly would please him. That went some small way towards easing the tightening guilt in my belly as I presented the original letter to the prince with an elegant bow.

I'd stolen hundreds, probably thousands of pounds worth of goods over the years and never felt guilty.

But somehow this was worse. Less... honest. At least when I robbed from people, I met their eyes, and when they saw my pistols, they knew exactly what was happening.

This? The way he thanked me so sincerely?

It had me backing away and wishing him well before I left.

I even meant it.

45

The next morning, I found Bastian waiting for me in the stable yard, a shit-eating grin on his face. I ignored his smugness and readied Vespera before riding out.

"Aren't you going to ask me?" A note of impatience entered his voice as we left the yard.

"Ask you what?"

He raised his eyebrows and indicated his expression. "Why I'm so pleased with myself."

"I thought that was just your face."

"Fine." He huffed and shrugged, as if hurt. "If you don't want to know the route..."

I bolted upright, making Vespera step sideways. "You have it?"

He kept up his hurt act for approximately half a second before giving me a conspiratorial look out the corner of his eye. "I do. They're planning to announce it next week, but I thought we could start practicing sooner."

"If we weren't riding, I'd kiss you right now."

His gaze flicked to my mouth, and I swore a flush of pleasure crept over his cheeks. It might've just been the cold. "Can I bank it for later?"

"If you're good."

"I'm always good."

We raced to the Queenswood, then walked the course, which looped all the way to the ancient part of the forest where I'd met him yesterday. There it rose to a rocky outcrop where it crossed the stream that provided fresh water to the fortified castle that had stood here before the palace.

The bridge was a solid stone affair and might've been constructed at the same time as the castle. But at a narrower part of the stream, just before it dropped into a waterfall, a series of stepping stones studded the surface. They'd make a quicker crossing, if they weren't too slippery and would hold a sabrecat's weight. I approached and peered over the edge. The falls dropped some fifty feet, their spray misting my skin.

"The rules don't say you have to use the bridge." Bastian nodded towards the stepping stones. "But they do stipulate that anyone who goes in the water is disqualified."

"Hmm." I eyed the bridge, which crossed almost seventy yards away. "To the bridge on this side and back on the other... That's got to be an extra four-hundred feet, right?"

"I'd say so."

"Worth trying, then." I clenched my jaw and urged Vespera towards the stepping stones.

It was a short jump for her to reach the first—probably a single pace if she was running. The same again to the second. Then the third was a leap away, but one she took easily, before jumping on to the forth and stepping onto the fifth and final stone. My jaw eased as we landed on solid ground.

A risk, but... the stones held without the slightest wobble. It would save time and could give us an edge if the other riders didn't know about the shortcut or didn't trust their cats to cross them safely.

We crossed back to Bastian, who gave me an odd look. "You made that look easy."

"Vespera and I have been working together a long time. I know what she can do, and we trust each other." I scratched behind her ear, and she pushed her head back into my touch.

"I can see that." He patted his cat's shoulder as he watched us. "Come on, I'll time you across both routes." From his pocket, he pulled a golden orb that made my stomach drop.

"Your orrery." I squeezed the reins. How was that possible? It was still in the box under my bed.

"Alas, no." He eyed me sidelong as he turned the loop that attached it to a chain. "I borrowed Asher's. Something happened to mine. Or should that be *someone*?"

I refused to meet his gaze and acknowledge my guilt.

After three turns, he pressed the bottom, and the panels making up the surface split apart. From between them emerged a tiny armature with a ball on the end. When I peered closer, I realised the lines etched on its surface were continents. Earth.

He held the orrery upside down and did something I couldn't see that made the tiny globe tick around like the second hand on a pocket watch. A moment later, his finger moved, perhaps touching some hidden button, and the globe stopped. When he pushed in the chain loop, the globe whirred back to its starting point, reset.

I'd thought orreries were just for marking the movement

of the planets and other celestial bodies, not... whatever that had just done.

His shoulders sank as he sighed. It wasn't the theatrical sigh he'd given earlier, but something soft and sad. "I wish you hadn't sold mine." He ran a finger over the miniature Earth. "It was my father's."

His father's. Shit. No wonder he'd looked at me so murderously when I'd taken it.

The back of my throat ached as his promise to get it back took on a whole new dimension.

I'd planned to eventually sell it, but I couldn't do that to him now. However, I didn't dare tell him I'd had it all this time. He'd go right back to that murderous look and maybe even act on it.

Regret etched its way between his brows. I couldn't picture this as the man who'd killed his own father, but I could see him as a grieving son.

Double shit.

"I'm sorry, Bastian. If I'd known..."

One corner of his mouth rose as he looked up from the orrery. "You'd still have done the same. You didn't know me. Why would you care? I was just a man on the road with gold." He shrugged. "If you're willing to risk entering this race with everyone at court seeing you breaking your unwritten rules... It must be for good reason—good enough reason to drive you to robbery, good enough reason to drive you to this. A stranger's sentimentality is nothing compared to that."

I opened my mouth to tell him he was wrong, but... As desperate as I'd been after the bailiff's visit, with no idea I was about to be offered an impossibly well-paid job working for Cavendish... No, I still would've taken the orrery, even knowing its sentimental value.

"Come on." He turned his cat towards the bridge. "I'll wait around that corner. You race to me, and we'll see how much quicker the stones are compared to the bridge."

When I tested the routes the second time, Bastian grinned as I rounded the corner. "You don't have to tell me which route you took." He held up the orrery. "The stones. That was a minute faster."

"A minute?" I huffed, catching my breath and patting Vespera's shoulder.

"And three seconds."

A whole minute and change. Races were won on less than that.

"I think we have ourselves a winner." He squeezed the chain the orrery hung from, and his gaze flicked to my hands on the reins. A feral light gleamed in his eyes as his canines glinted. "Kat, you are going to *destroy* the competition. And I can't wait to see it."

I chuckled at the ferocity in his voice as he said, "destroy."

"I guess the saying about counting chickens hasn't reached Elfhame. Come on, show me the rest of this route."

We rode downhill at a walk, letting Vespera catch her breath, keeping our eyes open for other obstacles along the course. A couple of fallen trees. Boulders. They'd all slow us. I wouldn't risk injuring Vespera, whatever the prize money.

By the time we reached level ground, the route cleared of obstacles and we raced back to the gardens. I won, of course, but he wasn't as far behind as yesterday.

"You're a quick study," I huffed as he drew to a halt at my side, patting his cat's shoulder.

He sat up, smile dazzling. "I have a good teacher."

I wasn't sure if it was his pride I picked up on, or if it was my own at his improvement, but warmth suffused me as we walked towards the stables. A large carriage laden with cases trundled out onto the drive, a red dragon crest glinting on its door.

"It's a shame the Caradocian prince had to go home."

"Hmph. A shame for him, perhaps. But better for us."

I cocked my head at him as though I hadn't already entertained the same idea. "You think this improves Dusk's position with the queen?"

"One less suitor in the running." He flashed me a grin. "While you train for your sabrecat race—which I hear he was a favourite to win, by the way—don't forget we're still in our own competition."

"But if Asher doesn't marry Her Majesty, I thought you'd prefer Cestyll Caradoc to 'win' over, say, Dawn."

He made a dark sound, not quite a laugh, and his eyes narrowed. "I'd prefer anyone to win over Dawn. Why Cestyll Caradoc, though?"

"They're secretive, but I heard the fae live amongst them. Is that not true?"

His mouth twisted to one side as he tilted his head. "Perhaps."

I arched an eyebrow. "'Perhaps'? That's not the kind of decisive answer I'd expect from the Night Queen's Shadow. I heard you saw all, knew all."

"I know plenty of things I shouldn't." His lips twitched, even though a frown shadowed his eyes. "As for fae who may or may not live in Cestyll Caradoc... Elfhame has been shut off for a long time, even from our cousins that remain elsewhere in the world."

"'Remain'?" An odd way to phrase it.

His eyebrows twitched together. "Do you not know?" He

sighed at my blank expression. "No, it's fae history. I suppose you wouldn't. Do you really want story time?"

"Tell me." It might be useful for my work, but I also wanted to know for curiosity's sake.

"Is this one of your questions?" His voice lowered, tightening my thighs, which made Vespera prance a couple of steps.

"Will you tell me if it isn't?"

"I'll take that as a yes." There was a flash of one canine before he sat back and rolled his shoulders. "We once lived across the whole world, almost as ubiquitous as humans are now, and far more diverse. But, like your kind, we warred with each other." Another sigh, this one from somewhere far deeper. "Unlike humans, however, we are slow to breed. Which is good, because otherwise, in our centuries, we'd have dozens of children."

Families with a dozen children weren't uncommon, but I couldn't imagine trying to wrangle twice or three times as many. "The world would've been overrun."

"Exactly. It would've collapsed under the sheer weight of our demand for resources. But..." He winced. "That slow reproduction rate came back to bite us in the arse after a wave of particularly terrible wars. Many died, and the human population exploded while we were struggling to recover. That left us relegated to small pockets of wild land as your ancestors tamed it for farming. We were isolated and for the first time, we weren't the dominant species on the planet."

"How long ago are we talking here?" I eyed him. He might only look a little older than me, but had he been there for the history he was now telling me about? Was it one of those "terrible wars" where he'd got the scar across his chest and stomach?

"Thousands of years ago. Long before my lifetime."

Perhaps not, then. I filed away the question of his age for another day.

"Our leaders held a council about the problem and reached the only conclusion people who'd warred for thousands of years could." His mouth curled as his eyes narrowed. "War. With the humans, this time. Teach them for taming our world, teach them that nature cannot be tamed for long. We killed many. But so too did our enemy."

He glanced at me, and I became keenly aware that I was part of the "enemy" in this tale.

Could they have wiped us out entirely?

He scowled towards the stables as another carriage left the yard. "We were arrogant—we thought they would be no match for our magic and superior weapons. But we were no match for their sheer numbers. And"—he exhaled, shoulders sinking—"we hadn't learned our lessons from our own wars. We were too few. And we recovered too slowly. By the time the war was over, our numbers were a tiny fraction compared to what they'd once been. Whole nations wiped out."

Where his scowl had been irritated a moment ago, now it softened and his gaze grew distant. I gripped the reins against the urge to take his hand.

"We retreated to islands and other places that could be protected. Albion was our greatest stronghold for a long while. But you finally got a foothold here, too." He eyed me sidelong with a rueful smile. "For a while, we tried to live in peace. And *for a while,* it was successful. But something happened."

"That's vague."

He snorted. "So are the history books. They disagree on exactly what, and it was so long ago that none of my kind who were alive to see it remain. Some say it was a tragic love—a fae king who loved a human woman... Who, of course, died. Poison or sickness—there are different versions of the tale. He lost his mind and massacred every human he could find."

I wrinkled my nose.

"It sounds stupid to me, too." He shrugged and rolled his eyes. "Maybe it was a human who killed her. Whatever his reasons, the humans didn't take kindly to that. They finally captured him and bound him in iron before a grisly execution." The reins creaked in his hands. "Once his son was old enough, he hunted down all the folk behind his father's death. Back and forth it went in revenge upon revenge, fae numbers getting fewer and fewer all the while. Blood soaking the earth."

How awful to see your species dwindling like that, wondering if eventually there would be none left. Surrounded by violence, where nowhere was safe for you or your loved ones. Was that kind of world worth surviving in? I chewed the inside of my lip, not liking the question and liking the fact I had no answer even less.

He huffed and shook his head, the skin around his eyes tight. "At last we had a ruler who had more brains than rage and she realised we would be wiped out if it continued. She parlayed with the humans and the two other fae leaders left in Albion. Their treaty granted us the land we now call Elfhame. She and another fae leader agreed, so they became the first Night Queen and Day King, sharing the kingdom. The third fae leader refused the terms. He would not be bound by a wall. So he left for the west and started the high mountain holds in what you now call Cestyll Caradoc. There were others too, the folk of Cantref Gwaelod and Ériu, and of course, the unseelie..."

I swallowed at the reminder of the unseelie. All this talk of other factions had made me forget about them, but now I had to wonder: was he really half unseelie?

"But we lost touch with our cousins over the centuries. My queen has started to rectify that, opening up diplomacy outside of Elfhame... and, of course, where Dusk goes, Dawn *insists* on following." He gestured towards the palace as we drew closer, nearly at the stable yard now. "Hence their suitor. Stars forbid Dusk gets an advantage over Dawn." He scoffed and wrinkled his nose. "So, there you have it. A brief history of my people and why I don't know what's happening in Cestyll Caradoc."

It sounded so... isolated. Was that why they'd opened up communications again after so long? An attempt to rebuild bridges with the outside world? Or was Cavendish right, and it was part of some plot against us? After hearing all that, the former sounded more believable. Alliances would help protect them, after all.

"Was that your last war?"

He laughed, dark and humourless. "Of course not. We didn't learn our lesson, even after so many were lost. The wars of succession were our most recent. Before my time, but..." His eyebrows twitched as he gazed into the distance. "My fathers fought in those. They took scars away from that conflict, and so did Elfhame itself. It unleashed horrors that still stalk the land, and some areas are... not safe."

All sorts of things could exist between the gaps in that vague statement.

In Albion, there were places in the deep, dark forests— places where unwary travellers disappeared, never to be seen again. Albion didn't even have the same level of intrinsic magic that Elfhame did—how much worse might their dark places be?

If we warred with the fae, what scars might it leave on our land?

Despite the sun warming my back, I shuddered.

When his silence stretched on, I realised he didn't want to say any more on the subject. At least not for now.

"Well..." I shook my head, thoughts jumbled by war and horrors that walked the earth. I wasn't sure I wanted to know what that meant. War sounded like a living nightmare.

Did Cavendish know all this? Any of it? He had to have some sort of fae contact to get hold of my necklace and the one he wore for power.

"That's... a lot. I think it's the most you've ever said to me in one go."

His smile was slow, lazy, dangerous in that way an apparently sleeping cat was still dangerous to any creature that thought it could sneak by. "Don't worry, Katherine, I'll claim on all your questions tonight, after the queen's dinner."

That set my face on fire just in time for us to enter the bustling stable yard. We'd spent a lot of time together today and yesterday, but riding hadn't allowed us to get physically close, and I'd tried to keep my focus on training. His promise sent a frisson of anticipation through me.

We said nothing more, just shared long looks as we dismounted and let stable hands lead our cats to their enclosures. He inclined his head and left while I forced myself to linger and see if I could pick up anything more about Cestyll Caradoc's sudden departure. I couldn't—perhaps because my mind was already on tonight and what I'd wear to dinner.

When I finally left the stable yard, I bumped into one of the rose-gold-haired sisters from Dawn. It was the younger one who'd said she'd let Bastian run rampant with her. Maybe that was why she glared at me.

But my skin tingled too warm to be chilled by her icy look, and instead I smiled at her sweetly.

I practically skipped to the palace.

THAT AFTERNOON, after washing and taking lunch with Her Majesty, I locked myself in my rooms and brought out Bastian's orrery. Even though I'd seen him do it, after weeks of idly trying here and there, it was a shock when I turned the chain-loop three times and pressed the bottom and... "*Voilà.*"

The plates covering the surface spread apart, and out poked a tiny globe. When I kept turning, the gaps widened, more planets emerged, and out fluttered a folded piece of paper.

"Jackpot."

But when I flipped the sheet open, it was covered in nonsense. *AGPEVVHGUILV*... Random letters—row upon row of them.

Face scrunched up, I peered inside but found nothing other than tiny gold cogs and toothed rails and all sorts of pieces of mechanism I didn't know the names for.

And yet Bastian had been so keen to get this back. Yes, it was his father's, but...

Was this nonsense note the reason he'd risked leaving the palace that night? That seemed likely. After all, why keep it if it was meaningless rubbish? It had to be some sort of code. A message, perhaps? Information for his queen?

I chewed the inside of my cheek. The question was, what information? Was he passing on Dawn's secrets... or Albion's?

I shook my head and closed the orrery, weighing it in my hand.

I should give the note to Cavendish. And yet...

When I won this race, he'd no longer be my boss. I'd leave my job and court, go back to the estate and enjoy my quiet life.

The thought wasn't as comforting as it should've been.

No more of Ella's outrageous innuendos. No more Bastian. I'd leave them behind, too.

That wasn't what I'd come here for. I'd come for a command and the queen had only sent that because Cavendish wished to recruit me. Out of his employment, there'd be no reason to keep me here, and with the prize money, I'd have what I needed. I could clear that arsehole husband's debt and save the estate.

I'd be safe.

Just like I wanted.

46

I left it a week, until the day before the race, before bringing Bastian's orrery down to our morning ride. After all, I had to pretend I'd gone to the trouble of getting it back from whoever I'd "sold" it to. I didn't want him to know I'd simply fished it out of the box under my bed.

Unlike floaty fae gowns, the fine wool of my riding dress allowed for pockets. In one of those pockets, I fingered the orrery's smooth shell and etched designs as I entered the stable yard. It was quiet today, with all the Caradocian prince's belongings and retinue long gone, and maybe that was what made me pause before crossing to Vespera's stable. Or maybe it was something else, some gut instinct.

Then I spotted it. In a quiet corner, shadowy darkness, Bastian speaking with a dark-haired man I didn't recognise. He was tall and handsome, but his rounded ears said he was only human. Their voices were too low for me to hear, so I edged around the yard.

I made it halfway before Bastian turned.

Shit.

Head whipping around, I strode towards Vespera's stable as if that was what I'd been doing all along. Once inside, I hauled her saddle from its stand, trying to ignore the speed of my heart, and greeted her before saddling up. The stable hands knew my routine now, so they'd taken to bringing her in from her enclosure early and leaving her tack ready. I appreciated their efficiency.

When I turned, a shadow stood in the doorway, dark against the daylight beyond. "Spying on me, were you?" His tone was playful, but my stomach still dropped.

If he only knew.

"I wondered who you were talking to." I shrugged, but he stalked closer. Maybe it was my guilty conscience making me wary, but I backed away until I hit the saddle stand.

"Mmm-hmm." He nodded, silver eyes on my mouth as his fingers sank into my hair. He crossed the line of my space and kept going until his hips met mine. In the dry, dusty air of the stable, his cedar and bergamot scent was refreshing and heady, filling my nose, curling over my tongue, sweetly suffocating.

"What are you doing?" Not that I didn't understand his intent—his eyes always gave him away when it came to kissing me, toying with me, breaking me apart.

But I had a race to train for.

He tilted my head up and gripped my waist. Somehow, my hands were clutching the front of his jacket, although I hadn't told them to move. "Giving you a little inspiration for tomorrow."

The words fluttered over my lips before he replaced them with his mouth, his tongue, a light graze of his teeth. Through my dress, his fingertips circled my nipple—he had an uncanny way of always knowing where they were and homing in on their tight knots of sensitivity. He could play me so well.

Too well.

My skin burned for him, but I wasn't only meant to be enjoying myself. This was still a job.

Arching into him so I made firm contact with his cock, I pulled the barest inch from his lips. "Who were you speaking to?"

He gave a crooked grin and pulled my head back before tracing my jaw with a line of kisses. "Is my flame jealous?"

I huffed a breathy laugh as he trailed down to my throat. "Like you were with Webster, you mean?"

He nipped the side of my neck, right at the point where it met my shoulder. I gasped, pulse spiking, its echo in my thighs and between my legs.

"Webster?" The light tone in his voice was forced, though.

I slid my fingers into his impossibly dark hair and gave a little tug. "Don't pretend you don't remember who he is."

He laughed softly, the breath tickling. "You really want to talk about him while I'm doing this to you?" He pinched my nipple, and I couldn't help but let out a soft cry. He gripped my thighs and pulled them around his hips, slipping one hand under my skirt and up my calf. "No, these sounds I wring from you—he doesn't do that. I know I have your attention." His smile was perhaps the smuggest yet, like he knew he had me and that I wouldn't leave, even though he'd left the door wide open.

Fuck him, but he was right.

And yet I wasn't so sure it worked the other way.

As he returned to my throat, teasing and nipping, that hand still working its way up my leg, I traced lines over his scalp. Just lightly. Just testing how long it would be before he stopped me.

"Is there someone waiting for you at home?"

He chuckled and pulled back to meet my gaze. "Ah, she *is* jealous." Nose brushing mine, he shook his head. "Is this a question for our bargain?" His trail reached the top of my thigh, teasing the edge of the lacy underwear Blaze had made for me.

"It seems you want to fuck me, but you don't yet have credit." I flashed a grin as I tightened my thighs around him.

"Then, no, there's no one important back in Tenebris."

I opened my mouth to point out how his answer could mean there was still someone in another town or city.

"*Or* anywhere else." He ran his fingers over my underwear, and I sighed at the pressure and the pleasure that came with it. "No one I enjoy doing this to quite as much as you."

His kiss drowned me. Or maybe it was his words. Either way, I lost myself in it for a moment as he kept stroking me, stoking the ember of my desire.

"I've missed you, Kat," he murmured against my lips.

"What do you mean?" My voice caught as he focused on my clit, the fine silk adding a different kind of friction compared to his bare skin. "We see each other every day."

"Yes, but it's all business. Training for the race. I barely get to touch you."

I scoffed. "You managed to arrange for us to meet other times. You could've done that again." I nipped his lower lip as though admonishing him. Maybe part of me *was* punishing him.

His pupils blew wide, leaving only narrow rings of glowing silver. "I've been busy," he growled.

I feathered my mouth over his, teasing him for once, and

slid my hand down his chest and under his jacket. When I found his pierced nipple through his shirt, I circled the pad of my thumb around then over it. A low sound hummed from his chest as he tensed against me.

More fool him for telling me the piercing made it more sensitive.

My reward was the stiffening of his dick pressing into my belly. For all I enjoyed his skilful hands and nimble tongue, I ached to feel it inside me. The part of me that found power in his reactions wanted to make him come, hard and uncontrolled. In me. On me. It didn't matter, I just wanted to know I'd caused it.

Maybe it was that I needed to know he was as easily undone by me as I was by him.

"Busy doing what?" Much as I'd realised Ella was right and I could enjoy my work, it was still work, and there were questions I couldn't shake.

Why *had* the Night Queen sent him to Albion when she normally kept him so close? Since the Caradocian prince had left, Asher had taken the favoured spot at the queen's side. Had Bastian planned the Caradocian suitor's untimely departure? Was Bastian a threat to my country, as Cavendish thought?

I slid my hands between us and undid the top button of his trousers.

"No." The cool, dry touch of his shadows clasped my wrists and pulled them away. He took several ragged breaths. "You know I can't tell you. But"—he pulled my now soaked underwear to one side—"I think you've asked more than enough questions."

Thumb circling my clit, he slid one finger inside me. As good as it felt, it wasn't the part of him I wanted. But my building orgasm didn't give a shit about that, especially when he added a second finger and smothered any more questions with a kiss.

It only took a few thrusts to tear me apart with a decimating climax.

As I sank back to earth, I somehow gathered my willpower and the strength of my thighs to lift myself off his fingers. "Stop."

His breaths were as heavy as mine as he pulled his hand away and met my gaze. Frowning, he canted his head. "What's wrong?"

I huffed and shook my head, skin still tingling and tight, like my body wanted more. He usually made me come at least two or three times, often more, so maybe I'd grown used to that and my body was now primed for it. Part of my brain had to agree—what the fuck was I doing, denying myself more of this when I was about to lose it?

When my job with Cavendish ended, so too did my excuse to be with Bastian.

"Nothing's wrong. But we have a—*erm*—different kind of ride planned for the morning. Not that I don't appreciate this one." I flashed him a grin and planted a quick kiss on his lips, squeezing my thighs around him before letting them drop. I shivered as my underwear tucked back in place over my sensitised flesh.

He gave a low chuckle and smoothed my skirts over my hips, though he kissed my throat at the same time, as though he couldn't bring himself *not* to. "Something tells me you're going to need to ride slowly."

"You're not wrong." Just the pressure from my thighs closing had me squirming. Riding was going to be some sort of torture. I swallowed, took a deep breath, and stamped down my desire. That wasn't easy, considering the firm touch of his lips and the way he held my waist, like he didn't want to let go. "There is one other thing."

"Hmm?" He nuzzled against my jaw, kissed my cheek and the corner of my mouth.

"This." I pulled his orrery from my pocket.

When I held it up and let it catch the scant light in the stable, his eyes went wide. It was the first time I'd seen him shocked. Truly shocked—a pure, unguarded reaction.

"I... I thought you sold it." He reached for it but stopped an inch away, as though afraid to touch it and find it wasn't real.

"I got it back." I pressed it into his hand and smiled at his soft exhale and the way his shoulders sank. "When you told me it was your father's, I felt terrible."

The knot of his throat rose and fell as he rubbed his thumb over its surface and turned it over in his hands. His eyes gleamed, fixed on it.

It was a long while before he twisted the top and pressed the bottom. The outer plates parted. When no note fell out, his expression didn't flicker. I held still, waiting for the question.

He closed the orrery and squeezed it in his fist over his heart. "Thank you, Kat. It means a lot to have it back."

"You're wel—"

He smothered the word with another kiss. A long one, softer than any we'd had before. Somehow this was the one that lit up my nerves all the way to my fingertips and toes, that warmed my heart, and had me sinking against the saddle stand.

Eventually, he pulled away and pressed his forehead to mine. "Come on, let's get you ready to win this race."

349

47

Inside my gloves, sweat slicked my palms as I rode Vespera to the starting line. The sun was still working its way to the height of noon, but it already shone bright and warmer than I'd have liked. At least it wasn't raining. That would've made the stepping stones too slippery to cross and the rest of the course treacherous with mud.

Despite not eating breakfast, my stomach churned as one-by-one the other riders spotted me joining their ranks. Eyebrows rose. There were several dukes entering for the prestige of winning and probably the queen's boon. A number of lower-ranking noblemen, earls and viscounts, who might've valued both the cash *and* pride. And just one other woman.

Mouth set in a grim line, Miss Ward met my gaze. She must've had the same idea as me—win the prize and her money troubles would be over for a while at least. Three thousand pounds would make her a decent dowry.

If I didn't win, I hoped she did.

I inclined my head at her as I searched for a place on the

starting line. No one moved over, her included. She scowled before looking away.

I couldn't blame her. Court hadn't been kind to her *or* her disgraced sister. Why would she expect me to be any different?

At last, Prince Valois urged his cat to one side. "*Madame.*" He bowed his head and indicated the space he'd made.

I thanked him as I took the spot, as well as a few deep breaths.

"I didn't realise you'd be entering, Lady Katherine, but I must say your presence makes winning much more difficult."

Shit. Did he know I'd been practising? "How so?" I raised an eyebrow at him slowly, as if it was just a casual enquiry.

"I'll spend all the race looking at you rather than the course."

I laughed, and in another version of reality, my heart might've sped at the flirtation from such a handsome man. But Bastian had ruined me—his words and his attention had taken root in my flesh and mind, and it was those I sought.

Double shit. I was buried far too deep and enjoying it far too much to make a grab for anything that might save me.

"Perhaps this will help." Bastian's familiar voice came from behind so suddenly, I thought I must've conjured it by thinking about him. But he came into view, pushing his sabrecat between mine and the prince's. "There, now you won't be so distracted, *Your Highness.*" His bright smile showed far too many teeth.

The prince's eyebrows rose and his eyes flicked from Bastian to me and back. "I see." He inclined his head and turned to the rider on his other side for conversation.

"No need to be rude," I whispered to Bastian.

"He's lucky he got away with just rude. He was much too

keen to have you next to him." He glowered ahead, shadows ghosting around his thighs and hands.

"You don't own me, you—"

"I know that," he snapped, the crease between his eyebrows deepening, shadows darkening. "If the man finds you attractive, I can't blame him, and vice versa. He's pleasing to look at. I'm talking about the fact Winthrop's sabrecat has spent the morning throwing its guts up, and they found lily petals in its stable."

That was a punch to my own already queasy belly. Lilies were poisonous to cats. No stable hand would put them anywhere near one of their charges. Every week, they checked the open enclosures and destroyed any toxic plants they found even the slightest sprout of. It couldn't be an accident. "Will the cat be all right?"

"All right?" Bastian's eyes shot to me like I was insane for asking. "Another runner's been sabotaged and you're worried about the animal?"

I stroked Vespera's shoulder, wincing at the word I'd been trying to avoid. Sabotage. "I am."

"The stable master is treating it, said it'll be fine. But"—he came closer, leg brushing mine—"that's one rider down already. You should be worried about yourself rather than someone else's sabrecat."

I shrugged and tugged the cuff of my glove. If it hadn't been in the way, I'd have picked at the side of my nail to release my fizzing nerves. "Why are you riding if it's so risky?"

"I might be able to keep someone off you."

I sucked in a breath, but when I turned, I found his attention fixed ahead.

Brows and jaw set in determination, shadows almost

hiding his hands entirely, I could see why many considered him so fearsome.

And yet...

He was entering the race not to win and give me the money, like some knight in shining armour, but to protect me while *I* won.

Plus, he'd helped me train. Having someone to race against had made me quicker. Knowing how much faster the stepping stone route was versus the bridge had made the decision to take the risk much easier. I'd only been able to quantify it thanks to him keeping time on Asher's orrery.

Then there was the book. It must've cost a ridiculous amount of money. I hadn't dared open it since that first night: I didn't want to want it as much as I did. Loving it felt dangerous, because it was such a perfect gift, something I couldn't have ever dreamed of existing, never mind possessing.

Aside from teasing me so mercilessly and often inappropriately in public places, he'd treated me with generosity and, dare I say, in his own slightly twisted way, *kindness?* Despite all the times he'd made me come, he still hadn't once taken his own satisfaction—at least not with me. And while that disparity left me uneasy, he couldn't lie, so part of it had to be because of what he'd said about hating to see me only half alive.

I felt more than half alive now.

That only made the grip of nerves on my stomach and throat tighter.

"Gentlemen," the queen called from a dais at the edge of the marquee, "*and ladies.*" She nodded to Miss Ward and me, and I was sure her mouth curved in the hint of a smile. "Take your marks."

Left and right, sabrecats shifted as officials stalked along the starting line, checking no one was over it. Once they gave the all clear, the queen lifted her chin and held out an embroidered handkerchief. "Remember, any use of magic will see all parties punished severely. Now, make your queen proud."

Her fingers parted. The handkerchief fluttered. And we ran.

Vespera surged forward, with me low over her back. Grass and dirt flew up as dozens of paws tore over the ground. Almost at once, Bastian fell behind. Or maybe it was that I pulled ahead, several others close by.

To the left, Eckington bent almost double, teeth bared as he yelled at his sabrecat.

Fur and saddle leather, determined faces, jostling shoulders and flanks. The air was thick with it all, and the heaving breaths of sabrecats and riders only added to it.

I clung to the reins and kept myself small and close to Vespera, counting to keep my breathing steady amidst the chaos. This first part of the course was narrow, made worse by the crowded start, but we'd be clear soon. I just had to hold on.

A cry from the right. Prince Valois slid to one side, saddle still between his legs. I reached out, but he was already falling. I looked back in time to see him and his saddle roll across the ground, disappearing behind paws and legs. A moment later, I caught another glimpse of him standing, running a hand through his hair, looking around as though confused about what had just happened.

I had a good bet.

Sabotage.

He was an experienced rider. For his saddle to have come off like that, someone must've tampered with it.

Keeping my entry secret until the last minute suddenly felt like an excellent decision.

"He's fine," Bastian shouted as he cut off my view. "Keep going."

I gritted my teeth and returned my focus to the course ahead. Beneath me, Vespera was a surge of muscle, a force of nature barely contained in flesh. I could feel the pent-up energy inside her, the potential, waiting for my signal to put on more speed.

Not yet. It was still early.

We ate up the grass path through the gardens. Me and half a dozen others led the pack, another group close behind, including Bastian on my tail, and the rest somewhere behind them.

A jolt rattled through me, followed by a flash of pain as I bit my tongue. My grip tightened, hands and thighs keeping me on Vespera's back as I found Eckington far too close to my left. Vespera snarled at his cat, and I opened my mouth to point out that he'd knocked into us, when his eyes flicked to me. They didn't widen in surprise.

He knew what he'd done.

His fingers flexed around the reins and his larger sabrecat veered this way again. To the right, another duke rode too close.

I had nowhere to go.

Eckington's booted toes dug into my calf an instant before his cat's shoulder barged into Vespera's. I jerked to one side, hips rolling to try to absorb the shock of impact, a muscle in my back twinging. If not for my legs anchoring me in place, I'd have slipped.

His nose wrinkled in a vicious sneer that chilled me. This

was deliberate. He wanted me out of the race. Maybe he thought a woman would be an easy target.

Again, he steered closer.

Fine. He could have this first stretch.

I pulled on Vespera's reins and loosened my legs around her, signalling for her to slow. Despite her pent-up energy, she obeyed, and we fell back.

He tossed a triumphant smile over his shoulder. "Ladies shouldn't play men's games."

Prick. I gritted my teeth and fought the urge to shout the word and push Vespera to full speed.

I fell in beside Bastian, who was tailing Eckington. His eyes smouldered with the same murderous look he'd had when I'd taken his orrery and Langdon had been cruel to me at the picnic. He loosened the reins and his thighs flexed as he tried to pull ahead and reach Eckington, but there wasn't space.

"What are you doing?" He bit the question out, shadows seething up his arms.

"Biding my time."

"If I could use my magic without getting you disqualified, he wouldn't have any more time left."

I wasn't sure whether to laugh or shiver. Maybe I'd spent too much time around him, because I chuckled. "He won't matter soon." I didn't remember my own voice sounding so cold before. Maybe it was the steel of determination. Perhaps it was my own rage packed beneath layers of ice.

I would win this race, and no arsehole duke was going to scare me off.

Jaw set, I steered to the far side of the pack, ready to speed into the space that would open up in five, four, three... two...

The instant we hit the Queenswood, I gave Vespera free

rein, keeping right. My height (or lack of it) and her smaller size allowed us to duck under low branches and hug the trees, clear of the other riders.

In that space, we sped, wind whistling in my ears, tugging at my hair, stinging my eyes.

We pulled ahead.

I never expected my years of highway robbery to pay off quite like this, but here I was, leading the race. Over the now-familiar forested course, that lead only opened.

We hit the halfway point, still in the lead. At two thirds, we pushed uphill around tight turns that forced us to slow. But the others had fallen so far behind I could only hear their thundering pace and shouts to their cats.

The river gushed ahead, full from a rainstorm we'd had yesterday afternoon. But the five stones still sat proud of the surface, and I steered Vespera straight at them, just as we'd practised.

One. Two.

On three came the familiar pad of her paw landing, then a jerk.

The world pitched and water rushed up to meet us.

I smacked into it, clinging to the pommel, breath bubbling out at the biting cold. Water stung my eyes and filled my nose. I had to grit my teeth against the panic of it closing over my head and the emptiness of my lungs.

Beneath me, Vespera's muscles surged as she tried to find her feet.

Something smacked into my knee, sending pain lancing through my bones.

At last, I broke the surface. The cold hit me as I gasped in as much air as my lungs could take. Vespera splashed and scrabbled for purchase as the stream swept us sideways.

The falls.

Shit.

"Come on." I released one hand from the pommel and placed it on her shoulder, even though the water tugged harder on my remaining grip, rushing around my chest.

We spun as she must've caught hold of something, leaving us pointing upstream. I huffed out my relief.

Then we slipped.

Another rock hit my heel. Another bruise. That wouldn't kill me.

But the falls might... and they were only a few feet behind us.

My heart thundered, louder than paws hitting the ground at the race's start.

"Come on, girl, you can do it."

We'd faced worse than this. The law had hunted us. The cold winter when I'd brought her inside so she wouldn't die of hypothermia. The lean months when I'd given my meat rations to her.

This couldn't end for the sake of a stupid race.

The world jerked, jarring my neck, as her back legs fell over the edge.

And stopped.

I didn't dare move. She lifted her head, eyes wide, and through the clear water, I spotted her front paws holding a submerged rock.

A slippery, wet rock with nothing for her claws to sink into. She wouldn't be able to hold on for long.

Ahead, the third stepping stone... wasn't there.

And behind me, Vespera's back paws scrabbled for purchase where there was only gushing water.

48

Cold water crashed into my chest, splashing my face, biting my fingers. One-handed, I groped through it, searching for something else I could direct Vespera to grab onto. I only found more submerged rocks.

A few yards away, roots dangled over the outcrop's edge. Tantalising, but too far.

Beyond the stepping stones, the bridge arched over the stream. The first of the riders hit it, but the waterfall's roar smothered the sound of their paws. Or maybe it was the clamour of my heart, which vibrated through my entire body.

"Help!"

They didn't turn.

Because they couldn't hear or because they didn't care?

The water's chill gnawed into my flesh, hitting my bones.

Over my shoulder, the drop stretched away, dizzying, ending on rocks. Falling meant death for us both.

"Please help!" I shouted again and again as Vespera's ribs heaved between my legs.

My eyes burned, my thighs too, from holding on.

I would do anything for survival... but there was nothing left *to* do.

"I'm sorry, Vespera." I stroked her neck, fingers numbing.

I'd brought us here. Wanting to win that money had made me take this risk. Stupid, stupid woman. What madness had made me think I could step out of safety and not pay the price?

A crack broke the air, then *creeeeeeak*. I barely spotted the tree falling this way before it sent a wave of water over us.

Somehow, Vespera held on.

When we emerged, me spluttering, her with ears flat, the tree crossed the stream, just inches from her paws. Gasping for breath, I stared as it took me far too long to register.

Wood. Claws. A much better grip.

But Vespera was way ahead of me as her shoulders heaved and she reached. We jerked as she held on to her rock with one paw, slipped, let out a low and uncertain roar.

Then her claws sank into the bark.

She huffed each breath, hauling us close to the fallen tree, and I eased my legs to give her space, only holding the saddle's pommel. My arms burned and shook.

She released the other paw from the rock and cupped that around the trunk. With a grunt and the scrabbling of her back legs, she pulled us up.

It wasn't dry land, but it was close enough. We were safe.

I flopped on her back, but ahead, a flash of colour caught my eye. The tree trunk rose to another rocky outcrop above us, its base in the air, uprooted. Just beyond that, red hair and a face looking back. The Dawn Court fae I'd seen near Caelus's rooms.

Had they just saved me?

Now she'd caught her breath, Vespera balanced her way along the fallen tree.

"Hello? Did you—?"

Before I could finish the question, they disappeared into the forest.

Vespera jumped to the riverbank, and I half dismounted, half fell from her back, landing on my hands and knees.

Solid ground. I could've kissed it.

Breaths sawed through me, raw and burning. Vespera crouched, catching hers, too.

"Good girl." I choked on the words as pressure built at the back of my eyes.

Fuck. That had been close. So close. Another few seconds and we'd have fallen.

"Kat!" Shadow-wreathed boots slid into view and strong hands closed around my arms, pulling me upright. "Are you all right?" Silver eyes wide, Bastian held me at arm's length and scanned me.

I nodded several times before I managed the words. "I'm fine. Just a little soggy."

Something that was half laugh, half exhale burst from him, and he pulled me against his chest. Shadows writhed around us like a stormy sea. "Fuck, Kat, you make jokes at the worst fucking times." He squeezed so tight I could barely breathe, but he was so warm, I didn't care.

Warmth and solid ground. That was all I wanted right now. Air felt like a lesser priority.

I clutched his shirt like it was a handhold over the edge of that waterfall and buried my face in it, in him, inhaling his familiarity.

"Your teeth are chattering. Here." He swept his jacket around my shoulders and stroked my cheeks, giving me another wide-eyed look as though he couldn't quite believe I was on dry ground either. His shadows curled and licked the air, calmer than before.

"Thank you," I murmured before pulling away. Although I wanted to press into his touch, I needed to check on Vespera —she'd been through more of an ordeal than I had, holding us above that precipice.

I half-staggered to her (maybe more than half) and leant against her shoulder while I gathered my strength. Less shaky, I ran my hands over her chest and legs and checked her paws. Her front claws were scuffed, but otherwise...

With a long exhale, I wrapped my arms around her neck. "Thank you. Such a good girl. The best. *Thank you.*"

Her spiky fur tickled my face, thoroughly drenched, and when I looked back, I found I'd left a trail of water. In the quiet, my hair dripped; the front of Bastian's shirt was soaked, too.

If I had the energy, I might've laughed at the picture we made. But I was dead on my feet.

He eyed me as though he could see that. I must've looked ghastly, judging by the concern etched between his eyebrows. "Are you going to be all right to ride back?"

"*I* am, but she needs a break. I can't believe she held us so long. I'll lead her back." I took her harness and tried to step forwards, but my knees decided they were no longer a solid but some sort of jelly.

He caught me before I hit the ground. "That's a 'no,' then. Come on, you'll ride with me and we'll lead her back." Arm around my waist, he paused and looked up at Vespera before giving her a scratch behind the ears.

Despite my soaked state, he held me against his chest as we rode back. He covered my cold hands with his, muttering about how I needed to get dry and he'd have a fire lit in my rooms immediately. The way he said it sounded like he'd burn everything on that fire.

"You really don't need to worry." I even managed to say it without my teeth chattering, though my eyelids kept drooping. A bone deep weariness dragged on every inch of my body. But we were out of the Queenswood now, in the sunshine, and the marquee rose not far away—nearly back at the palace where I could fall into bed.

"Kat"—his arm around my waist tightened as he spoke right in my ear—"the stepping stones were fine yesterday and the day before and all last week. Then suddenly today, they're not?" He leant his head against the side of mine; his exhale tickled my cheek. "Don't tell me that's an accident."

I shivered, not entirely at the cold. "What are you saying?" I knew, though. I bloody knew.

"If anyone saw us training, they'd have realised you'd be at the front of the pack and that you'd choose the stones over the bridge. This was sabotage. And you were the target."

I was saved from responding as spectators swarmed around us, asking what had happened, exclaiming at my sodden condition.

Ella's face was amongst them, eyes wide. "Are you all right?" she mouthed.

I nodded and tried to give a reassuring smile.

A less welcome face peered out from the crowd too, craning over their heads to get a look at me. Uncle Rufus. I shrank into Bastian's hold as his look swept over me, assessing. After a moment, he nodded to himself and the hint of concern that might've been in his expression disappeared.

All was well—his ticket to lordly introductions was safe.

And that was when I saw Cavendish. He didn't look this way, just stood talking to the queen. The cold in my bones turned to ice, creaking and aching with a horrible certainty.

I'd fallen in the water. I was disqualified from the race.

And I was stuck working for him.

49

I took a long, hot bath and sat in front of the fire for most of the afternoon, but nothing could shift the cold that had seeped into me. Ella brought me cake, but I couldn't do much more than poke it around the plate.

Someone had targeted me with sabotage. It sounded ridiculous. Who in the world would want to sabotage *me*? I wasn't a threat to anyone. I wasn't powerful or dangerous. I was just a noblewoman caught up in the games of men.

However, court life didn't stand still for the sake of a little backstabbing. That was its lifeblood. So that evening, I readied myself for a ball. The guest of honour would be Eckington, since he'd won the race. It would be a miracle of self-control if I didn't wring his bloody neck.

My bath had revealed several bruises on my legs, including a spectacular one on my knee, so I entered the gardens wearing the deep teal gown. Maybe to make up for the lack of a thigh slit, its neckline plunged deeper than any I'd worn so far, almost reaching my belly button. Gold chains held it together, so I wasn't in danger of bursting out, and stars decorated the neckline and skirt. They winked in the flickering light of hundreds of lamps dotted around the gardens, and tiny crystals glinted where Blaze had sewn them into the pleats and gathers.

Earlier today, I'd received another box from her with a note attached. *Thought you'd get more wear out of this than another gown. B. x*

Inside had been the other garment I now wore: a cloak made of the turquoise fabric Bastian had given me with the book. She'd scattered celestial symbols across it. With every movement, the light silk glimmered like moonlight on water. As beautiful as that was, the shoulders were my favourite part. Made from stiffened leather and edged with pale gold, they looked like pauldrons from a suit of armour.

After today, armour was exactly what I needed.

Now the calendar had turned to September, this garden ball would be one of the last outdoor events of the year. A number of ladies wore long-sleeved gowns, and there were fewer slits in skirts. Blaze had chosen well to make me a cloak. Like my fae-worked pistol, the fabric was a marvel: despite its lightness, it kept me just the right side of warm in the cool evening air.

I'd barely entered the ball's pooling light when I felt Bastian's gaze on me. He stood with Asher and a pair of ladies who seemed to be paying Bastian a lot more attention than the Dusk suitor. I couldn't blame them—this morning, he must've cut a dashing heroic figure, carrying me back from my misfortune. Most people probably thought he'd rescued me.

There was no sign of the red-haired fae who actually *had* saved me.

For once, I approached Bastian, rather than waiting for

him to come to me. That chill still sat in my bones, and the idea I'd been sabotaged highlighted just how alone I was at court. Cavendish was meant to be my ally, but he hadn't been able to prevent it. Behind all the smirks and flirtation, Bastian was supposed to be my enemy and yet it felt like he might be my only powerful ally in this whole place.

And a foolish part of me wanted his comfort.

That foolish part was the silly girl who'd loved stories of romance and adventure, staying up late to read them to her sister. She was the girl who'd hoped to one day marry for love. She'd been innocent of duty, of *reality*.

One tiny seed of her had survived my wedding and the truth of our finances. When eighteen-year-old Avice had appeared on my doorstep, freshly eloped with a man she loved, that seed had sprouted. It had made me help her flee Uncle Rufus and Papa.

And I'd lived to regret it.

She, however, had not. Lost at sea or murdered in some pirate attack—I didn't know the particulars. No one did. Only that she hadn't been seen since boarding a ship.

But I knew enough.

Love had got her killed. And that had been the poison to destroy the final sprout of foolishness in me.

Love wasn't practical or sensible or useful. Just deadly.

And although what I felt for Bastian wasn't love, thank the gods, it was still *something*.

Something that carried me across the wooden flooring they'd laid over the lawn and straight to him.

When I was a few yards away, he cut off from the group and closed the distance. He touched my arm, bright eyes skipping across me. They looked faintly golden tonight, sucking up the lantern light.

He opened and closed his mouth in an uncharacteristic show of hesitation before squeezing my shoulder. "I can't decide whether I should ask how you are first or"—he shook his head, gaze skimming down me—"tell you how beautiful you are. I knew that colour would look incredible on you. Are you all right? And do you know you are, quite literally, stunning?"

I scoffed, though his praise went some way towards thawing the ice in my bones. "To your first question, yes, just a few interesting bruises." I winced and flexed my tender knee. "And to the second... no, but thank you."

"Hmm, I prefer it when you say 'please,' but 'thank you' might be my third favourite." His teeth flashed in the briefest grin.

"Third? What's second?"

"My name."

"I'll have to remember that, *Bastian*."

He gave a low hum of pleasure. "But, seriously"—he stroked my arm—"are you sure you're all right? You look pale." He feathered his thumb over my cheek before letting his hand drop, as though he remembered we weren't meant to be touching like this in public.

"Honestly..." I looked out over the growing crowd like that would make my admission safer. "I wish you would take me away from here and just hold me like you did after the race."

He clenched and unclenched his hands. "We could go somewhere quiet. No teasing. I'll be the perfect gentleman, if that's what you want. I'll hold you as long as you need."

I couldn't meet his gaze. Too dangerous, especially when my stomach was doing odd, fluttery things. I clasped my hands together against the urge to hug myself. "Thank you. I... I can't disappear right away, though."

He sighed. "This thing *has* only just started. I don't give a solitary shit, but I suspect ducking out now would break one of your rules, wouldn't it?" Head canted, he gave me a rueful smile.

"You know me so well." I rolled my eyes.

His smile faded. "Not well enough."

Something blocked my throat and I couldn't come up with any reply.

We stood that way for a long while, gazes locked, something I couldn't place hanging in the air between us, until a footman approached and offered us drinks. I grabbed a glass of deep red wine, grateful for the interruption.

Much as things between us had always been flirtatious, it felt like our relationship was changing, and I wasn't sure I liked or wanted it. This was meant to be work, and I'd come to terms with enjoying that work. But it couldn't be anything more.

I sipped my drink and almost choked on it as I spotted a familiar head of red hair. Uncle Rufus. He'd somehow secured an invite, and Caelus was sure to be here. Maybe I could get his introduction out of the way.

"Kat?"

I jumped, blinking up at Bastian.

"You went all still and even paler. I thought maybe that drink had killed you." He eyed my glass theatrically, then glanced in Uncle Rufus's direction, where I'd been staring.

My chuckle came out hollow. "No, but I do have some family business to attend to."

"That sounds fun." He pulled a sardonic face that almost cheered me up. "So, family business, a couple of dances, then we disappear?"

It sounded so simple. I ached to say yes. But... "Is that *allowed?*"

He pushed my hair over my shoulder, then ran his hand down my back and pulled me close—closer than we should've been in such a public place. "You can do whatever you wish, Katherine."

I knew it wasn't true, but I wanted to believe. Good gods, how I wanted to.

Biting my lip, I nodded. "A couple of dances and a circuit of the ball—I think that should be enough. But if Eckington comes anywhere near me, I can't be held responsible for what I might do."

He laughed, the sound as dark as the gardens beyond the lantern light. "Don't worry, I hear the guest of honour has found himself indisposed."

I skimmed the crowd. No sign of Eckington. "What happened?"

He smirked and took a sip of his drink like he was trying to hide it. "*I* happened."

I widened my eyes. "What did you do?"

"I hear he broke his arm... and maybe his nose."

My heart sped. "You mean *you* broke his arm."

He shrugged. "I was there."

"Bastian! You can't just go around—"

"He could've got you killed." His eyes blazed, almost as intense as the ferocity in his voice. In the dim light of the ball, shadows gathered, roiling like storm clouds. They were no match for his scowl, though. "He's lucky I left him alive. When I find out who broke that stone, they'll wish they were dead."

I stared up at him, unable to blink or form words. He hurt Eckington because he'd threatened me? After I'd run into him so afraid, he'd asked whether I wanted him to kill Langdon, and I hadn't been sure whether it was a joke, but now...

"Wait, Langdon's nose. That was you."

He scoffed, but the way his canines showed made it more of a snarl. "Who did you think it was?"

"I assumed his delightful personality had pissed off someone else."

"The way he spoke to you, Kat..." He shook his head, the muscles in his jaw ticking.

I didn't know whether to shake him or kiss him. No one had ever fought a battle on my behalf—normally, I had to back away as everyone expected of a lady. Violence wasn't an answer, but...

Hadn't I been eager to see Lara's killer hang? Not only for justice, but for a moment's vicious pleasure at seeing him pay. Of course, Cavendish would never pay—his position protected him. But if I could get away with venting my anger on her behalf, would I?

I honestly couldn't say. And I didn't know how to feel about the fact Bastian had been so enraged by someone else's treatment of me.

Maybe I wasn't the only one who felt this shift in our relationship.

"I'm not sure I should thank you. It might encourage you." I swallowed and shook my head. "But I have that family business to deal with." The thought of Uncle Rufus had my stomach clenching.

Bastian's gaze flicked to my knuckles whitening around my glass. "Fine," he said softly, leaning in close enough that he could've kissed me, "but I'm whisking you away at the first opportunity. That's a promise."

50

I carried the warmth of that promise with me across the floor, marking Caelus's position near a statue on a plinth, and approached Uncle Rufus.

The closer I got, the more the music pressed on my ears. The bare skin of my arms and chest felt too light, like a breeze might blow me away. Every muscle in my legs tensed, insisting that I should be running from Rufus and not towards him. But there was no room for instinct.

With a bright, tight smile, I greeted him. "The Dawn suitor, Lord Caelus is here. I thought perhaps I might introduce you?" My voice came out high and inwardly I cringed at the uncertainty of "perhaps" and "might" and the way it raised at the end like a question.

"And here I was thinking you'd forgotten your family duty. It looked like you were going to keep me waiting until next year." He smiled slowly, eyes cold and glittering like ice. "But I think you understand that wouldn't do. You were always much better behaved than your sister, especially after your little lesson."

The world pitched, and it was a battle to hold still. He'd called what he'd done to Fantôme a lesson before.

Rictus smile in place, I gestured towards Caelus and started in that direction. Despite the cloak, goosebumps flooded my arms, like my soul was trying to leave my body in a thousand different places.

"Do you have any idea how rare fae allies are in Albion?" Rufus whispered at my side. "Friends in Dawn Court will make our family unstoppable. Everything I do is for the Ferrers name. Your father understands that—you should, too."

Family duty. Of course.

It was why he and father had been so hard on Avice. She'd struggled to bend herself into the shape of a perfect lady. Or even an imperfect one. Maybe there was some way I could've helped her behave, but that was a chance long lost.

In a roundabout way, it was also why he'd killed Fantôme. A lesson in obedience—one he'd felt I needed to make me a good wife. I'd tried my hardest, moulding myself into compliance. But I'd still failed—no heir and a husband I barely saw. However much that suited me personally, it was a gross failure in wifely duty. One the rest of the world could see only too clearly.

Those battles were in the past. Now, at court, winning the right person's favour might set him closer to earning a title. As the second son, he had none, where my father was a viscount.

Titles brought lands. And lands brought wealth.

What benefits might friends in Dawn Court bring the Ferrers name?

As though he sensed me approaching, Caelus turned, hair

gleaming and glinting. "Ah, Katherine." He smiled slowly, not even sparing a glance for my uncle. "I was just admiring this pretty little thing." He slid his hand around the statue's calf...

It flinched.

It wasn't a statue at all, but a woman painted white and draped in cloth like one of the ancients. It was only then I took a closer look at the other plinths surrounding the ball's open space and realised they moved, gradually changing poses.

"But now I have something worth looking at." His gaze trailed down me, making my cheeks burn.

I clasped my hands tighter. His was the kind of look my father would've birched my palms for—exactly the reason he'd bought me the fae-worked pistol.

At my side, Uncle Rufus shifted, his arm just happening to brush mine. That man never did anything by accident.

"You're too kind, Lord Caelus." *Please, gods, don't let him say anything inappropriate about me calling his name.* "I wish to introduce my uncle, Ser Rufus Ferrers." I stepped to one side, making myself smaller so he could take centre stage.

Caelus sniffed and nodded to Rufus before turning back to me. "I hope you weren't too injured in the race, Katherine. It would be sacrilegious for anything to spoil such intriguing beauty."

I dropped my gaze like a lady was supposed to. Consequences catching up with me again.

"My niece is a charming girl, isn't she, Lord Caelus?" Rufus smirked like a cat who'd just caught some small creature and now held it under one great paw. "Run along, Katherine. I have some business I'd like to discuss with our new friend."

Over sooner than I could've hoped. I bowed my head and backed away, though my feet itched to run. Caelus watched me, frowning as Rufus closed in on him.

When I turned, I came up short, finding my path blocked by Prince Valois. "Your Highness!"

"Madame Ferrers, I hope you will do me the honour of a dance." Eyebrows raised, he held out his hand.

This wasn't part of my plan for the evening, but it would be rude to refuse him. So I let him lead me onto the dance floor.

Unlike Bastian, someone had taught him the finer points of manners, because he held me at a respectable distance and made entirely appropriate small talk. It was a kind of relief, his grip on my hand and waist letting me settle back into my body so I no longer felt so light and untethered.

"Thank you for watching out for me in the race this morning," he said in the midst of our polite chitchat. That had to be his real reason for asking me to dance.

I scoffed. "I only looked over my shoulder and was relieved to see you get up. I'm sorry about your accident."

He raised one eyebrow, the twist of a smile on his lips. "And I'm sorry about *your* 'accident.' So many of those today. I hear Eckington himself had one *after* the race, no?"

I eased into the next step, as smooth as ever, but my heart jerked in my chest. Was he implying I'd had something to do with it? Which, in a way, I had, but only after the fact. "I heard the same."

His teeth flashed in a vicious grin that would've been a match for Bastian's if he'd had longer canines. "Couldn't have happened to a nicer man. I saw what he did to you. I'm glad his actions caught up with him."

The next moment, his expression softened into something more amiable and he returned to small talk for the rest of the dance.

When the music stopped, he escorted me from the floor

with a rueful smile. "I hope your *amoureux* doesn't mind me borrowing you."

My face burned to hear Bastian called my lover outright. It seemed the rumour mill had done as I wanted. Not that he'd been exactly subtle. "I'll assure him of your good intentions."

Prince Valois chuckled before bowing and leaving me. I wish I'd seen his face when he turned and found a dozen young women gathered behind him, like a dainty mob.

No sign of Bastian, so I went and fetched a drink. I needed one after facing Uncle Rufus *and* Caelus. This table had a variety of wines, and just as I was deciding between a rich valpolicella and a fruity rioja, I felt a presence at my side.

"*Such* a shame about your accident." One of the rose-gold-haired sisters smiled down at me, expression much too bright.

Teeth gritted, I grabbed the nearest glass, suddenly no longer bothered whether it was rioja, valpolicella, or even blood, as long as I was away from her. But when I went to turn, she caught my shoulder in a grip as hard as steel.

"Now, now, are these the manners they teach you in Albion? *Tsk, tsk.*" She leant in, violet eyes wide, mouth down-turned. "I was merely commenting on how *sad* it was that your little stepping stone toppled and you fell into the water. Terribly, terribly sad."

Her words gripped my throat. I hadn't told anyone exactly how I'd ended up in the water, and I couldn't imagine Bastian having a friendly chat about it with anyone from Dawn. "*You.* You sabotaged me."

She scoffed and shook my shoulder, grip moving closer to my neck. "As if I'd get my hands dirty. Silly girl." With a vicious smile, she came even closer—another inch, and we'd have been kissing. "Your serpent already has the favour of one queen. I couldn't have you winning him a boon from another, could I?"

Like I was meant to agree with her. I huffed and bit my tongue against the desire to shout that I'd wanted it for myself, not for anyone else. I could've used it to get a divorce.

But shouting wasn't allowed. Instead, I lifted my chin with a cool smile. "Look at you, grabbing a lady at a ball. Your enmity with Dusk makes a fool of you."

Perhaps she hadn't expected a reply, because her eyes widened and she loosened her grip enough for me to pull from it. Expression fixed, I turned and stalked away, draining my glass in one gulp.

"Your obsession with the Serpent makes a fool of you," she called.

It was an effort not to fling my empty glass at her.

Ahead, shadows rippled, and when I looked up, I found Bastian approaching, shoulders squared.

The sharpness of his face, the dangerous beauty, the blazing intensity of his eyes—it stopped me in my tracks. It stopped my breath, too, making the rest of the ball recede into a distance of fuzzy shapes and muffled music.

Fuck. How had I ever thought I could resist him? How hadn't I thrown myself upon him at first sight? Unfathomable.

My skin burned, suddenly too tight. I tugged at the neckline of my gown.

He cast his gaze over me and I swore I could *feel* it trickle over my throat, my breasts, my belly, pooling between my legs. "Are you...? Did she...?" Jaw solid, he went to stride past me, but I placed a hand on his chest.

I left it there, soaking up his heat and the hardness of his muscles. It made my head spin. "You promised me a dance."

Nostrils flaring, he glanced past me, though I couldn't

remember why he would do so. With a sigh, he nodded. "You're right. Best not to make a scene here." A deep breath that rose and fell under my palm, then he took my hand and led me onto the dance floor. Something tight and hard entered his movements, making them more clipped than usual, more efficient.

Anger, I realised. It excited me, setting my heart racing.

Why hadn't I let him—*made* him fuck me yet? Why had I only taken his tongue and fingers? It didn't make any sense.

I blinked, and we were already dancing, waltzing across the floor, spinning, spinning, spinning.

Trusting his lead, I slid my hand down his chest and under his jacket.

"Kat? What are you—?"

Through his shirt, I grazed a nail over his nipple, making him jolt. It ran through me—power, the evidence of his pleasure, as heady and dizzying as good, strong alcohol. "You said I can do as I wish." My voice sounded like it was coming from very far away and much too close all at once.

He snatched my hand away. "Some rules still stand."

I huffed my disappointment and instead pressed against his body, letting his leg come between mine with each step. "You have astonishing self-control," I purred, looking up at him from beneath lowered lashes. I licked my lips slowly, wishing they were occupied with his mouth or cock... or any part of him, in fact.

He watched the motion, his own lips parting before he clamped them shut as if remembering himself. "If I lose control of the situation, people die."

My laugh echoed around us. "That's very dramatic. I didn't realise orgasms could be so deadly."

"I mean in all of life. My work involves many strands that need careful management."

I cocked my head. "And why does that mean you don't get to come? Or am I just part of your work?" The heat of anger mingled with desire, making my gown unbearable against my skin.

His brows lowered. "Is this a question in our bargain?"

"Are you just avoiding answering?"

"Veto."

"It wasn't part of the bargain. You can't—"

"I'm vetoing this whole conversation. New topic."

I arched into him. "I don't want to talk, Bastian, I want to feel you come in my—"

"Kat! What are you...?" Eyes wide, he pulled me to a halt.

Somehow, my gown was hanging off my shoulders. But it was still on my body, and that was far too much clothing.

I needed him. Wanted him. Why had that ever been a problem? It seemed so silly to care about anything other than riding him, pleasing him, taking him, letting him do whatever he wished to me right here, right now.

Even though we'd stopped dancing, the world still spun as Bastian pulled my gown back into place.

"Stop it." I swatted his hand away—or at least tried to. "I want to be—"

"Kat?" That was Ella, her face swimming into view. I couldn't decide whether to be glad she was here or angry that she was close to Bastian. "Are you all right?"

"I'm wonderful." I cupped her cheek, thumb tracing her lip. Maybe her *and* Bastian. She wouldn't deny me, if I asked very, *very* nicely.

"Asked me what?" She frowned and caught my hand before her gaze flicked to Bastian.

I must've said my thought out loud. I giggled.

"How much has she had to drink?" She tugged my dress back over my shoulder. How did it keep falling down? "And how long has she been trying to strip for?"

"I am *here*, you know. And one glass, to answer your question."

"Shit." Bastian crowded close, which was perfect, and I sank against him. "This isn't drink. Kat, where's your necklace? The pearl one you always wear."

I touched my throat. Nothing there. "My special necklace." Though I couldn't remember what made it special or why I bothered wearing it. Seemed like a bad idea right now. I didn't want to be wearing *anything*.

"I felt magic on it before, and now I know what magic that was. It blocks fae charm. I thought she was immune." He sighed and shook his head before peeling my hand from his stomach where it was sliding down to explore.

"Come on." Ella put an arm around my shoulder, leaving a trail of fire everywhere she touched. Oh yes, both of them at once. That would be divine. "Let's get her away from here before—"

"Lady Fortnum-Knightly-Chase," some distant voice called.

Bastian swept me to one side, his broad back blocking my view.

Not that I was interested in them, whoever they were. Not when I had these interesting buttons to undo and then I'd have access to his bare chest and—

"Damnation," Ella muttered. "The queen wants me." She looked from Bastian to me, then off in the direction of the voice, torn.

Maybe she didn't want to take me up on my offer. Shame. What would another woman feel like?

"Go." Bastian nodded, catching my fingers as they fiddled with the buttons of his shirt. "I know a queen is not to be denied. I'll make sure she's safe."

Ella glanced over her shoulder again before straightening to her full height, which wasn't great. The way she pointed at him, though, she might as well have been a giant. "Bastian Marwood, I don't care if you're the Night Queen herself. If you harm a hair on Kat's head, I will personally mine a hunk of iron, make it into a blade, and hunt you down."

His low chuckle hummed through me. "Understood. There's nothing I want less than to hurt her. Besides"—he shrugged, and I stared at the way it bunched the muscles and rippled up the side of his neck—"I'd never take advantage of a human affected by charm. It's cheating."

"So comforting," she muttered. "Kat, I'm going to leave you with Bastian." She said it very loud, like I was a naughty child or a confused old woman.

I was neither. I just *needed*. Bastian. Sex. To come a hundred times. To do whatever he asked. To please him.

"Just do as he asks and... uh... behave."

I laughed and kissed her, falling forward as I lunged. If not for her and Bastian catching me, I'd have landed face first on the floor.

I was still laughing when Bastian ushered me away from the ball's lanterns and his shadows deepened around us. I sighed at their cool touch, a balm for my feverish skin. "What are you going to do to me in the dark, Bastian?" I bit my lip and looked up at him.

"This." The world swung, and I gasped, no longer sure where was up or down.

When I blinked, I found myself looking at... "This is your back." He had hold of my legs, the hold firm but much lower than I'd have liked. "You've swung me over your shoulder." I laughed again, head spinning, and tried to reach his arse, but it was just out of reach. "My arms are too short." I pouted.

"I didn't have you down for a groper."

"I didn't have you down for a kidnapper. Not that I'm complaining. Where are you taking me? Are you going to ravish me?" Another giggle bubbled out of me.

"I'm taking you to my rooms."

With a long sigh, I sank against his back. "At *last*."

51

I didn't remember much of the journey, just that he carried me over his shoulder and I took the opportunity to touch every inch of him I could. He tensed when I traced the points of his ears, and that was the only time he swatted me away. Interesting.

At last, he put me down in his sitting room, and I leapt into his arms, kissing him, wrapping my legs around his waist. "Bastian," I sighed between kisses, but he was stiff under me. And not in the way I wanted.

"Kat. No." With a firm grip, he peeled me off and held me at arm's length.

"I'm finally in your room. What's the matter?"

"You're not really here. This isn't *really* you. You're under the influence of charm. And"—he sighed—"it seems you're highly susceptible."

I pulled and twisted against his hold, but it was even firmer than it had been in the library. With a frustrated grunt, I put all my bodyweight against his grip. It didn't budge.

He raised an eyebrow at me. "Are you finished?"

I glared back, skin fizzing with irritation and heat and raging need. "Why didn't you just leave me at the ball if you didn't want me?"

"And risk someone else finding you in this suggestible state? I don't think so."

My hands clenched and unclenched, greedy for touch. "What about my room? You could've taken me there."

"I know you're safe here."

"'The safest place in the building'—I remember. What bullshit."

He frowned, leaning back. "Pardon?"

"I said it's bullshit. I'm not safe from *you*, am I?" I sagged in his hold. "I'm... I'm... I'm a fool."

That Dawn Court woman had been right. I was a fool for him. In the space of months he'd undone so much of what I was... I didn't even recognise myself anymore.

His expression tensed as he searched my face, eyes and grip softening. "Kat, you're not—"

I threw myself at him to stop that pitying look.

But once more, he disentangled himself from my grasp. The burning of my skin grew unbearable—only he could quench it, and he refused. "Bastian, please, just—"

"Let's have a drink, hmm?" He gave me a crooked smile. "Then we can talk."

"I don't want to talk."

"We can not talk, too." His smile turned wicked, full of dark promise.

"*That's* more like it." I waved him towards the decanter, and he returned with two glasses. I eyed him over the rim as I sipped mine, mentally undressing him.

This time, in my mind, I didn't tell him to leave his trousers on.

"Ah-ah." He caught my hand, which had somehow reached the buttons of his trousers. "Drink first."

"I didn't have you down as the type to need Dietsch courage." I chuckled and downed the rich brandy. "There, happy now?" I upended the glass to show him it was empty. "Now, fuck me until I forget my name."

I laughed, the sound echoing in my ears again and again. He caught my glass before it hit the floor.

When had I dropped that? And when had the room started throbbing?

Rubbing my temples, I frowned at the pulsing walls. "Bas... Bastian?" My eyelids drifted as my arms grew heavy. I dropped onto the settee. "What...? You put something in my drink."

He winced. "You need to sleep this off until we get your necklace back. It was the only thing I could think of to calm you down."

Even though I couldn't reach for him, my skin still sang for his touch. I made a little sound of frustration. "Don't you want to fuck me?"

With a sigh, he sat at the end of the settee. "There are few things in this world I want more."

I managed to slide my foot into his lap and tug at my dress, but my body weighed too much to move more than that. "Then do it. *Please*."

He huffed a laugh and shook his head. "It's unfair to use that word when you know what it does to me." He took my foot and rubbed the sole, wringing a whimper from me as the firm stroke of his thumb lit up my whole body. "But... The way you acted when I stayed in your room." He frowned at his work, now circling the ball of my foot. "So quiet. So still. At one point I thought you were dead, but then I heard you take the smallest breath, like you were trying to hide and not be heard."

He swallowed and looked up at me. "Something happened, didn't it? Your husband or... I don't know."

I found myself holding my breath. I was so used to being able to read people and thus knowing things they hadn't told me, I'd forgotten I could give away things I didn't mean to.

He kissed the sole of my foot. I didn't even remember taking my shoes off. "When we make... When we sleep together, I want you to know it's something I'm doing *with* you, not *to* you."

With. To. Such small words. Such a gulf between them. It shook me to realise I'd never seen the difference or thought of sex as something done together rather than something done to me.

He gave a soft smile, no canines or wickedness. "One day, Kat, you will beg me to be with you, and you'll mean it. No fae charm, nothing clouding your judgement. And when you ask me, freely and wholly, *then* I will take you to my room and take my time showing you how it always should've been."

Despite the sluggish sinking of my eyelids, my pulse throbbed in every part of me... not wholly with desire, but...

It was something sweet and bitter, something sad, something that needed softness rather than the hard greed of lust.

It stung my eyes, and I hated it.

"Nonsense," I muttered, chest too tight. "I haven't had it worse than any other noblewoman in an arranged marriage."

He shook his head, holding my feet close to his chest, letting them soak up his warmth. "I've seen trauma, Katherine. I know what it looks like. It's picking your cuticles when you think no one's looking. It's the most controlled woman I've ever met running headlong into me because she's blinded by terror. It's the way you lay beside me, as still as a corpse." The muscles in his jaw feathered, and the scar through his lips paled as his mouth flattened. "For your husband's sake, I'm glad he's dead. If he wasn't, I'd have to do it myself."

I shivered. Not at his threat, but at all he'd said before. All the reactions I thought I'd kept in check or at least hidden... and he'd seen them all.

To escape it, I stopped fighting and let my eyes sink shut. Arms came around me, lifting me, and it felt like I kept going up, up, up, until I floated somewhere above the moon.

"Are you still there?" he asked softly.

"Mmm." I nodded.

"Your necklace. Do you know where it is? Did you take it off?"

I shook my head, nestling against him.

"Did someone else?"

"Don't know."

"Do you think it came off by accident?"

Such a shame about your accident.

"The woman from Dawn..."

"What did she do?"

But I was drifting somewhere warm.

It shook, tugging me back to my heavy body and tender bruises.

"Kat, stay with me a little longer. We need to find your necklace. What about the woman from Dawn?"

"Touched my shoulder." She could've taken this necklace he was obsessed with. "Just before we danced."

"Right." He lowered me into something softer than clouds, and I let out a moan. It felt like someone was cradling my brain in fog and sweet-smelling mist. "The one I saw you with, rose gold hair?"

"Mmm." I might've nodded, but I wasn't sure I could move anymore. I didn't want to, not when this cloud felt utterly wonderful.

"You've done so well, love. Just one more question." Silence for a long while as I sank deeper and deeper. "Where did you get the necklace from?"

I managed to make my tongue move, even if it was so I'd have the peace to keep sinking. "He gave it to me." Months ago. Months and months and months.

Pearlwort to save you from the faeries. Pearlwort to guard your heart.

"Who?"

He'd said one more question. This was cheating now. I tried to open my mouth to tell him so, but it was very far away and didn't listen to my instruction.

"I'll get it back for you." Something warm touched my cheek. I'd have pressed into it if I could summon the strength. "Rest well, my ember."

52

I woke more well-rested than I'd been in... in... gods, I didn't know. Years? The scent of cedar and bergamot enveloped me, and that was what made me bolt upright.

This wasn't my bed.

This wasn't my room.

On the beside table sat my pearlwort necklace. The whole of last night came crashing back. "Oh gods." My face burned.

No sign of Bastian, but I grabbed the necklace and scrabbled to fasten it around my neck. "Fuck. Fuck!"

A knock at the door.

"Uh. Come in?"

Bastian appeared in the doorway, crooked grin in place, hair *out* of place. He still wore his suit from last night; he must've slept on the settee. "I heard you swearing, so I knew you were awake."

"I... I am *so* sorry. I don't know—"

"Don't."

Mouth opening and closing, I blinked at him. "But I acted like... I was out of control. Like a madwoman, like—"

"Like someone under the influence of fae charm." He shrugged. "That wasn't your fault. In fact..." His mouth twisted to one side. "It might've been mine."

How the hells did he figure that? I cocked my head.

"When you didn't respond to it before, I thought you were immune, so I..." Another shrug. "Well, with how close we've been, you're probably more attuned to me than you would've been. You didn't react that strongly when we met on the road, did you?"

I'd never felt anything like last night. I shook my head, not entirely trusting my tongue. Hells, after last night, I didn't trust *any* part of my body. I had, quite literally, thrown myself at him.

Fuck me until I forget my name. Fire engulfed me. How long until it burned me to ashes so I could disappear from this conversation?

"You see? You have nothing to apologise for. I should've given you something to ward off charm a long time ago." He winced, the wrinkles around his eyes charming as they spelled out that rare sight: vulnerability in the Bastard of Tenebris. "I'm sorry I didn't."

I touched my necklace, reassuring myself it was still in place. "How did you get it back?"

"I found it discarded in a bush." He gripped the edge of the door. "If I wasn't supposed to be maintaining some semblance of peace with Dawn, I'd be paying her a visit this morning." His knuckles whitened.

I couldn't tell him she was responsible for sabotaging the stepping stones. He'd already promised to make that person wish they were dead.

"The bathroom's at your disposal. When you're ready, I'll help you sneak back to your rooms."

And that was the end of any reference to last night. It was as though I hadn't made such a scene. Outwardly, at least. Inside, I replayed snatches and moments and especially her voice.

Your obsession with the Serpent makes a fool of you.

She wasn't wrong.

WHEN I RETURNED to my rooms, Seren was already there, fiddling with jars on the dressing table. She gave my gown a pointed look, raised her eyebrows, and curled her mouth into a slow grin.

"It's my job," I snapped, sweeping the cloak from my shoulders.

"Oh, of course it is." She shook the half-full jar of preventative. "Well, he wants to see you. Same place, immediately, etcetera, etcetera. You know the deal by now."

Oh joy. I bit my tongue. "Fine, but I'm getting changed first."

"Probably a good idea." She giggled and went back to "tidying." It was more like just moving things around without any specific aim.

Much as I dreaded these meetings with Cavendish, this one was probably well-timed. I couldn't tell Bastian about Dawn's attempt to sabotage me, but I could tell him. Since he didn't trust the fae, he must already have someone spying on one of their contingent. Had they got wind of the plan? Did it come from Dawn Court's official channels, or was she acting independently? The latter seemed more likely—I couldn't imagine the Day King or his immediate advisors having any idea who I was.

Fifteen minutes later, I knocked on the door to Cavendish's office. Undoubtedly later than I should've been. I smoothed the wince from my face as I entered at his command.

"Katherine." Voice warm, he said it like I was a welcome friend. "Won't you sit?" With an indulgent smile, he gestured to one of the armchairs that faced his desk.

The back of my neck prickled as I approached. He'd never —*never* offered me a seat before.

"You've had quite a scare," he added, as though sensing my hesitation. "How *are* you?"

I sank into the chair, gripping its arms. "Just a few bruises, ser. Though, yes, it was a little frightening."

His smile widened, though I couldn't work out if it was that he liked my honesty or my fear.

Now I was locked in this job with no hope of escaping until my debt was paid, I had to ensure he trusted me. I had to do everything I could to please him. And yet I didn't want to give him any of Bastian's secrets—not his real ones, anyway. Cavendish wouldn't find out from me about Bastian's ability to split in two.

Still, there were things I could tell him.

"I've found out who sabotaged me."

Fingers steeping, he raised his eyebrows. "Have you, now?"

"Dawn Court."

Chuckling, he stood and came around the desk. He shook his head as he approached. "It's so delightful how you say that as if I didn't know. Sweet girl." He stroked my hair, then cupped the back of my head, gently bringing me to look up at him.

Damn, his network was quick at gathering information. "How did you find out? Are you spying on them too? Will they be punished?" The questions tripped over each other, even though I should've known better than to ask them. I blamed my fear from the race, the lingering effects of charm—so many things that threatened to unravel my usual control.

"I knew they were planning it."

My breath stilled. My face tingled in time with my pulse as it grew harder, louder. He couldn't mean...

"I wanted to see if the Bastard would save you. And he did." He leant over my chair, bringing his crotch close to my face. His gaze lingered on me, a distant smile drifting onto his lips as though he was imagining something else and not seeing reality.

"You knew." Maybe I shouldn't have been shocked—not after he'd killed Lara. But she'd been in his way; I was working *for* him. Yet he'd risked my life to satisfy his curiosity.

He knew about the plan, yet he thought *Bastian* had saved me. Then he didn't know about the red-haired fae. The more I thought about it, the more I was sure they'd toppled that tree to help me. The question was, *why?*

"Of course I knew." He chuckled and ran his fingers along my jawline, then down my throat, rubbing it.

My skin crawled, and my nails dug into the arms of the chair. I had to stay still. Had to. I couldn't anger him by pulling away.

Still. Still. Still. Obedient and good. Please him. Keep him happy.

The thoughts burned.

"I must say, I'm impressed that you've inspired such devotion in him. Though since I hear you're still taking the preventative, I shouldn't be surprised."

My heart dipped, missing a beat. He knew that too? The only way... Seren. Of course. She didn't only work for me, did she? She was spying on me for Cavendish.

Still smiling, he went on, "I expect your reports to grow a great deal more interesting from here onwards. Unless, that is"—his eyebrows inched up—"you're inspired to devotion yourself?"

Cold dread trickled down my spine. It felt like a blade made of ice cutting me open. What I felt for Bastian wasn't love, but it was *something*. And Cavendish couldn't know that.

Be what he wants you to be.

I shook my head. "No. No devotion."

"Good." His thumb trailed up my chin to my lips, pressing so hard it hurt. "Good girl."

I was trapped. I couldn't back away—from him now, or this job.

It would be the death of me.

The thought rang through me with sudden certainty. There was no escape. I just needed to survive long enough to save the estate—at least then Morag and Horwich would have a roof over their heads. They'd be safe.

"Now"—he dragged his thumb away, and a coppery taste touched my tongue—"I have a request for you." He smiled as he straightened.

The alarm bells in my head were deafening. He'd never requested anything from me, only *told*.

"You're my star operative, Katherine. You're very precious to me, you know." His gaze roved over my face and hair before he kneeled.

He *kneeled*.

I blinked, refusing to believe what I was seeing. He didn't seem the type to kneel for anyone, even his queen.

But here he was on his knees in the space between my legs, hands resting on my cheeks. "And yet you test me. My resolve. My patience. And I've realised why." He smiled slowly. What might've been a kind expression on someone else was chilling on his face. "I've pushed you too hard, too quickly, stretching you to your limits. Limits need to be tested gradually—that's the only way to push them further. In this request, I won't push you."

My pulse thundered through me, making my eardrums ache. What was this request that he had to butter me up so thoroughly before asking?

"Everything, even the strongest steel snaps at some point." He brought his hands to my shoulders, toying with the hair tumbling over them. "This is your decision."

I managed to swallow, but my throat was still thick. "Like when you killed Lara?"

"That was an order you disobeyed. I'm *asking* you to do this."

I wanted to tell him he was so fucking kind. I wanted to scream the worst words I knew at him. I wanted to hit him, throw the contents of his desk at him. I wanted to make him pay for Lara's death.

But none of those things were obedient. None of those things would get me anywhere except for six feet under.

"What are you asking me to do?"

"Poison Bastian Marwood."

The words hit my eardrums and bounced back off, echoing, deafening, piercing me with pain.

Poison Bastian Marwood.

No. I couldn't. Why would he want that?

I opened and closed my mouth. "What did you...?"

"I want you to poison Bastian Marwood." He smiled like he'd just asked me to pass the sugar. "He's a danger to my court, and you're in the best position to get close to him. He trusts you."

I wanted to laugh.

Because I wanted this to be a joke.

"I pushed you too hard with Lara, and I understand I'm asking a lot now." Cavendish squeezed my thighs—I was too shocked by his request to even react to it. "Take some time to think it over."

With that, he stood and went to a cabinet behind his desk —the same one he'd taken the vial from that would make Bastian drowsy. It now felt like a test—if I could slip him a few drops of that, I could pour poison into his drink.

The lock clicked as he opened the cabinet and pulled out a tiny vial of purple liquid. Maybe my mind was too frazzled from... from *everything*, because I could've sworn it glowed faintly, throwing dim purple light on his fingers.

They say poison is a woman's weapon. Ella's words came back to me as I stared at the vial.

It was beautiful, in a way. Like Bastian—beautiful and deadly.

"Aconite." He shook the little bottle and held it up to the light. "Such a pretty thing. Such a deadly thing. Mixed with a little magic to render it undetectable." His teeth gleamed, edged with purple light. "You could pour this in spring water and the colour would disappear. No one would ever know."

I wasn't sure I drew breath the whole time he spoke. The edge of my vision pulsed in time with my heart, dark splotches edging in, like black spot creeping over rose leaves.

"That's all for now." He squeezed the vial in his fist and returned his attention to me.

My shock must've leaked onto my face, because his lips thinned. "I'm not a monster. I'll simply do whatever is required to keep my realm safe. I'd expect you to understand that. After all, isn't your estate *your* realm? And here you are at court, fucking a man you barely know, all to keep it safe." He lifted his chin and, with a wave of his hand, dismissed me.

I jerked my way to the door, mechanical. Somehow, my stiff fingers got it open. I was halfway out when he spoke again.

"You may disapprove of my methods, Katherine, but we aren't so different."

53

I needed to get out.

The sooner the better.

It was hopeless, but I'd paid off almost half the bailiff's warrant. I had to try.

That was what took me to Win the next afternoon. She'd taken to appearing at court once a fortnight, selling goods, getting rid of unwanted gifts, helping gentlemen procure presents for their mistresses. She was right—court provided a roaring trade in luxuries no one wanted to ask too many questions about.

I hugged the book of roses to my chest.

It was the most expensive thing I owned and the least complicated. Cavendish had provided the money for all my gowns and jewels—he'd be well within his rights to demand them back if I managed to leave his service.

But this was mine. It shouldn't be, though, not when I'd got it from Bastian through false pretences.

So I showed it to Win, whose eyes went so wide I feared

they'd fall out of her head.

"Do you think you can sell it?"

"Oh. Oh yes. I can sell the shit out of this." Her cheeks took on a feverish flush as she nodded, flicking through the pages. "I've never seen anything quite like it. I don't know how to price it." She frowned, touching a petal and giving a soft huff.

I clasped my hands together against the desire to snatch it back and call off the deal. I shouldn't want it. Wanting it was dangerous. I needed money and safety more than I needed a pretty book.

But its scent still drifted up my nose and for a fraction of a second, I could've been old Kat pruning roses on a warm summer's day, blissful in her garden of ignorance.

"Maybe I'll set up an auction." Win nodded to herself, rubbing her chin. "There are some collectors of fae-worked—"

The door crashed open. I flinched, sucking in a sharp breath; she yelped and hid the book behind her back.

Bastian stared from me to her and back again, body wound so taut, his arms trembled. His nostrils flared. "Why can I smell roses?"

I gripped my hands tighter. I had no answer.

"Bastian." Win smiled, clutching her chest. "You made me jump. I don't have anything for you today, but—"

"Give me the book."

"We were just—"

"Give. Me. The. Book." He held out his hand to her, but his eyes drilled into me.

She obeyed, movements slow like he was a wild animal she didn't want to startle.

His knuckles went white as they closed around the book. "Leave us."

Her sigh was pure relief. With a wincing smile, she scuttled out the door and eased it shut.

Bastian frowned at the book. "Why?"

"I was just showing—"

"Don't fucking lie to me, Kat." His eyes closed. "I know what she is. You were selling this to her. I want to know why." When he looked at me, it reminded me of snowmelt—cold sharpness softening. Like I'd hurt him.

It pierced me. But... "You said it was mine. I could do what I wanted with it."

"But... this?" He shook his head. "*Why?*"

"I need the money."

He scoffed, nodding at my gown. "You need the money? You said that about the race too, but look at you. You don't look like you need anything—not anything money can buy, at least. This was a gift." He raised the book, its gilded cover glinting. "It was meant to be something for you to enjoy. The touch, the smell—I thought you'd find pleasure in it."

"I have a duty and it isn't to pleasure." He knew nothing if he thought otherwise. "What use is pleasure to repair a leaking roof? What use is pleasure when I have a bailiff to pay? How does pleasure help? Or beauty? Or the fact I love that fucking book?" I hadn't meant to say that. I wasn't meant to want the damn thing. I needed to rein my tongue in before it ran away with me. "It helps me with nothing. It isn't useful or practical."

"Useful? Doesn't it make you smile? Doesn't it make you happy? Doesn't it fill you where so many things have emptied you?"

I stilled, his words landing like punches. "I don't deserve —I don't *want* it."

He scoffed again, bitter this time. "That's a lie. You meant what you said the first time. You don't think you deserve it, do you? The book and what it makes you feel—what it represents."

I tore at my cuticles, trying to ignore the desperate pound of my heart against my ribs. "I *don't*. I told you when you gave it to me."

This wasn't only about the money. I couldn't bear to have that book in my room, looking at me, a reminder of how every time I spoke to him, it was a lie.

A reminder of what Cavendish had asked me to do.

"Do you have any idea how few people get what they deserve? Fuck *deserve*. And fuck the bailiff. You're resourceful—Hells, you're the fucking Wicked Lady; I'm sure you'll find another way to pay. Take what you *want* for once, not only what you *need*." He gripped my shoulders and I could feel in the tightness that he wanted to shake me. "Gods damn it, be a little selfish."

"Take what I want?" I laughed. That was the only possible response to such a ridiculous, impossible request.

He searched my face until my laughter stopped and I stood there, breaths too fast, too deep. Where he'd been all quivering tension, now his shoulders sank and his mouth turned down with an edge of sorrow. "Who did this to you, Katherine?" His voice dropped to a low murmur.

I blinked up at him, not understanding the question. *Did what?* This was just who I was, the way the world was. At least, the way *mine* was. He made it sound so easy to "be a little selfish," spelling out the vast distance between the planets we lived on.

His gaze was too heavy though, like the silver in his eyes was lead and I had to bear all its weight. I looked away, but he caught my cheeks, touch light where before it had been so hard.

"Who made you deny yourself so much? Who hurt you so badly your only protection was to persuade yourself you wanted nothing at all? Who told you pleasure was wrong? Who said beauty was pointless?" His chest rose and fell like saying all that had been an effort. "Tell me, and I'll make them die a thousand deaths."

I clenched my jaw. He was wrong. This was just the way of the world. He didn't understand: he was a man, he was fae, and he was powerful. Different rules applied.

How dare he think he knew me and my life so well? "You know nothing. Don't think that just because you've been inside me, you know how my mind works."

"This has nothing to do with where I've touched you, Kat. It's what I see you do. You can't even allow yourself a bloody book. You enjoying it and keeping it isn't going to bring about the fall of human civilisation."

Wrong again. I was meant to be earning money and securing my estate. I wasn't meant to be enjoying books or balls and certainly not finding pleasure in the arms of the man I was spying on.

I swallowed back the things I couldn't say and the anger spiking through me. Anger wasn't safe. "I'm just trying to survive. You have no idea what that requires."

"Survival is a slow death. No one can keep treading water forever—it's just a slow way to drown. If their situation doesn't change—if no lifeline comes or they don't find a boat or solid ground—they will sink." His eyebrows knitted together even tighter as he searched my gaze. "I don't want to see you sink, little ember."

I flinched, flayed bare by his words, nerves exposed to the

stinging air. "Don't call me that. Don't... just... don't." I swatted his hands away, unable to bear his touch.

Because it tempted me. It made me want to believe the things he said.

It was the greatest danger I'd found in this entire palace.

"Katherine, then." But he still wore that heavy look. "I don't care what I need to call you. I just want you to listen. Survival alone is not enough. There comes a point when you need to *live*."

My hands curled into fists, fingernails cutting into my palms. How dare he presume to tell me my own business? How dare he try to tell me how to live?

He opened his mouth to speak again, but I leapt in first.

"No." Fuck reining my tongue in; I let it loose. "Why do you care, anyway?" I cursed the tremble in my voice—it was anger, but it sounded much too close to breaking. "This is just a fake relationship, remember? A bargain. You'll be disappearing back to Elfhame when the queen chooses her suitor." My finger shook as I pointed at him. "*You* can be as selfish as you like—there'll be no consequences when you disappear out of my life. I'm the one who'll still be here. I'm the one who'll have to tidy up the broken fucking mess you leave behind."

Eyes widening, he opened his mouth again, but I couldn't take a moment more. I needed to escape. Not just Cavendish and his job, but Bastian, too.

Blood boiling, I swept from the room.

He was wrong. It didn't matter how easy he made it sound to take what I wanted. *He was wrong.*

54

I spent the rest of the day stewing. I lost track of how many times I asked, "How dare he?"

Swanning into my life, telling me how I should live it. Questioning whether I really needed money. Stopping me selling that bloody book.

Fine. He thought it was so precious, he could keep it.

By the next morning, my temper hadn't cooled. I scowled my way through breakfast with the queen as Ella pointed out, waving a sausage at me. I couldn't bring myself to tell her about the argument.

The other ladies-in-waiting were abuzz with the arrival of a new queen from across the ocean. She'd been kept sequestered since her arrival. Meanwhile diplomatic talks went on behind closed doors, but the latest news was she'd be presented to court and finally meet the queen tomorrow.

"I hear her husband is quite a specimen," Ella murmured. "And she's a beauty herself. I can't wait to see them. Would it cause a diplomatic incident if I were to proposition them *both*?"

Not even her inappropriate joke and waggling eyebrows could lift my mood.

Once Her Majesty let us go, irritation still filled me with raw energy that couldn't be vented by pacing around my room. Instead, I donned a cloak (*not* the one made from his fabric) and stalked out into the gardens.

The late dahlias in scorching orange and pink did nothing to improve my mood, but at least I could stride along the paths and suck in cool, fresh air.

Who made you deny yourself so much? Who hurt you so badly your only protection was to persuade yourself you wanted nothing at all?

I didn't deny myself. I just had other priorities. And I did want things. I wanted to pay off the bailiff and keep a roof over Morag's and Horwich's heads, *and* my own. I wanted security, safety. And... And...

What did I want beyond that?

I walked the length of the gardens and found no answer.

Once, I'd wanted romance and adventure and even love. When I realised I couldn't have those, I scaled back my desires to something more realistic. Breeding pretty roses. Creating beauty through flowers. A contained, safe life that took comfort in small pleasures.

And once the illusion around our estate's finances fell away, I wanted only that.

The *illusion* of safety.

Because I'd been paying off the bailiff for a few months now, but I'd still come inches from death at the top of that waterfall. I'd still been targeted by sabotage. I was *still* entwined with Cavendish—a man who killed with *carte blanche.*

I'd dedicated myself to battling for survival, and yet I was still dangerously close to losing that fight.

Survival is a slow death.

Maybe Bastian was right. In that one thing, at least.

Did I really want to die having denied myself some little scrap of... of...?

My eyes burned and I couldn't even push my thoughts towards the word. Scrubbing my face, I dragged in a breath.

Did I really want to die having denied myself some little scrap of joy?

Enjoy the book. Eat the cake. Sleep with Bastian.

Because next week it could all be over. *Memento mori.* Remember, death.

Although I questioned Lara's choice of partner, I couldn't deny she'd enjoyed him. And she'd always seemed *happy*. That was part of her allure—an inner glow of what looked like joy.

And however dangerous it was, I felt something when I was with Bastian. I felt something *for* him.

I'd lied to him yesterday. It wasn't *just a fake relationship.* Not anymore.

We hadn't crossed a line, we'd obliterated it.

I didn't only seek him out to spy on him. I didn't just want his information *or* his pleasure. I'd gone to him at the last ball because I wanted his comfort. He wasn't any of the things I'd first thought—a bored aristocrat, an arrogant fae... an enemy.

He was fierce. Protective. Sly. Smart.

And he made me feel things I'd never given myself space to experience before. Troubling things. Beautiful things.

Useless things.

When I looked up, eyes burning, I found myself at the rose

bush Webster had bred and nurtured. No flowers remained, just rose hips left on its branches to feed birds over the coming winter. They would help the robins and sparrows survive, but the flowers had come first. And even though they'd faded and died, I still held the image of their perfect, bright beauty in my mind.

I rubbed my chest, savouring the feel of my heart thudding beneath skin and bone, the way it sped at the danger of it all. The feel of living, not just surviving.

If working for Cavendish was going to be the death of me anyway, I would live a little first.

55

I sat with my decision the rest of the day, prodding it, testing it. *When you ask me, freely and wholly...* Maybe it wasn't a decision made wholly—I chose this with my mind and body, rather than my heart. Hearts were treacherous things, leading us down dangerous paths. But I chose it with free will and at least as much excitement as trepidation. The trepidation was mostly about facing Bastian after that argument.

But duty came first, and the next day that duty involved helping the queen get ready for her audience with this visiting queen. For the Duke of Mercia's death, we were all back in mourning. I'd had enough of wearing black, but it was a reminder of my decision to live.

We gathered in the throne room, anticipation buzzing through the crowd. A new nation. A pirate queen. It was the stuff of legends.

"I hear she's originally Albionic herself, that's why she's

come." Ella rubbed her hands together. "I can't wait to see them."

"Just make sure you wipe the drool off your chin."

"What?" She rubbed her chin. "Where?"

Chuckling, I patted her shoulder. I opened my mouth to tell her it was a joke, when Bastian and Asher ascended the dais. I sucked in a breath and held it.

It had been a few days since I'd seen Bastian and his looks struck me afresh, like smelling the first roses of the year after a winter without them.

He and Asher took positions of honour at the queen's side. It was the first time the queen had brought any of the suitors onto the dais with her at an official event. Was it a sign of her favour or just posturing for the benefit of this other queen? Uncle Rufus had said fae allies were rare—having two at her side was sure to make a statement about Albion's power.

A short fanfare cut through all conversation and the doors opened. I couldn't see the pirate queen entering—one of the frustrations of my height. But I caught a glimpse of a uniformed man, perhaps the same height as Bastian or a touch shorter. His mid brown hair bore a streak of shocking white above one eye. Ella had heard right—he was gorgeous, with a strong jaw and cheekbones you'd cut yourself on. Before I could take in anything more, he disappeared behind a sea of heads.

"Presenting Her Majesty, Queen Vice of Sanctuary, First of her Name, the Stormblade, Queen of... Pirates. And Admiral Consort, Knighton Blackwood."

Everyone but the queen—*our* queen—bowed, and I took my chance to look past the lowered backs and—

That face.

I knew that face.

The last time I'd seen it had been in my stable yard, blurred through tears as we hugged goodbye. She hadn't been so tanned then or so tall, but she'd always been beautiful.

This wasn't possible. She was dead.

The room spun away as Queen Elizabeth came down from the dais, arms outspread. She spoke, but the sound came out slow and distorted, dipping in and out of comprehension.

Pain in my chest, I pushed through the crowd before it could block my view again.

Because my sister stood before the queen, lips moving, eyes bright. Alive.

Alive.

I didn't dare blink in case I broke the spell.

Unless... it wasn't her. Maybe this was just someone who looked remarkably like her. Maybe I was misremembering— after all, it had been years since I'd seen her... since anyone had.

It couldn't be.

Impossible.

Avice was dead. Lost at sea. Killed by love.

An older blond woman presented something covered in cloth, which Avice removed with a flourish. A sword. There was more sound, pressing on my ears as though they needed to pop.

"... Excalibur, the blade of the rightful ruler." That was my sister's voice.

Vice, Queen of Pirates.

Ay-viss and *Vice* sounded nothing alike, but take the *A* off Avice...

Queen Elizabeth took the blade and held it aloft. The room bowed once more, leaving clear air between Avice and me.

My heart thundered as slowly, slowly, she turned this way. If she didn't recognise me, I'd know it wasn't her. If she did...

I couldn't comprehend that far ahead. It was too big. Too much.

Her mouth dropped open. Her eyebrows rose.

She knew me.

She knew me.

I could only stare and tremble as she approached.

Not possible.

She reached out, stopped short. Her eyes were the wrong colour: Avice's had been brown, where the ones staring at me were a deep sea blue. "Kat?"

Not possible.

I swayed, knees in danger of giving out. "Avice?"

She dipped her chin, an uncertain smile wavering on her lips.

"You're..." Maybe I was having some terrible and wonderful hallucination. I held my breath and reached out, both wanting to check this was real and not wanting to know if it wasn't.

My fingers wrapped around a warm arm. She was real. Solid.

"I thought you were dead, but..." My eyes burned, blurred. My sister.

My sister.

"But here you are."

"I'm sorry." Then her arms were around me, engulfing. "I am alive. I am real. I swear. I will explain it all."

My brain stuttered over the idea, over the details of her vanilla scent and the fact my face was against her chest. How had she grown so tall?

411

Squeezing, I nodded and took a deep breath. She was real. And she'd explain. That was all that mattered.

At last, she pulled away and smiled down at me for a moment before turning. Unerring, her gaze landed on Bastian.

He watched me, hungry, perhaps still a little angry, a hundred questions in his eyes.

You want me to fuck you over the throne or...?

Warmth flushed my skin, burning away my shock.

Avice canted her head at me in a look that asked even more questions.

I cleared my throat. "We have a lot to catch up on."

She threw him another glance, mouth a flat line. "Apparently so."

"You'll have time for that later," Queen Elizabeth said from nearby. "But for now, I believe you requested a meeting." She raised an eyebrow at Avice.

My sister squeezed my hand. "I'll find you as soon as we're done."

I nodded as she walked away, my mind still tripping over the fact of her existence.

The sister I'd mourned for the past four years was alive.

56

Less than an hour later, a message came for me in the form of the blond woman who'd presented the sword to the queen. Ella had told me the blade was Excalibur and apparently some of those sounds I hadn't really registered were gasps as the legendary sword was formally returned to Albion.

"So you're the famous Kat." The woman, Perry, gave me a warm smile as we threaded our way through corridors towards Avice's suite. She'd introduced herself as Sanctuary's ambassador to Albion. Between her tanned skin and blond hair, she looked like a Viking from one of my old adventure books. Yet her elegant aqua gown and the smile lines around her eyes made her less shield maiden and more goddess of home and hearth or the summer sea.

I caught her giving me a similarly evaluative look. Normally those looks in court were all cool calculation that asked "What can I get out of this person?" Yet hers was as warm as her smile and more curious than calculating.

"Vice has told me so much about you."

I rubbed my forehead. "I'm not sure I'll ever get used to hearing people call her that."

"This must all be quite a shock." She squeezed my shoulder. "Probably a stupid question, but are you all right?" Although she was a few inches shorter, there was something about her that made me feel like a child who'd come running into the house with scraped knees.

It made me ache for simpler times.

"I..." I massaged my temples. "I think so."

I bit back a laugh when I found myself entering what had previously been the Caradocian suitor's suite. I bet the chamberlain was counting himself lucky the prince had left. Otherwise, with all these suitors at court, he would never have found space suitable for a visiting *queen*.

Queen. My sister.

My head throbbed.

We found her pacing before the fireplace, her husband, Knigh, pouring drinks from a decanter as a small grey cat watched from perilously close to the fire.

I stopped, struck again by the fact Avice's face looked back at me. Not quite the same—those different eyes, that height, plus the past few years had carved away the childish fat that had remained on her cheeks at eighteen. But it was still her. How?

Other things had changed, too, like the fact she was a queen. Again, *how*?

Remembering myself, I went to bow.

"Don't you dare." She fixed me with a wide-eyed look and strode across the room. "You don't ever bow to me." With a chuckle, she threw her arms around me.

"But you're a queen."

"It's... complicated." She pulled back and cupped my cheeks, searching my face. "I can't believe you're really here."

"*You* can't believe it?" I scoffed. "You're meant to be dead. I don't..." I shook my head. "I don't understand. What happened?"

She shared a look with Knigh, then another with Perry. "That's a long story."

"A *very* bloody long story." Knigh's mouth twisted to one side. "One that requires a drink." He held up the decanter.

Perry cleared her throat and curled up in an armchair. "*And* dinner. We'll never get through the whole story without something to soak up the alcohol. I've asked them to bring it up when it's ready."

"Wise choice." Avice chuckled and stroked my hair before offering me a chair by the fire. "You look so well," she said as I sank into it.

The grey cat jumped onto the arm and sniffed my shoulder. I held still. Her sniffing went to my cheek, tickling, before she plopped into my lap and began kneading.

"Well, Barnacle has claimed you." Avice shrugged, as though helpless to do anything about it. "You're hers now." Amusement fading, she surveyed me. "Last time I saw you, money was tight, but..." She gestured at my gown. "And you're at court. That can't be cheap."

Smoke and mirrors. I shifted, pretending it was because I was settling down for this long story rather than because of my discomfort. Barnacle gave a short *miaow* of irritation before circling and curling up in my lap.

"Sorry, little one." I scratched the top of her head, grateful for the excuse to delay my response.

If I confessed my money woes, that would lead to questions about how I could afford these expensive gowns. I might've confessed this new line of work to my sister—after all, she'd kept my highway robbery secret all these years. But telling a foreign queen was a different matter.

A treasonous matter.

I disguised my shiver by fussing the cat. "Situations change in four years." It was an answer Bastian would've been proud of—not technically a lie, but not the exact truth, either. "But, come on, you'd better start this story if we're to stand any chance of sleeping tonight."

"Well." She flopped onto the settee opposite my armchair. "First, I should probably introduce my husband by a name you might recognise. Knighton Villiers."

My eyes almost fell out of my head. "The man you were *meant* to marry?"

He gave a soft laugh as he brought over my drink. "When have you ever known your sister to do anything the straightforward way?"

"That's a fair point." I grinned up at him. "It's good to meet you, Lord—"

"Just Knigh. You're my sister now." He pressed the drink into my hand before joining Avice on the settee.

"I suppose so." I hugged my glass as Avice fit herself into the crook between Knigh's arm and chest, sharing a look with him that made my insides twist like climbing wisteria vines.

I couldn't say what was in that look, but it was warm. It was wanting and wanted. It was belonging and freedom. Comfort and ferocity. A hundred things that should have warred but instead balanced each other into wholeness.

Avice sighed, sinking against him. "Where do I begin?"

He kissed her brow. "At the beginning, love."

416

Of course.

It was love. The kind of love my childhood self had dreamed of and wanted. A want that I'd stamped down. A want that had died with my sister.

Or so I'd thought.

57

The story was as long as Knigh had promised. Between the three of them, they told it over drinks, then dinner, then tea, followed by more drinks and a late supper. It was gone midnight by the time they finished, and my head spun with shipwrecks, battles, and sea monsters.

But the thing that really crept into my flesh and bones was the sense of belonging she'd found at sea.

It was a relief that we ran out of time for me to tell my tale. It wasn't much of one. Husband still useless but thankfully absent. Highway robbery. Summoned to court. That was when it grew complicated.

Avice and Knigh escorted me back to my rooms in the small hours. Although they'd been sequestered away, Perry had been allowed to mingle at court, so she'd told my sister about Lara's apparently unsolved murder. Walking back alone was out of the question.

Over the following days, we spent every moment we could

together. They were due to leave soon, and gods knew when I'd get another chance to see her. That meant I saw little of Bastian and only at formal events. I blamed Avice's presence, but perhaps there was a little cowardice involved, too.

Speaking to him would involve some confessions I wasn't sure I was brave enough for yet.

However, there was one unexpected bonus of having a pirate queen for a sister—I hadn't caught so much as a glimpse of Uncle Rufus. Seemed I wasn't the only coward.

There was one buzz of drama that eclipsed the excitement about the Pirate Queen's presence—for a day, at least. Early one morning, a gardener was turning a compost heap and unearthed a body. At first, speculation rushed through the palace that Lara's murderer had returned and taken another victim. But when it became clear the poor man had been there some time and was too decomposed to identify, interest soon waned.

I wondered about the man. All we knew was that he wore simple clothes. The Watch couldn't even work out his cause of death. Though after seeing their handling of Lara's murder, that wasn't saying much. But he'd had a life and hopes and plans.

Memento mori. Another reminder of my decision to enjoy whatever time I had.

I was thinking of that on my way to Avice's suite for dinner when a figure in black came round the corner. My stomach spasmed at the sight of Cavendish as, for the first time outside of his office, he actually acknowledged me, inclining his head. "Lady Katherine."

"Lord Cavendish." I stopped and bowed, heart hammering, even though this public setting had to mean I was safe from his usual attentions. I started away, but he leant closer.

"I'm sure Her Majesty is pleased you've been reunited with your sister." He gave a stiff smile that didn't meet his eyes. "But you would do well to remember you are at court to do a job." His eyebrows rose before he continued down the corridor.

My absence from Bastian's side had been noticed, then. It was a far more subtle reminder than I'd have expected from Cavendish. No hair-pulling, for starters. I swallowed and glanced over my shoulder, but he didn't look back.

Avice was leaving tomorrow, so I'd throw myself back into work then. I hurried to her rooms.

We'd been parted for so many years, a little distance lingered between us. I hadn't told her about my financial problems or spying. But I enjoyed spending time with her, Knigh, and Perry, and I'd miss her. She'd invited me to Sanctuary, but I'd declined. I had work to do here, and I doubted the queen would grant me permission to leave—not when Cavendish could pull any strings he wanted to keep me here.

Still, we had a fun evening with good food and good company, and after dinner we retired to the chairs before the fireplace. The evenings were growing cooler now, promising a snowy winter.

I couldn't help but notice how Knigh watched Avice as she fetched more wine from a cabinet. My husband had never looked at me like that.

Knigh had already set our empty glasses on the table, ready for topping up. Throughout dinner, they'd worked together to make sure all the different bowls and plates reached Perry and me. They also worked together in telling stories of their adventures—finishing each other's sentences, adding amusing details.

They made a good team.

Might Robin and I have made a good team if I'd tried harder? If I'd been a better wife—gone to him a virgin and given him an heir—would that have made him stay and help fix the estate's finances? He *was* useless, so maybe not, but it might've at least stopped him from gallivanting around Europa and spending so much money.

In a different version of the world, was there one where he looked at me like that?

My sister had married for love. Although she'd got that wrong the first time, it had set her on a path that led to Knigh. You didn't need to read people to see it was a powerful, passionate love; it practically hummed through the air every time they made eye contact.

Like now, when Avice reached over the low coffee table and glanced up at him. She bit her lip, but it did nothing to disguise her smile of pleasure.

"You two..." I shook my head. I hadn't meant to say anything out loud. I blamed the free-flowing wine at dinner.

Avice raised her eyebrows at me, topping up the glasses. "Us two?"

"I just... It's funny that you were *meant* to marry. I remember how much you hated him." I shot Knigh a wide-eyed look. "Oh, sorry, I—"

Avice chuckled and passed my drink. "Don't worry, he knows. I told him as much to his face."

He arched one eyebrow. "On more than one occasion."

Perry scoffed, curling up in her armchair. "Quite heatedly, as I recall."

As Avice passed, Knigh pulled her onto his lap. "But I wore her down," he said, squeezing her thigh, before rescuing his drink from her hand.

Perry's face screwed up, eyes narrowed in thought. "And how many times was it you tried to murder each other?"

Avice shrugged, wine sloshing. "What's a little attempted murder between spouses?"

Arm easing around her waist, Knigh shook his head. "I lost track of the number of times you threatened to cut my tongue out with my own dagger."

I couldn't tell whether this was all a joke or serious. I cocked my head at Perry.

She widened her eyes at me. "Oh, they really have. That was all *before*, though." She smiled at them over her glass. It was warm, and yet... some sadness tainted her gaze. Perhaps because they were leaving tomorrow and she was staying behind.

Or perhaps it was the same tinge of sadness that coloured me. Yes, Avice had found love, but she'd been through an ordeal to get there and now she stood—well, *sat* before me, a different person with a different name. The girl who'd tried so hard to fit the mould had died and been reborn.

"But here you are, quite obviously..." I gulped my wine and shook my head as it slid down a bit *too* smoothly. "You adore each other, don't you?"

Avice gave an over the top sigh. "Damn it, Knigh. I thought we were so subtle about it, too."

Knigh spread one hand, the other stroking her hip. "I really don't know how she worked it out."

I gave him a lopsided grin. "I'm good at reading people."

They laughed and the sound warmed me.

Who was this woman laughing and making jokes, sprawled on a settee? She wasn't acting like a lady. And yet...

I felt more myself than I had in a long while.

THE NEXT DAY, I dropped off a report for Cavendish with more useless information. After that, I was heading to the stable yard to say goodbye to Avice and Knigh, when a summons arrived from the queen. I cursed, but there was no denying *the* queen, even if your own sister was *a* queen.

Over the past few days, Queen Elizabeth had taken to spending time in the palace conservatory, and I found her there, surrounded by plants and ladies-in-waiting, Excalibur on the table. The sword emitted a faint hum that I more felt than heard.

"Dear Katherine, I've missed you." She smiled and patted the seat beside her. "Sister to a queen! Come and tell us about her."

I did, keeping things as general as I could. My loyalties lay with Albion but also with my sister, and this request tore me between them. Still, the queen seemed satisfied, and as soon as I could slip away, I ran down to the stable yard.

But I found only a tearful Perry. Avice and Knigh were long gone.

As I left with an arm around Perry's shoulders, I found Asher standing to one side, slumped as he watched the ambassador with an odd look.

When I met his gaze, he drew a long breath and pulled upright, as though remembering himself. "Katherine." He bowed his head, then swept away towards the palace.

I was still frowning at his odd behaviour when we entered the first courtyard, and the sight of a familiar head of red hair sent a shiver through me. "Uncle Rufus," I said with a bright smile.

"Katherine." Above the curve of his lips, his eyes remained as cold as ever. "I need a moment with you"—he gave Perry a pointed look—"alone."

She stiffened at my side, eyebrows drawing low as she eyed him. "Kat, do *you* want me to leave?"

I wasn't sure what she saw, but she understood something wasn't right.

I made my smile brighter. "It's fine. This is my uncle."

What else could I say? *Please don't leave me with him; he terrifies me?*

I had to pat her on the shoulder before she would leave.

Once she was out of earshot, my uncle's attention snapped to me. "I have need of one last favour from you."

My stomach dipped, half with trepidation about what this favour might be, half with anticipation of being free of him.

"Yes?" My voice rasped.

"You're to come to a meeting with one of my new friends. Tonight, nine o'clock. North corridor."

My heart missed a beat. I hadn't been to that part of the palace since the day Lara was killed. But I nodded mechanically.

"Good. Keep the night clear and wear something pretty."

One night, then I'd be free.

58

I couldn't eat dinner; I just pushed it around the plate as my stomach pulled into a tight, hard ball. "It'll all be over soon," I whispered to myself.

Accompanying him to a meeting had to be either to put this "new friend" at ease or to elevate his position, since I was a lady-in-waiting.

I'd planned to go to Bastian this afternoon and finally clear the air after our argument. But with this looming over me, I couldn't face it. He would have to wait until tomorrow.

For a second, I smiled—when I woke in the morning, I'd be free of my uncle's demands.

I just had to endure a little longer.

I dressed quickly, choosing a velvet gown of blackened green, the colour of an emerald viewed through smoked glass. One eye on the clock, I brushed my hair and rifled through my jewellery before choosing to wear none but the pearlwort necklace.

Then there was no more putting it off: I made for the north corridor.

Every third wall sconce was lit, leaving the halls dim, with darkness pooling in corners and alcoves. My heart was a heavy thud in my chest, like it ticked the seconds until I'd be free from my uncle.

I squeezed my hands together and counted my breaths to keep them slow.

It didn't stop me half leaping out of my skin when he loomed from an alcove. "Good, you're on time." His gaze skimmed over me before he gave a nod of approval. "That will do." He planted his hand between my shoulder blades and propelled me along at his side.

We rounded several corners and walked down winding corridors. I didn't know this older part of the palace and soon lost track of where we were.

"What is it you need from me, Uncle Rufus?" My voice sounded thin and echoing in the silence of the bare stone halls.

"You're to entertain my friend for the evening. He's taken a liking to you."

I blinked, feet keeping pace even though my heart stumbled. He didn't mean... "Entertain?"

A sigh blasted through his nose. "You're a married woman, Katherine, and I know you've been whoring yourself to that fae from Dusk. Don't play innocent." He speared me with a look. "You're spending the night with Lord Caelus."

My feet fell still. I told them to move, to keep going, to obey, but the shock flooding my body was more potent than rational thought.

Consequences catching up with me.

"Don't suddenly get precious about who you take to bed. I

hear your husband is back in the country. What would he say if he found out what you've been up to?" His lip curled in a sneer as he grabbed my arm and yanked.

It jolted through my joints, enough to jerk my feet into walking.

I could do this. I'd endured the selfish fumbling of Robin Fanshawe: I could endure Caelus.

Yet, something colder than the north wind engulfed me, lifting goosebumps across my flesh.

My stomach balled even tighter as we turned more and more corners. "Why?" It was a small, pathetic sound. "There are other women at court prettier than me. There are *professionals* and courtesans. Couldn't you take one of them to him?"

He snorted. "Yes, but I'd have to pay for them. Besides, it's *you* he wants. What man wouldn't want to say he'd had his enemy's woman?" A cruel smile sharpened his features, and I was grateful his eyes stayed on the route ahead. "Don't you know men want what another man has? Fae are no different."

I could do this. I could. It was no different from marriage. I'd done it for years.

But I'd endured my useless husband before I'd known better.

Now I knew what pleasure was.

This would be another lungful of water in that slow drowning death Bastian had spoken of. And hadn't I decided to live a little before the reaper caught up with me?

I twisted away. Uncle Rufus must not have been expecting it, because I slipped from his grasp. "I don't want to."

Eyes wide, he stared at me. It was the first time I'd ever seen him genuinely surprised. But it was gone in a moment, replaced by a sneering chuckle. "Do you think it matters what you want?"

"Please, Uncle Rufus." I looked up at him, beseeching. If there was anything warm inside him, any speck of pity or humanity, this would appeal to it. "I'll give you money instead. Or another favour. Anything but this."

All trace of that chuckle vanished. "Are you disobeying me?" His voice had dropped to a soft murmur, prickling the back of my neck.

"I... no... just... Can I do something—?"

Hand on my throat. Back slamming into the wall.

I froze, barely breathing as he held me there.

I didn't so much feel it as watch, like I stood outside peering through a window at something happening inside, just a silent observer.

"You remember this, don't you?" A slow smile showed his teeth.

"No." My voice was quiet and so very distant, shunted out of the way by fragments of somewhere else.

A dark sky. Soil between my toes. Something I didn't want to see behind me.

I flinched from the shards of memory threatening to pierce through the blank space in my mind.

A tiny corner of my brain shrieked at my body to *move*, to do something.

I should pull on his hand, get it off me. I should claw at his face. I should stab him with a hairpin.

But stillness was safer. Stillness was a way to hide. Stillness let me pretend I wasn't really there.

"You remember what I told you then? You remember the lengths I'll go to." His grip tightened, making my breaths wheeze.

The sound pressed on my ears, bringing pieces of a memory I didn't want.

Night closing in. The silence of the grave. My own urine trickling down my legs.

"You remember you are expendable."

The corridor darkened. Black branches spread overhead. Dewy grass grew underfoot.

I don't want it. I don't want to remember. I don't...

59

I'm walking through the forest on my family estate. The sky above is dark—black branches against a black sky, stars twinkling in between.

I'm not alone.

Uncle Rufus walks behind me, carrying a lantern. His footsteps whisper and creak on twigs and dead undergrowth.

I was still crying about Fantôme when he barged into my room a quarter of an hour ago, dirt on his hands and boots. Unsmiling, he ordered me out of bed. "Stop those useless tears. You want to bury your cat, don't you?" I barely had time to put on a dressing gown and slippers before he marched me outside.

"Just ahead." His voice shatters the silence.

The lamplight picks out shapes under the trees. A mound of earth, something wrapped in sacking, a spade. The light disappears in the depths of a yawning hole.

He's already dug the grave. That's... almost kind of him. Maybe he feels bad about Fantôme and this is his way of showing it.

I glance back and try to smile. But there's nothing kind in his

430

face.

"There's your cat." He nods at the burlap-wrapped shape, and that's when I spot the white tail sticking out.

My burning eyes blur, and I have to swallow down more tears. My poor Fantôme. She trusted me to look after her. And I failed.

He jerks his chin at the hole. "Get on with it, then."

I pick up her wrapped body. As I clutch her to my chest, she seems lighter somehow. "I'm sorry," I whisper too quietly for my uncle to hear.

I reach the edge of the hole. It's large, a bit longer than I am tall, and dips away into pure darkness as Uncle Rufus stands back, the lamp at his feet.

"I can't see."

His mouth is flat, his eyes cold. "You don't need to see to know what way is down."

I don't want to throw her in. She's had enough ill-treatment for today... for her short lifetime.

I swallow and climb into the hole. It smells. Earth and dampness, the rotting of years upon years of leaf mulch and bark—the scents I'm used to in the forest.

But there's something else.

Something thicker, deeper. Something that blocks the back of my throat and makes my stomach heave. Decay and rot, like an animal long dead.

It crawls down my back, a reminder that Fantôme is gone, even though I hold her in my arms.

I almost turn my ankle when I reach the bottom, but I catch myself before I fall.

Holding my breath, I lay her down. She's so small compared to this grave.

"Are you ready to see now?" Uncle Rufus approaches, only his head visible over the edge of the grave, then his broad shoulders, his

chest. *Finally, he lifts the lamp, and I have to shield my eyes against the sudden brightness.*

When I can see again, I steel myself to face Fantôme. I should witness her in her final resting place before the earth locks her away. I owe her that much.

The sack's rough brown burlap is rendered gold by the lamplight.

But it doesn't lie on rich, dark earth.

Fabric, muddy and sodden, still green in places. And something in it, pale against the dirt. Several somethings, all long and thin. Buttons and boots, too. A shiny brass belt buckle.

Long, blond hair.

Empty eye sockets. A crack above them.

It takes me long seconds to understand.

A body... a skeleton now.

The old decay I can smell.

My heart thunders to life as though it can battle the death around me. A scream catches in my throat, coming out as a whimper. Gasping, I stumble into the side of the grave and climb up, damp earth cold on my fingers and toes.

When I reach the top, his smile is colder. He catches me by the throat, holds me still.

"Do you see, now?"

I pant, pull on his hand, try to back away. His grip tightens.

I don't know how long I stare up at him. Who is she? How did he find her body? Why has he brought me here? We need to report this, try to tell—

"Do you recognise her from your stables?"

I blink at him, mind replaying his words again and again until I can make sense of them. Green. The colour the stable hands wear. Long blond hair. It's Dia. Several years older than me, she used to work with the sabrecats. She taught me how to clean their claws.

She ran away four or five years ago, leaving a note to say she was getting married. But...

"She disobeyed my orders." Uncle Rufus bares his teeth, which are yellow in the lamplight. "You know such disobedience requires punishment."

I shiver, palms hot at the memory of the birch being slashed across them.

"Only a few lashes, but she fought. And that was when she had a little accident." He taps my forehead in the same place there's a crack on the skull.

No one ever questioned the contents of her note. Except it wasn't hers, was it?

She never left the estate.

"Lesson learned. Obey orders. Accept your punishment. Isn't that right, Katherine?"

I stare up at him, not taking in the words as anything other than sounds rising and falling.

He killed Dia. By accident, perhaps. But he buried her here in the woods and hid the fact she was dead. That doesn't sound like an accident to me.

I swallow past his grip. "Why?"

"I told you why she's dead. And you're not stupid, so you must be asking why I'm showing you this." He smiles again and forces me back a step.

My feet squelch into the mud at the edge of the grave. My slippers must've come off as I clambered out.

"To teach you a lesson, of course. You made that sabrecat disobey me. You made a fool out of me."

"I didn't. I taught her commands in—"

His grip cuts off my words, my breath. My eyes water, and I try to pull his hand away.

It does nothing.

433

I dig my fingers in harder. When that fails, I use my nails.

He doesn't so much as wince.

He looms over me, nose wrinkled, eyes burning as his fingers bite into my flesh. "Like an untrainable sabrecat, an untrainable girl is a danger to her family. You're not going to prove to be untrainable, are you, Katherine?"

I claw at his hand, wriggle in his grasp, kick his shins, try to scratch his face.

It's no use. He's too strong, and a realisation curdles in my stomach...

I'm powerless.

So I shake my head.

And he smiles. "Good. I'd hate for it to be your grave next."

I try to drag in breaths but only manage tiny, wheezing gasps that creak in my ears. My face tingles. Dark splotches bloom on the edge of my vision, like night closing in.

I'm dying. I'm going to die here. This will be my grave.

My heart thrashes in my chest like it can join the fight and save me.

"It's your duty to do as you're told, marry who you're told, and give your husband heirs. All that's required of you is obedience and silence. Nothing more." He pushes me back another step.

No. No. Please. I try to say it, but I have no breath to say it with.

My lungs spasm. They burn, desperate for more than this thin wheeze.

Another step. My feet slip and there's nothing beneath them.

He has me over the grave, some still sane part of me registers.

I scrabble at the mud, toes digging in and catching for an instant before they slip away into the void again. Tears in the corners of my eyes, I cling to his arm, trying to take some weight off my throat.

He can't mean this. He can't mean to kill me. Not like this.

But then I meet the cold depths of his eyes. They glint like ice. And, worst of all, they look right through me, like I'm a pane of glass.

Like I'm nothing.

He does mean it. And the story about Dia is true. He killed her. He killed Fantôme.

And he's about to kill me.

Warm liquid trickles down my legs.

"You will obey your family. You will protect your family. You are a silent and pretty pawn in the business of men. The sooner you understand that, the safer you'll be."

But I'm his family—his niece. He's meant to protect me.

He's turning grey... the whole night is. My grip on his arm loosens, muscles growing weak.

I croak, "But—"

He lets go.

Air rushes into my lungs. I'm flying. Falling. In darkness.

For a moment it's beautiful, euphoric, as my brain lights up and the black splotches disappear.

And I can breathe.

Then I crash. The air blasts from my lungs. Pain thunders across my back and shoulders where I hit the uneven ground. The world goes dark, light, dark.

I blink. I might've been unconscious for a few seconds, because the light's different, like the lamp has been moved.

Wheezing, I drag in breath after breath—I'm winded, but it's still better than his hold on my throat.

I roll to my side, trying to stand.

Staring back is darkness.

Two pools of it. Empty. Unseeing. Futile and broken. A promise of nothing.

Cold understanding shoots through me. I cry out and try to roll to my feet to get away from Dia's body. I'm lying in her grave.

"Don't." Dirt rains down on me.

I ball up, shielding my face.

He looks down at me from the graveside. "You need to learn. Your sister is bad enough, but she's still young. I won't have both my nieces out of control. Keep still."

I stare up at him. From this angle, the lamp carves his face in pure light and deepest shadow, like a contorted mask at the theatre.

His mask is cruel and as icy as the cold seeping into my skin from the soil below.

"You will lie there until I say you can leave. Every time you move"—he lifts the spade into sight—"you get buried a little more. Do you understand?"

I blink my gritty eyes. This is insanity. It can't be real. I'm in some horrible nightmare. Maybe if I lie here long enough, I'll wake.

I nod.

His eyes narrow and he ducks out of sight. A moment later, soil tumbles over my feet. I gasp, but manage to hold still when his face appears over the edge of the grave again.

He means this. All of it.

"Do you understand?"

This time, I don't nod.

I'm not here. Not really. This isn't reality.

He smiles, though there's a twinge of disappointment in the curl of his mouth.

I whimper as something crawls by my bare foot. Another spadeful of dirt covers me.

I'm not here. That isn't my foot. I can do this. I can obey.

Still and silent as the grave, I lie there with the cold of the soil seeping into my bones and my nightgown growing sodden from the mud, and I wait until I'm allowed to leave.

"Get your fucking hands off her."

60

"Get your fucking hands off her."

The voice didn't belong in that memory.

From a distance, I watched as Uncle Rufus's jaw tightened at the interruption. "This is a family matter. It doesn't concern you."

"Maybe not. But it concerns her, and if she had the power to tell you to get off, she would."

Bastian. Somewhere behind my uncle. I couldn't crane past to see him. I couldn't do anything. My body had shut down. I was dying. There was only the cold in my every fibre, saying death was coming.

"Think of it that she's speaking through me," Bastian went on, voice edged with razor blades. "So I'll say it once more, just in case you didn't hear the first time..."

He appeared at my uncle's shoulder, mouth close to his ear. "Get. Your. Fucking. Hands. Off. Her."

Eyes so wide, I could see the whites all the way round, Uncle Rufus spun away, releasing me. He stared up at Bastian.

"Better." Except Bastian's lips didn't move.

When my uncle turned, he found himself face to face with another Bastian. His second self.

My uncle's jaw fell slack as he stared from one to the other.

When he turned again, trying to escape, another figure blocked his way—this one formed of shadows.

Eyes bulging, Uncle Rufus made a strangled sound.

I should've found pleasure in this. But I couldn't feel anything, only creeping cold, bone-deep and numbing.

Both corporeal Bastians smiled. It wasn't as cold as ice, like Uncle Rufus's smiles—this was colder, as cold as the space between stars. "The only reason I'm not halfway through tearing your head from your body is because it's clear she doesn't need to see any more violence right now." They said it as one, voices a twin chorus of clipped consonants and barely contained rage.

And that rage was a beautiful thing, in a quiet and terrifying way. In the way a serpent approached and struck in perfect silence.

Shadow-Bastian stepped to one side and Uncle Rufus fled.

"Kat?" Bastian closed the space between us, his other selves watching my uncle's retreat. He cupped my cheek, and the sudden blazing heat of it made me want to pull away.

But I couldn't. I had to obey. To be good. I had to keep still and do as I was told.

"Katherine?" He searched my gaze. "Look at me. Look at where you are. Feel the wall behind you, the floor beneath you. You're here. You're safe."

I could only stare as various sensations crept back into my body. First was my heart, racing, racing, racing like it could hammer its way out. My fingers clung to the stone wall at my back, sore and stiff. My skin was clammy with sweat, and moisture gathered in my shoes and down my legs. I'd wet myself.

I must've said it out loud, because he shook his head. "It's all right. Don't worry about that." His voice was pitched low and soft, soothing against my frayed nerves. "You're safe. You're here. See?" He stroked my hair, the feeling far too gentle to belong in what I'd just seen. "Tell me where you are."

"The palace." My voice still sounded distant, but maybe not so far away as it had been before.

"That's it. Good. Good." He nodded and held my shoulder.

It was like an anchor. Solid. Heavy.

I let out a long breath, eyes sinking shut. This was real. He was real. So was I. That other thing... I turned away from the rawness of the freshly torn open memory... It had been real once. But a long time ago. Not now.

"Hey, eyes open. On me." His grip on my shoulder squeezed, and my eyelids fluttered open. "Good. You're doing so well, Kat. Is there somewhere you can go? Somewhere you feel safe?"

Nowhere was safe. Nowhere.

I managed a faint shake of my head.

"I suspect he knows where your rooms are." His jaw ticked, then he exhaled, expression softening as he stroked my hair again.

I sank against the warmth of his touch—it was a bright light against the dark cold of that grave.

"Do you want to come to my suite? It's guarded; I'll make sure they know not to let your uncle through."

The safest place in the building. The only place he couldn't reach me.

I nodded and let Bastian take my hand.

439

61

I remembered nothing about walking through the corridors, only arriving in Bastian's suite and him using that magical lock on the door.

I didn't want to think about what I'd just seen, but every time I closed my eyes, that grave awaited me.

"Shit, you're shivering." Bastian stepped into view, reaching for my arms, then stopped short. "I don't know what happened there. Is it all right if I touch you, or would you prefer I don't?"

"It's fine. I'm fine." My voice came from very far away, not quite sounding my own. "I just need a drink and some sleep." My answers to everything. I didn't want to think, didn't want to feel, didn't want to exist, just for a while. A bottle would take me there.

He gave me a gentle smile and rubbed my arms, his touch like fire against my ice. "Not yet. If you sleep now, it'll be worse. Let's get you something dry to wear, though."

He disappeared, and I hugged myself. I didn't want to sit

and get the furniture wet. Besides, moving seemed like a lot of effort when my body felt like I'd lost a boxing match.

Had I really held that memory locked away all these years —half my lifetime ago? Uncle Rufus wasn't just cruel and manipulative, using fear to get what he wanted—he was a murderer.

I had no idea how long it was before Bastian reappeared. Time was a fuzzy concept, a bit like the space around me that seemed to shift and wobble at unexpected moments, even though I knew the walls were solid.

"Here we are." He held out a bundle of white cloth.

I stared at it, blinked. What did he want me to do with that?

"Shall I help you?"

I shrugged.

It didn't matter. I was broken. I couldn't see straight, think straight. The world was cruel and dark. My own mind had betrayed me, first hiding that memory for so long, then drowning me in it instead of fighting back.

Nothing mattered.

And he couldn't help me.

"I'm going to put this on you, all right?"

I dipped my chin. He could do what he wanted to me. Didn't matter.

Holding my gaze, he slid my gown over my shoulders and let it fall to the floor. A dim and distant part of my mind pointed out this was the first time he was seeing me actually naked. Our encounters usually involved my clothes being pulled out of the way, not off. But he only looked at my face.

"Arms up."

I obeyed, and he slid the white cloth over my hands. For a blessed moment, there was just white as it passed over my head.

White nothingness. Close to oblivion. But not quite. My brain still worked. *What he did to you. To poor Dia. Murdered. Her body. That night. That night. That night. If you'd been bad, he would've killed you.*

When I emerged from what I now realised was a shirt, my eyes burned and my lip trembled.

Bastian's brow crumpled. "Oh, love." He pulled me against him.

"But I wet myself. I'm dir—"

"I don't care." He squeezed me like he really didn't care that my legs were still covered in my own piss.

His tight hold was a shell, holding me in my fragile body, holding back memory and thought. I cowered into it, letting my silent tears soak into his shirt.

Gods knew how long later, he pulled away and searched my face. "I'm going to run you a bath. You're fucking freezing." He swept the dampness off my cheeks with the pads of his thumbs. "Will you be all right here for a minute?"

Nothing was ever going to be all right. But I nodded.

When he backed away, I thought I might fall. My legs were so tired, my body so heavy. But I held still as he made his way to the bathroom; he didn't take his eyes off me until he disappeared through the door.

For every minute he was gone, I slid a little further inside. Outside was a harsh place. A bad place. One I didn't want to know.

"Kat?" He was here, close, touching my shoulder. "Come on, let's get you warm."

I went wherever he led me, letting the world pass in a haze that was too bright, too sharp. "Brandy." That would push everything to a more comfortable distance.

"Not wise, I'm afraid. Though I'm glad to hear your voice."

I sighed and hunched into myself.

The huge bath was full. That probably should've excited me—the first time I saw it, I'd wanted to try it out. But I could only stare at it, no spike of emotion inside.

There was some movement, then he appeared next to me, jacket removed. I frowned at his exposed shirt with its sleeves rolled up, not able to understand.

"We're getting in now, all right?" He pushed my hair over my shoulder, slid his hand down my back, then lifted me against his chest. Everything about it was so gentle, it tugged at more tears, though I couldn't say why.

We. My mind snagged on the word, sluggish.

"But your clothes. They'll get—"

"I don't care." He walked down the steps, and even in my deadened state, I couldn't help but sigh when the water hit me. Hot, almost uncomfortably so.

I might've let out a moan as it closed over my shoulders. It soaked into me, burning away that deathly cold until it only remained in my marrow, like ice lingering in shadows on a sunny winter's day.

"There," he murmured against my hair. He still held me against his body, sitting on what must've been a submerged seat built into the bath. "You've stopped shivering." Beneath me, his muscles eased.

We sat there a long while, the water's scent eventually breaking through my shuttered senses. Lavender and chamomile, sweet and soothing. I also registered that the room was only dimly lit with glowing orbs bobbing though the air. Fae light.

"Kat?" He tilted my cheek towards him. "Good, you're still awake."

"Why can't I sleep?" If I couldn't drink, sleep was the next best escape.

"Soon, love." He rested his head against mine. The weight of his arms around me and the warmth of the water held me here and now, reminding me of my body and reality. "Just stay awake a little longer, then you'll be safe to sleep. Otherwise, you'll go right back to the memories you were lost in earlier."

Part of me wondered how he knew this, but I was too tired to pull on that thread.

"You're safe here. After this, you can do whatever you want. Sit by the fire, on the settee, sleep. My rooms are your safe place."

Nowhere was safe. Nowhere. The world was a dark and dangerous place. Safety was only an illusion.

But he went on, "You can even tell me to go away, and I'll wait outside, guarding you. Anything you need, I'll get."

It should've warmed me, pleased me, made me smile, made me *something*. But I felt nothing, just the icy core that remained at the centre of my bones.

Eventually, he carried me from the bath and set me on the floor, dripping. I frowned at the drenched shirt that came to my knees as he pulled a towel around me.

He followed my gaze. "I didn't want you to think I meant this as anything sexual." He wrapped the towel tight until I was cocooned and could barely move. I should've felt trapped, but... something about the tightness was comforting.

In his room, he helped me change into a dry shirt and a huge dressing gown before disappearing behind me and reappearing in dry clothes himself.

He gave me an odd frown, bemused perhaps. "You haven't moved." He looked at the bed, then back at me.

I followed his gaze, not understanding what I was meant to have done. Had I displeased him?

"You've done so well." Gently, he propelled me towards the bed. "It's safe to sleep now." He peeled back the blankets, sat me on the soft mattress, and pulled them up around me. "Do you want to be alone, or shall I stay?"

I didn't know. Alone was like the grave, though. I'd lain in there alone. Cold. Dark. Terrified, but having to hide it.

"Kat, love? Come back to me." His hand was on my cheek, his face close, filling my whole field of view.

I blinked, heart racing. "Stay. Please stay."

He slid in and curled around me, chest to my back. "Light or darkness?"

"Not darkness."

"How's this?" He pulled out his orrery, twisted the chain-loop, turned the central section, and did something else I couldn't follow as his hands moved too quickly. It opened up, and as the fae lights around us grew dim, it threw light onto the walls and the canopy above the bed.

Dark purple and midnight blue, with tiny points of light. The night sky, but... different. I'd once seen a book in a friend's library that was full of illustrations of space. Some had been speculation about what it might look like, others showed views through powerful telescopes. This was like those illustrations, turning the room into another realm, one that wasn't light or dark.

"Yes." The terrible tightness I'd been carrying all day eased. "I like it."

"Good. Here..." He curled my fingers around the chain. "If you wake and you don't know what's real or what's memory, remember that this is real and solid. Run your fingers over the links, feel the metal, listen to the way it clinks when it moves."

He squeezed me and closed one hand over mine, keeping it on the chain. "Listen to my breaths. Feel my warmth around you. No matter what happens, remember, all of this is real."

I rubbed my thumb along the links, letting each one press into my skin as his words pressed into my weary mind. *All of this is real.* It carried a weight, one I didn't understand, but that seemed more than just the orrery and this moment. As my eyelids drifted, the thought slid through my fingers like sand.

"Sleep, sweet love, sleep well and deep. I'll be here when you wake."

Above us, the stars spun slowly, and I spun away with them.

62

The next day, I couldn't face the thought of getting out of bed. But I had duties beyond this room, no matter how much that made me cringe. Estates, bailiffs, spymasters... I didn't want there to be a world outside —at least not one I had to think about.

I stared at the wall. I should get up. I should get up. I should...

Behind me, Bastian moved, replacing the warmth of his chest with a long sweep of his hand down my back as he sat up.

"I should go," I muttered into the pillow. "The queen will have brunch soon. She likes us all there."

"She does." He pulled the blankets around me and stroked my hair. "But that doesn't matter. She has other ladies-in-waiting. I'll take care of it. I'll say you're ill."

I couldn't summon the will to argue and instead let myself sink back into the mattress.

"You don't need to worry about anything other than what

447

you need right now." His voice drifted over me as the world faded. "Tell me, and I'll make it so."

I spent most of the day sleeping, only waking to drink water (there was always a cool glass of it by the bed) or go to the toilet. Bastian kept the bedroom door open and stationed himself in an armchair opposite it, where I could see him if I sat up. Not that I did often.

Exhaustion had taken root in me, creeping through every muscle, knotting in my mind.

And I succumbed to it.

Sleep meant I didn't have to do anything, think anything, be anything. I welcomed it with open arms.

But it betrayed me.

Night. Damp earth. Pale bone. The stink of death.

I clawed at it, trying to keep Dia's body from mine. If she embraced me, her death would seep into me, stealing my breath, and I'd join her in the grave forever.

"Kat, it's a dream." Bastian's voice shattered the memory-turned-nightmare. "It isn't real."

Dragging in searing breaths, I blinked and found myself in his bed, soaked in my own sweat, gripping his clothes. A scratch marred the smooth skin of his cheek, and his shirt was torn.

I snatched my hands away and clutched my chest. "I'm sorry. I'm sorry." I'd hurt him. That would displease him. That meant punishment. I shook my head. "Please don't. Please. I'm sorry. I didn't mean to."

"Kat." He caught my fingers, which now clawed at my own flesh as I fought for air that didn't seem to come, no matter how much I gasped. "It's all right. You're not in trouble. You're not in danger. Just breathe with me."

He held my gaze and inhaled, long and slow.

It was impossible. I couldn't. I needed to get more air, quickly. Nothing was going in. I was going to die.

"Katherine." Voice firm, he squeezed my hands. "Do as I tell you. You can do that, can't you?"

Lungs spasming, I nodded. Do as I'm told. That was my everything. That was safe.

He placed my hand on my stomach, just above my belly button. "Feel the breath here. In through your nose." He inhaled again, long and slow.

I clamped my mouth shut and followed, though my chest twitched, begging me to suck in greedily, rather than draw in slowly.

"That's it, good. And out." He blew through his mouth, nodding encouragement.

I copied, though my breath ran out before his, and I sucked in another.

"No. Not yet." He pressed my hand into my belly. "Not until that's gone right down."

I blew out, shaky.

"Good. Again."

He led me through another set—in slowly, out fully. I managed to follow this time. The tightness in my chest eased with each rise and fall of my hand until I could breathe normally on my own. He gathered my limp body into his lap, and I let exhaustion claim me once more.

I LOST track of day and night as I lived in a loop. Sleeping, drinking, staggering to the toilet, sometimes waking from horrible things I didn't want to remember. Always, Bastian was there, a watchful sentinel. Sometimes I found him working, other times reading, but always on that chair or at my side.

One day, I woke with two voices drifting through the open door. One was Bastian's, the other... I closed my eyes and listened.

"... change in meeting venue?" Asher, maybe?

"I'm not leaving my suite, so it's here or not at all."

"It was just a question. No need to get like that about it. I swear I've never seen you so tetchy before we came here." A pause. "I *wonder* why."

"Do we have business or are you here to speculate on my state of mind?"

Asher chuckled. "There's always business for the likes of us, Bastian, you know that. The queen has made her intentions known."

"Then the alliance is secured?"

"There are some negotiations I need you for first."

Bastian grunted. "I told you, I'm not leaving my suite until—"

"Then after she's better. But I need you to manage this. The queen's expecting it."

The door pulled to, leaving it only open a crack. I could've focused and listened in. I should've. But I couldn't gather the energy, and working for Cavendish felt like a distant torture— something that belonged outside these rooms. Instead, I let the hum of their muffled conversation lull me back to sleep.

When I woke, the door was wide open with no sign of Asher. Still, I wondered...

"What exactly is it the Night Queen's Shadow does?" I asked on my way back from the bathroom. I hadn't been able to face running a bath—that seemed an insurmountable task. But I'd noticed the sharp stink of sweat on myself, so I'd washed in the sink. This part of the palace had hot running water, and I'd taken my time scrubbing it into my skin. I was ashamed to admit it was the first time I'd washed since that first night.

Bastian placed the letter he was reading facedown in his lap and raised an eyebrow at me. The corner of his mouth twitched. "What exactly is it a lady-in-waiting does?"

I scraped my nail along the trim of the armchair next to his. "I entertain my queen, attend to her... do as I'm told."

He scoffed. "Perhaps our roles aren't so different after all. You're talkative today. Feeling better?"

No, but this teasing conversation let me pretend things were normal for a while. "You didn't answer my question."

He gave a long sigh that seemed to come from somewhere deep inside. "I do what needs to be done."

"Including being incredibly vague."

Mouth twisting, he inclined his head. "Including that."

I should find this out for my job. It was just work. Not sating my own curiosity. Not at all.

Liar.

"What else?"

His stubbled jaw tightened as he stared at the fire. He wouldn't answer. Either he'd remain silent or shift the subject. He hadn't touched me in anything approaching a sexual way since that night with my uncle, but this was the kind of time he'd pull out that card. Anything to escape answering.

"Quiet things."

I stilled at the sudden sound of his voice.

"Subtle things. Bloody things. Sometimes bad things." His

mouth flattened, and he straightened in his seat. "I *earned* the name Serpent. When I heard it, I chose the snake for my sigil." He gave a humourless laugh. "If people were going to call me that, well, I'd own the name and the fear that went with it. Fear is a useful tool, after all."

Mouth dry, I swallowed. I hadn't realised the nickname had come first. What had he done to earn it? My tongue wouldn't cooperate to ask.

At last, his gaze cut to me. "I've done awful things, Kat. Some I'm not proud of. Don't think that just because I've helped you, I'm some noble hero. I'm the villain in many other people's stories."

A villain? I couldn't believe that. A villain didn't treat me the way he had. They weren't so gentle; they didn't get into a bath fully clothed so I would feel safe.

"I can see what you're thinking. Don't fool yourself. I do what's required—whatever that may be." He balled up the letter, knuckles going white as he squeezed. "I've seen what happens when people don't, and I won't live in that horror."

He tossed the paper into the fire and watched as the flames licked at it, first singeing, then catching yellow and red at the edges, before engulfing it entirely. "I'll do what I must, no matter how much my feelings might disagree." He glowered at the paper turning to ashes. "You should remember all this when you find yourself tempted to trust me."

Too late.

When my inner alarms cried danger around Bastian Marwood, it wasn't for my life. It was for my heart.

I scratched the fuzzy trim, digging my nail right in. "I don't believe you."

"You should. My kind can't—"

"Yes, you can't lie. You've mentioned that, and so has

every damn story I've ever read about the fae."

He bristled and opened his mouth to go on.

I held up my finger. "You believe those things about yourself, so to you it is true. But that doesn't mean it's *the* truth with a capital *T*. You can't lie, but you can be wrong."

His lips pursed. "Hmm. I don't know whether to be irritated that you're telling me I'm wrong or touched that you'd perform such a feat of mental gymnastics to make it so I'm not a villain."

"No mental gymnastics required." I gestured at our surroundings. "You haven't left this room in days. You must be neglecting your work—I'm sure it isn't all papers that can be tossed onto the fire. All this to look after some nuisance human."

"Don't say that. Not ever." He frowned, but there was a softness in the downward turn of his mouth. "Your pain, your fear, what you've been through—that isn't a nuisance. *You* are not and never could be."

That didn't seem right, and it made my shoulders curve inwards. So much for teasing conversation and my pretence of normality.

"Let me worry about my work, but rest assured, it isn't being neglected. I've made arrangements so I can stay here."

For me.

The cold that lingered in my bones rose, cloaking me in goosebumps. I didn't deserve so much attention, so much patience. He'd also had a chest of my clothes brought here. Yet I couldn't even thank him for it.

Thanks. Such a simple word, but the letters might as well have been fish bones for all they stuck in my throat, and I sank into sullen silence. The weight of his kindness crashed into me, leaving my body as heavy as it had been that first night.

"Now we've cleared that up, would you like something to eat?" He gestured to a side table loaded with several plates. Cheese, cold meats, sandwiches, apples, pears, and black-berries.

My stomach twisted at the sight and I turned away. "No, thank you. I think I'll go back to bed." I drifted to the bedroom, his gaze boring into my back.

There was no more talk about whether he was a hero or villain, but the next day, he tried to tempt me to eat again. The day after, he brought out the best weapons in his arsenal: an array of biscuits and cakes that any other time would've lit me up with joy.

But joy seemed stupid now. Another illusion.

That evening, I lay alone with the orrery's light show, not quite dozing, not fully awake, when he came in and the bed shifted behind me.

"Kat? I don't know if you're awake, but... I have a confes-sion." His voice wavered, uncertain.

That was the first thing that reached through my haze.

"I'm worried about you."

That was the second, making the back of my throat ache.

He drew a long breath. "I've never been so scared in all my life."

And that was the third. The way he murmured it so softly, like he didn't want to say it out loud. He didn't seem like someone who felt fear, never mind admitted it.

I didn't know what to say, how to respond, just that some-thing inside me cracked.

"It feels like I'm watching you drown and there's nothing I can do about it. I'll keep trying, but... please don't give up." He smoothed my hair and kissed my head before leaving.

63

The next day, when he offered me food, I took a bite of an apple. It tasted of nothing, but I smiled at him and chewed. When I took a second mouthful... there was something sweet. With the third, a note of tart green apple.

Before I realised, I'd finished it.

I wanted more sweetness, so I took a cake next. Coffee flavoured, and I tasted it all. The bitterness, the caramel notes, the sugar, the icing so sweet, it almost made me swoon as it melted over my tongue.

When I cleared the crumbs from the plate, my stomach still felt empty.

"You might want to take it slowly," he said as I gobbled down slices of buttery chicken and minted lamb.

"I'm hungry." I clutched my belly. "Famished."

He pressed his lips together but didn't stop me.

Eventually, I'd had enough and flopped onto the settee

with a groan. My stomach gurgled, making my face burn. "Sorry, I—"

"Don't apologise for eating. Ever."

I didn't know what to say to that, so I rubbed my belly while it grumbled about the sudden influx of food.

The silence stretched on, not entirely uncomfortable.

"That night... how did you know where I was?"

The corner of his mouth feathered as he shuffled through the papers in his lap. "While your sister was here, I... I missed you. As soon as I heard she'd left, I went looking for you. You weren't in your rooms, so I hunted through the palace. And then I found you with that man." His jaw clenched, the pale scar standing out as his lips pressed together. "I smelled you first, your scent with that of someone related to you. Then I smelled your fear, and *then* I came around the corner and saw his hands on you." He took several deep breaths, nostrils flaring. "If we'd been in Tenebris, I would've let my shadows rip him apart."

The look on his face—it was no joke.

Several more breaths, then his gaze slid to mine. "I know he hurt you, not just then, but before. I know there's something very wrong that isn't only down to him scaring you that night. And I know you want to hide from all those things, even if it means hiding from the entire world."

My heart pounded, clashing with whatever was happening in my stomach. A cold sweat broke out on my forehead.

I had to look away. His eyes were too penetrating, too dangerous. He saw too much.

"If and when you want to talk about it, I'm here."

My stomach lurched. "Oh gods." I jolted to my feet and ran to the bathroom.

Everything I'd eaten came right back up. Thankfully, I made it to the toilet. I heaved and heaved, drenched in sweat, and as the vomiting abated, I became aware of a hand rubbing my back. My hair wasn't in my face, either. When I sat up, I found it being held back by shadows and Bastian kneeling beside me.

I scrubbed my face, wishing myself a million miles away. He wasn't meant to see me like this. What must I look like?

"I should've stopped at the apple."

He gave a rueful smile and passed me a glass of water. "I should've slowed you down, but I was too relieved to see you eating."

I swilled the water around my mouth and spat it down the toilet before closing the lid and flushing. With a sigh, I sat against the tiled wall. His shadows slid from my hair, whispering over my shoulders and back to him.

"I have to admit"—I sipped the water, forcing myself to take it slowly—"this isn't exactly the behaviour I'd expect from someone people call the Serpent. The breathing. Knowing exactly what to do when my mind's unravelling, how to bring me back to the here and now."

He looked away. A beat later, he sighed and sat against the wall opposite, knees bent, forearms resting on them. He still didn't meet my gaze, just stared at his hands, and I was about to change the subject when he finally said, "My father. He has episodes where he relives the war. He saw things... did things."

"You mentioned scars. Wait... *Has?*" Present tense.

One side of his mouth rose. "I have two fathers. Unlike here, our marriages aren't restricted to one man and one woman. When they call me the Bastard of Tenebris, it isn't entirely accurate." That rise of his mouth turned into a twist.

"They were married when they adopted me. This belonged to *Baba*." He pulled the orrery from his pocket. "And the one who's still alive, whose trauma overwhelms him sometimes, I call *Athair*. They're different words for father in our old tongues."

"Like we have father or papa or pa."

"Exactly." He nodded, twisting the outer plates of the orrery, opening and closing it.

"It must be hard seeing your *athair* dealing with something so horrific."

He turned the orrery until all the planets peeked out, one-by-one. "I don't like to see the people I care about suffer." His gaze shifted past the orrery to me.

I was the coward this time—I had to look away. "My father was very strict." I didn't know why that came out, just that it felt like the right thing to fill the gap and turn us away from what he'd just said without saying.

I heard the draw of breath that signalled he was about to speak. I wasn't ready for whatever it might be, so I jumped in. "Especially after my sister was born. I now know that's because she isn't his. Mama did a deal with a fae to get pregnant." Avice had told me during her visit—her magic came from being half fae.

Bastian shifted, one leg straightening. "Oh?"

"It was years since she'd had me, and she was desperate for another child, so..." I shrugged. "Fae bargain, it was. The fact this fae lord could give her what he couldn't left Papa paranoid and insecure. I understand that now, but as a child..." I shook my head. "He just changed overnight. It was confusing. Frightening. But not as frightening as his brother Rufus."

Goosebumps crept over my skin. My heart beat a little faster.

Swallowing, I pressed my palms into the tile floor. Cool. Smooth. The ridge between tiles, full of rough grout. I wasn't there, I was here with Bastian and safe—or at least as safe as life got.

"He killed my sabrecat cub in front of me and Avice. I was fifteen. She was only eight." It gripped my heart. I should've protected her from that sight. I should've stopped it.

Only... if I'd tried, I'd have ended up with Dia, wouldn't I?

In the periphery of my vision, I could see Bastian's slight movement—clenching his hands into fists, perhaps. But I stared at the hem of my borrowed shirt, at my knees just below that, at the way they were still red from kneeling as I vomited.

"I can't see the exact moment. Like my mind refused to hold on to the image. I think I'm glad." I traced a sharp spot on the edge of a tile again and again—an anchor point, keeping me focused. "But that's not the only thing..."

I rubbed my feet together and bit my lip as my eyes burned. No tears. Just tell him. Some of it, at least. If I told someone else, maybe that would purge it from my mind and it would have less hold on me.

"Kat," he said, voice soft, "you don't have to—"

"I want to." I let my head fall back against the wall and counted the shell curves that decorated the ceiling. "There has always been this blank memory. I just had a few images that I couldn't make sense of and sometimes they'd bubble up. Nighttime. Earth. The forest. I didn't know what happened until..." I tugged the shirt's collar though it was nowhere near my throat. "When he held me and... and... that was where I went."

"You didn't just remember, you relived it."

I nodded, eyes so hot, it was a wonder tears didn't stream down my cheeks. I kept my head tilted back and didn't dare blink. "I was there," I whispered. "I couldn't even see the corridor anymore. I saw everything my mind had refused to. I could smell it, feel the mud on my feet, his grip on my throat as he threatened to kill me."

I didn't remember telling my body to move, just that I found myself curled in a ball.

"Oh, Kat." Bastian's warmth seeped into my chilled body as he gathered me close. "Love. You're safe now. I'll make sure he never touches you again."

I knew what that meant. "No." I dragged my head up from my knees and met his gaze. "I don't want you to do to him what you did to Eckington."

A shadow of the cold fury from the corridor slithered through his silver eyes. "I'm not going to break his arm or his nose. I'm going to break *him*."

"*No.* He's my uncle."

"I don't give a shit if he's one of the gods themselves. He needs to be punished for what he did to you and stopped from ever doing it again."

"He's family. You may not care, but it matters to me." My heart gave a heavy beat as I edged too close to those rumours about his father. But... he couldn't have killed him. I saw the sorrow whenever he spoke about him, how much the orrery mattered to him.

"You can *find* family." He searched my gaze, deep lines etched between his eyebrows. "You don't need someone like him."

"Maybe not, but it's my choice. I have a duty to my family

—my blood, and he's part of that, no matter what he's done. I can't change or let go of it."

His jaw rippled, and every line of his body went hard.

"Promise me you won't kill or harm him."

"I can't do that." His canines showed as he spoke, halfway to a snarl.

I clutched his cheeks. "Promise me, Bastian. *Please.*"

He held so still, I wondered if perhaps he hadn't heard me. Then he blasted out a breath. "For fuck's sake, Katherine. You know I can't deny you." His eyes squeezed shut. "Fine. I promise I won't kill or in any way harm your Uncle Rufus until and unless you free me from this promise." With a sigh, he opened his eyes. "Happy?"

"Thank you." I stroked his cheek, and he grumbled before standing.

"Come on, sitting on this cold floor isn't good for you. What do you want to do instead?" He helped me up.

"Honestly? Sleep some more." I gave him a rueful smile. "I'm exhausted."

"As you wish." He scooped me up and started from the room.

"I'm not too exhausted to walk." A chuckle bubbled through my words.

He stopped and squeezed me against his chest. "I don't care. It made you almost—*almost* laugh."

He carried me to the bedroom, the slightest spring in his step.

64

The next day, my attempts to eat went better. I stuck to just an apple at first, and when my stomach didn't reject it, I tried a little bread and cheese. The flavours sliced through the grey haze of exhaustion. When I looked up, I found Bastian watching me, a smile on the edge of his lips.

"Are you laughing at me?"

His expression smoothed, and he shook his head. "Never."

"You've definitely laughed at me before."

"Never at you eating. I like seeing you enjoy food, especially now. Did you realise you made a little sound when you bit into the cheese?"

My face went hot. When had I lost such awareness of myself? "Cheese is good."

"It is. One of the best foods, if you ask me."

"I'd drink to that." I raised my eyebrows at him in question. I hadn't had a single drop of alcohol since arriving.

He watched me a long while, the look that stripped me

bare. "One won't do any harm." He gave me the choice between brandy and whisky. I chose the former, and he poured one for me and a whisky for himself.

We sat in companionable silence by the fire as I savoured the sweet apricot and peach notes of my brandy. I hadn't noticed those when I drank it the night of Lara's death.

That felt like a year ago, though it had only been a couple of months. And the first time I met Bastian on the road? It could've been a lifetime ago. His face was still as achingly gorgeous, but now I found it was an ache I enjoyed.

His gaze, tinted gold by the fire, slid to me. "What?"

"I was thinking about when we first met." The brandy made me say what I was actually thinking, rather than jumping to a lie.

Except... no, it wasn't alcohol. It was this cocoon he'd built around us in his rooms. Like there was no outside world. Like we weren't from nations that could find themselves enemies as easily as allies. Like I wasn't being paid to spy on him and doing a poor job of it.

This place was safe—perhaps not just for me, but both of us. That was why he'd told me about his father's trauma and had confessed his fears for me. That was why I'd been able to speak of my uncle.

I swallowed, throat suddenly thick. "The night before I met you, I had a strange encounter with a fox."

His eyebrow flickered a fraction. "Oh?"

"It didn't seem entirely... fox-like." I laughed a little at myself. "Later, I thought maybe it was you, but you can't turn into an animal, can you?" I narrowed my eyes at him. "And even if you could, I don't think it would be a fox."

He chuckled and swirled his drink, looking at it as his cheeks perhaps went a little pinker. "No, it wasn't me. What animal do you think I would be?" he asked casually—a little *too* casually.

"I'll tell you, if you tell me what you know about that fox first. I can see you know *something*."

Lips pursing, he slid his gaze to me. "You're too good at reading people. That's a dangerous ability."

"Dangerous for you, you mean."

"Naturally."

I held his gaze a long while, but he said nothing more. "Are you going to tell me, then?"

"I was on the road the night before you stopped me, but so were others. The fox being one of them. Their scream alerted me, so I turned back."

"Why were you out? You aren't supposed to leave the palace."

"Are you lecturing me on rule-breaking, Wicked Lady?"

I huffed into my glass, steaming its sides. "No, but... it's a risk—not just to you, but to your whole diplomatic mission. Why take it?"

"There are wards around the palace grounds that mean we can't send messages."

"Then the legends are true—there's iron in the palace walls?"

"There must be, because no magic can pass through. And the city is too busy—too many eyes. So I have to ride further afield to send word back to Tenebris. When I heard the fox's scream, I knew I'd been followed. I turned back and decided to come out the next night, when the rain would wash away my tracks and scent. But..." He gave me a sidelong look as he sipped his whisky. "Someone had other ideas."

I sank a little deeper into my chair and shifted my attention to the brandy.

A long moment passed. "What did you do with the note that was in my orrery?"

I held still, but goosebumps crept over me. "I burned it." The lie spilled out of me without thought, like my speeding heart pushed it through my tongue in the same way it pushed blood through my veins. Was he doing all this because he knew I had it and hoped kindness would get it back? If it was a message to Tenebris, it could contain secrets about Albion. Hadn't he said he'd do whatever was required?

What would he do now he believed I'd burned the note? And was it worse than what he'd do if he knew I had it still?

I dared to look at him.

Swirling his whisky, he nodded slowly, though his shoulders had slumped. "Well, we've got what we wanted, anyway, so I suppose it isn't the end of the world." He gave a crooked smile. "Your queen has chosen her future husband."

I sat up, eyebrows rising.

"It's Asher. Dawn will be sick when it's announced."

I chuckled into my brandy, heartbeat calming. "Good." I pictured the rose-gold-haired woman's expression when she heard. *Please, gods, let me be near her when she finds out.*

"I didn't think you were so invested."

"I'm..." I nearly said *invested in you*, but I bit my tongue. "I'm aware a fae king will be best to secure the magic of the royal line, but I didn't want it to be Dawn. Not after..." My brandy sloshed against the side of the glass as I tilted it. "The woman who took my necklace..." When I dared to look up, I found him sitting straight and still, alert. "She's the one who sabotaged the stepping stones."

His knuckles whitened. That murderous look lit up his eyes.

I swallowed. "Don't kill her."

His jaw flexed and I could practically hear him pull it open before he answered. "I can't." He downed the last half of his drink and slammed the glass on the table. "Something as overt as that could cause all-out conflict between the courts. I can't risk that, however much I might want to." He gave a bitter smile. "I'm sorry, Kat. I knew they were acting against us, but I didn't think they'd target you directly. That was foolish of me."

I ached to know what Cavendish had found out about Dawn. What were they doing against Asher and Bastian? Had he acted to neutralise them? Was Caelus's request for me purely because of Bastian, or had he bought my lies in the hall near his rooms? Either way, it was his doing, not Bastian's.

"You don't need to apologise."

But Bastian didn't look up. For a long time, he stared into the fire, brow knotted, hands fisted.

Eventually, we shifted the conversation to lighter matters, and I must've fallen asleep on the armchair, because I woke to find him carrying me to bed. "Bastian?" I looked up groggily as he turned away from pulling up the blankets.

"I'll be through in a while." He slipped from the room, and a moment later, I heard the faint clink of the stopper being removed from a decanter.

A SHOUT WOKE ME. Bolt upright, I searched the room, eyes wide in the dim fae light that drifted through. No one here. Not even Bastian.

A sound came through the door. Movement. A muttered word too quiet for me to decipher.

Chest tight, throat tighter, I slipped from bed and grabbed the poker from the small fireplace in his room. One of the bobbing fae lights followed as I crept out.

In the sitting room, I found no intruder, just Bastian sprawled on the settee, eyes shut, shadows seething around his hands.

He must've cried out in his sleep. Shoulders sinking, I dropped the poker.

Deep lines between his eyebrows, he shook his head. "Stop. We can't." The head-shaking grew more violent, and one leg kicked straight. "No. They're only civilians." His chest heaved now, punctuated by whimpering, as he raised his hands like he was protecting himself.

His fear thickened the air, clutching my heart. What did he see? What nightmare was he trapped in? "Bastian?" Careful to avoid his thrashing, I knelt at his side. "Bastian? You're dreaming, it's just—"

A tendril of shadow shot at my outstretched hand. Its chill touch made me gasp, but when it flicked across my skin, a soft momentary touch like a snake's tongue tasting the air, it eased. Winding around my wrist, it tugged me closer.

"Bastian, wake up." I let the shadow press my palm to his cheek. Burning skin, slick with sweat.

With a tearing gasp, he jerked, and his eyes shot open. Chest heaving, he stared up at me. "What are you...?" His eyes flicked around, and I knew the moment he realised this was real and whatever he'd just seen wasn't, because he gave the deepest sigh I'd ever heard.

I stroked his cheek, finding more moisture pooled around

his eyes. Not just sweat. "It's all right," I murmured. "You're safe. It was just a dream."

He shook me off and dashed at his eyes. "I wasn't the one in danger." He turned from me, pulling away into the back of the settee. "Go back to bed, Kat." A tremor caught his voice and his breaths were still ragged. "I'm fine. It's no less than I deserve."

I scoffed. "Deserve? I didn't think you believed in that word."

No reply.

When I stroked his shoulder, I found him shaking. "Bloody hells, Bastian." I eased onto the settee and lay behind him.

"What are you doing? I told you, I don't—"

"Deserve any comfort?"

"I don't. I've done bad things, Katherine." His voice no longer shook, but there was a tension in it that cut me. "The kind of bad you don't come back from. And I let down Lara. We still don't know who killed her."

The brandy left in my stomach curdled. I couldn't tell him the mystery was solved. If Cavendish ever found out...

Bastian curled away. "These nightmares are the least I deserve."

"Fuck deserve." I couldn't comfort him by telling him the truth, but I could hold him.

I pressed against his back and wrapped my arm around him.

He tensed, no doubt about to push me off, but... he just held there as if unsure whether to resist or surrender.

Under my palm, his chest thrummed in a wild beat. "Your heart's racing." I buried my face in his hair, breathing in cedar and bergamot, and it gave me the strength to argue. "We don't have to talk about this after tonight. But right now, you need someone here for you. You saved me before; let me save you tonight."

He held still and I could practically hear him trying to decide. Under my hand, his heart calmed, and around us, his shadows eased to gentle ripples. Yet, his body remained tight.

"Please." I said it against the nape of his neck.

A shiver chased through him, followed by the tension in his muscles melting. He sank into me and let me curl around him.

"I have you, Bastian. The dreams are gone now, and I'll guard you against them until daybreak."

He pulled my arm tighter, pressing my hand into his chest. In the dim light, his shadows slithered across the settee and drew a blanket over us.

Gradually, his breathing slowed and the frantic beat of his heart became something steady and strong.

He slept, but I couldn't.

I couldn't poison him, either. Not after this.

Whatever he might've done for his queen and country, it was as dim and distant as the memories that haunted him.

Much closer and far brighter was the feeling in my chest. It wanted this man when he was vulnerable, brutal, or kind. And even if it couldn't have him, it wanted him safe.

He was no monster. Whatever he said, he was no villain. Not in my tale.

I couldn't keep working for Cavendish, not just for my own sake, but for his.

65

The next day we didn't speak of it, but his nightmare lingered in the air and in a mutual softness between us. We went on like it for a couple of days until I realised I was looking after him almost as much as he was looking after me.

And that meant it was time to go outside. I wasn't fine but well enough to face the world and be part of it once more. Hells, I was even well enough to register pay day was coming up, and that meant another letter to Morag and another step closer to paying off the bailiff.

"Are you sure?" Standing in the doorway to his bedroom, Bastian kept his expression so flat, I couldn't tell if he was relieved or sad at the suggestion I return to my suite.

"No?" I raised one shoulder and adjusted the neckline of my dress. It felt odd to be wearing my own clothes rather than one of his shirts. "But I don't think I ever will be entirely."

A crease flickered between his eyebrows, a softness in his eyes. It said, *You don't have to.*

A KISS OF IRON

But I did.

The rest of the world wasn't going to disappear, no matter how much I wished it. And the longer I stayed out of it, the harder it would be to return.

I didn't think he'd force me to stay, but he might tempt me.

Shoulders back, I drew myself up to my full height. "I'm sure enough."

He dipped his head, one side of his mouth rising. "Then that's good enough for me. But if you need to escape again—"

"This is 'the safest place in the building.' I know."

No surprise, he insisted on escorting me back, and when we arrived, he also insisted on going in first to check my suite.

I trailed after him. My rooms were as messy as I'd left them. "Good to see my maid hasn't suddenly developed a work ethic in my absence." I flashed Bastian a grin. "Not sure my nerves could take such a radical change in the world."

Though...

"Huh." I couldn't help but smile as we entered my bedroom, because not only was my rose bush not dead, but it was covered in flowers. Despite the fact we were months past the season, here I stood in *October* stroking a velvety petal. "I take it back. I hadn't realised she was so green-fingered."

Bastian leant on the bedpost, watching me with a private smile.

I looked down at the rose, wondering if he'd replaced it with a fae one, perhaps to get rid of Webster's gift. But, no, it still had the scar at the base where it had been grafted onto the rootstock, and the tag with Webster's handwriting poked from the soil.

"What?"

471

"It wasn't your maid. I asked Ella to come and water it for you."

"Ah. That makes a lot more sense." As did the fact he'd been thoughtful enough to ask. My heart tripped over a beat.

Fuck.

I was lost. Utterly. Willingly.

Somehow, I managed to swallow and followed it up with a casual shrug. "Does this mean you're satisfied there are no murderers or monsters hiding under my bed?"

"All clear," he sighed. "Which means I have no excuse to march you back to my rooms."

Every alarm bell in me went off at once.

Because I wanted.

Good gods, I wanted.

Smoothing the front of my gown, I pushed those thoughts and troublesome feelings down.

"Bastian, I owe you—"

"Nothing."

"No, I need to say—"

"Please don't." He pushed off from the bedpost and closed the distance between us. "Don't." He cupped my cheek and pressed his thumb to my lips, like he was afraid I'd try to speak. "I owe far more than I'm owed, and I have no problem paying off my moral debts in your direction." He slid his hand back, pushing the hair from my face.

"Thank you."

He sighed, eyes shutting. "And yet you still did."

"Of course."

He opened his eyes, a weight in them like there was more to his words than I understood. "I don't deserve your thanks, Kat."

I lifted my chin. "Fuck deserve."

472

He huffed a laugh and placed his hands on my shoulders. "Good night, troublesome woman." He bent closer, and I held my breath.

But his lips only pressed to my forehead before he turned away.

It had been a week of comforting touches and gentleness, and I'd assumed that was to give me space to recover. Part of me had thought of his rooms as a border not only to the outside world, but between my recovery and the way our relationship had been before.

Yet here we were, beyond that boundary, and he hadn't taken the chance to kiss me.

It was the vomiting. Or pissing myself.

He'd been kind, yes, but after what he'd seen, he didn't think of me as he once had.

And all the while, the shape of him, the scent of him, the sound of his voice—everything about him had imprinted on me. I carried the mark on my heart and my body. Perhaps even my soul.

"Kat," his voice came from the door, and I spun, "if you need me, you know where I am. You're always welcome back. And here..." He fished in his pocket and threw something at me. "In case you struggle to sleep."

I only caught a flash of gold before my hand closed on it. Smooth and round, attached to a chain. His orrery. "Bastian, I can't—"

But when I looked up, he'd gone.

66

No sooner had Bastian gone than Seren appeared with a summons to Cavendish's office. I raised my eyebrows at the clock—nearly eight o'clock in the evening. This would be our latest meeting.

Still, I trod the familiar route to his office and braced myself before entering.

His unblinking stare hit me at once. "Oh, so you do still work for me, then?" Lips thin and pale, he stood and stalked around the desk.

"Of course, ser." For now, at least. I was a couple of days off my third pay day, which would put us at more than half the debt cleared. I would see out the next two months by feeding him useless information, get my wages, finish paying off the bailiff, then resign. It would mean no roof repairs, but at least I wouldn't have to continue working against Bastian. My pulse sped at the idea of escape and how Cavendish might react.

"I've been unable to find you, so that must mean one

thing." His eyes narrowed. "You're meant to seduce him, not *live* with him."

"I was ill." That was Bastian's cover story. Not entirely a lie, just a sickness of the mind rather than of the body.

"Yet I assume you've heard the news of Her Majesty's forthcoming engagement?"

"She chose Lord Mallory."

His cheek twitched. "She did. And the wedding gives us the perfect opportunity to poison Marwood. As his liaison, you've been chosen to pour the mead."

Us? I could've laughed.

I clasped my hands so tight, the knuckles ached. "Perhaps it's Dawn you should be focusing on, ser. I haven't seen Bastian hurt anyone, but it was a woman from Dawn who sabotaged me in the race, *and* she took my necklace. If she could plot all that, what else might they be doing behind the scenes? I'm sure whoever you have spying on them knows more."

He gave a deep sigh, eyes rolling. "Your little accident. You're still going on about that?" He shook his head as he approached, eyes spearing me in place. "Don't you understand? If you'd won that race, you wouldn't be working for me anymore." He picked up a lock of my hair and examined it, mouth curling slowly like smoke from a forest fire. "And you are useful to me. My favourite piece on the board."

I wasn't just any piece on his board—I was a pawn. Useful and entertaining, but ultimately expendable.

But he'd given this pawn a choice. I lifted my chin.

"I won't poison him."

His mouth spread into a grin. "Oh, she's decided." He laughed, the sound chilling my veins. "You've caught feelings for the Bastard."

475

I shook my head.

Still laughing, his hand closed around my throat. I froze, the world suddenly sharp and bright like ice. My feet dragged on the rug as he backed me into the wall.

"Oh dear, Katherine." He sighed and pressed against me, pushing his thigh between mine.

I couldn't move, could barely breathe. My heart stuttered in my chest, like a flame about to gutter out.

"Is this all it takes to make you believe a man is good? How trite." Head tilted back, he peered down his nose at me as he rubbed his leg over my apex.

I'm not here. This isn't happening to me. This isn't real.

But a dark, cold grave and Dia's pale bones waited when I tried to drift away.

"I didn't realise women were as led by their pussies as men are by their cocks."

That wasn't what had helped me decide. It was nothing to do with sex.

Was it? My husband's bad treatment hadn't left me so desperate that I'd fallen for the first man to show me a little kindness.

"Maybe if I fuck you a few times, you'll do anything *I* say." Cavendish watched me as though searching for a response.

I could do nothing but take shallow breaths and cling to the wall and my sanity as dark branches spread overhead.

No. The wall is real. This room. This vile man's thigh between mine. Not that... Not there.

At last, he eased his leg away and slid his hand up my throat, forcing my chin up. "You heard what he did to his father, didn't you?"

And I didn't believe it.

He paused like he wanted an answer. Summoning every scrap of strength, I nodded.

"And yet you still decline my offer." His mouth tensed, but he released my throat.

I remained pinned against the wall, gasping.

"Very well. You ask him how his father died and see what he says. After all, he's a fae—he cannot lie. When you have the truth, then give me your answer."

He produced a familiar vial from his sleeve and shook it. Its purple glow turned his face a ghastly shade that reminded me of bruises and bodies.

With a nod towards the door, he dismissed me.

I jerked my way over and yanked it open.

"And Katherine?"

I stopped, but couldn't bring myself to look at him.

"Choose wisely."

67

Ella was in my rooms when I returned. Seren had let her in before leaving, and truth be told, I was glad I didn't have to be alone. She squeezed me tight and gave me cake and let me ask about inconsequential things like the latest gossip at court. Eventually, she did leave, but I had Bastian's orrery, and the starry lights from that lulled me into sleep.

The next day the queen remarked upon my "illness" and pallor, but otherwise it felt like another day as a lady-in-waiting. After dinner, I found a message on my mantlepiece, even though the door to my suite was locked.

Sorry for my absence today. Meetings upon meetings. Deep joy.

I'll find you tomorrow. Could use your help. Would be good to see you.

Yours, B

He wanted to see me. Was that out of concern, for this help he mentioned, or just for the sake of seeing me?

I lay in bed reading the note again and again by the orrery's dim light. By the time I fell asleep, I still didn't know what to make of it.

The next morning, I'd dressed and was brushing my hair when a knock sounded at the door. Ella was early today. "Come in," I called from my bedroom.

The face that appeared behind me in the mirror wasn't Ella's. "Bastian." I spun, almost dropping the brush.

He stood in the doorway, leaning against the frame, one corner of his mouth rising as he took me in. "You look well."

I glanced back at the mirror. The purplish shadows that had haunted my eyes since my encounter with Uncle Rufus had mostly faded, though the queen was right—I still looked a little pale.

"So do you."

Did his back straighten a fraction?

I cocked my head at him. "Were your meetings incredibly exciting?"

"Oh yes, thrilling." He crossed the threshold into my room. "But I didn't come here to talk about treaties and your queen's engagement."

"You need a favour from me."

"I'd like your help, but..." He stopped at arm's length, hands clasped behind his back. "No obligation. If you don't want to, it's fine. I don't—"

"Bastian, I know what no obligation means." I grinned at his stumbling. What had him tiptoeing around the request? "Spit it out."

"I'm going to an event tonight to gather information, and it would help if you came with me. But..." He looked away, tilting his head side to side. "It isn't the usual kind of event."

"This isn't spitting it out. What are you dancing around?"

The skin around his eyes tensed. "It's a fae-hosted party. A... private function."

"Good gods, would you just—"

"Sex. It's a masked party where people go to have sex."

Like Ella had mentioned. "Oh." My cheeks heated.

"Not that we'd have to. Most people drink and drape themselves over each other, especially since this one involves humans. Your kind are still getting the hang of being more open about their bodies. The masks have made some loosen up, but not all."

"And you want me to go with you."

"I want to get information from someone, and they'll be more relaxed if I seem... preoccupied. And..." He swallowed. "I don't really want anyone else all over me."

I laughed, part at him, part at myself.

His eyebrows clashed together. "Like I said, you don't have to—"

"Yes."

His mouth fell open. "Yes, you'll—?"

"I'll go with you to this party tonight." I rubbed my chest. A tension I didn't know I'd been carrying had dissipated with that laugh.

"I was expecting you to decline."

"The Kat you first met would've. But..." I looked away, cheeks growing even warmer. "To be honest, it's a relief. After the way we said goodbye, I thought..."

Good gods, it felt like a ridiculous thing to say after all he'd done for me over the past week. Did I have no gratitude that he'd put his life on hold?

He hooked a finger under my chin and raised it until I met his gaze. "You thought... what?"

"That you weren't interested in me like that anymore. And... I suppose this is just work. You just want my help, right? I wouldn't blame you if—"

"Kat?"

I clamped my mouth shut.

"When did you start spouting such utter nonsense?" He shook his head before coming closer, his breaths fanning my lips. "After what you went through, I wanted to wait until you were ready. Does your temporary transformation into a blathering, adorable idiot mean you're ready to be my ember or has a changeling taken your place?"

His words did odd things to my insides, "adorable" and "ember" in particular, though for vastly different reasons. I nodded.

"Which one?"

"First one."

For a beat, his mouth curved, then it was on mine. Sweet, gentle, tender, it began, like he was reacquainting himself with the shape of me. His hands smoothed down my arms and around my back, pulling me close.

Maybe I'd been wrong before about safety only being an illusion, because this, this space in his arms, it *felt* safe.

I tiptoed up to him, hands on his chest for balance, and when I opened my mouth to his questing, he continued his mapping of me. His tongue traced the roof of my mouth, wringing a whimper from my throat. One hand cupped the back of my head, the other anchored my waist.

Everywhere he touched, tendrils of sensation awoke in me, and like ivy tearing through the mortar between bricks, he broke apart the ice that had lingered in my bones.

I was free.

Perhaps my body gave me away, perhaps in a soft moan, because that was when our kiss grew heated. My tongue upon his, our breaths coming faster. Hands on my backside, he lifted me, and I looped my legs around him, greedy for more touch, for more reminders of how he felt.

A moment later, my back bumped into something hard, and he pulled an inch from my lips.

I had to blink a few times before I registered: he had me against the bedpost. With a soft laugh, I threaded my fingers through his hair and ran my thumb along the edge of his ear. His groan rumbled into my chest as his cock twitched.

"So, maybe a little bit interested?" My voice came out breathy.

Pupils wide, he watched me and leant into my touch. "If I didn't have a meeting to hurry to, I'd gladly spend the next few hours showing you how very"—he pressed me into the bedpost, cock growing harder against my pussy—"very"—another grind that shot pleasure through me—"interested I am in every part of you." He squeezed my arse and nipped my lower lip. "But we'll have to settle for this... at least until later."

He said "settle" but somehow his mouth was back on mine, lighting me up as he palmed my breast and ground against me.

Fuck, I didn't want him to stop. "Do you really have to go to a meeting?" I gasped the words around kisses that grew more frantic by the moment.

"Don't say the M-word to me right now." His voice carried a low, rumbling edge, and he pinched my nipple like that was a punishment.

I yelped as pleasure pooled between my legs. "Meeting."

He shook his head. "Katherine, I thought you were obedient." He pinched again, harder, wringing another cry from my throat. "Such a bad girl today."

I bit my lip, squeezing my thighs around him. He hadn't pushed my hands away, so I stroked up to the point of his ear, greedily eating up the sight of him shuddering. "Meeting."

Only the thinnest line of silver remained around his pupils as, with a low growl, he crushed me into the bedpost and bit my neck.

I let my head loll back, drunk on the fact I'd won a reaction from him and the power it represented. Being touched by him was sublime, but touching him soared into something truly divine.

In the distance, a clock chimed.

"Fuck." Breaths heaving, he pulled back. "I really do need to go." He glanced down and clenched his jaw. "How the hells am I supposed to walk into a meeting like this?"

When he lowered me to the floor, I couldn't help guffawing at the obvious bulge in his trousers.

He glared at me, nostrils flaring, but a twitch at the corner of his mouth gave him away. "Damn you, Katherine. You really are the wickedest woman." Eyes closed, he took in several long breaths, then backed away. "I'll have an outfit sent to you for later." He reached the door, and it was only once he was gripping the frame that he opened his eyes. "Unless you have something suitable? And by that, I mean entirely *un*suitable." He gave me a rakish grin, gaze skimming down the high-necked gown I'd chosen for brunch with the queen. His knuckles whitened.

My pulse hummed in every part of me, as much at the look he gave me as at the way he'd just ground me into the bedpost. "I have just the thing."

There was a flicker of surprise on his face before he bit his lip and backed out of the room. "Then I will very much look forward to seeing you later. Be ready at nine."

With another deep breath, he was gone.

I dropped onto my bed. How the hells was I supposed to focus on *anything* for the rest of the day?

68

I was sitting on the settee watching the door when the knock came. Three fast raps that echoed my pounding pulse. I drew a shaking breath, checked the pins holding my hair up, and smoothed the front of my outfit.

"Outfit" was a very loose term.

I wore one of Blaze's lingerie confections, a skin-tight black lace bodysuit cut high over the hips that left my legs bare. Most scandalous of all was the bust—a wide satin sash tied in a bow was the only thing covering my breasts. One tug on the end, the bow would untie, and I'd be exposed.

But Bastian would have to wait until the party to see it. I couldn't walk through the palace in a scrap of lace, so I wore a black robe. Thick ruffles around the hem made it look like a gown rather than a glorified piece of lingerie.

With a last check my breasts were contained by the bow and the robe, I called, "Come in."

When the door opened, my breath caught. In head-to-toe black, Bastian stood there. Perhaps not so different from his

485

usual clothes at first glance. However, the trousers were tighter, showing off his muscular thighs, and as he entered, light from the corridor ghosted through his shirt where the fabric was ever so slightly see-through. It hinted at light and shade, sketching out the shape of his body beneath.

He stilled when his gaze landed on mine. It trailed across me, slow as poured honey, pausing at my cleavage, the nip of my waist, the point where one thigh crossed over the other. It ended on my bare feet. With all my agitated pacing, I'd kicked off the dainty lace slippers that completed the ensemble, and they lay in the middle of the room.

The knot of his throat rose and fell slowly as he stalked closer. "I suddenly no longer want to go to this party."

"Oh?" I cocked my head as I took his offered hand and rose. "What would you rather do?" As if I didn't know.

Again, his gaze travelled my full length, this time snagging on the tie of my robe. "For starters, I'm fascinated by what I'll find under this." He ran the tie between finger and thumb.

"Just you wait." I smiled sweetly up at him, fluttering my lashes.

"And the worst thing is, I have to." Clenching his jaw, he took a step back. "Sometimes, I really hate my job. I assume you're planning to wear these?" He scooped up the lace shoes, a faint smile easing into place as he looked at them.

"Well, I wasn't going to walk the halls barefoot. What're you smirking at?"

"They're so small." He shook his head and knelt at my feet before offering one shoe with a flourish. "*Madame*."

Chuckling, I stepped into that one, then the other, enjoying the feel of his deft fingers easing the tight slippers over my heels. Of course, being Bastian, he couldn't resist sliding his hand up the back of my leg, eyebrow rising when he reached my bare thigh. "Kat, are you wearing *anything*?"

I swatted him off. "You'll have to wait and see," I said with a shrug, as though my heart wasn't drumming a wild beat on the inside of my ribs.

"I'm glad you wore black, because I got you this." He produced a mask from his pocket—black lace even finer than my bodice. He tied it in place, careful not to knot my hair or ruin the coiled style I'd pinned it into, before tying his own plain black mask in place.

Its darkness only emphasised the glow of his eyes, and no one at court had hair quite the same colour as mine. But I'd read enough adventure stories to understand—masks didn't always hide identities, they merely let us divorce ourselves from them. Albeit temporarily.

Tonight I was not myself, and the rules Lady Katherine Ferrers tried to live by didn't apply.

Arm-in-arm, we set off. We made for the older part of the palace, where the hallways wound like warrens. He explained everyone referred to each other as "Stranger" at these events, even if they knew their identities.

My pulse dipped as we passed the corridor Uncle Rufus had dragged me down.

Bastian's hand closed over mine. "Are you all right?"

I nodded, and we continued on.

After a few more corners, he tapped a complex pattern on a set of double doors before turning to me. "Remember, if you change your mind at any time—"

"Just say." I squeezed his arm. "I know."

When the door opened, a masked servant ushered us into an antechamber and held out her hand for my robe. The moment of truth. I swallowed, fingers closing around the tie.

And stayed there.

I wanted to untie it, but it was as though my hand hadn't received the message about the old rules not applying.

Bastian's arm slid around my shoulders. "I think she'll wait until we get inside. It's a bit chilly in here." He gave the servant a disarming smile.

She bowed her head. "Of course, ser. Your host has stipulated one edict for his guests." She gestured to a side table laden with sherry glasses. Despite his apparent ease, I felt Bastian stiffen. "Everyone is to drink one before they enter."

"I see." The smile stayed on Bastian's lips as he led me to the table. Each glass was full to the brim with a clear liquid that swirled with an iridescent shimmer like mother-of-pearl. "*Arianmêl*," he murmured, his tone suggesting he spoke between gritted teeth.

"Alcohol?"

"No. This doesn't cloud your judgement in the same way as alcohol, but it does lower the inhibitions."

"Perfect for the occasion, then." I raised an eyebrow at him.

"For the party, yes, but not for our purposes. It makes fae more forthcoming with the truth."

"Surely that's ideal for gathering information?"

"If I didn't take it, perhaps. And there's another interesting side-effect." He stroked my shoulder through the semi-sheer silk of my robe. "It renders humans unable to lie."

My stomach dropped. "Oh."

No lies. It was an ability I'd taken for granted.

But I still had silence.

"Do we turn back?"

"Turn back?" I snorted and tossed my head the way I imagined my sister might when faced with a challenge. "Never." I handed him a glass and scooped one up for myself. "Bottoms up."

Eyebrows raised, Bastian chuckled. "Is that what humans say? Interesting."

We clinked glasses and drank.

It didn't burn on the way down. No, this was far more soothing, lulling almost. Warm, like a lover's touch. Sweet like honey. It slipped down my throat and coated my tongue, its flavour like the first sunny day of the year.

My head spun as I looked up and found Bastian watching me, his cheeks flushed. A low hum of pleasure spread from him into me. The tension disappeared from his muscles as his hand splayed over my lower back, and he pulled my hips against his. "You've gone that colour I love so much." He grazed his mouth over my cheeks as though he could feel the colour or taste it. His hands trailed to my waist and gripped the tie of my robe. "Are you ready?" he murmured against my ear. The breath of his words tickled my skin, making me shiver.

I nodded. No hesitation.

I wanted him to see me. I wanted him to consume me. And I didn't care how many people watched.

A wicked smile claimed his mouth as he tugged the bow undone. With a sweep of his fingers, he pushed the robe off my shoulders and let it pool on the floor.

Those perfect, scarred lips parted. His gaze roved over me, lingering on the bow over my chest and the sheer lace.

Biting his lip, he rubbed the bow between finger and thumb. "Like a gift. Except, I've never known a gift to destroy me as much as I think you're going to." He laughed softly as he bent his face to my neck and angled my head to give himself better access. Teeth, mouth, tongue, he kissed the nook between neck and shoulder as though he would devour me.

I arched into it, clinging to his shoulders like they might help me survive the onslaught of sensation. It streaked through me until I trembled.

"I've never seen anything so perfect." His hands skimmed over my back and my arse, up to my hair, like he couldn't decide where he wanted to touch me more. He whispered in my ear, "I love..." His breath caught, and he pulled away as though realising where we were. "The way you look. I love it."

His throat bobbed, and he gave me a long look, eyes hooded. "I would say you should wear fewer clothes more often, but I'm not sure I'd survive if you did." Scoffing, he shook his head. "Listen to me babbling, and we're not even in there yet."

When he nodded, the servant opened the next set of doors, and, hands on my shoulders, chest against my back, Bastian steered me inside.

69

Giggles and groans formed a chorus with the hum of quiet conversation. Clinking glasses chimed, and somewhere beneath all that, a lone cello played, low and sensuous.

At first glance, it seemed like a normal party. People lounged on settees and armchairs, drinking. Four more sat at a card table, bets piled high. One couple stood against a wall, deep in conversation.

Except...

On the settees and armchairs, women sat draped on the laps of partners, some wearing scant lingerie like I did, others wearing nothing but their masks. Two kissed as the men beneath them held their thighs and slid their fingers under their lacy garments.

A blond woman lay across a dark-haired woman's lap, backside bare as she received a spanking. My mouth might've dropped open as the spanker then bent and kissed her "victim," sliding her hand between her thighs.

At the card table, one man was shirtless and the other naked. One of their opponents smiled at the clothes piled up amongst her winnings. The other woman sat back, panting as the table wobbled suspiciously.

As for the couple against the wall... They were less deep in conversation and more—well, it looked like his cock was deep in *her*.

My heart played staccato percussion to the cello's deep, sweeping melody. It felt like the floor itself throbbed as we passed from that room into another. Ahead, an empty wing-back chair beckoned, and around us, more guests kissed and touched and fucked.

Definitely not a normal party.

Bastian's thumbs worked the muscles in my shoulders as he bent to my ear. "While we're here, where can I touch you?"

"Everywhere."

"Hmm." I wasn't sure if it was thoughtful or pleased, but the sound hummed into my back as we stopped before the chair. "You are good, Katherine." He circled to my front, lifted my chin, and gave me a deep but all-too-brief kiss.

I half-staggered after him when he pulled away, which made him chuckle softly and catch my shoulders. "And impatient."

He sat and patted his lap.

I obeyed.

For once, it wasn't out of fear of punishment if I didn't, but because I *wanted* to loop my arms around his neck and get as close as possible.

He pulled my thighs over his, so I sat sideways, and traced his fingers over the bone of my ankle. "Keep your ears open," he murmured as he kissed just below my ear. "You never know what secrets people might spill in a place like this."

Listening was easier said than done when my pulse rushed in my ears. Beyond that, a very quiet and distant part of me cried danger. But it was easy to ignore her, with *arianmêl* still sweet on my tongue and Bastian's hand snaking up my calf.

This might be forbidden and scandalous and break a million rules.

But they were other people's rules.

For the first time in my life, I didn't care what anyone else thought, only what *I* thought.

I wanted Bastian.

Not for my job. Not for information. Just for myself.

I thought he was incredible and intriguing and a hundred other things that meant I couldn't tear my eyes away from him.

Maybe it *was* obsession.

But I didn't fucking care.

I pressed against him, circling my arse over his cock. He answered with a shaky exhale and one hand tightening around my waist.

Behind me, a conversation drifted through the cello music. "... heard she came to these."

"Only strangers come to these parties, remember? But I heard the one who killed her wasn't a stranger."

The next words were muffled. "... covered up, because he's high-ranking."

"Well, you're not covered up." A giggle. "Why are we talking about this when I'm about to put my mouth around your dick?"

"An excellent question."

There were no more words, just another giggle followed by a groan of pleasure.

Bastian's spiralling fingertips had reached my thigh, all controlled movement, but his breaths came from between parted lips.

I couldn't tear my gaze from the sight, not when I wanted those lips kissing every part of me. "Anything useful?"

"Hmm." He shook his head and nuzzled against my neck. "It's a little hard to concentrate."

I didn't bother to bite back my grin—that had to be the *arianmêl* at work. "Is something the matter?" I circled in his lap and traced my fingernails over his scalp, teasing the skin right behind his ears.

"You're playing the part well, love." He spoke against my skin, squeezing my thigh. "A little too well."

"And yet you're holding back." I grazed the edge of his ear and took a wicked sense of victory at the sound of his breath catching.

"Oh, really?" He pulled back and arched an eyebrow at me, a flash of challenge in his eyes.

I shrugged, all nonchalance even though my heart rate kicked up at his look. "You'd normally be inside my underwear by now."

The grin he returned was wicked as his grip shifted. His thumb dipped between my thighs, not quite reaching my apex. "You have me all figured out, don't you?"

I rolled my hips, tilting into his hardness. "I think I do."

He gritted his teeth, nostrils flaring as he squeezed my thigh. "I'll give you a chance before I let go of my grip on the reins. I'm only giving it to you because of where we are and the fact of your inexperience." His nose grazed mine, and he gripped the back of my head, forcing my gaze on his. "Do you *really* want to play this game, Katherine?"

"Yes."

As simple as that one syllable.

It lit up his eyes, his smile, more hellfire than sunshine. "First of all..." He slid his hand up my thigh and drew the length of his thumb along my centre. My breath hitched, caught up in the pleasure of that friction. "I don't need to be inside your underwear to make you come, *Wicked Lady*."

"And second?"

The flash of his canines was a warning, but I was too slow.

Shadows rolled off his shoulders and seized my wrists. "Second, I don't recall giving you permission to touch me." They pulled my hands behind my back, forcing my body to arch. The position pressed me harder against his cock and thrust my breasts forward. "That's better. But any more cheek from you, and I'll have them take care of that lying little mouth of yours, too. Understood?"

I wasn't just his ember, because good gods, I *burned*. Even in this slip of lace, I was too hot, my skin tingling in time with my speeding pulse.

"Yes, Bastian," I whispered, enjoying the way he smiled as I said his name.

"Good."

The word pleased me almost as much as the friction of his fingers rubbing through my lace underwear.

"And third..." He took advantage of my arched back to lower his lips to my breast and, through the satin bow, grazed one canine over the peak.

The hard point sent pleasure streaking through my body, lighting up every fibre, brightest between my thighs. My leg kicked out, as involuntary as my nipple pebbling. His laugh was low and as dark as the shadows snaking around my ankles and clasping them in place.

"As I was *trying* to say, *third*, I prefer your hair down."

Something—it had to be more shadows—whispered against my scalp. A moment later, a dozen hairpins fell to the floor, and my hair cascaded over my back. "Perfect." His hum of approval vibrated into my breasts as he kissed them.

I panted out a laugh. "You could've just asked."

He gave me a sidelong look, still lavishing attention on my cleavage. "Where would be the fun in that?"

I watched him work, the little frown of focus drawing fascinating lines between his eyebrows.

Despite his touch stoking fire in me, a dark corner of my mind wondered who else had seen that look on his face. *Arianmêl* might mean I didn't care about other people's thoughts, but I couldn't entirely escape my own.

"Did you do this with Lara?"

His stroke over my underwear slowed as he looked up with a faint smirk. "Why? Are you jealous?" His eyes widened. "Oh, you are... of a dead woman, no less."

My cheeks burned. It was a silly question and to envy a dead woman, ridiculous.

Stroking my cheek, he bent close to my ear. "I didn't. Because I didn't want to use a party like this as an excuse to do this." His finger slid beneath the lace bodice and inside me.

I tried to keep still, but I couldn't hold back my whimper.

"As an excuse to be seen with her so publicly. As an excuse to show her off." He nodded across the room, where a couple watched us from a dark corner. "I only want that with you, my flame. I so love to be scorched by you."

He *did* still find me attractive—lusted after me, even. The knowledge bloomed in my chest, thriving and bright, like weeds flowering in the poorest soil.

I turned my head and caught his mouth in a searing kiss. It said what I couldn't. How pleased I was at his admission.

Gratitude for all he'd shown me. A need that I couldn't confess.

He pulled away enough to murmur, "I'd planned to fuck you with my shadows tonight, but I couldn't resist feeling you." He made a low sound as he plunged into me. "So wet, so hot, so tight."

My body hummed on the verge of crescendo. It made my breaths heave, but I'd never known him so talkative, and my curiosity burned almost as much as my flesh.

"Why don't you ever come?" Even now, I could feel his desire digging into my backside as he stopped me doing anything about it.

"What makes you think I don't?"

"You walk away still raging hard."

"'Raging.'" He scoffed and slipped another finger inside me. "I'll show you raging one day." His voice took on a gravelly quality that vibrated into me. "Do you have any idea how many times I had to make myself come after the library, just in order to think straight?"

An answer at last. It wasn't that he didn't *want*. It had to be his need for control, as if his climax would hand some of that over to me.

My laugh was breathless and wild. "Fuck, I love *arianmêl*."

He chuckled before sucking the fluttering pulse point in my throat. "So do I. Even if you are taking advantage of me."

I was about to reply when a shadow fell over us.

70

Despite the mask, I knew the chestnut brown hair that glinted in sunshine when there was none. Caelus.

Bastian pulled me tight against his chest and lifted his chin in question.

Caelus smiled slowly. "What an interesting guest you've brought, Stranger. Do you care to share?"

Bastian's fingers stilled, and I could feel the tension in his chest as he bent to my ear. "Do you want him, too?"

The question made me blink. Maybe I shouldn't have been surprised by it—Bastian liked to ask what I wanted. Still, with someone from Dawn?

"Enmity doesn't stand in these parties." His fingers crooked inside me, dragging a gasp down my throat as he pressed on a sensitive spot. "And I wouldn't let it come between you and something you wanted."

Caelus's sky-blue eyes seared into me with raw, undisguised lust. His hands clenched and unclenched like he needed to use them for *something*. With his fae bone structure and lithe muscles, he was undeniably attractive, and yet...

I shook my head.

"A pity." But he nodded and retreated to a settee opposite, where he was soon joined by a man and woman.

I trembled as Bastian teased the point inside me and my clit at the same time. "Is he the one you wanted to get information from?" The words did not come out quite that coherently.

His brow furrowed. "Information?"

"The reason we came here."

"Fuck information. I only want you."

But I kept glancing at Caelus, finding him watching me as the man beside him lowered his face into his lap. The sight of his hunger only made my body tighter.

It said I was desirable. Powerful.

Bastian followed my gaze. "I love the way they watch, and yet only I get to touch." He grazed his teeth over my throat and sucked on my pulse, drawing me tighter still. "Do you want me to make you come while he watches, my sweet flame?"

"Yes." It came from me in a strangled gasp. "I want him to see I'm yours."

Not only was I powerful, but Bastian was my choice. *Mine.* Not one foisted on me by an arranged marriage or one I made purely for money—not anymore.

He made a low sound, deep in his chest. "Say that again."

I lifted my head and met his gaze. "I want him to see I'm yours."

He smiled slowly, eyes lowering to my mouth. "Whose?"

"Yours, Bastian." I couldn't keep in my cry as his pace sped, making stars flicker on the edge of my vision. "I'm fucking yours."

"Then let him watch you burn for me." His kiss was devastating, deep and slow, hitting every point that he'd mapped before and knew wrung me out.

I came apart on his hand, and he consumed my cries as my body became pure flame, white-hot, blinding.

There was no room. No party. No Caelus. Just my pulse and his touch.

At last, I sank in his lap, eyelids fluttering as his shadows loosened their grip and soothed my skin.

"That's my sweet flame." He pressed kisses on my mouth and jaw, nuzzling into my neck.

Across the room, Caelus stared at me, lips parted, hand fisted in the hair of the man whose head bobbed in his lap.

Perhaps he hadn't expected me to go through with it.

But tonight I wasn't Lady Katherine. I was a different creature entirely. Something free.

Something that lived.

For now.

Memento mori.

"Bastian," I murmured, cupping his cheek and making him meet my gaze. "Take me to your room and show me how it always should've been."

He stilled, the only movement his eyes searching mine.

"I mean it. I decided a long time ago."

His brow furrowed. "This is the *arianmêl* talking."

"No. That drink has only made me speak my mind more and fear less. It hasn't changed what I think, what I feel, what I *want*." With the pad of my thumb, I traced the scar running through his lip, down to his chin. "I want you, Bastian... I want *us*."

"For your bargain?"

I shook my head. "Not for that. Not for anything else. Just

because *I* want this, I want you, and I want it to be real. Do you?"

"You mean it." The words came out on a breath, almost a laugh. He gripped my cheeks. "Then yes, Kat. I want it to be real. Stars above, I don't think I've wanted anything in my life more than I want you."

Then there was no room for words.

It was a kiss of madness. A kiss that held nothing back. A kiss that etched itself upon my heart.

Around it, we stood and half-stumbled from this room before he picked me up and carried me through the next. Legs around his waist, I tugged at his hair, the buttons of his shirt, kissed his throat, nipped the throbbing pulse there. I rubbed his ears and consumed his moan, high on it and the fact he was letting me touch him.

The fact that tonight, I'd finally make him come apart as he had me.

We made it to the antechamber. There was no sign of the servant as we crashed into the wall, knocking the table and sending glasses shattering. The sweet fumes of *arianmêl* surrounded us, intoxicating as they invaded my nostrils.

He ground into me with a low groan, and I kept up my torment of his ears. His cock twitched against me, hard and ready.

"Now, Bastian," I whispered upon his skin, tearing at his shirt. "Now."

"A stronger man would say no." He kissed his way down my throat, my chest, then closed his fist on the loose end of the satin bow and looked up at me with something approaching pain. "But you have undone me, Katherine. You are my poison. And I'm not sure I want the antidote." He pulled, and the bow came loose.

The instant my breasts were exposed, he palmed one and closed his mouth on the other. Lost in the feel of that and his other hand slipping under my backside, I let my head drop back against the wall. He teased my sensitised flesh through the lace, making me arch to find more.

"Please."

"Fuck." He pulled the fine fabric aside and started on the buttons of his trousers. "You're going to destroy me, ember... flame... fucking forest fire. I'm ash for you."

Eyes shut, I savoured the anticipation as he sucked on my nipples and freed himself. This. At last. I'd feel—

"Unhand my wife."

71

My heart stopped.

That voice.

The world cracked as my past came crashing into it.

Bastian made a low, growling sound, my flesh still in his mouth. "Fuck off. We're busy."

"I can see you're busy *with my wife*."

"You've got the wrong woman. Her husband's dead."

I pushed Bastian away and covered myself. That was when he went still.

When I tore my eyes open, I found myself face-to-face with the man whose absence had made my life, if not happy, then bearable.

Ten years my senior, Robin Fanshawe looked every bit his age and then some tonight. The grey streaks at his temples had spread through his mousy brown hair. His nose had thinned, and he peered down it at me. Narrow lips pursed above a weak chin, just as I remembered, though deeper lines bracketed them now.

As he shook his head, the trembling of his jowls made it clear he'd eaten well these past few years. "Dead, Katherine? Is that what you told him?"

It was when he said my name that Bastian flinched.

"Kat?"

I couldn't answer. That drink meant I couldn't lie, and the truth...

The truth was worse than anything else.

Bastian's chin feathered down as though a nod could prompt me to answer.

"I never said..." My heart leapt to my throat, blocking any more words. It didn't race, it just boomed, loud and hard, shaking me.

His tanned skin paled several shades. He blinked at me, then slowly disentangled himself.

Without a word, he swept from the antechamber.

"I must admit, when your uncle wrote to me, I scarce believed—"

"Shut your fucking mouth, Robin."

His eyes bulged. In a decade of marriage, I'd never sworn at him—not out loud, anyway.

Witness the magic of *arianmêl* and the things it made me brave enough to say.

Yet, it hadn't made me say or do anything that wasn't true. I wanted Bastian. I was his.

I ran after him.

"Wait, Bastian, please."

His back continued down the hall, shoulders square.

"I'm sorry, I didn't mean to..." But something stilled my

tongue. I *had* meant to keep it from him: Cavendish had told me to. "I haven't seen him in years."

Fastening the bow over my chest, I drew level with him. He didn't look at me, just kept marching down the corridor, hands fisted at his sides.

"I changed my name back—it's like we're not even married anymore. It's only a technicality."

"A 'technicality'?" He stopped and turned wide eyes upon me at last. "Only a technicality? Kat, you have a fucking contract with that man."

"So?" I spread my hands. "It's only paper. It doesn't matter."

He advanced, looming over me. "It matters to me." His shout bounced off the stone walls, pushing me back. "It's a contract. A deal. These things are sacred."

"What the hells does that mean?"

"It means that all this time, I've been breaking a taboo without even knowing it. It's forbidden to keep spouses apart."

I scoffed. "Suddenly you care about the rules? And as for 'keeping us apart,' he's already done that for our entire marriage."

"This isn't funny. And it isn't just a rule. We never break a deal, a bargain, a contract. Whatever the fuck you want to call it—we do not break them. 'My blood is bound in bargains.' That is what we are."

His silver eyes blazed, boring into me like he could see all the bargains we'd made written upon my skin.

"So breaking arms and noses is fine... threatening to kill people is fine... but breaking a contract is an unforgivable sin?"

"How could a human understand?" Jaw rippling, he stared

at me for three heavy heartbeats before turning and storming off down the hall.

I had to run to keep up, rounding several corners, calling after him. "Bastian. Stop. Wait."

He did not.

We reached the doors to his suite and he threw them open. "Leave me alone, Katherine." He stomped inside.

"No." I charged in after him, catching one door before it slammed. The impact jolted up my arms, bruising the heels of my hands. "I've obeyed enough. My father, my uncle..." I almost said Cavendish but bit my tongue just in time. "Even you."

Back to me, he tore off his mask and threw it on the floor. His shoulders heaved with each heavy breath.

"Look at me."

He bowed his head.

"I said *look at me*."

When he finally turned, his whole expression was clenched, tight and hard. Blinking, he snapped his eyes to me.

I searched in those eyes for something of the man I knew. The one who'd seen I was more than just Lady Katherine. The one who'd looked after me in my darkest days. The one who'd made me feel—who'd made me *live*.

A stranger stared back.

I peeled off my mask and looked up at him, bare. "Bastian, please..."

He flinched, maybe because I used that word. In an instant, the weakness was gone, replaced by sharp, forged edges—the steel blade I'd seen when we'd first met.

I inched closer, clutching my chest. Something inside it tore, like thorns grew there. "You're making it sound like I've done something wrong by being with you, but it feels like this is the first right thing I've done in my life."

I swore the tiniest chink opened in his steel mask.

Toe-to-toe with him, I stopped. "Maybe I should've told you, but I refuse to regret the rest of it." Gritting my teeth against the waver in my voice, I drew myself to my full height. "I refuse to say any of it was wrong. You're the one who told me I should *live* my life—that I should have my cake and eat it."

His shoulders eased as he exhaled through his nose.

Giving in. I'd got through to him. I sighed, heart easing, thorns withdrawing.

"Oh, well, good for you." He smiled, too many teeth showing. "As long as *you* don't regret it, that's fine." The smile turned into a snarl as he bent close. "Never mind that you took away my choice in whether I broke that taboo. As long as Kat had fun, that's all that matters."

With a hiss, I took a step back like he really was a serpent and had bitten me.

"Tell me, Kat, was it fun riding my fingers, knowing I was helping you break your contract?"

His words stung, venom seeping through my veins. "That isn't—"

"Were you laughing while my face was buried between your thighs?"

"It wasn't like—"

"Was it all the more fun knowing I had no idea about your secret?"

Now my hands fisted. "You fucking hypocrite."

There it was. The *arianmêl* talking.

His eyes widened.

I lunged forward, only an inch between our faces. "Don't

you try to pretend you give a solitary fuck about rules or laws, mister left the palace, broke two noses and an arm, snuck into Caelus's rooms, associates with a fence *and* invited her to the palace."

My voice wasn't my own. I'd never sounded so firm, so angry, so... strong.

"And"—I pointed right in his face—"you have secrets too, so don't pretend you're so bloody innocent. What about your father?"

The question that had lurked in the back of my mind finally slithered free.

Bastian went still.

For a long while there was only the ticking of the clock on the mantlepiece, until at last he swallowed, straightened, and lifted his chin. "You really have gathered a lot of information about me, haven't you, Katherine?"

I stood my ground, even though a chill crept over my flesh.

"Fine. I'll tell you about my father. This"—he touched the side of his lip where the scar threaded through—"and this"—he ripped his shirt open, buttons pinging across the room as fae light silvered the smooth scar across his torso—"are my mementoes from killing him."

The breath caught in my throat. I found my head shaking. "No, you didn't."

"I did." His smile was ice. "What you heard is true. I killed my own father."

That wasn't possible. Not with how sad he'd seemed. Not with how much he cared about his orrery.

"It was an accident, then?" I nodded, encouraging him to agree. He could tell me. I'd listen.

But he only shook his head.

"You..." My voice came from very far away. "You killed

him... deliberately?" Tingling fingers gripped together, I willed it to not be true. *Shake your head again.*

"And a princess. Beheaded her. Delivered her head to my queen." Smile brightening, he spread his arms as if presenting himself to me, his audience. "What did you expect from the Bastard of Tenebris? The bastardy isn't *technically* true, but the sentiment? Well..." He gestured at himself. "Here I am."

He said it with such feral delight, I couldn't doubt the truth of his words. I wanted to, though. There had to be some other explanation.

"I don't believe you." My voice was small and fragile.

"Then you're a fool." He loomed over me, a sharp smile on his lips.

I held still, refusing to back down. "What happened? Tell me." That would clear this all up. It had to.

"You want an explanation? Fine." As he drew in a breath, his shoulders squared and his spine straightened, taking him to his full height. It made him look more inhuman than ever. More angry than ever.

I clenched my fists against the threatening shiver.

"My father was a traitor twice over. In the wars of succession, he didn't choose the Night Queen—he was an enemy general." His gaze slid over my head and into the distance.

"When he turned coat to the Night Queen and betrayed the other side, he turned the tide of war, too. If not for him, it might still be raging now." With a twitch, his nose wrinkled. "As punishment for starting off on the wrong side, my queen branded him a traitor, took his titles, and made him work in her stables. Because of something that happened before I was born, I had to grow up in the shadow of the traitor general, in hay and shit, rather than in luxury."

And he cared about luxury? I frowned up at him, losing

sight of the man I knew as he became more and more the stranger.

"Why do you think people were so keen to call me a serpent? They already saw me as a traitor, tainted by my father. You know what they say about apples not falling far from the tree. I shouldn't have been surprised when he betrayed the Night Queen and joined her daughter in a coup attempt. Maybe he fancied himself a queenmaker." Another cruel smile, though tension laced the skin around his eyes. "I was glad to prove my loyalty and escape his bad name."

A coup. Just as Lady Ponsonby had said. Hadn't I thought the details of her story carried the ring of truth?

At last his gaze returned to mine, and he lifted his chin, as imperious as a king. "I walked in there and I hacked the life from him. Then I went after the treacherous princess and I took her head."

My mouth dropped open, the faintest sound falling from them. Because I couldn't form any words in response.

Hadn't I wondered all this time? I'd told myself it was impossible, but a corner of me had known I didn't ask because I didn't want the answer.

I'd been wrong about Bastian.

He wasn't an ally I could rely on. He couldn't keep me safe. If he'd turned on his own father, he could turn on me. I couldn't trust him, and I couldn't trust my feelings about him.

I'd been so, so wrong. He'd done that to his own father; what might he do to me? I wasn't safe with him. Not at all.

His gaze skipped between my eyes as his smile wavered. "I can see exactly what you think. And I hate to disappoint you, love, but I did warn you."

The world spun as I backed away. Oh, he *had* warned me. And I hadn't listened.

Cavendish and Lady Ponsonby had warned me, too. Even that rose-gold-haired fae woman had, in her own way.

By the time I reached the door, I was shaking.

Bastian inclined his head, eyes empty, smile bored. "Goodnight, Katherine."

72

When I got back to my rooms, I found Robin inside.

Some *arianmêl* must've lingered in my system, because I asked, "What the fuck are you doing here?"

He gasped, pasty cheeks turning red.

I couldn't blame him. The rage in my voice shocked me. Where had it come from? Except... that desire to watch it all burn—it had always been there, trapped beneath my fear.

"I hear you were fed some fae concoction, Katherine, so I won't punish you for speaking to me in that manner. But you'd do well to watch your tongue."

A distant alarm bell rang through my bones. But it was quiet, and I found I didn't care.

"The chamberlain gave me a key, since you're my wife." His mouth twisted. "You may have forgotten that fact, by the look of you, but others still hold some regard for the sanctity of marriage... even if it is to a whore."

"How dare you?" My arm snapped back, ready to slap him.

He caught my wrist and squeezed. Crowding over me, he lifted his chin as though in victory.

He might have my hand, but I still had my tongue.

"The sanctity of marriage?" I bared my teeth at him. "Where is that when you're fucking your way around Europa?"

The backhanded strike rang through my face, through the room. Jagged pain opened in my cheek, bringing with it the taste of copper.

His eyes widened as though he'd surprised himself.

After all, he'd never hit me before.

It still tingled in my skin, but the pain of it was nothing compared to the way Bastian had looked at me minutes ago. My chest was wide open, flayed and raw from that.

Yet the sting from Robin's strike was also an answer.

It wasn't that I'd gone to him without my virginity. It wasn't that I hadn't given him an heir. It wasn't that I'd failed in any wifely duty.

He didn't treat me badly because of me. He treated me badly because of *him*.

That more than the strike made my eyes burn. It had never been me.

No matter what had happened tonight, Bastian had shown me that. Whoever he might be, however bad an ally, he'd shown me I deserved better than my husband.

"Enough," Robin muttered, voice shaking as his hands clenched and his shoulders squared. Maybe he thought he'd brought these tears to my eyes. "I will challenge this man to a duel and clear this whole incident up."

My mouth dropped open and something trickled down my lip. When I wiped it, my fingers came away red. I laughed at the sight.

The look he gave me said I was half-mad.

Good. That might scare him off.

"Go ahead and duel Bastian." I smiled, and from the way he recoiled, there must've been blood on my teeth. "He'll kill you. It'll save me from this joke of a marriage."

"You're insane." An uneasy laugh bubbled through his words as he backed away.

"You're probably right. You don't want to stay in here. Never know what a madwoman will do to you in your sleep."

Not taking his eyes off me, he circled to the door.

"Leave the key," I bit out as he opened it.

"Gladly." He fished it from his pocket and tossed it on the floor before backing out.

I slammed the door shut, locked it, and dragged the armchair in front of it before sinking to the floor.

My head throbbed, half ringing with Robin's back-handed strike, half with Bastian's words. Tears burned my eyes, salted my throat.

I curled up in the spot where Bastian had knelt to put on my shoes and prayed that I'd wake and find this had all been a horrible dream.

It hadn't.

I woke, stiff and sore, with an imprint of the carpet on my thigh and dried blood on my lip.

Arianmêl was the worst drink in the world. Unlike when I drank alcohol, all of last night remained in my consciousness with needle-sharp clarity. With every movement, it pricked me deeper until I grabbed the brandy bottle and drained it.

The gods had to hate me, because I couldn't stay in my room and work my way through the emergency bottle I'd stashed in a cabinet. Today was the official announcement of the queen's choice of suitor. In a couple of hours, everyone would gather in the conservatory. We'd have the joy of and listening to some terminally dull speeches about the joyous occasion and the treaties and trade deals that had been agreed along with the engagement.

Going through the motions of getting ready, I downed more brandy.

It made the situation seem less bad.

Bastian wasn't really upset that I was married. It was the fact I'd concealed it from him, which had him understandably hurt and furious. And in the face of my accusation—I winced at the memory of my defensiveness—he'd lashed out. That was all the stuff about his father was. A way to push me away... punish me, even.

He'd had a chance to cool off now. Today he'd be more reasonable.

We could clear all this up with a simple conversation.

By the time I made my way to the conservatory, a hip flask hidden beneath my gown, the world felt a bit softer and I was actually smiling. Lush, broad-leafed foliage filled the space, brighter and thicker than I remembered. It stole my breath, made my smile even wider.

Since Asher was the man of the hour, he had a spot on the dais by the queen's empty throne. Bastian had been relegated a few rows back, behind the remaining suitors. Their position in the front rows was meant to ease the hurt of rejection.

As Bastian's liaison, I, of course, had a seat reserved next to him, with Perry and Ella on my other side. I eased past them, still smiling despite their furrowed brows and shared glances.

Bastian didn't look at me.

He also didn't look at me when I wished him a good morning, but he did give the slightest nod.

I squeezed the orrery to give myself strength. But the moment I opened my mouth to speak again, the herald called us to stand for Her Majesty's arrival.

Dressed in vibrant emerald green, she passed, face serene as each row bowed in turn. This wasn't a marriage for love, but perhaps the fact she'd had some choice in the matter gave her this level of peace. Maybe it was all a mask.

We remained standing for the first speech, and I took advantage of the fact my short stature hid me from view to lean towards Bastian.

"Look," I whispered, "about last night... I'm sorry. I didn't mean to upset you."

His eyes remained fixed ahead, but his jaw feathered.

"And I didn't mean to mislead you, it was just... You assumed I was a widow, and it was easier than explaining the truth."

He glanced at me, then back at the dais. His eyes widened as they returned and landed on my cheek.

I'd covered the faint bruise with make-up, but maybe he spotted the telltale swelling. My stomach turned at the thought of his pity. And I didn't need this conversation to be derailed by his anger at Robin, either.

"It was cowardly of me not to tell you, and I'm sorry."

When he returned his attention to the speech without saying a word, I wanted to scream at him.

Something. Anything. Even if it was to tell me to shut up and die.

"Bastian, please—"

From the row in front, Lord Winthrop turned and glared back at us.

With a huff, Bastian grabbed my wrist and pulled me out of the row. Several pairs of eyes followed us. He herded me to the back of the room and stopped in a small, sheltered space behind a column. Sharp creases cut between his brows as he looked down at me. "What?"

"I'm trying to explain and apologise and... you're giving me nothing."

"Go on, then." He folded his arms. "Explain."

I sucked in a long breath and pulled back my shoulders. "I didn't want to be married to him—I *never* did. I didn't choose it. He's awful, and yet I'm chained to him." My stupid eyes filled with stinging tears as the full and horrible truth of it hit me. I could change my name, but I couldn't change the fact I was trapped in that marriage. I gritted my teeth in a desperate attempt not to cry.

Bastian's fingers bit into his biceps as he leant a little closer.

"Truth be told, I wish I was a widow. It would be easier." I'd never admitted that before, though I'd had plenty of dreams where a message had arrived informing me of Robin's death in some foreign country. The worst part was always waking up. "But I'm not. And although I let you think I was, I'm still not in that marriage through choice. My heart isn't in it."

It's yours. But how was I meant to say that when he was still looking at me with such cold distance, more a stranger than the man who'd cared for me?

517

So I swallowed and said the closest thing I could. "I didn't lie when I said I was yours." My voice cracked, and a useless tear escaped.

The creases between his eyebrows softened, less angry, more... confused? Or sad, perhaps? He caught my tear on his knuckles, the touch gentle enough to crack some vital part of me.

But I didn't want him to pity me because I was crying. I wanted him to understand. I wanted him to still want me. My lip trembled, and I caught it between my teeth before raising my eyebrows in question.

He held my gaze a long time, the glowing depths of his eyes as unfathomable as the moon itself. At last he exhaled, shoulders sinking, and I dared to hope.

"You're still married, though." His mouth, his jaw, his shoulders hardened, and those silver eyes went as distant as the moon. "You can't be mine."

I dug my nails into my palms to hold myself together, because the pain in my chest was too much.

He leant away, the creases between his eyebrows sharp once more. "And I meant everything I said last night. I saw how you looked at me when you heard the truth. I know what you think of me."

Clenching my jaw until it hurt, I shook my head.

Yet he nodded. "I decided my queen was more important than my father. I chose my position at court over him." He leant closer, the corner of his mouth rising softly, like he regretted being the bearer of bad news. "I know you want it to be a horrible misunderstanding. I know you want me to be some secret hero. But I told you I was the villain in someone else's story."

Where was the lie? How could it hide amongst these words and the ones he'd said last night?

I shuffled through them and when that turned up nothing, I clawed them apart, desperation seizing my throat.

He didn't want me anymore. And maybe in a horrible way, it was just as well, because this was not the man I knew... or thought I did.

"When I cut him apart, I knew exactly what I was doing, Katherine." He said it softly, the same tone he used when he touched me. "Just as you knew exactly what you were doing when you concealed your marriage from me."

I flinched. "They aren't the same at all."

He snorted. "No, you didn't kill anyone, but at least I've never lied about my crimes. Everyone knows who I am—*what* I am. You knew exactly what you were grinding up against at that party. I only found out once your husband appeared."

And that was it. A second strike from his acidic venom.

It crept through my veins like a slow death as he backed away and returned to the engagement announcement droning on.

Bastian wasn't some misunderstood hero with a violent, protective streak. I didn't know why he'd helped me in the race or saved me from my uncle. But it didn't make him my ally. It didn't make him my *anything*.

Because he wasn't mine at all.

73

After the speeches, footmen cleared the chairs for a drinks reception in the conservatory. Around me, the blooming tropical plants were grey and scentless. The wine had no flavour. I could barely hear Ella and Perry's chatter.

I circulated with them, somehow maintaining control. Close attention would've revealed I was drinking too quickly to be ladylike. I deposited empty glasses next to plant pots and grabbed a fresh drink every time a tray passed me by.

Speaking of close attention...

"Kat?" Perry touched my shoulder, eyebrows drawn together above her smile.

Ella squeezed my other shoulder as I blinked from her to Perry. "She asked if you were all right."

"You're being very quiet today, and..." Perry's green eyes flicked to my cheek.

I might've been able to withstand Perry alone, but add the

crease of Ella's brow, even though she advised against frowning because of wrinkles, and my eyes instantly burned.

I drained my wine to wash away the sudden thickness in my throat and hugged the glass to my chest. "What do you do when you find out someone isn't the person you thought?"

Ella pressed her lips together, her delicate nostrils flaring. "When someone shows you who they are, believe them."

Perry shot her a frown. "Well, yes, but... it isn't always that simple." With a gentle smile, she extracted the empty glass from my grasp and took my hand.

The tender way she looked at me sent me right back to childhood. If not for our surroundings, I'd have crawled into her arms and let her tend my wounds, physical and emotional.

"Sometimes"—she stroked my knuckles—"people put on an act that isn't their true self. Maybe to push you away. Maybe to punish themselves. I've seen it first-hand and the destruction that comes after. You can't always be sure whether you're seeing the truth or the mask they want to hide behind."

At least with Bastian, I could be sure he hadn't lied. Which meant Ella was right, and I had to believe him, no matter how much it hurt.

"What did he do, Kat?" Ella's voice trembled, not with upset, but with building anger that had her lips pale and tight. She stared at my cheek.

"This? No." I touched the tender skin and ran my tongue over the jagged cut inside. I had enough control over myself not to wince, so maybe they wouldn't think it so bad. "I was drunk last night and fell." It was easier than admitting I'd let Robin hit me.

"Darling, if he found out..." Her gaze flicked to Perry. "If you're in danger..." She pressed her lips together.

Perry cleared her throat. "I sense there's more you two need to talk about. I'm going to go and find somewhere to deposit this"—she indicated my empty glass—"and give you some time alone." She squeezed my hand before disappearing into the crowd.

Ella ushered me away to a quiet bench overshadowed by ferns and broad-leaved palms, with a table full of cakes beside it. "Kat, if he hurt you because he found out you were spying on him, there's no telling what else he might do." She tilted my head to one side, frowning at my swollen cheek. "If he did this... I fear he isn't the man we believed."

I could've laughed to hear my own thoughts parroted back at me. But I was too hollowed out for laughter.

She bowed her head. "Maybe he *is* a risk to Albion. Isn't that what Cavendish feared all along?"

I frowned. That didn't seem right.

My gaze sought him out, some stupid part of me thinking it would be a comfort. He stood on the dais, deep in conversation with Asher and the queen. The only other person up there was Cavendish, who watched the exchange, expression flat. But his arms gave him away, crossed, one finger tapping on his biceps.

Was Ella wrong or did I just *want* her to be?

With Asher as our king, Bastian would have access to all kinds of information about Albion. He'd have access to the queen herself.

If he or the Night Queen meant us harm, they would have all the opportunity in the world. Nowhere would be safe, not even my estate. Mama, Morag, Horwich, Ella... they'd all be in danger.

And no, he hadn't hit me, but he had betrayed his own father. He was *not* the person I'd thought.

When I turned back to Ella, she held out a small plate with a miniature lemon cake on it. "You look like you could use the sugar to help the bitter pill go down."

I groaned. "The truth is the worst medicine."

When I took a bite, it was ashes in my mouth.

I dropped it back on the plate and gave Ella an apologetic smile. "Langdon was right."

She pulled a face and scooped up the rejected morsel. "Him? *How?*"

"Maybe I shouldn't have my cake and eat it after all."

THE DAYS DRIFTED by in a dull haze. I told myself it was winter closing in, but I didn't even half believe that. I forced food down my throat mostly so I could stomach the brandy I drank once I returned to my rooms. At least Robin was avoiding me —I didn't see or hear anything of him. He'd apparently done enough.

After the announcement, the other ladies-in-waiting started deferring to me, leaving me the seat closest to the queen, letting me choose her outfits when we helped her get ready. I'd been given the role of pouring mead for the coming wedding ceremony, and Ella whispered that it had made some envious.

Idiots. They wouldn't envy me if they knew.

Except, I had been the idiot. How hadn't I realised what Bastian was?

Gorgeous, seductive, all that attention on me? Of course he was too good to be true. I could only attract the very worst men, it seemed.

Cavendish was right—he'd blinded me with pleasure. Worse, I let myself be blinded. I let myself be seduced when I was meant to be the one doing the seducing. I'd lost track of why I came here. I'd lost track of my duty, of the only thing that truly mattered.

Two more payments and I'd be free of the bailiff's warrant. The estate would be safe.

I just needed to get through these two months, and then I'd never need to see Bastian Marwood again.

I certainly wouldn't need to sit through his judgemental looks. Every time I entered a room, his eyes snapped to me, sharp as steel. This meeting with Cavendish, Asher, the queen, and her archdruid to discuss arrangements for the wedding was no exception.

It cut me at the same time as it brought my thorns to the surface. What the hells gave him the right to judge me? I'd only had an affair; he had murdered his own father. One vastly outweighed the other.

He acted like they were the same.

Irritatingly, the more I stewed over it, sitting straight despite the weight of his gaze constantly turning to me, I started to see *some* similarities.

He'd never lied to me about his father. I simply hadn't asked. And over time, getting to know him, I'd chosen to believe the rumours couldn't be true.

Equally, Bastian had chosen to believe I was a widow, since I behaved like one. I'd never lied to him about it. He simply hadn't asked.

Killing my own blood was a moral line I wouldn't cross.

And adultery was a moral line he wouldn't cross... at least not knowingly.

Seen through that lens, the two things weren't so different.

If he'd been raised to feel as strongly about adultery as I did about killing a family member, perhaps I could understand.

It didn't make me feel better.

If anything, it was worse, because I'd unwittingly made him break a taboo. It made me more complicit in hurting him.

And yet...

I shouldn't feel sorry for him. I shouldn't care about his hurt.

I should be cursing his name.

And on a logical level, I did. The still-sensible part of me knew he wasn't the man I'd thought, but the foolish rest of me mourned him.

As we sat side-by-side, the foolish girl in me missed the touch of his hand on my thigh, hidden under the table as he reached higher and higher.

I reminded her of what he was.

Ruthless.

Dangerous.

Although he might not be my enemy; he also couldn't be my ally.

So, day by day, I let the thorns grow in that raw space in my chest. They were more useful than what had been there before.

They would protect me where my heart had not.

74

That evening, Ella came to my rooms and flopped on the settee.

"That good a day?" I raised an eyebrow at her over my glass. It was filled with more brandy than she'd approve of and was my second of the evening. Tonight I was breaking all the rules, apparently. Anything to dull the sharp way Bastian now looked at me.

"The best," she sighed, rubbing her forehead.

I placed a tumbler before her and poured. "Say when."

She watched the deep amber-bronze slosh higher and higher before finally nodding.

I sat back in my armchair, and stared at the mirror above the fireplace, trying not to think about how its silver was a lot like a certain fae's eyes.

I had to forget about him. The sooner the better. It would be easier once I returned to the estate and didn't have constant reminders, like the settee we'd sat on the night he'd stayed.

Duty. That was what mattered. To the estate and to the people I cared about. I'd make sure Morag and Horwich had a home and food and pay.

It didn't light me up, though. Inside was just as dull and grey as the overcast day.

And my glass was already empty.

When I sat up and filled it, I waited for Ella's scolding about how the way alcohol would make my skin red and undo all our hard work. It brought a half smile to my face. Something that could be relied upon. Something that showed she cared. Something that I would miss when I went home.

Only she didn't stop me.

I poured a little more, almost to the brim now. Nothing.

That was when I registered she hadn't even tried to fill the quiet with gossip or a salacious story.

Curled up around her glass, she sat staring at the coffee table. Her furrowed brow was practically inviting wrinkles to set up permanent residence on her perfect skin.

"Ella?"

She jumped, sucking in a breath, eyes shooting to mine. "Hmm?"

"You've just let me pour myself a second drink without so much as an arched brow. What's wrong?"

"I'm fine." Gaze sliding away, she tugged at the high neckline of her gown.

That in itself was wrong, too. Ella always wore clothes that showed off her petite figure. It was one of the reasons I'd put so much wood on the fire this evening—she'd promised to visit and she always felt the cold in her gauzy dresses. But this gown was one I hadn't seen before with a lace collar that stood halfway up her throat.

Then the way she tugged it...

The back of my neck prickled, and I straightened my spine as a chill raced over my skin.

Not fine. Not fine at all.

And here I'd been absorbed in my own woes.

She was hiding something, and it made my own throat tighten in sympathy... in horrible certainty.

I approached the settee. It was only a few paces, but each step felt like a mile.

I couldn't say how I knew exactly, just that I did. Maybe it was purely the gown and the way she'd pulled at the neck, or maybe it was that one victim recognised another.

My heartbeat was deafening by the time I eased into the seat beside her. "Show me."

She shot me a frown, delicate nostrils flaring. She didn't say a word, but her eyes said, "Don't make me."

I pushed the caramel hair back from her shoulder and dipped my chin. "Show me."

A muscle in her jaw quivered before she dropped my gaze and pulled down the delicate collar.

Angry red marks marred her creamy skin, deepening to purple in places. They made my heartbeat thunder, because I recognised their form.

Long and thin, around her neck. The ghosts of fingers.

Like the ones I'd seen on Lara's body.

"Who did this to you?" My voice came out soft and cold, like night-falling snow.

Ella shook her head, pulling the collar back over the bruises. "It wasn't my target. She didn't—"

"I know." More of that chill certainty whispered through me, raising the hairs on my arms. "It was Cavendish, wasn't it?"

Her head bowed. She said nothing.

Hands fisting in my lap, I drew a long breath around the tightness of my heart. "I know it was him, because he did the same to me. He slammed you against the wall, holding your throat, didn't he?"

Her eyes shot to mine, wide. Had she also believed that she was the only one? Swallowing, she nodded.

"Right." I was on my feet. I didn't remember telling my body to stand, but I wasn't the one in charge anymore. My feet carried me to the door.

"Kat? What are you...?"

It was one thing to hurt me, but Ella?

Sweet, kind Ella who, despite whatever had made her cynical about men, still stepped out into the world with gentle (and sometimes outrageous) cheer.

No.

"Stay there." My voice was not my own. Maybe that was what made her obey.

My skin fizzed as I stalked out into the corridor. I could barely contain my breaths as heat filled me, engulfed me. It was a wonder the carpets didn't burn to ashes as I walked over them.

How dare he? How dare he lay a fucking finger on her?

I marched to that familiar door, lifted one shaking fist, and hammered on it.

Never let it be said that I didn't have good manners.

No answer.

When I tried the handle, I found it locked.

Jaw creaking, I paused and listened. No sound inside.

Nails digging into my palms, I dragged in a deep breath and turned around.

Fine. I couldn't see him tonight, but tomorrow...

I left a note at our drop point saying I'd reached a decision about his "request." That would get a meeting out of him quickly.

And then, there'd be a reckoning.

75

I made Ella stay in my room that night. I wasn't sure if it was so I could comfort her or so her presence would comfort me. Confirmation she was alive, even though Cavendish had closed his fingers around her throat as he had Lara's.

I set Bastian's orrery to project stars on the canopy over the bed and stroked her hair as her breaths eased.

Sleep wouldn't come for me, though.

Lying there, I could only stare up into the slowly drifting stars. I could understand why Bastian had broken Langdon's nose and Eckington's arm.

The buzzing fury surging through me had wanted to rip Cavendish apart when I reached his office.

Perhaps it was just as well he wasn't there and I had this time to cool off. Tearing him to shreds might've felt good, but he was stronger than me physically, more powerful politically, and he had the weight of court and the queen on his side. Did she have any idea what he was?

I gritted my teeth, but it did nothing to quell the bitter taste flooding my mouth as I realised I couldn't destroy Cavendish.

But I could tell him to stick his fucking poison where the sun didn't shine.

It played out in my mind, repeating the moment I would tell him I was quitting and that he'd have to do his own dirty work. It didn't help me sleep, but it did make me smile.

I'd overpaid the bailiff every month so far. That would buy me time while I worked out how to gather the rest of the funds. I did have a little extra money squirrelled away from my work as Bastian's liaison—that granted a small sum. I'd have to hit the roads hard at night, sell honey and any surplus vegetables. But I'd broken the back of this debt, and Bastian was right—I was resourceful. I'd work something out. Enough to escape Cavendish.

Undoubtedly, he would threaten me. Maybe worse. But I was prepared. I could endure it.

Ella made soft sounds and snuggled close to me, but otherwise, she slept soundly, even when the door clicked and Seren slipped in.

The orrery threw glinting lights over her face and hair as she stood in the doorway.

I'd assumed she was merely his spy—a willing servant. But was she as much a victim held in his grip as Ella was? As I was?

"He wants to see you," she murmured.

"Now?"

Her blond ringlets dipped with her head, less bouncy than usual.

I slid out from the covers and Ella's arm and dressed in

silence. Black felt like a fitting choice—not for mourning, but to go with my mood.

When I reached his office, I found him at his desk, flipping through a notebook covered in spidery script.

"What did you do?" My voice was low and flat.

"I do a lot of things, Katherine." He looked up from his desk, gesturing at the black-covered notebooks surrounding him. "You're going to need to be more specific."

"To Ella."

"Oh, that." He returned to the notebook with a shrug.

With a shrug.

He'd gripped her throat hard enough to bruise, and now he *shrugged* about it.

The flames in me licked to life.

"I asked you a question."

He must've heard the change in my voice, because his attention snapped up from the desk, his eyebrows rising. "She was disobedient. And you seem to be heading in the same direction, *Katherine.* Do you need reminding of your place?"

"I know my place." Teeth gritted, I smiled.

Good gods, did I know my place.

I always had.

But the difference was, now I knew I'd survived worse than him. I'd been held over a grave, threatened with burial in it. I'd watched my own uncle murder my sabrecat cub. I'd been bent into compliance by him when I was still a soft and tender fifteen-year-old.

I'd set in that shape, hardened in the mould. And I might never straighten out of it, but I also couldn't be scared any more than I had been that night.

"And it isn't here. I'm done."

His eyelids fluttered. "You're...?"

"Done. I'll work until the end of the month, then I'm going home."

"And the Bastard?"

"I won't be poisoning him."

His upper lip twitched. "That man must be exceptional in bed."

I held still, even though his words made my stomach dip.

"To still be so loyal to him, even after he's rejected you so harshly." The smirk glinted in his eyes, cruel and alert. "Tell me, did he enjoy meeting your husband?"

The breath huffed out of me. "You knew." Of course. At our very first meeting, he'd instructed me never to tell Bastian.

"I wish you valued specificity more. *What* did I know?"

"You knew marriage was sacred to fae and acting against it was taboo."

He tapped a small oxblood red book on the shelf behind him. "'Know thy enemy,' as wise Sūnzǐ said. Most fae marriages include clauses that allow for other relationships if everyone involved is aware and consents. Under those circumstances, fucking someone else doesn't come between the married parties. But Albionic marriages include that pesky 'forsaking all others' clause, don't they?"

My tongue pressed to the roof of my mouth. A decade ago, it had formed those words. Technically, they were part of my contract with Robin. Not that he'd ever given a shit about it.

"When I chose you, the fact you were still married was the only mark against you. But a little deception cleared that issue right up, didn't it?"

He'd known all along, and he'd made me unwittingly complicit. My stomach hollowed, and I gripped my hands together to keep from clutching it. He'd set me up to win Bastian *and* to lose him.

"You see how alien he is?" Cavendish canted his head. "He isn't human. He doesn't value what you value. He doesn't see the world as you do. Did you ask him about his father?"

"I know what he did. It changes nothing." A lie. It had changed everything, except for this: "I still won't poison him. You'll have to find someone else to do your dirty work."

And this was where he'd threaten me. Maybe even kill me outright.

Still, it was better than continuing as his pawn.

"Very well." With a sigh, he lowered his head. "It's a shame, though."

His tone made me tense. And... no threat? His shoulders even sank, like he was giving in. It prickled between my shoulder blades like the sensation of being watched. I bit my tongue.

Lips pressed together, he shook his head. "Poor Ella."

That blew a cold wind over the fire of my anger, making it gutter. I swallowed, throat tight. "What do you mean, 'Poor Ella'?"

"Just that with you being so fond of her, it would be a terrible shame if something found its way into her drink."

"You—"

I clamped my mouth shut against the name I'd been about to call him.

Think, Kat. Be sensible. Be smart.

Despite the anger smouldering in me, I had to remember control. I held myself tight and met his gaze. "You're asking me to choose between Ella and Bastian."

He chuckled. "Oh no, no, no. I wouldn't do that."

The breath eased from me.

He smiled, head canted, fingers interlaced on his desk.

"Either you poison Bastian, as I've asked so patiently. Or I take care of him *and* Ella."

All the air sucked from the room.

I went very still. The whole world did.

Either Bastian died, or he *and* Ella did.

I stared at Cavendish, eyes burning, and I willed it to not be true. A joke. A very unfunny joke. But he just sat there, smiling like this was all perfectly reasonable.

He tilted his head further, like he was waiting for my answer.

I didn't want to pick an option, because they were both awful.

Only it didn't matter what I wanted. Hadn't I been told that enough? Hadn't I *witnessed* that enough?

It had *never* mattered what I wanted.

Especially not when it came to Cavendish. He'd framed it like a request, but like dealing with Lara, he'd only ever given the illusion of choice.

I didn't move, but inside, I crumbled.

One dead or both.

It was no choice at all.

"Open the cabinet." I stared at the place where he stored the aconite.

He stood slowly, as if not wanting to spook me. He needn't have worried—my feet were rooted to the spot.

The lock clicked, echoing in my ears like a replacement for my pulse.

A moment later, he stood before me, the vial of purple liquid in his outstretched palm.

"Do you accept this duty for your country?"

I didn't want to.

But I took it.

"Poison may be a woman's weapon," he said as I ran my thumb over the faceted glass, "but it has its uses, however cowardly."

Just the sound of his voice burned in me. The injustice. The casual cruelty. The sheer fucking hypocrisy.

"Cowardly?" I scoffed, watching the way my movement sent the poison's light dancing across my hand. "Is it cowardly to play with substances that are just as likely to kill you as your target?"

The words came from the thorns knotted inside me. It was a dark place, darker than the ancient part of the Queenswood, darker than Bastian's shadows.

"Is it cowardly to calmly drip death into someone's glass, knowing you'll have to face the moment when their eyes widen and they realise what's happening?" I'd have to do that. At some point Bastian would realise he'd just consumed death that I'd dripped into his drink, and he'd look at me with accusation, anger, hurt.

Cavendish's eyes widened as if he could see the thorny, flowerless branches snaking through me and it made him wonder who—*what* I was.

I lost myself in the pretty shift of glass and purple light. "Isn't it funny that poison is looked down upon? And clever tricks and traps and seduction." Like Ella's cosmetics—she'd called those women's weapons.

"Anything that relies on techniques where we stand a chance? Cheating, cowardly, weak. But lopping someone's head off with a sword or pummelling them with your fists? Honourable and fair." I bared my teeth and squeezed the vial. "Strange how the only valid weapons are ones that rely on brute strength—a domain where you'll beat us every time. So says a system made by men."

I was trapped in that system. Surrounded by men more powerful than I could ever hope to be.

But, fuck, was I angry about it.

Not just angry for me. For Dia. For Lara. For Ella. Even for my sister, who'd been forced to flee and change her name and identity in order to find somewhere in this gods damned world to become herself.

It fizzed in me, corrosive and vicious. Anger was not safe. Especially not at him.

But maybe *arianmêl* had left a permanent mark on me, because I just couldn't bring myself to care.

"You have power over us—physical domination, fear. How are we meant to win when you can hold us down and strangle us with your bare hands?" My eyes burned with the image of Lara lying dead.

But my rage burned hotter.

It made my smile a spiked thing that I pointed at him. "Poison, though? It puts us on a level footing. No wonder men don't like it."

Cavendish had paled, and now I'd stopped, he opened and closed his mouth before speaking. "And *I* don't like your tone."

Poor thing. I almost pitied his discomfort. He didn't seem the kind of man who was used to it. He certainly wasn't used to his pawns talking back.

But I didn't want to be a pawn anymore. I didn't even want to be on the board.

"Will you poison him or not?" His tone was clipped with warning.

He'd pushed me to this. And I might not have a choice about doing it, but I could choose how it would happen and what came after.

"These are my terms. I will see out this month as your spy.

I will poison Bastian Marwood." I counted each item on my fingers. "And you? You will pay me a very handsome bonus. You will not so much as think about harming Ella in any way, shape, or form. And afterwards, I'll return to my estate and live out my days in peace, never—and I mean *never* to be bothered by you or this court ever again. Are we in agreement?"

He drew a long breath, straightening, becoming the composed spymaster once more. "Katherine Ferrers, you have a deal."

76

Over the following days, court grew smaller and quieter, like it was cutting back for the winter. Other than the Frankish and Dawn Court delegations, most of the other suitors packed up and headed home, which meant fewer social events.

That suited me—I didn't feel very social.

I struggled to think about much other than the vial of poison locked away in my bedroom. It burned its way into my dreams until I had to move the lockbox from under the bed to the bottom of the wardrobe.

The only thing that stopped me from hiding in my rooms was trying to cheer up Ella. I stopped by her rooms or invited her to mine. Some nights, Perry joined us, too. They were the only two people who managed to drag a laugh from me— Perry with her piratical adventures, and Ella with her sexual ones. It was a balm to see her smile.

The queen spent a lot of time in the conservatory, often alone. I didn't know much about the warm climate plants in there, but there seemed to be a lot of flowers, considering the cool weather.

One morning, as I led Vespera back from a ride, I bumped into Webster and asked what he'd put on the roses to bring them into bloom again.

"That's the thing." He glanced left and right before bending closer. "Nothing. I haven't done anything different this year, and yet they're flowering in the middle of October. The lad who looks after the hothouse plants in the conservatory says the same thing. Reckons it's magic from those fae." He shot a glare at the palace. "Strange times, if you ask me."

I chewed my lip, eyeing the roses we passed. Even they couldn't make me smile. I'd be going back to my estate soon and there'd be no flowers there. I should get used to being away from them.

"How is your shrub getting on? I'd... love to see it."

When I turned, I found him watching me with eyebrows raised, mouth twisted to one side. I didn't understand what the look meant. Hopeful, maybe? It felt off, like there was some meaning I missed.

"It's doing well. Like these, it's flowering again."

"Lady Katherine." Perry stepped out from behind a bush, a bright smile in place. "So good to see you. Will you walk with me?" She gave Webster a pointed look.

He ducked a bow and hurried off.

Brow furrowed, Perry watched him retreat. "Are you all right?"

"Uh... yes?" I patted Vespera's shoulder. "Shouldn't I be?"

"Didn't you see the way he was looking at you?"

"What? Webster? How was he looking at me?"

Perry offered Vespera her hand to sniff before squinting at

me, head cocked. "Or his comment about wanting to see the rosebush? Really? Ella said you were good at reading people."

This was like when I'd first come to court. And I'd had enough of this place and the things people didn't say in it.

"Please, Perry,"—I rubbed my temple—"just spell it out."

"Where is your rose bush?"

"In my room."

"And he said he wanted to see it, yes?"

"This is *not* spelling it out."

She rolled her eyes. "Good gods, woman, he was fishing for an invitation to your bedroom."

I laughed.

She did not.

As we made for the stable yard, I wondered, though. It was an odd thing for him to hint at, though servant-aristocrat affairs weren't unknown—just ask the stable hand I'd given my virginity to.

What was truly disturbing was the fact I hadn't read it. The raised eyebrows—a hopeful question hidden in his remark. The twist of his mouth—an awkwardness in the asking in case he was rejected. And Perry's sudden appearance —a rescue.

I was losing my touch. Sleepless nights and alcohol. The constant weighing knowledge of the vial of poison and the fact I would use it in a matter of days.

The sooner I went back to the estate, the better.

THE NEXT AFTERNOON, I had a final fitting with Blaze. Since I had an official role in the wedding ceremony, I had to wear a traditional robe.

Traditional didn't seem to come into Blaze's vocabulary, though. She stood back, pouting at the way it hung around me, apparently unsatisfied, even though she'd cut it as low as possible. "I cannot work with this shape. It's all wrong for you."

Ella sighed, throwing her hands in the air. "It's what's required for the ritual."

"You Albionic folk and your rituals." Blaze huffed, rolling her eyes.

Today, I was inclined to share her sentiment. I'd always enjoyed the calls to the gods and the elements, the offerings on the altar or in the soil. But this morning I'd attended a wedding rehearsal at the grove, which put me in Bastian's presence for three excruciating hours.

During a moment where we had nothing to do but stand back while the archdruid spoke to the queen and Asher, I bent a little closer to him. At his side, his hand flexed, but he didn't move away.

"I have to say I'm surprised," I whispered as the archdruid handed a small bowl of honey to the queen.

Bastian arched an eyebrow without looking at me. "By?"

"I thought you'd have me removed as your liaison at the first opportunity."

"I see no need for that." His gaze flicked this way, not making it as far as my face. It paused on my hands, where I'd picked the cuticles so much they'd bled. "I understand the role comes with a stipend, and you need money. You may as well stay in post until I leave."

The guilt stabbed me. After everything, he endured my

presence as his liaison for my sake. "Thank you," I muttered, frowning ahead.

"Which, you'll be glad to hear, will be soon now this has been secured." He gestured to the soon-to-be-married couple as they shared honey to ensure their marriage would be sweet. Good luck to them—it hadn't worked for mine.

"I'm leaving at the end of the month," I blurted. Gods knew why. Maybe some childish attempt to let him know I'd be leaving before he did.

His eyes shot to me and for the briefest second, his brow crumpled.

I shouldn't care. But it felt like a victory, even if it was smoothed away in an instant.

His throat bobbed. "Where will you go?"

"Back to the estate, of course."

"But your husband... It's his house, isn't it?"

"Everything is his." The slumbering rage that I'd discovered inside myself raised its head and clipped my words short.

"Can't you end the—?"

"Don't you think I've tried?"

Asher and the queen turned at my rising voice, eyes wide.

I sucked in a breath and bowed my head. The heat in my cheeks wasn't shame, though.

This whole situation was ridiculous. And having to explain it to Bastian was just the icing on a particularly shitty cake.

"I requested a divorce from the old queen," I muttered, voice back under control. "She denied me. If I'd won the race, I would've used the boon to get it granted, but we both know how that went."

"You have to get someone else's permission to end your own marriage?"

I could feel his stare—it needled my skin. Where once it had warmed me, now it only reminded me of how powerless I was in my own damn life.

"I had no choice at its beginning. Why should I have a choice about its end?" And now, here it was, coming between me and something I *had* chosen. I gave a humourless laugh— if it wasn't laughter, it would be tears. "This is how it is for human women. I'm my husband's property."

His eyes widened before dipping away from mine. "I didn't know. It isn't like that in Elfhame."

I flashed him a bitter grin. "How could a fae understand?"

He made a low sound and wrinkled his nose. "I've never heard anything so barbaric."

I bit my tongue against another retort. *Surely killing your own father is more barbaric than that.*

And now, standing here in my sitting room while Blaze fitted me for a robe to wear while I poisoned him didn't help my foul mood. I chose silence and let her and Ella discuss me like I wasn't there.

"And what is it you're asking me to add in?" Blaze peered at the sketch I'd given her, sent from Cavendish.

Ella shrugged. "A pocket for smelling salts."

"A hidden pocket in the sleeve for smelling salts?" Blaze arched one delicate eyebrow, which disappeared behind her fringe. "Yes, 'smelling salts' are popular at our Frankish court, too." Her mouth twisted to one side.

I kept my face neutral. She knew exactly what the pocket was for, and it wasn't anything to do with ladies fainting.

Ella smiled sweetly. "We thought Her Majesty might get light headed with the... emotion of the event."

"Oh yes, I'm sure. So much emotion for her arranged marriage to someone who's practically a stranger." Blaze gave us each a flat look before shrugging. "It is not for me to question my clients and their specifications... only their taste." She scowled at my robe again. "And I truly do question it in this instance. But"—she sighed—"it must be, I suppose. I will, of course, ensure you look beautiful, Kat."

Before she left, she kissed me on each cheek and gave me an odd look. "Be careful, *ma chérie*," she whispered. "Smelling salts are a dangerous game." She held my shoulders. "Farewell."

So final.

I frowned at the door as it closed behind her, a creeping realisation lifting the hairs on my arms.

When I left court, Bastian wouldn't be there to say goodbye. He'd be dead.

My throat closed.

I shouldn't want to say goodbye to him. I should be glad to rid us of a dangerous enemy and pay off the last of my debt while doing it. That's what a dutiful woman would feel.

Maybe I wasn't so dutiful after all.

Besides, the man I wanted to say goodbye to didn't even exist. He never had. The tears standing in my eyes, threatening to spill, they mourned the person I'd thought he was.

When Ella saw my face and pulled me into her arms, it was that man I let myself cry for.

77

The grove was decked in flowers—roses and the tropical orchids and hibiscus from the conservatory, even though they'd eventually die out here in the cold. Lanterns made from coloured glass added cheerful light to the dull autumn day, making the trees seem less bare.

At my position by the speckled sarsen stone altar, I stared out over the gathered faces, waiting for the moment I had to pour the mead. A glass for the queen, one for Asher, one for Cavendish, acting as Albion's witness, and one for Bastian, as Elfhame's witness.

I longed for a drink myself, but I hadn't dared sneak more than a gulp of brandy this morning. Not when I had such an important job to do.

The secret pocket in my sleeve weighed me down, and when I blinked, for a horrifying second, every face in the crowd was Bastian's.

He isn't who you thought. This will save Ella. Steel your heart.

I told myself that over and over again as the archdruid

spoke of the value of alliances, the honour of a marriage blessed by the fae, and other meaningless things.

As he explained the importance of the libation, he glanced at me. My signal. Stomach churning around that single gulp of brandy, I turned to the table set up behind the altar. The glasses glistened, too sharp, too bright. The mead caught the autumn sun, its amber tones glinting like gold.

I should've drunk more.

I couldn't do this.

Kill Bastian? What was I thinking? I'd been angry, hurt… stupid. And even if Cavendish was right and he was a danger to my country, that didn't mean he deserved to be poisoned. There had to be some other way.

The first glass clinked as I took it from its stand with shaking hands. I sucked in a breath, feeling dozens of eyes turn to me rather than the archdruid, who went on about how mead had first been the drink of the gods. The next glass made no sound.

Now I had hold of myself, I glanced up at Cavendish, who stood a few paces away, watching the ceremony. I uncorked the mead and poured all four glasses, gaze boring into him. He ignored me, even as I took the queen's glass to her and Asher's to him, presenting them with a bow, just as I'd practised.

It was only as I stood with Bastian's glass in my hand that Cavendish finally looked at me.

Utter calmness governed his face. There was no hint that he was about to, through me, kill a man.

His calm sent my heart lurching. "If I don't do this, you will, won't you?" I whispered, voice lost in the bare branches of the grove. "Like you did Lara."

The faintest crease marked his brow.

His public persona was so controlled, even in a moment like this, where I came perilously close to disobeying.

Not for the first time in Cavendish's presence, the back of my neck prickled. But this time it wasn't at his lecherous look or inappropriate touches, it was...

Something felt off.

That controlled furrow of his brow spelled out confusion.

As I flicked open the vial hidden in my palm, I adjusted a lock of hair from my face, taking my time, watching Cavendish all the while.

Cavendish, who took every opportunity to admire my hair, gaze caressing it as often as his hands did.

But not today.

As I tipped aconite into Bastian's glass, he turned and approached the altar, ready for his part in the ceremony. The poison disappeared into the mead. Colourless, scentless, just as Cavendish had said.

My heart boomed in my ears, slow and loud, as I followed him to the altar.

Something was wrong.

Very wrong.

His mannerisms, so controlled, less... elegant, somehow. His eyes held no hint of smouldering cruelty that took delight in seeing me afraid. He hadn't so much as glanced at my hair or cleavage.

This wasn't just a man wearing the mask of a public persona.

The world beyond the altar faded away into the grey and brown of almost-bare autumn trees. The only things in focus were here. The only things that mattered were here.

I took Cavendish his glass and kept my eyes on him as I bowed. Still neutral, disinterested almost, and not in that fake-bored way Bastian liked to hide behind. My gaze snagged on the open collar of his robe.

He took his glass. When I only stood there staring, his eyebrows rose and he glanced at the remaining drink.

I swallowed and fetched Bastian's glass.

Something not right. Something about Cavendish.

Mechanically, I circled the altar, each step towards Bastian taking a lifetime as I stared at the honey-gold mead.

Gold.

Cavendish's necklace... which there was no sign of disappearing into his robe. He *always* wore it. Always. It was so important, he'd had it repaired after Lara's murder.

Unless...

He'd never acknowledged me outside his office, aside from that one time during Avice's visit, when he'd reminded me that I had a job to do. I glanced at the queen, who flicked me an impatient look. I *did* have a job to do—three in fact. Spy for him, lady-in-waiting to her, and liaison to Bastian.

And his behaviour now versus in his office... If it weren't impossible, I'd have said he was a different person entirely.

What if I wasn't working for the queen's spymaster?

It sounded like madness, even in my own mind, but...

If—*if* that was true, what would be the ripples from today?

Protecting Albion from a threat, perhaps. But what else?

Poisoning Bastian in the middle of the queen's wedding would cause a diplomatic incident between Albion and Elfhame. With my position at court, it could be considered an act of war.

And Bastian had told me exactly what war between fae and humans was like. Death. Destruction. Nowhere and no one would be safe.

My heartbeat was like the bailiff's pounding at the door.

The same dread I'd felt that day swept through me.

Options. If I told him about the poison, it would still leave us just as diplomatically screwed, albeit he'd still be alive. Alive and able to lead the Night Queen's forces against us with all the intelligence he'd gained while he was here.

Fuck. No. Not an option.

I stared up at him, one step away.

Time was running out.

His face was still, neutral, but I swore there was a flicker of softness in his eyes. It might've been wishful thinking.

It didn't matter. I didn't know who or what Bastian was, exactly, but that could wait until after. Right now, I needed to keep him alive.

I dropped the glass.

And Bastian—fucking Bastian moved in a blur, catching it without a drop spilt.

He straightened, frowning at me, the faintest question in his eyes. "Are you all right?" he breathed.

I snatched the drink from him.

"Kat, what're you playing at?" His eyes widened at me, and murmurs rippled through the guests. I didn't look directly at the queen, but I could feel her spiky tension needling the air.

"Give me the bloody mead," he whispered.

"Don't drink it."

"Are you joking? It will be a massive insult to your queen if I don't, and an insult to mine if you try to spill it again. The ceremony would be ruined. Hells, maybe even this whole alliance."

A shadow passed over me. Cavendish looked between us, one eyebrow rising fractionally. "Is there a problem?"

"No." Bastian's mouth curved as his gaze bore into me. "Katherine was just about to give me the mead, weren't you?" He tugged the glass from my grip.

That heart-pounding continued, hammering on my eardrums like someone wanted to get in.

He wanted this alliance. He'd worked towards it—all those meetings. Yes, it would benefit Elfhame, but didn't Albion benefit, too? That was how alliances worked.

The shifting light turned the mead from gold to amber to pale wheaten yellow as he lifted it.

I blinked up at Cavendish.

He tilted his head at me as if trying to work out what I was doing. This wasn't a man anticipating his enemy's poisoning.

No options left.

I lunged and tore his robe open.

A collective gasp sucked the air from the grove. Bastian paused, the glass almost at his lips.

I stared at Cavendish's bare chest. No necklace.

I didn't work for Lord Thomas Cavendish, the queen's spymaster.

I never had.

The pounding broke through: my ears popped, and knowledge bloomed in my mind, clear and certain.

Some things were more important than mere survival.

And I did not want to live in a world torn by fae-human war. I certainly couldn't leave the people I loved in that nightmare.

Besides, hadn't Bastian said mine was a life half-lived? I was only losing half a thing, but if it prevented war... it was worth giving up the tooth and nail grip I'd held so long.

I grabbed the mead.

I gulped it down.

Sweet and alcoholic, the floral spiciness of honey. No taint of poison. Just as... whoever the fuck I worked for had said.

I dashed the glass upon the ground, its breaking shattering the silence. Let them think me mad. I'd already torn the spymaster's shirt open, and hadn't Robin said I was insane? If this was just the action of a love-sick woman who'd been rejected by a fae lord, there would be no war.

Hundreds of pairs of eyes stared at me, round with surprise.

One silver pair, though, they bulged as Bastian's whole body stiffened, not quite surprised, but something else. "No." His hands closed in the air above the broken glass.

But I didn't have time to puzzle out the thoughts of Bastian Marwood. I needed to get out of sight before the poison took effect. If anyone realised the truth behind my theatrics, this would all be for nothing.

With unCavendish still out there, Albion wasn't safe yet.

I fled from the grove.

I had no idea how long I had left, but whatever it was, I needed to make it count.

78

I ran to my rooms, no sign of the poison's effects yet.

If I wasn't working for the queen's spymaster, who the hells was I working for? It had to be someone who'd benefit from Albion and Elfhame being at war... or at least not being allied. The key rattled in the lock as my hand shook.

That was shock, not poison, right?

Either way, I didn't have long. An hour, maybe?

I hurried inside, grabbed paper and pen, and began a message for unCavendish. When I'd visited his office uninvited, I'd found it locked, so I couldn't just appear and count on finding him there.

My mind whirred and tangled as I wrote.

He'd leered so close to me, I knew he wore no mask or clever stage make up. The face that looked so like the one I'd just seen in the grove was very real.

A twin, then? Or someone who just looked incredibly similar?

Surely Cavendish would know if he had a twin. Whoever unCavendish was, he wasn't working with the real man.

Then there was the necklace.

UnCavendish always wore it. Bastian had said it was a fae symbol for magical power. My tingling fingers crept to my own throat. My necklace was also magical, almost certainly fae-worked. And the poison glowed with some magical aspect. So, he had easy access to fae items.

My gaze slid from the note to the open drawer of the desk and the gleam of my fae-worked pistol.

How do you think we go about killing each other?

UnCavendish had lied to me, so he couldn't be fae.

Wait. *Had* he lied to me?

He is a danger to my court.

My court. Not *ours.*

If unCavendish was from Dawn Court, that was no lie.

That meant...

"A changeling."

Normally in the stories, they killed or kidnapped a target and took their place. This one must've kept the real Cavendish alive and worked around the fringes, occupying his office while he was engaged elsewhere. At our first meeting, hadn't he appeared in his office soon after I'd seen him in the throne room? Yet he'd looked unflustered.

By the time I'd finished the message to unCavendish saying there was a problem with the poison, my hands were tingling.

I might not last to see this through.

My chest tightened, threatening to crush not just the place where my heart had once been, but the sharp thorns that had taken its place.

I wrote another note, this one much shorter.

E. Our Cavendish is not Cavendish but an enemy of Albion.

If I died before I could resolve this, at least Ella would be warned. I knew she worked for the same man I did, since she'd told me he always wore the necklace. Even if I couldn't stop him, she could. I hid the note in my lingerie drawer. Ella would want to help clear my belongings, and she knew I'd find it excruciating if anyone else saw the scandalous underwear.

I grabbed my pistol, loaded it, and hurried to the west corridor and the dragon tile, where I left my message. Someone had to be monitoring it. Out of curiosity, I'd once checked the spot an hour after I'd left information and it had already been collected. Today, with his plan falling into place, he had all the more reason to keep a close eye on the drop point.

Heartbeat sluggish and loud, I went around the corner. I angled my pistol until I could see a distorted version of the corridor reflected in the polished steel.

If no one came, my plan was buggered. Well and truly.

I waited. The grandfather clock at the end of the hall *tick-tock*ed, each second clunking, lost forever.

At last, a familiar shape appeared at the other end. Chestnut brown hair, servant's clothes. Webster.

He could just be here for—

He stopped at the tile, bent, and lifted it.

He worked for unCavendish.

I rubbed my chest with numb fingertips. I hadn't told him personal secrets, no, but I'd spilled another kind of truth to him. I'd shared my passion for plants; I'd waxed lyrical about roses. I'd let him see that part of me.

And he'd been spying on me all along.

No wonder he always appeared whenever I went in the gardens. After Perry's comment, I'd assumed he had a fondness for me.

Perhaps it was because I was dying, but the betrayal cut deeper than I'd expected, spiking pain in my chest.

In the warped reflection, he straightened and hurried back the way he'd come.

Following, I rubbed my face. That tingled now as well, and the slow tolling of my heart wasn't normal.

And that pain... it wasn't the betrayal.

Fuck.

"Hold on, Kat," I whispered. "Just a bit longer."

When I reached the junction before the corner Webster had disappeared around, a dark figure stepped into my path.

"Lady Katherine." Prince Valois smiled down at me, but that faded as his eyebrows pinched together. "Are you all right? You look very pale."

"I'm fine. I just need to—"

Deep in my gut, pain seized my breath. Other than a gasp, I made no sound, but I had to clutch my belly. It felt like something was ripping it open.

"*Madame!* You are not fine." Warm hands closed on my shoulders and ushered me back the way he'd come.

I wanted to follow. The warmth was comforting. The grip was firm, safe.

But nowhere would be safe if I didn't stop unCavendish.

"This way. We need to get you a doctor. Here, let me—"

"No." The muzzle of my pistol pressed into his chest.

He blinked down at it, brow creasing. "I see."

"I'm sorry." I backed away, gun still trained on him. After a few deep breaths, the pain subsided enough that I could straighten. "This shot is meant for someone else, but I can't let you stop me."

"Stop you from doing what?"

I shook my head, now at the corner. The pain was a sharp point dragging through my gut. "Stay away from the north corridor. I... Lord Cavendish might not be as he seems."

The last thing I saw before turning away was his look of utter confusion.

I ran, head pounding, chest tight, and made it to the north corridor in time to see Webster disappear into Cavendish's office.

Gasping for breath, I waited in an alcove. I shouldn't be this breathless or bathed in this much sweat. Every heartbeat shouldn't be so painful.

The aconite was weaving its way through me, insidious tendrils creeping through my veins.

I waited.

And waited.

Webster didn't come out.

Fine. I'd have to confront him as well as unCavendish. He had to believe he was also working for the real spymaster. Once I revealed the truth, he would help me tackle the impostor.

The click of my pistol echoed down the corridor as I cocked it.

With it hidden up the billowing sleeve of my robe, I entered Cavendish's office for the last time.

79

It wasn't the dramatic entrance I might've hoped for. My stomach chose that exact moment to spasm again, and I staggered under the weight of the pain.

UnCavendish turned from the fireplace, a candelabrum on the mantlepiece lighting him from behind, casting his face in shadow. "I wasn't expecting you here so quickly. I only just received your message."

Teeth gritted against the whimper that wanted to come out of me, I took in the room. No sign of Webster. Had he left through a hidden door, perhaps?

UnCavendish lifted his chin and sniffed. "Why can I smell aconite?" His eyes widened, a million miles away from the controlled surprise I'd seen on the man in the grove half an hour ago. "Did you spill the poison?"

"I'm asking the questions." I levelled my pistol at him. "What the hells are you?"

A beat more of surprise, then his teeth flashed in a soft laugh. "You're smarter than I thought. What gave me away?"

559

"Necklace. You're wearing it now, aren't you?"

"Ah, of course." He tugged open the collar of his shirt, revealing that telltale glint of gold. "Blasted thing. To maintain this form so long, I need a power source."

This form, then... "You *are* a changeling. And..." I checked behind me, but we were the only two here. "You're Webster."

His smile was slow, somewhere between pleased and cruel. "At least I can get rid of this now."

With a shudder, his body rippled. The brown of his hair flipped through every colour I'd ever seen and settled on ashy white. Like Ella's riffle of playing cards when she shuffled, his clothing flicked and merged into his skin, which still flashed through endless colours. At last, it ended on a dark charcoal grey.

He stood before me in Cavendish's shape, but an inverted black-and-white image. His unnerving eyes pinned me—the whites black, the pupils white.

"*This* is much easier to maintain."

The only thing he wore was the necklace, the tiger's eye flaring bright.

"How? How could you live alongside the real Cavendish without being found out?"

"By being clever, of course." He scoffed. "I didn't wander the halls as him, ready to bump into the real person by accident."

Then the man who'd scolded me for neglecting my job during Avice's visit had been the real Cavendish. Why hadn't I stopped and talked to him a moment longer? If I'd asked him a question, I might've realised that wasn't the man I worked for. But of course, that was exactly why unCavendish had told me never to approach him in public. I squeezed my pistol.

"Then how *did* you wander the halls?"

"No one sees the servants." His mouth curled, revealing glossy black teeth. "Webster was very handy for that *and* for keeping an eye on you. It got a little dicey when they found his body. Good thing it was too decomposed for anyone to identify him."

My stomach turned, setting off another clench of pain. I ground my teeth through it as sweat broke out on my forehead. Poor Webster. He'd been a real person, someone with a life and hopes for its future. "You killed him just to take his place."

"He was expendable." He shrugged. "He might even have become my favourite form if you'd invited him to your room." Those strange eyes trailed down my body. "But, since you didn't take the bait, I can't decide. Was it better playing Cavendish while I toyed with you or choking the life out of a woman while wearing her lover's face?"

My blood ran cold and my heart did something strange, making me flinch. "Langdon... You lured Lara to that room by pretending to be him. You killed her while in his shape."

His face flickered and changed to a black and white version of Langdon's, sneering at me just as he had at the picnic. "I could kill you in the Bastard's shape, if you like?" With a smirk, he shuddered and his face riffled again. For a moment, it was Bastian leering at me. "No? You don't look like you like that idea." He shook his head and became unCavendish once more. "This gives me so many options." He fingered the star pendant and let it drop to his bare chest.

I touched the pearlwort necklace at the hollow of my throat. "Skin contact." He had to wear it under his shirt not only to hide it, but to make use of the power.

He inclined his head. "Skin contact. You've learned so much, Katherine. In an odd way, I'm proud of you. Look at how much you've grown from the woman with tear-stained cheeks who stood before me at our first meeting, so clueless to the ways of court. And now here you are." He sauntered closer.

How hadn't I seen it before? That deadly grace was not human.

Or maybe he'd always hidden it and now didn't bother to.

"Solving your own mystery. Threatening me with that little gun. It's a shame you missed the part where changelings are fae and fae can only be killed with—"

"Iron, aconite, or fae-worked weapons." I flashed him the side of the gun, showing the clockwork mechanism far too intricate to be human.

He stilled, eyes growing even wider in genuine surprise.

But instead of victory, I felt only pain. It doubled me over, pushing tears to the corners of my eyes. I bit back a whimper —I wouldn't give him the pleasure of hearing my pain. "Fae-worked, arsehole," I grunted out. "Now back off."

"Hmm." The skin around his eyes crinkled, but he didn't back away. "The cat *does* have claws. How delightful. And here I was thinking you helpless *and* clueless. But..." His eyebrows rose a second before the corners of his mouth did the same. "But *that smell*." He chuckled, the sound chiming and echoing in my ears over and over, dizzying. "Oh, you silly girl. You've taken the poison. A sudden attack of conscience about killing the dashing Bastard of Tenebris?"

"I realised you weren't Cavendish." Merely speaking had sweat pouring down my back. The room spun, slow like my pulse. "I realised it would cause war."

"And you couldn't stop him drinking it any other way, so you just *had* to throw yourself at the poison and drink it for him? How romantic. How tragic." He came another step closer, and I backed into the desk, grateful for something to lean against.

"Then again," he went on, "I didn't expect anything more from the woman who stood before me that first day. So desperate, you pressed into even my touch." His odd white-pupilled eyes trailed down me, lingering on my hair and the low neckline of my robe.

Still, he stayed out of arm's reach, and I was glad for that. The numbness in my hands had spread and I couldn't entirely feel the pistol anymore. If he struck, it would probably fall from my grip.

"No wonder he so easily convinced you to take poison for him." He scoffed, disdain written in the wrinkle of his nose. "Killing yourself for a creature who doesn't give a damn about you, who can never love you. How sad. How pathetic."

"You're wrong." Bastian had told me about the war waged for love. Teeth gritted, I raised my chin. "Fae can love."

He laughed and splayed his fingers over his chest. "Oh, I don't mean *fae* are incapable. I mean the Bastard is. You know he killed his father and isn't even sorry about it?" He clicked his tongue, head shaking. "A monster like that? No, he cannot love. Cannot care. Not for his father. Certainly not for you, however delightful that hair of yours, those luscious curves, that beautiful face. Oh dear"—he cocked his head—"though it's looking pale now."

He was wrong, and maybe, in my hurt, I'd been wrong too. I'd seen emotion on Bastian's face. Regret over his father's death, even if he'd done it deliberately. He'd cared for me in his rooms, feared for me. I'd read those things in him.

But unCavendish was right about my pallor. I was dying. No escaping that.

I could do one thing first.

"Well, drink it up." I swung my pistol towards his chest. Head would be better, but with this tremble in my arms, I didn't trust my aim. "Because it's the last thing you're going to see."

There was a tendril of sensation left in my finger. It curled when I told it to, squeezing the trigger.

But the tendril in my gut squeezed at the same moment.

Pure, white-hot pain. It blinded me, seizing my body. Together with the crack of my pistol shot, a cry filled the room.

Only when I blinked and found myself clutching the desk and panting did I realise it was mine.

UnCavendish still stood before me. His chest wasn't torn open and bleeding. He just stared at his arm, where a thin trickle of pale grey blood seeped between his fingers.

I'd missed a lethal shot.

"You little bitch." He turned his glare on me and advanced. "That actually hurt."

"Reload," I whispered, like that would make my body obey me. "Reload."

If I could just do that, I stood a chance of ending him before this poison ended me.

When Papa had gifted Avice and me our pistols, he'd made us practise loading until it took seconds. I could do it in my sleep.

The gunpowder flask and shot spilled onto the desk as my fingers spasmed. The room warped and twisted. I grabbed the flask, sucking air between my teeth and trying to battle the pain writhing in my stomach. A losing battle, I knew, but I didn't need to win. I just needed time.

Black spots flecked the edge of my vision, spreading like rot.

I spilled gunpowder down the muzzle and into the pan, getting as much on the desk as in the pistol.

Nearly there. Nearly.

I shook a lead ball from the case, but my arms sank like they were made of the same stuff.

The gun slipped from my nerveless fingers. Its clunk on the table was like the clunk of the grandfather clock counting down the seconds I had left.

But this one was not followed by another.

Agony had me in its grip, dragging my spine taut, destroying the world, letting darkness close in.

I didn't know how long passed, but when I blinked, I found myself on the floor, no sign of my pistol, unCavendish standing over me.

I'd failed to load it. I'd failed to stop him.

"You thought he cared for you." He shook his head, something almost sad in his eyes as he surveyed me. His hand went to the dagger at his belt, but he didn't draw it. "Stupid, stupid girl. I tried to tell you."

I stared up at him, every breath an effort, my pulse stumbling and skipping.

This was it.

He didn't need any weapon—he could just watch the poison take me.

There was a sound—the door opening? I didn't have the strength or the control over my body to turn my head.

"Touch her and die."

80

UnCavendish's laugh was ice in my ears. It merged with the cold creeping through my body.

Understanding crept much more slowly. I knew that voice...

"Too late, Bastard. I've already touched her many, many times." I caught the edge of a wide smile as unCavendish lifted his head. "And you're far too late to save her life. She's half dead already, like the rest of her kind."

On the very edge of my narrowing vision, dark hair, seething shadows, and a face I knew very well indeed.

Bastian. Jaw solid. Eyes burning with cold fire.

It hurt to look at him. Alive. Without pain. And so fucking beautiful it broke my stuttering heart.

"A changeling." His voice was gritted. "I should've known."

I had to get up. Lying here was too vulnerable, too useless.

I tried. All I managed was a sluggish raise of my arm, and even that was agony.

"You hadn't worked it out?" UnCavendish canted his head. "I'm disappointed."

"I knew someone was working against us. I just didn't know who."

"And you never will. There'll be no witnesses to this." With a hiss of pain, unCavendish took something from the desk. It was only when the gold inlaid stag came into view I understood it was my pistol.

He took out the ramrod and tamped down the shot I'd partially loaded, muttering about his arm as he glared at me. "She'll be dead soon, and it's rather convenient that you're here, too. Such an easy story to tell. The jilted lover takes poison and shoots the man who rejected her." He tossed the ramrod on the desk.

Bastian made no move to stop him or come closer. Maybe he didn't realise it was the same fae-worked gun I'd threatened him with on the road. I tried to tell him, but agony caught my throat and turned it into a hoarse cry.

He twitched, eyes flicking to me for an instant. "No, I don't think that's how the story goes."

"Isn't it? She's dying, Bastard. It's just a pity I never got to hold that pretty flame hair while I fucked her." UnCavendish gave me a lingering look. "But knowing you became so infatuated with my spy? That makes up for it." A wide grin spread his lips as his gaze slid back to Bastian.

Thrumming with tension, he stood in silence.

As that quiet stretched on, unCavendish's expression soured. "You don't seem terribly worried that she's lying here dying. I thought your obsession would make you want to keep hold of your possession. Yet here you are talking to me like you have all the time in the world." He cocked my pistol.

Now Bastian smiled. "That's because I was stalling for time while I got behind you."

Above me, unCavendish twitched. "Behind me? But you're—"

Steel erupted from his throat. Pale blood rained upon me.

In the sickening spin of the room, Bastian's face loomed over unCavendish's shoulder.

His double.

Teeth bared in vicious pleasure, he twisted the blade and wrenched it out.

UnCavendish gurgled, incomprehensible words bubbling from his mouth. He clutched his throat, like he could hold the wound together.

But just like there was no hope for me, there was none for him.

He went still.

The world turned as grey as the changeling's blood. Then the Bastian from the doorway was at my side, cradling me against his chest while his other self dumped unCavendish's lifeless body on the desk.

"Kat?" He shook me, wide eyes darting between my rolling ones. "You idiot. You beautiful, fucking idiot."

I tried to focus on the ceiling, the hair falling in his face, the movement of his perfect lips as he talked. But the only things that anchored me were his eyes. They glowed in the dim room, like twin moons overhead. I breathed a laugh at the foolish thought.

He cupped my head, pulling my face closer to his until he filled all of my tunnelling vision. "Don't you think I knew this was coming?" His voice choked. "Don't you think I was prepared?"

"I don't... understand." It took all my strength to push the words out, each one painful, and they still creaked, barely audible.

Eyes gleaming, he stroked my cheeks. If only I could feel it. His nostrils flared as he shook his head. "I took the antidote before the ceremony."

The antidote. To aconite.

Then he knew I'd tried to poison him and that was what had me in its grip.

"I'm sorry." My eyelids drooped. "At least we stopped him, though... Everyone's safe."

You are safe.

I wished my fingers still had some sensation in them. I'd have stroked his cheek one last time, written the scrape of his stubble on my nerves, taken the memory of it away with me.

The room grew darker as pain wrung me out. The scream pierced my ears, and around me, Bastian's hold tightened.

"No. No! You're not allowed to die yet." He shook me, and I forced my eyes open. I'd have cursed him for it, too, if I'd had the breath. "That thing is dead, but it was working for someone else."

Everything wheeled round and round as I rose. It was like the room moved around me, rather than I through it. How strange. How funny.

I hung in his hold, so heavy, so tired, long moments between each beat of my heart.

There was a thunk of something wooden, and a sense of movement, but I couldn't keep my eyes open a moment longer.

"Kat? No, don't you dare use that as an excuse to give up. I still need you."

I faded away on his words.

81

I drifted in and out of being. Moments, images, voices came and went, some I could make sense of.

Bastian's face, his eyes wide and red-rimmed. Everything about him tight and jerky.

Asher, mouth and brow pinched, brown skin ashen, shaking his head.

Crashing. The high tinkle of breaking glass.

"Stop it! There's none left. You took the last of it today."

"Make more."

"It takes a week, Bastian. I have a batch brewing, but it won't be ready for days. And she'll be dead by then."

Dead by then. She. He meant me.

"There must be something."

My body, cold on the outside, burning in the middle, being poked and prodded. Air wheezing through my lungs.

"She's... it's not looking good. Without the antidote..."

Their words faded as I sank into darkness.

There was no pain in the deep black. I could stay here, floating in nothingness. It was a mercy, really.

But something wrenched me. Agony, beyond pure, beyond blinding, beyond deafening. I was it and it was me.

I came to, screaming.

"I'm sorry, love." Close by, Bastian's voice cracked, and I realised the wrenching was his arm around my shoulders. "I'm so sorry. But you need to sit up and drink this."

"Do you think she can?" Asher's face swam into view, distorted by my tears.

"Of course she can. She's strong. She's endured worse than this."

I wasn't so sure. *Nothing* was worse than this. I could normally keep quiet despite pain, but this decimated my control.

Something pressed to my lips, and I drank.

Bitter. Familiar. "Coffee?"

Asher's eyebrows shot up. "You can talk. Yes, coffee. I need to get your heart rate up."

My stomach spasmed around the warm liquid. "I don't—"

It came back up, bending me double. I didn't even know what I vomited into, onto, just that it felt like razor blades being dragged over my soul.

I lost my grip on the room and floated away again. But this time, stuttering images played across the darkness.

Thorny branches growing at impossible speed, twisting upon themselves, slithering over me, holding me paralysed.

Maybe it wouldn't be so bad. Death. Bastian was right—I'd been half-dead a long time. Now I could sink the rest of the way into oblivion.

Black roses budding, blooming, dying. Death was only natural.

I'd achieved nothing with my life half-lived. I hadn't even saved the estate. Morag and Horwich would be homeless, jobless.

There was the distant shriek of an animal caught in a snare. I thought I glimpsed red hair between the tangled branches before they hissed, forked tongues tasting the air as they became serpents.

Not real. It isn't real. A tiny island of self stood still at the centre of their writhing bodies. I clung to it, listening to its lucid voice.

"The book," I croaked somewhere in my delirium.

"Shh, love." A weight settled on my forehead. "Save your strength. You need it to fight this."

I sank under the weight, falling through grey, black, white, nothing, serpents licking my fingertips. But I couldn't go. I needed to tell him.

Eventually, I found I could move my mouth again. "Sell..." I blinked. "The book."

The light was different, and Bastian's face was on my other side, like I hadn't only blinked between words.

He shook his head, face creased. "This again?"

"Get the money to Morag." That would save the estate.

That would be enough.

"... Never done from fae to human before. I don't know if it will—"

"Do it."

A glow lit behind my eyelids, followed by a sharp pinprick of pain in my arm. I flinched, but someone caught my wrist.

I managed to push my eyes open.

Blood. Tubes. Something in my arm. A narrow, sharp pain compared to the rest of my body that felt like I'd been battered down a dozen staircases. I reached for it, but something cool closed around that wrist too.

"Kat?" Bastian's face above me. He smiled, but there was something fragile in its tightness. "Hello, love." A shadow of warmth reached through the numbness of my skin. "It's so good to see you."

"I can't feel my hands and feet."

"It's all right. You will soon. Asher's fixing you."

Something tickled the crook of my elbow, the same spot that had hurt a moment ago. I tried to lift my head to look, but I couldn't move. I could only make my eyes follow a trail of crimson passing through a tube sticking into his arm. "What's going on?"

"I'm giving you my blood."

"Hmm."

Comforting blackness came rolling in.

"No, no, no. Kat? Stay here."

I clung to the voice. I *liked* that voice. Even in my numbed state, it was a balm, warm and soothing, spreading through me. It pushed back the pain in my veins, like ivy claiming a broken ruin.

My eyelids fluttered open, and I was rewarded for my effort by the sight of the most gorgeous man I'd ever seen.

"That's it." His nose was an inch from mine. He cupped my cheek, holding me in this room, in the light. "Good. Stay right here with me."

"Bastian?" I would've reached for him, but something still gripped my wrists.

"It's me. I'm here. I won't leave you."

I needed to... I sifted my jumbled thoughts, looking for the thing I needed to do. Something important. Something I needed to say before I fell into darkness again.

Ah. *There.*

"I'm sorry."

"You have nothing to apologise for, love. Don't worry about anything. Just hold on and we'll get you better."

"So tired..."

I thought I just blinked, but when I opened my eyes again, that sharp pinprick had gone from my arm and nothing held my wrists.

"She's awake," he called across me.

"That's a good sign. Try to keep her that way."

The pain... it had gone. I took a deep breath, enjoying the stretch of my lungs, the cool feel of the air. "I'm alive."

"You are." He squeezed my hand. I could feel the warmth, the calluses at the base of his fingers, even the slight clamminess that suggested he'd been holding mine a long while.

I could feel all of it.

Including the guilt.

I'd almost inflicted this on Bastian. Whatever he was, however foolish he made me, I hadn't stopped caring about him. Wars and alliances aside, I would never have forgiven myself if I'd hurt him like this.

"I'm so sorry."

He arched one eyebrow. "Didn't I say you had nothing to apologise for?"

"But I spied on you."

574

He nodded, no surprise widening his eyes or raising his eyebrows. He must've heard enough in unCavendish's office.

"And I almost poisoned you."

His expression darkened into a glower. "I wish you had."

"And I'm so, so sorry." Tears pushed on the back of my eyes. "I should've told you, but..." My voice cracked. "I was so afraid. I thought he'd kill me. I thought I'd lose the estate. I couldn't get away."

"Shh." He shook his head. "He's dead now. He can't hurt you. I just need you to focus on getting better so we can find out who he was working for. See? Just because he's dead doesn't mean you get to shirk your responsibilities and swan off to the next place. I need you."

My exhale was almost a laugh, but my chest tightened around it. "Don't think I'm very useful at the moment."

His smile flashed, as warm as the feeling that had spread through my veins earlier. "You're useful to me." He kissed my forehead, but... I couldn't feel it.

I blinked, eyelids sluggish.

"Kat?"

The darkness crumbled over me like damp earth.

"I'm sorry."

"You already said that."

I tried to shake my head and failed. "This is for... I can't hold on."

"Shit. Asher? What's going on?"

Asher appeared over me, holding my eyes open, peering into them. His face screwed up. "My magic fixed the antidote in your blood before the transfusion, but... it isn't sticking in hers." He shook his head. "It's only having a temporary effect. The changeling must've done something to the poison to make it... I don't know, resist the antidote somehow?"

I drifted on his words, eyes closing.

Something shook me. "No, Kat. Please. Look at me." Bastian gave a hum of approval when I held his gaze. "Then give her more of my blood."

"You only have so much. If I bleed you dry, it'll kill you."

"If she dies, it'll kill me."

I battled to keep my eyelids open. Gods, were they heavy.

Bastian shook his head, movements darting. "There has to be a way."

"What do you want me to do, Bastian?" A note of frustration streaked Asher's voice. "I can't heal poison. It's beyond my abilities. Luminis's healers might be able to, but—"

"Then I'll take her there."

"And her husband? Her Majesty won't let you cross the border without his permission."

"Then I'll get it." Bastian shouted for a guard, voice fading as I slipped away in the spaces between my slowing heartbeat.

82

Asher was talking when I next became aware, his low voice comforting. That point of pain was back in my arm. I couldn't move, but warmth bloomed under my skin.

"... I'll stay to clear the diplomatic mess."

"What mess?" Bastian grunted. He'd promised not to leave me, but our earlier conversation was little more than fragments scraping against each other.

"Have you not been listening? You do know why we came here, don't you?"

"Get to the fucking point, Asher."

"Their queen has said she won't marry me. Her magic has been awakened by that sword. The plants in the conservatory. The roses still blooming... We should've realised. She doesn't need to marry to shore up her power. She has her own now."

"Then fix it while I return to Tenebris."

They fell quiet, but something picked at the back of my

mind, like my fingers when they couldn't stop picking at my cuticles.

I'd apologised, so it wasn't that. Something else... something from Cavendish's office.

My eyes rolled. I had to open them. Had to ask about...

"Kat?" Bastian's voice, closer now.

The warmth spread up my arm, pushing back the pain once more, giving me space to think.

The warmth of the antidote in his blood.

That was the thing picking, picking, picking.

"How did you know to take it?"

"What?"

"The antidote."

He flinched before smoothing his face and shaking his head. "That's not important right now. You need to save your strength for the journey. Asher's doing another transfusion to prepare you. We're setting off as soon as—"

"Bastian." I had to be feeling better, because my voice was firm. "Tell me how you knew to take the antidote."

Something cracked in the moonlight of his eyes, and he looked away. "I knew you were spying on me."

I blinked, expecting to find serpents and thorns crowding my vision, because this had to be more of the strange delirium I'd seen as death had drunk me down.

But that had all gone. This second transfusion was apparently doing the job.

Exhaustion lapped at me, eroding my ability to stay awake, but it wasn't that same terrifying oblivion that had tugged on me earlier.

I could focus now, and I saw how Bastian couldn't bring himself to look at me.

"You... *knew*? Since when?"

The scar running through his lips paled as he pressed them together. "Soon after you arrived."

"Why didn't you say?"

A muscle in his jaw feathered. "I needed to know who you were working for. Flush them out." He finally met my gaze. "I needed to get close to you, and I could only do that if you were oblivious."

My heart dipped like the ground beneath me had been pulled away. Some cruel corner of me laughed.

The irony. Oh, the fucking irony.

"You needed to get close to me... Like I needed to get close to you. So looking after me, helping me, protecting me..." The words scorched my throat. "You just wanted me to trust you."

That muscle in his jaw went solid as he bowed his head.

"All so I would slip and give you information. Just like I wanted you to." I laughed, bitter and breathless, as my chest tightened. This time, it was nothing to do with the poison.

He'd known. All along, he'd known.

We were the same, and yet...

"I tried to quit. I tried to find a way out."

He grimaced. "The race."

"*And* the book. If I got enough money to pay the bailiff, I would've saved the estate, and then I could've told him where to stick his damn spying." My voice cracked, and I hated myself for that weakness. But maybe I hated him more, because I went on. "Because I didn't want to do that to you anymore. Because... it became real. Or at least I thought it did."

"It was. It only *started* as a way to get you to trust me. After that, it was real, Kat—*so real*. That's why when your husband showed up, I couldn't—"

"No." I managed to point at him. It should've been a

victory, but it was only exhausting. "I fed him useless information to keep him happy. But you kept going. Even after you knew about my marriage, you kept me as your liaison so I would poison you. You wanted me around so you could follow the trail back to your enemy. You kept using me."

His shoulders sagged. Giving in.

Of course he was giving in. Because there was no argument he could make when I spoke the truth.

And fuck, the truth cut.

Yes, I'd tried to poison him. Yes, I'd spied on him. No, I didn't deserve my bitter hurt.

But like he'd said, *fuck deserve.*

He'd taken it all a step further. He'd worked his way deep under my skin to my most vulnerable places and made me feel new things. He'd made me think there might be more to life than just survival.

Cruellest of all, he'd made me hope.

"I'm such a fool." I shook my head, setting the room spinning wildly. "The changeling was right. You never cared about me. You were just using me to find him."

"I'm sorry." He stroked my cheek. My body was too heavy to pull away. "I wanted to tell you. It wasn't only—"

"You did it, Bastian. You found him and you killed him. Well done. Mission accomplished."

Since I couldn't leave, I closed my eyes, shutting him out, losing myself in the heavy exhaustion.

The warmth of his blood spread through my empty chest, slow and sweet like honey, like an embrace.

But that was a reminder that my last one had been from him, carrying me here.

And he'd been using me all along.

EPILOGUE
BASTIAN

The instant I stepped through the shadow door, Elfhame's magic hummed through me. Normally it was a comfort.

Not tonight.

The snow, the familiar tent with a cheerful fire burning outside, the cedars branching overhead, and the night sky beyond. It all faded compared to the red-haired form in my arms.

I touched Kat's pale cheek. Her dark lashes didn't flutter, even as the cold air swirled around us, carrying the promise of more snow.

"Kat?" I shook her. "Little ember? Can you hear me?"

Nothing.

Dread seized my throat.

"Bastian?" Faolán's great hulk unfolded from the tent flap, followed a moment later by his human wife, Rose.

My gaze snagged on her strawberry blond hair, a pale whisper of Kat's.

Yet she stood. She breathed. She smiled at me, though it wavered with uncertainty.

Kat couldn't do two of those things, and the third... I hadn't felt her chest heave in my arms for too many seconds. Her eyelids still didn't flutter.

My pulse pounded at the overwhelming outrage of it.

Placing one hand on Rose's shoulder, the shapechanger frowned. "What are you doing back already? I didn't think—"

"Shut up, I can't hear..." I held my breath and pressed my ear to Kat's chest, trying to ignore the desperate spike of my own heart. Through the blankets, softly...

Ba-dum.

It was a long time before the next beat came.

Slow and erratic, but her heart was still going.

Thank the fucking Stars above.

I allowed myself a moment of holding her close before I dragged in a breath and strode to Faolán. "Where's your stag?"

He stepped between me and Rose, hands raised. "Bastian, your friends..." He jerked his chin at the snowy ground.

Except where the snow should've been painted silver by the moonlight, there was only darkness.

My shadows.

They spilled around us, obliterating the snow under their crashing waves.

In my arms, movement. A soft murmur. "Beautiful... useful..." Her head shook, eyes still shut, eyebrows tight together.

"Your stag," I gritted out. "I need it."

"Who is she? What happened to her?" Rose peered around Faolán, reaching for Kat.

I tensed. "Get away from her." My voice thundered, not just mine but my double's and my shadows'.

The ground trembled. Snow shook down from the cedar's branches. A startled bird flew away with a squawk.

Power rumbled in my nerves, drawing on Elfhame's native magic.

Useless fucking power. I could suck it all up and it wouldn't save her. I was not a man made for healing.

A warning growl came from Faolán. "Control yourself."

I blinked. My shadows had spread in all directions, forming a lake of darkness.

Fuck. He was right.

If I lost control and let them consume everything, that wouldn't help Kat.

Deep breaths.

My chest was still raw with every inhale, but I felt a little less like I was about to fell every tree in a mile radius.

I nodded to Rose, not trusting myself to form a decent apology out loud. "Your stag. Now." A faint purr of power still ran through my words.

With a huff, Rose led the way to the back of their tent, her long legs covering the ground quickly. Not quickly enough.

I glanced at the stars as we reached a pair of tethered stags. One lifted his head and sniffed the air. The other rolled his eyes and backed away from my shadows.

"How far are we from Tenebris?" My shadow door was anchored to a bracelet Faolán wore—a quick way for me to reach him when he was working in the field. But it meant I didn't know where we were exactly.

"Seven or eight hours' ride."

I went rigid.

Too long. Too far.

In my mind, Kat upended that glass again, draining its deadly contents.

It was an iron blade running me through.

And worse, so much worse, the wonderful idiot did it for me.

Rose rummaged under blankets draped over a stand. "The saddle's just—"

"No time for that." I mounted the first stag and adjusted Kat, so she sat across my lap. The instant I had her secure against my chest, I bellowed for the stag to gallop.

We rode east, against the moon.

I let the stag choose his course—I'd had the creature bred from good stock. He was intelligent enough to not want to break his own leg and strong enough to ride for hours.

Instead, I turned my attention to Kat. Her breath fanned my cheek. That was a good start, settling the roar of my heart. A stroke of her cheek. "Katherine? Love?"

Her lashes fluttered. Her green eyes rolled before settling on me. "Bastian? What...? There were thorns and snakes... and one bit me."

"No, you're with me. You're safe. I'm taking you to healers who'll be able to help."

She shook her head and frowned, eyelids drooping. "Is this real now?"

"It is. I told you before, 'No matter what happens, remember, all of this is real.' I meant it, Kat. This is real. We are real. I meant every word." My voice cracked, blocking my throat with painful splinters.

"I don't..." She made a soft sound and fell limp in my arms.

It was only once I'd checked she still breathed that I bent to the stag's neck and whispered in the oldest tongue, the language of the earth and stones itself, "Faster. Faster. I'll see you rewarded in the Underworld."

With a snort, the creature put on a burst of speed.

I felt every breaking breath, every crash of his hooves upon snow. I heard the roar of his blood pumping too fast. This speed would kill him. And part of me mourned that. But I needed to get Kat to Tenebris as quickly as possible.

Whatever the cost.

WE MADE it in five hours. Sun paled the horizon as we rode into Tenebris. Lights drifted through the streets, kissing the stone walls carved of basalt and labradorite. Soon they would pale to pure white alabaster and pink-veined marble as Dawn Court ascended and my city shifted into its daylight twin, Luminis.

Kat hadn't stirred in the past hour.

The stag collapsed in the street, and I pressed my hand to its brow and thanked it. With Kat in my arms, I ran the rest of the way.

Folk from Dawn and Dusk—the former venturing out, the latter heading home—passed me. Some did a double take when they saw my face. I didn't have time to care what they might think of the Night Queen's Shadow sprinting through the streets as the sun rose and turned Tenebris into Luminis.

Every breath ripped through me as I skidded into the House of Healing. The pale stone walls were blinding after the half-light outside.

A tall woman glided towards me, hands clasped together. I

recognised the cream-coloured hair bound in braids down her back—she'd healed the wound on my chest all those years ago. Her face betrayed none of that, though she had to know who I was. In fact, her face was far too fucking serene. Didn't she understand this was an emergency?

"Heal her." My voice boomed in the silence of their entrance hall. "She's been poisoned."

With a gentle tilt of her head, the woman took in Kat. Unhurried, she raised her eyebrows. "Hmm."

"Didn't you hear me? You need to—"

"She's dying."

"I know that. That's why I fucking brought her here." My shadows inked the marble floor, lapping at the base of the columns. "Aconite."

Head tilting, the woman's eyes narrowed like she was listening to something in the distance. "Not just aconite. There's a magical additive, too. Interesting."

"Yes, terribly fucking interesting. Now save her."

"She's dying. And the sun's up, Serpent. Dawn rules now. Your orders don't stand." The healer backed away, hands spread as though there was nothing she could do.

No. There had to be something. *Something.* Kat couldn't die like this. She'd only just started to live.

"I'll owe you."

That broke the healer's serenity—her pale blue eyes flashed wide.

I bent close, so she'd understand I meant this. "Anything." Power rumbled through the word, and dust hissed from the ceiling.

"Calm yourself, Serpent. We will save your human, and you will owe us." Her smile said I'd regret our bargain.

But I didn't care.

I followed her through a small archway and laid Kat on the bed inside. I answered her questions about the poison, about the treatments Asher had tried. I let her take more of my blood.

I did everything she asked, because I'd do anything to get rid of the heaviness in my heart.

I didn't want redemption. Redemption was for people who took their wrongs back. I'd do the same terrible things again in an instant, and I'd undoubtedly do a hundred more before my life was over.

But if I did something good in the world, it might fix some of the cracks, even if they weren't the ones I'd caused.

And helping Kat had always felt good.

Until today.

It had been bad enough to watch her suffering as she slipped under the poison's grip, but seeing her face as she'd realised the truth...

It was like someone had poured aconite down my throat and placed iron under my tongue. Bitter and burning, it made me want to throw up everything I'd ever eaten.

And I shouldn't care... But whatever she'd lied about, whatever taboo she'd let me unwittingly break, she didn't deserve this.

In this one thing, it seemed I did care about deserving.

She lay on the healer's bed, hair splayed over the pillow, face almost as pale as the marble walls. She looked so small, empty, almost.

Not the woman I knew who'd just started taking up space in the world. Not the woman whose laugh filled me. Not the woman who'd lived too long trapped by fear, and had finally—finally started to experience life so keenly.

No, this was a shadow of her, even smaller than she'd made herself in front of her uncle.

The thing inside me that had spent the past several hours cracking broke a little more.

Because she was still married, so I really, *really* shouldn't care.

She was forbidden. Tempting.

Not only for my body, but for my mind, my soul... and the place in my chest that ached, but I didn't dare name.

She was dangerous.

Equal parts beauty and grit, a raging inferno under a veneer of cool innocence, and the most dangerous creature I'd ever faced.

Because if she died, I wasn't sure part of me wouldn't follow.

*Kat and Bastian's story continues in **A Touch of Poison**.*
Pre-order and send your proof of purchase to claresagerauto@
gmail.com to get the opening chapters ahead of release and be in
with a chance of winning a hardback copy.

Read on for a note from the author...

AUTHOR NOTE

Welcome to Tenebris-Luminis!

I hope you enjoyed reading this first part of Kat and Bastian's story as much as I did writing it.

It was something of a rollercoaster, I'll admit. I always outline my books before writing them, but these two... they didn't entirely follow the plan. (For one thing, they had a lot more steamy times than I'd planned.) But I love the adventure they took me on!

(And I want to reassure you... despite where we've left these two, I'm an optimist at heart and I always promise a happily ever after for my main characters... They just might need to go through a few "challenges" first. *Insert evil laughter here.*)

In these author notes, I generally speak a bit about some of my inspiration and research, as well as how a story relates to my other books.

Honestly, I started writing this note a few times and kept coming back to this...

I never intended for this to be a book (or series) about female rage.

But here we are in 2022 (it's December as I write this) and *gestures at **everything***.

I started off listing some specific examples here, but... you know what? There are too many.

In short, men in power are still fucking us over. Hells, so are men out of power.

We've all seen the documentaries and news reports about abusive, high profile men who still somehow land that next big role; we've seen the women who come forward and aren't believed, the friends with partners who are... not right.

We all know or have been the woman in a crowd who was touched, the one who was followed, the one a man just wouldn't leave alone. Either first-hand or through a friend, we've all known that guy who got nasty when he was rejected.

It's fucking exhausting. And terrifying. And rage-inducing.

AUTHOR NOTE

When I wrote my previous series, *Beneath Black Sails*, I was so fucking exhausted from it all, I wanted to write something lighter that didn't include that BS, and it was a welcome break. But I couldn't keep on like that... not when the world was sending me so many reminders.

So with *A Kiss of Iron*, I sank into it. Apparently I sank deep. And I appreciate you joining me on this dive.

But don't worry, there's plenty more female rage to keep us going for the rest of the trilogy.

Kat is still deep in the rage and the fear.

Ahead of giving this book to my beta readers, I was expecting someone to ask why she doesn't tell someone else about Cavendish (well, unCavendish) or her husband or her uncle.

No one did.

Because they all understood.

And now I sit and think about that, it makes me a bit tearful.

Because it means they knew and you probably do too...

It isn't safe for Kat to speak up. She is trapped in a dangerous situation and locked in her own fear. And although she starts to find her rage by the end, she's still bound up in a lot of trauma and fear, and she isn't safe yet.

And I want to say to you...

It's OK to be afraid. It's OK to not speak up because you are afraid or because you're unsafe. You are not to blame.

You never were.

There are other things I could say, but they're in the book or they're to come in Kat's story. I'm better at speaking through made-up people—that's why I write fiction.

...

Well, there's no smooth way to segue out of such a heavy subject. And there shouldn't be.

This is the point I'd normally talk about my other books and how they relate to this one, but honestly, that doesn't feel right after all this. All I'll say is that all my stories are linked in some way, with characters who crossover between series.

I love history and mythology, so it's always a treat fleshing out a new part of the Sabreverse world. Most country/place names are based on old names for those places, usually in one of their native languages. Albion is a fairly well-known old name for England and Wales. Cestyll Caradoc is my own invention, meaning Castles Caradoc—Caradoc being a part-legendary, part-historical figure in Welsh folklore.

As for Kat and Bastian...

I don't want to spill too much in here, but the experience of writing Kat was a different one for me.

For one thing, a lot of my heroines are warriors of some sort. Ariadne in my *Stolen Threadwitch Bride* was my first foray into writing a woman who had no skill or training with weapons and I found that a fun challenge. But Kat... she's a fighter of a different kind.

Then, as I wrote her, all these parentheses started coming out. I don't think I've used a single pair of brackets in any of my published books, and yet they litter *A Kiss of Iron*. As I was revising the story and trying to decide whether they would stay or go, I realised *why* they'd come through in Kat's voice. Kat lives her life in parentheses—little gaps between what she can say out loud.

And Bastian... ah, Bastian. I don't want to give too much away, but I hope you enjoyed getting a glimpse of his point of view in the epilogue. Needless to say, our Shadow has his own baggage that you'll learn more about in the rest of the series— we've only just scratched the surface of all the things he's carrying. ;)

I'm excited for what's to come with their story, and I'm looking forward to sharing it with you in 2023.

In the meantime, if you enjoyed *A Kiss of Iron*, please consider leaving a review on Amazon and/or Goodreads—reviews help other readers find books they'll also love... and it gives you someone to squee about them with. ;)

I always love hearing from readers—feel free to drop me a line (clare@claresager.com) about your favourite characters or moments or tag me in social media (I'm on Instagram the most @claresager) when you post about KOI.

You can also keep in touch by joining my newsletter here: https://claresager.com/freebook/ I share sneak peeks, behind the scenes news, and some giveaways, as well as a couple of free stories that are only available to newsletter subscribers. It's where you'll find out first about *A Touch of Poison.*

Thanks again for joining me on this adventure—I can't wait to share the next part with you.

All the very best,

Clare, December 2022
        x

PS – I've put together some bonuses like phone wallpaper of the character art and a playlist over at: https://claresager.com/koibonuses/

ACKNOWLEDGEMENTS

I always say in my acknowledgements that, however it may appear, books are never—*never* the product of just one person.

With that in mind, I consider myself incredibly lucky to be able to thank the following people in no particular order...

Carissa, Lasairiona, and Tracie—the best author wives I could wish for. You three keep me sane(ish) and keep me going. Thank you so much for your support, your love, your advice and feedback, and, most of all, for listening to me whine. I count myself so, *so* lucky to have you in my life.

Alyssa and Andrew, Andra, Clare, Erika, Karolina, Laura, Mariëlle, and Noah—what a team of beta reading/editorial geniuses! Thank you for your time, patience, encouragement, and excellent suggestions (and for all the BetaBooks emoji reactions—they give me life!). I appreciate you, and this book wouldn't be what it is without you.

My very many author friends—I'm blessed to have too many of you to name, but special mentions for this book go to

Sacha and Meg for being smart and inspiring badasses and wonderful friends.

The epic and lovely Nate Medeiros—thank you so much for the STUNNING poison bottle and rose imagery used in the naked hardback cover design.

Maria Spada—for the gorgeous cover. I hope the story lives up to the lushness of your design! And I can't wait to show off your other covers!

Natalie Bernard and Anna Henri—for the incredible character art included in the hardback. I had your paintings on the screen as I wrote. Thank you for the inspiration and for being so wonderful to work with. <3

My friends and family—first of all, family members, you shouldn't be reading this book. I mean... yeah, maybe don't read book 2. Or at least pretend that you haven't. Things are going to get... interesting. And I don't need to know you've read that shit! That aside... I know I can be an antisocial creature, so thanks for your patience and still hanging around. I hope seeing this, it all makes sense now. ;)

Deedee and Dash—for walking across the keyboard and yet still being endlessly adorable as you keep me company while I write. (BTW, I wouldn't mind fewer "gifts.") Chirrups and chin scratches to you both.

ARC readers, BookTokkers, Bookstagrammers, book bloggers, and readers of all kinds—for the emails, the messages, the fan art, the fan music, the beautiful photos, the viral videos, the thoughtful reviews, the star ratings, the frantic messages you send your friends telling them they MUST READ THIS BOOK, and for everything in between and far beyond. I don't think you understand just how important you are, how powerful, and how wonderful. You help us authors keep doing this. THANK YOU.

I'm the kind of person who always saves the best for last, so the final thank you has to go to Russ. My partner in crime and chaos (and board games). My best friend. The one who knows me best. (Yeah, sorry about that!) Thank you, love. <3

ALSO BY CLARE SAGER – SET IN THE SABREVERSE

SHADOWS OF THE TENEBRIS COURT

Gut-wrenching romance full of deceit, desire, and dark secrets.

Book 1 – *A Kiss of Iron*

Book 2 – *A Touch of Poison* – Coming 2023, pre-order now.

BOUND BY A FAE BARGAIN

Steamy fantasy romances featuring unwitting humans who make bargains with clever fae. Each book features a different couple, though the characters are linked.

Stolen Threadwitch Bride

These Gentle Wolves – Pre-order now for March 2023.

(Featuring Rose & Faolán as seen in the epilogue of *A Kiss of Iron*.)

BENEATH BLACK SAILS

An enemies-to-lovers tale of piracy, magic, and betrayal.
Featuring Kat's sister Vice. Complete series.

Book 0 – *Across Dark Seas – Free Book*

Book 1 – *Beneath Black Sails*

Book 2 – *Against Dark Tides*

Book 3 – *Under Black Skies*

Book 4 – *Through Dark Storms*